ath

'Absorbing, charming and funny, *A Brush with Death* heralds a fresh and welcome new voice in crime writing. Susie Mahl is also a welcome new detective: witty, warm and very inquisitive.'   Antonia Fraser

'It's a big fat BRILLIANT!!!!'   Amanda Prowse

'This is a crime novel for mystery fans sick of gore and sexual violence. Just curl up and lose yourself happily in this world of animals and toffs – closely observed by a beady-eyed artist turned amateur sleuth who realises all is not as innocent as it looks and is determined to do something about it.'   Ruth Dudley Edwards

'A delicious new voice in crime writing... Excellent on the English aristocracy and written in a fine, wry style, we will hear much more of Miss Mahl.'
Daily Mail

'A riveting, charming and very funny new crime series from the fabulously talented Ali Carter.'
Piers Morgan

'The first book in a promising new series will remind you of *Downton Abbey* and Miss Marple, except that this Miss M is a pet portraitist with a penchant for rather expensive underwear, and it's purely for her own pleasure.'   *The Bookbag*

'An entertaining read, and one that had me up to the wee small hours.' *Crimesquad*

'Carter is a fresh and welcome new voice in crime writing and Susie Mahl a very different new detective.' *Crimereview*

'Brilliantly enjoyable; coolly observed.' *The Tablet*

'*A Brush with Death* is the first in a charming new series about pet portraitist and amateur sleuth Susie Mahl, and the debut novel from animal enthusiast Ali Carter.' *Crimereads*

'*A Brush with Death* is a perfectly English mystery, with an abundance of all the right jokes, details and muddy dogs. Author Ali Carter's first book is a lovely romp and shows promise for a wonderful tongue-in-cheek mystery series.' *Foreword Reviews*

'Animal lovers, Anglophiles and fans of humorous, socially observant whodunits will look forward to the next Susie Mahl mystery.' *Publishers Weekly*

'Fans of country-house cozies will delight in this series debut.' *Booklist*

'Its rich details on the British leisure class may interest fans of *Downton Abbey* and G.M. Malliet's "Max Tudor" mysteries.' *Library Journal*

'A fun read.' *Sussex Life*

'*A Brush with Death* is a charming and amusing murder mystery. It contains great character observations and is written with humour. She brings to life the world of the aristocracy and everything which goes with it. A pleasant change from the dark Norwegian noir genre. It is definitely a book to take on holiday.'

Country Wives

Praise for
The Colours of Murder

'It's a rare talent that creates a work that is both whip smart, fast paced and at the same time gloriously genteel. Carter is that talent.' Amanda Prowse

'This is a well paced and exciting read. More please!' Alexander McCall Smith

'Charming description of how "the other half live". The characters come alive and are very entertaining... I loved it.' *Promoting Crime*

'A Christie homage whose upper-crust humour targets readers who recognise the differences between a country house and a stately home.' *Kirkus*

'The gentle pace of an episode of *Midsomer Murders* and the intrigue of an Agatha Christie novel.' *Sussex Life*

A TRICK OF THE LIGHT

ALI CARTER

A Point Blank Book

First published by Point Blank, an imprint of
Oneworld Publications, 2020

ISBN 978-1-78607-768-4
ISBN 978-1-78607-769-1 (eBook)

Printed and bound in Great Britain by Clays Ltd, Elcograf S.p.A.

Oneworld Publications
10 Bloomsbury Street, London, WC1B 3SR, England
3754 Pleasant Ave, Suite 100, Minneapolis, MN 55409, USA

Stay up to date with the latest books,
special offers, and exclusive content from
Oneworld with our newsletter

Sign up on our website
oneworld-publications.com

For Geordie, Jack and Laura
Lang may yer lum reek

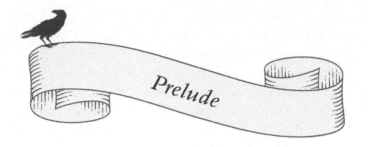

Far above the old walls of Auchen Laggan Tosh house, a full moon crept from beneath a heavy cloud. An owl hooted in the garden and pines swooshed in a gale. Laughing, swaying, the young Earl and Countess of Muchton and their friends stumbled into the hall. A grand wedding party on the neighbouring estate had finally petered out and now all were safely home.

The guests, a couple, great friends, wished their child's babysitter on her way and off she went into the night. It was late, and nothing was going to stop these four from heading straight to bed. Nevertheless Eliza, Countess of Muchton, popped the usual sleeping pill. 'Darling,' she told her husband, Robert, 'I like to take one just to be sure.' He grunted as he wobbled down onto their four-poster bed. Alcohol, not drugs, sent this man to sleep.

Out went the lights and in no time Eliza exhaled an elegant snore. Robert shuffled under the covers as he drifted off. Once again, he couldn't be bothered to remove his shirt, boxers and socks, not that this troubled his wife – she'd long given up trying to control him. Robert was an unreformed alcoholic, and Eliza had made her peace with the situation – alcoholism wasn't something to be 'cured'. She poured her energy into creating a loving home, one where the children could thrive. Mother Nature had not yet blessed her with any, but she had youth on her side and lived in hope.

The Earl and Countess of Muchton's marital bed was so huge neither ever disturbed the other in the night. Whenever Robert's dreams took a turn for the worse he would break into an anxious sweat, unbeknown to his wife.

Tonight, these dreams began full of glamour; the wedding had been up there with the best. Their neighbours, one of the oldest families in Britain, had spared no expense giving away their daughter. Eliza had sparkled amongst the other guests, she'd taken some of the best family jewels on an outing around her neck. Countless compliments had come her way, and those dazzling diamonds now lit up her husband's drunken dreams. Robert's mind indulged in rich and rare reflections and, as he wrestled under the covers, a subconscious smile appeared on his face.

But soon the dreams darkened, and the worst of his nightmares encroached. His late father loomed above. No matter Robert had been only six when his father died, he could clearly make out those domineering words: 'Make sure to keep hold of the family fortune.' But Robert had always lived beyond his means. Relied on the diminishing family trust to keep afloat.

Here now, fast asleep, he ruffled off the covers and slid out of his side of the bed. There must have been something particular in the alcohol tonight: he'd never actually sleepwalked before. But nothing was going to stop him now – this man was on a mission.

Having grown up at Auchen Laggan Tosh, he knew its architecture inside out. So, when in stockinged feet he wandered from the room you could pretty much guarantee his friends in the opposite wing didn't wake.

But their young child was never at peace in a house that groaned and, as the wind whistled through a rotten sash window, the child lay in bed quivering, eyes shut... listening.

Robert tiptoed around the landing, flicked on the light in a particularly dark corridor, and crept along the floorboards. He creaked open a bedroom door and a shaft of light followed him in. He was totally oblivious to the child in the corner whose heart beat terrified in a little chest.

It's a fact that when children are frightened very young they don't tend to tell their mummies and daddies. Not a whisper of the night-time wanderer. Not a hint of the strange mission of this man in a trance, who didn't have an inkling someone was watching. This only child fell straight into the trap: avoid at all costs being called a *fool*.

Forty-five years on and what happened that night lies buried. Robert, 9th Earl of Muchton, has passed away aged seventy-seven, leaving behind his wife and their twin sons – Fergus the heir and Ewen the younger.

The house, Auchen Laggan Tosh, boasts the presence of a king...but behind the door the past lingers. Earls in succession have fought, lost and won. Lives have been taken early and others have lived long. Women have been widowed and children died. Money has been made and gambled. The life of a Muchton is a rollercoaster. Good luck, I say, to the current Earl.

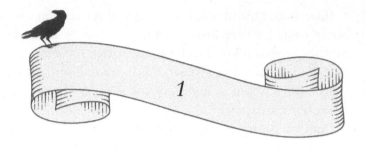

1

O ver a humpback bridge I went, the river Trickle below. I knew the name from the 'literature' I'd been sent back in January, when the Earl and Countess of Muchton had first asked me to be resident tutor on their Life Drawing and Landscape Painting Course.

Five-day tutored Life Drawing & Landscape Painting Course

Monday 23–Friday 27 March
Run in the wonderful setting of
Auchen Laggan Tosh Estate,
home of Fergus, 10ᵗʰ Earl of Muchton and his wife, Zoe.
Standing amidst 12,000 acres of Highland Scotland
with an abundance of wildlife, Auchen Laggan Tosh is
a Palladian mansion, designed by the architect Robert
Adam in 1761. It overlooks the river Trickle and is
secluded but not remote, the town of Muchton merely
four miles away.

Woo hoo. This invitation could not have come at a better time. I'd been back at home in Sussex after yet another singleton London Christmas with my dear parents Joseph and Marion, and I'd needed something – anything – to put in my diary and perk up the dismal, short, wintry days.

'You've been recommended by our great friend Suzannah Highbridge, you drew her Labrador last summer,' is how it all began. 'I've visited your website and your talent as a draughtsman and painter would, we feel, fit the concept of the course perfectly.' The Countess of Muchton wanted *me*.

A spot of Googling and I'd found a picture of the hosts, gleaned from last August's *Muchton Village Monthly*. The Earl and Countess were nice-looking, so the camera reports in the scene of them cuddled up on the stone steps of their pile, liver cocker spaniel sitting at their feet. Fergus's full head of salt-and-pepper hair and the look of self-assurance on Zoe's face suggested to me this pair had left their twenties well behind; might even be fast approaching their forties. Now, seven months on, I wouldn't be surprised if there's a baby brewing: almost inevitable that the later a couple commit the quicker a little squealer pops out. Not to mention the enormous house in the background crying out for an heir – someone to continue the custodial chain and keep all those treasures within the family.

I'm an oil painter and pet portraitist by profession, and although I've never tutored before, I've been to enough classes to know how it's done. So, almost from the moment the Muchtons' email pinged into my inbox – 'We have a small class of eight signed up and we'd be delighted if you fancied making the trip north for the first of what we hope to be repeated courses' – I was eager to accept. This residency would shake up my routine, introduce me to a new crowd and earn me some much-needed pennies, and – here's hoping – if I make a success of it there may be further tutoring opportunities to come.

Home, in Sussex, is a heck of a long way from the north of Scotland, and I let out a squeal of relief that I had reached the Muchtons' drive at last. Bump, bump, bump my car went as I gripped the steering wheel and tried my best to negotiate the divots. It was so dark outside there was no way of seeing the Highland landscape and I could only imagine infinite moorland with a fresh dusting of snow. The flakes, delicate and beautiful in the car headlights, were landing softly on my windscreen and disintegrating before the wipers got their wicked way.

Du-Dump, my car went through one final hole in the I'm-desperately-in-need-of-a-repair drive and I drew on to what felt like gravel. Several outdoor lights flooded the way and I swept in front of the imposing house. Oh jeepers – there's an almighty drag on my steering wheel – I must have picked up a flat tyre. Never mind. I've made it here, no need to worry right now.

I parked a respectful distance from the front steps next to an unbranded minibus and turned the ignition off. *Brrrr* it's cold. Better not hang about. So, grabbing my suitcase from the back seat – my art materials could stay in the boot for the time being – I rushed towards two hefty external curved stone staircases. I'd never been to a house with an entrance like this – an upside-down horseshoe, good luck spilling out. With no obvious door on the rusticated ground floor, I scampered up the right-hand steps to find a way in. My hot breath in the cold air was one step ahead of me until we reached the smooth dressed stone of the first floor. Wow. This was some place. I stopped and looked up, the snow fell in my eyes and the sudden piercing shrill of a bird in the sky sent me lickety-split bursting through the Corinthian portico. No way was I going to hang about and ring a bell.

Surely someone had heard me enter? But no one came, so I waited patiently in the cold, dilapidated neo-classical entrance hall. There was a dim electric wall sconce glowing, only just bright enough for my eyes to dart in and out of empty alcoves, rise up a fluted ala-baster column, cling to the corner of the Corinthian capital whose broken leaf had dropped as if it were autumn, scoot along the high-coved cornice, paint peeling along the way, then spiral up, up, up the full height of the house into one big, black sinister dome. The silence was magnified in the empty void and as my gaze fell from the glass cupola down to the hall I felt myself break into a cold sweat. Pull yourself together, Susie, I said – if you're going to be a good tutor you must muster more confidence than this. But there wasn't a singly homely attribute in here. No flowers, no stray shoes, no junk mail, no coat hooks, no wafts from the kitchen and no chitter chatter. I wanted to curl up and magic myself back home. I suddenly missed the smell of my new pomegranate diffuser, the stripy tea cosy I'd knitted in a flash of way-beyond-one's-years in December and the sheepskin slippers I splashed out on at New Year.

I took in a deep breath and drew what sense of belonging I could from Robert Adam's harmonious proportions. But that only went so far...where was everyone? I knew I'd got the right day – I'm so (some would say boringly) organised I could never get something like this wrong. But, as I waited and shivered and stood there feeling lonely, I picked up on a tinge of sadness in the atmosphere. Have I come to an unhappy place? Or does it just need a lick of paint?

Straight ahead of me was an arch leading into the main body of the house where an imposing staircase came straight down from the second floor in one fell swoop. Opening its jaws in arrival to the newcomer. A welcome of sorts. All of a sudden, a liver cocker spaniel came rushing down it, doing his very best not to trip on his ears.

Yes. A pet. There's nothing like a dog to make a house a home. Perhaps this one has been longing for a friend?

'Hello, poppet,' I said as he approached me, wiggling his bottom on the black and white marble floor. Wiggle wiggle wiggle it went as his beady eyes glazed with excitement and I felt myself smile at last.

My hand shot out to pat him, but this dog wasn't going to let me cuddle him just yet. He paused a few feet away, looking up at me, now thumping his tail.

Thump, thump, thump it went and the longer I waited for a human being to appear the more ominous the sound became. I felt a tension build between us – this pet was weighing me up.

'*Hello...*' I called out, and the dog began to whine. Then, following my second slightly louder, less quivery 'Hello', came a 'Coo-ee, who's there?'

The spaniel turned to look and through the arch emerged the bright lustre of flame-red hair, tucked and tied above the shoulders of a woman dressed in a cosy long kilt. 'Zoe Muchton,' she said as her hand shot out, and with the same speed a smile appeared on her face. By no means a beautiful face, but one that wore expression well and left me in no doubt this woman was genuinely pleased to see me.

'You must be Susie Mahl. Well done for finding your way here.' (This meant everyone else had arrived.) 'I do hope the snow didn't cause you any problem. It's only just begun falling. I rather like it. A layering on the roof gives a little bit of insulation. It'll make the bedrooms ever so slightly warmer. A good thing, wouldn't you say?' Her eyebrows rose with enthusiasm and her pupils swelled.

'Yes. But,' I told a slight fib, 'your house doesn't feel cold to me.'

'Nonsense.' Zoe looked down at the dog, which had come to heel. 'You and me, Haggis, we know how cold it can get. Haggis, this is Susie; Susie, this is Haggis. I think you're going to be the best of friends.'

I bent down and ruffled his ears, craving some love in return. But no, Haggis's eyes were fixed on his owner, worried she might bark if he dared share his affection.

'Now, come, Susie.' Zoe tapped me on the shoulder and I followed her through the arch. 'Dump your luggage there at the bottom of the stairs. Haggis will guard it and we'll go into the sitting room and get the introductions over with. The sooner we have the sooner we can all relax.'

Her energetic arm stretched for the handle but a BANG to our left stopped her in her tracks. I turned, startled. A skin-headed man in a tweed waistcoat and hunting-stockinged feet stumbled his way through a door behind the stairs. The keeper I'll bet.

'Stuart?' said Zoe with a sing-song in her voice.

'*Can I have a word?*' He was frantic.

'Now's not the time, I'm afraid, we have a house party, you know, for the painting week and they've only just arrived.'

If Zoe isn't flustered then neither am I. Well, at least I'm trying to convince myself of that.

Stuart wasn't taking no for an answer. 'I've been away this afternoon, yous sent me to pick up a roll of tweed fer the mill, but Donald just rang to say he saw lights doon by the river.'

'Now?'

'Maybe as much as an hour ago.'

'Who was it?'

'No idea. When he headed doon the drive he only just caught the tail lights of a car taking off.'

'How odd.' Zoe raised her hand to her chin. 'We have had people coming and going so it must have been one of them.'

'But Donald's certain someone was at the riverbank. Said he could see the torch fer his window.'

'Well, well, I'm sure it's nothing to worry about. We can discuss it further tomorrow, not now.' Zoe, lady of the manor, had the upper hand.

'Hmmm. Well. Right ye are then, I'll drop in first thing. Make sure youse lock your doors tonight.'

'As we always do, Stuart. I'll come to *you* in the morning. First thing after breakfast.'

That was that. The man turned to leave and Zoe,

without any further ado, burst into the sitting room. 'Everyone,' she announced as the door shut behind us, 'this is Susie Mahl.'

Eight faces were staring at me from comfy sofas and chairs. The fire crackled, my legs wobbled, and all of a sudden I felt slightly sick.

'Sweetheart,' beckoned Zoe, although there was no need, as the Earl of Muchton had dropped his end of the conversation and crossed the room.

'Susie, welcome, I'm Fergus.' His firm handshake made up in strength what his overall appearance lacked. I think Zoe must wear the trousers in this house.

'Thank you for having me.'

'It's wonderful to have you *all* here.' Fergus's gaze cast across the room and rested on his wife with a look of satisfied congratulation: at first glance it seemed they'd certainly assembled a remarkably diverse group.

Zoe, full of beans, touched my arm and whispered in my ear, 'I'm terribly glad to see you're in a polo neck. Some of these lot look distinctly unprepared.'

'Right,' said our hostess. 'From left to right, let's see if I can remember…This is Jane Atkinson…'

'Silent "t",' said Jane, a hoity-toity woman with I'm-happy-post-menopause-letting-myself-go-a-bit written all over her ample figure. 'You pronounce it *A*…kinson. I always think it's better to put people straight from the beginning.'

'Yes, of course, I am sorry.' Zoe moved on. 'Felicity Jennings, that's right, isn't it?'

'Yes, hello, Susie,' said Felicity, and Jane turned to give her a smile. I think these two come as a pair.

'Hello, Miss Mahl,' said a man getting up and marching

across the room in a pair of red trousers so sharp on the eye they'd clearly been bought for the occasion. 'I'm Rupert Higbert.' His brash hand shook mine, after which he retired to stand next to Fergus.

'Susie,' said Zoe. 'We must congratulate Lianne Madaki and Shane Taylor, two A-level students from London who won sponsored places on this week.'

'Hiya, Susie,' said Lianne, showing no signs of a chill despite her scantily clad figure.

'All right, Miss Mahl.' Shane gave me a cocky wink.

'That's great. Well done, you two. So clever.'

Zoe continued to the end of the group. 'Araminta Froglan-Home-Mybridge and Giles Chesterton, another set of A-level students.'

I did well not to smirk at the name of the skinny girl with a dimple in her chin.

'It's lovely to meet you all,' I said as the door behind me opened.

'And...' Zoe turned, 'here he is, Louis Bouchon.'

Oooh – it's a turn-up for the books to have male company of about my age.

Zoe smiled as if introducing an old friend. I wonder if Louis is here as a visitor, a student or both?

'Hello, I'm Susie.'

'Hello, Susie.' This Frenchman's handsome head gave a nonchalant nod as he passed by and settled in the one free armchair.

Fergus began, 'As I have you all gathered, I'd like to run through a few things. Do take a seat, Susie. Here.' He pulled a very unsteady-looking bamboo chair slightly out from the wall. I sat down, it collapsed, everyone laughed.

My goodness my bottom was sore.

'I'm so sorry,' I said, getting up.

Fergus offered his hand a fraction too late.

'Don't be,' giggled Zoe, 'it's absolutely not your fault.' She stretched out her foot and pushed the broken pieces into the skirting board.

'Here.' Louis tapped the arm of his chair and I crossed the room to perch my poor bottom next to him.

'To continue,' said Fergus, 'I hope you've all brought the timetables we sent you. If not, Zoe can muster up a couple of spares.'

'What's muster, Mr?' said Shane as Giles let out a snort.

'I meant Zoe will get you another one. But that's by the bye.' Shane still looked confused. 'What I want to say is, firstly, Zoe and I would like to welcome you *all* into our house and we do hope you will get a lot out of the forthcoming week. It goes without saying, we're very lucky to have Susie Mahl here as our tutor.' Fergus paused, I blushed, he then cleared his throat and continued. 'This is a residency for all abilities and Susie is on hand to help you throughout. In a moment Zoe will take you round the layout of the house and show you all to your respective rooms. Following this you're free to do as you wish until dinner; it'll be in the dining room at eight.'

Fergus's delivery was military to a T, literally – he must have had a spell in the armed forces. Quite a wise career move, between graduating and inheriting, if a non-negotiable future awaits. Why bother building a career if when Daddy dies you'll have to chuck it in? Passing the time learning the skill of organising people and forming a solid group of front-line friends, all within an institution that represses independent thinking – what an advantage.

'Do any of you have any questions?' said Zoe, softening her husband's tone.

No one said a thing and before you could catch a rabbit we were being whisked round the stately reception rooms of the first floor.

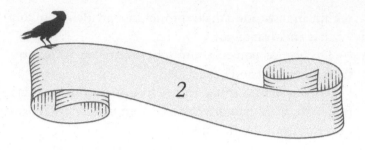

2

Lights flicked on and off as we were taken in and out of vast spaces, the atmosphere of the eighteenth-century Grand Tour reverberating in the architecture and its decoration. Pilasters, cornices, pediments and lintels were scattered throughout. But the painted ceilings, no matter what their colour – pale green, pale blue, pale peach, white, dark blue, dark green, dark red – cracked before our eyes, and with just a few remaining flecks of gold leaf clinging to various mantelpiece reliefs the splendour of the past was hard to grasp. The paintings, on the other hand, were in great order, cleaned and hanging in spotless frames. When I'd asked whether one particularly striking dog was a Gainsborough, Zoe replied, 'As none of you have been here before, Fergus will, I'm sure, make allowances and give you his once-a-year tour of the pictures at some point.'

Louis, who'd been dragging his rather nice suede Derby lace-ups ever since the orientation tour began, made an effort to reach my side. I had assumed he was bored having seen it all before, but when he said under his breath, 'I'd be interested in having a tour of the paintings too,' I realised I'd judged him too quickly – he was here as a student not as a guest of the family after all.

As Zoe pushed open a door into the drawing room, it let out a musty exhale and in we went.

'Fergus and I don't often use this,' she said, flicking a switch. Yellow light cast down from a dusty crystal chandelier, settling on various pieces of drab furniture. 'But I thought I'd show you anyway.'

'Not many paintings in here?' came Rupert's rhetorical question as he stared at the darker rectangular patches on the green walls. They were particularly noticeable in artificial light.

'We recently moved them to some of the spare rooms,' Zoe said. 'Felicty, you've got a nice portrait in yours.'

'Ain't look like you *ever* use this room?' said Shane.

'Very occasionally,' said Zoe. 'That fire,' her forefinger shot out towards a carved wood surround, 'throws out the heat when it's lit. But come on, no time to dilly-dally.' We were shuffled back out the door and on into a pretty much empty adjacent room.

'This one we call the music room, it's where you'll be drawing. I assure you these floor-to-ceiling windows let in a lot of daylight.'

I bet they do; there's a string of them running the entire length of the mottled deep plum wall.

'Easels and drawing boards are over there,' Zoe's head nodded at the opposite wall, 'and as you can see we've pushed bits of furniture to one side.'

That's all that's in here, no paintings, no flowers, no side tables, no figurines, no magazines, no rugs, and despite my critical reaction to the similar un-homely effect earlier, I'm rapidly beginning to understand: the

Muchtons don't have the vast sums of money their surroundings demand. Keeping on top of maintenance in a house of this scale must cost a bomb – Zoe and Fergus's coffers simply aren't deep enough. No surprise they're filling their house with strangers, running sign-up-and-pay courses to bring in a penny or two. But can money buy a remedy for the melancholy within these walls? And if so, they're going to need an awful lot of it to achieve the revamp.

Zoe was striding towards the far end of the room. 'Susie,' she said as she thrust back a folding door, 'you can expand into the billiards room if needs be.'

'Billiards is another name for snooker,' red-trousered Rupert translated to Shane.

'But,' said Lianne, 'why's that called a billiard room...'

'Billiards,' corrected Jane.

'*Billiards* and this a music room if they ain't got no snooker table or sound system in them?'

'Once upon a time,' recalled Zoe, 'they had a billiards table and a piano in them and maybe one day in the future they will again.' And with that ambitious thought we were all paraded into the library.

This room, or 'snug' as Zoe said they tended to refer to it, had bookcases lining the walls. A lovely old-fashioned arrangement. I couldn't help tracing a finger along the complete works of Sir Walter Scott, the collected poetry of Robert Burns, and on into a selection of John Buchan's rip-roaring tales.

Zoe caught me out of the corner of her eye and smiled. 'You must all feel free to borrow books while you're here but please remember to put them back before you leave.'

'Thank you,' I said as I helped myself to *The 39 Steps*.

The bookcases were interrupted by a little fire waiting to be lit, and set back from it, covered in dog hair, was a semi-circle of sunken soft furniture – I think Haggis likes to curl up in here.

'More than a trace of cigars,' scoffed Giles, proud at having identified the smell.

'No smoking in the house any more,' said Zoe. 'But this is where you can watch telly and play board games. They're in that chest over there.' She pointed up the other end of the room towards the only window. To the right of it there was a tall, elegant, Victorian writing bureau with a carpet-covered trunk lying beneath it.

'If you do light the fire, which you may at any time, please, *please*, always put the guard in front of it and make sure to shut the door when you leave.'

'Does anyone play bridge?' said Jane *A*(t)kinson.

'Far too complicated for me,' Rupert said, shaking his head.

'I do, at Cotswold Ladies' College,' said Araminta, who apparently prefers to be called Minty.

'I'm so pleased to hear they still teach you,' said Jane, 'it was part of the curriculum there in my day.'

'You went to my school?' said Minty.

'Yes, I'm an OC.'

'OC?' Felicity was confused.

'Old Cotswoldian, it's what members of the former pupils' network are called.'

Zoe took us out of the library (I can't quite bring myself to call it a snug) and paused for a moment at the foot of the stairs. 'Before we go up, I'll just point out that door,' she said; it was behind the staircase. 'If you go through it, first on your right is the door to the basement, that's where the drying room is.'

'Expecting rain, are we?' said Rupert.

'It's Scotland,' said Giles.

'There will be rain and sun,' smiled Zoe. 'But regardless, I'd like you all to keep your outdoor kit in the drying room, please. It makes for a tidy house.'

'Of course,' said Felicity with a tremble in her voice.

Zoe gazed at her, making sure everything was all right, and Jane for some reason squeezed her friend's hand.

'Now,' Zoe's focus was back on the door behind the stairs, 'if you go through there and turn *left* down the corridor and enter the second door on the *right*, you'll find the dining room. I won't show you now as Mhàiri Bannoch will be laying up.'

'Mhàiri?' said Jane, rather acutely.

'Yes, you don't know her, do you? That would be extraordinary.' Zoe tee-heed at the possibility.

'No, no. I just wanted to get her name straight. It's Mhàiri not Mary, yes?'

'Yes, Maaaaarie,' said Zoe, opening her mouth wide as if encouraging us all to do the same. 'She and her husband Donald have been here for years, part of the architecture of this place.'

I amused myself wondering if they needed a makeover too.

'Okey dokey, time to go upstairs.'

I bent down to pick up my suitcase and all of a sudden Shane was hanging by my side, reaching for the laces of his white trainers. Lianne nudged his behind and whispered, 'You don't have to do that here.'

I'm in Shane's camp. I don't understand why anyone would wear shoes upstairs, especially rural folk what with animal dung, wet weather and all that, but they do, and you know what – either there are very good cleaners in the country or carpets don't get as dirty as us born-townies would think.

Facing us as we went upstairs was a console table on the landing covered in photographs of Fergus and Zoe. A pre-offspring collection of romantic duos – one from their wedding day, a let's-lie-down-in-the-heather shot, and a couple of staged, possibly engagement photos. Jane leaned in to have a better look, but it was Felicity who paid the compliment, 'What a gorgeous couple.'

Zoe's eyes sparkled and she almost looked pretty. 'Thank you,' she smiled. 'Now, spread yourselves out along this side of the landing.'

It was a square design, open to the stairwell with a gallery around it. A delightful collection of oil sketches crowded the walls and I could just make out the signature E. Landseer Harris. I'm surprised they're Landseer, as I've only ever seen his large majestic Scottish paintings. Those are a bit much for my taste but these little gems are absolutely lovely, great big loose brush strokes on wood panel.

'So,' said Zoe with her back against the wall, motioning to her left and right, 'these are the north-east and north-west wing corridors and directly opposite are the south-east and south-west wing corridors. We have plenty of rooms and half as many bathrooms.'

She pointed under an arch to her left. 'Fergus, Haggis and I are down there, and, Louis, if you trot down the

north-west wing,' she was now pointing at a dark corridor on her right, 'you'll find the first door opens to
the Blue Room, yours. Rupert, you're just beyond Louis,
there's a bathroom between you to share. Donald should
have carried your bags up by now, that's if you all labelled
them.'

'Is there time for a nap?' said Rupert.

'Yes, yes, do have a bit of time out before dinner.' Zoe
took a step further along the landing, and flung open a
door. 'Felicity, your en-suite twin is in here, and Jane,
here you go, yours is just a bit further down...a small
double.' She flicked a switch and the whole house fell
into darkness.

'Blast,' she stamped her foot, 'there must be a fault.'

Giles's mobile phone lit up.

'*Fergus*, *angel*,' Zoe hollered over the banister. 'We
have a problem.'

Fergus had a torch in hand at the bottom of the stairs.

'I realised,' he mocked. 'Hang on there and I'll go to
the fuse box.'

'What are you going to do?' said Jane, rather boldly I
thought.

'Anyone got a candle?' called out Rupert.

'Don't worry, the lights will be back on in a sec,'
reassured Zoe.

'OoooOOOooo,' mimicked Shane, but before any of
us had time to feel frightened the lights were on again.

'Voila,' rejoiced Zoe.

'Darling?' Fergus was coming up the stairs.

'Yes?'

'The Rose room's wiring is faulty. A spark came out
the box when I flicked the switch.'

Zoe marched straight into what was going to be Jane's room.

'No, my love,' said Fergus. 'The electrics are faulty, the lights in there won't work. I've turned them off at the main switch.'

Zoe came back out with Jane's suitcase in her hand. 'I am terribly sorry about this.'

'You can share with me?' offered Felicity, hovering in her doorway.

Fergus's and Zoe's eyebrows rose, both hoping Jane would say 'yes please'.

'Can't you fix it?' said Jane, staring at Fergus.

'I'll try and call our electrician tomorrow, but I'm afraid we won't be able to sort it out tonight.' He took charge of the suitcase in Zoe's hand.

'My room's lovely,' said Felicity. 'There are two large single beds.'

Jane forced a smile and in she went.

'Right,' Zoe continued, 'everyone else, follow me.'

Tapping a relatively new door under the arch of the south-east wing, she explained, 'This is locked, it isn't used.' Then, continuing on around the square she went under an arch opposite and flicked a switch. Sporadic energy-saving light bulbs began to glow and as we waited for them to brighten she informed us, 'This is what we call the children's corridor.'

It was glum to say the least and smelt exactly how you'd imagine a cold old house's childless children's corridor would. The lights came up to speed and Zoe's kilt swung from her hips as she trotted down the well-worn drugget carpet. 'There are two bathrooms to share. I suggest girls take one and boys the other.'

The first door on her left took a shove from her shoulder before it scraped across a crowning wooden floor. We all hovered in the doorway as she went in. There was a sunken single bed pushed up against the wall and a wardrobe against another, opposite. A pokey curtained window with a few ragged hardbacks piled chaotically on its ledge faced us. Zoe read out the label on the moleskin bag. 'Giles Chesterton, you're in here. But, before you make yourself at home, come and I'll talk you through the plumbing.'

Into a large carpeted bathroom we all went.

'Urgh,' said Lianne, peering into the deep bathtub.

'Oh,' said Zoe enthusiastically, 'don't worry about those stains on the enamel, they're from years of dripping water. Brown but not dirty.' Then, holding her hair back with one hand, she bent to give the cold tap a firm twist – it didn't make the slightest bit of difference; the water continued to drip.

'Look,' said Zoe, who was now walking towards a china crapper. Honestly it was, Thomas Crapper's genuine article, the name stamped on the cistern high up on the wall. 'I want to show you how to pull the chain.'

Giles's nose made a noise as he held back a laugh and Zoe proceeded, with no idea what had amused him. 'You must draw this wooden handle down until the water comes. A little old-fashioned quirk.'

Once she'd demonstrated the method we left the bathroom and, thanks to labels on suitcases, most rooms and people were quickly paired off. 'Susie,' she said, heading for the semi-darkness at the far end of the corridor, 'here's where you are.' Mustering strength, she flung the door open. A great gust of freezing air shot out.

'Oh gosh.' Zoe rushed in to slam the little window shut. 'Sorry about that. I've been airing the house. I do hope you'll be happy in here.'

'Yes, thank you,' I smiled, longing for her to lend me a blanket.

But she left, pulling the door shut behind her.

I put John Buchan's *The 39 Steps* on the side table and dumped my suitcase on the floor. I felt lost and cold and low. The wallpaper was peeling at every join, the iron bedstead conjured wartime hospital scenes and the curtains, only moments ago flapping outside, were wet. I took in a deep breath and the pervasive smell of must shot up my nose. That hard-to-grasp-hold-of essence of green shrubbery letting off steam in a particularly damp and lacking-in-daylight part of the garden. Down by the pond, round the back of the boat hut. In I breathed just to make sure. Yup. Damp.

I kicked off my shoes and then, in the hopes it would warm me up, unpacked as quickly as I possibly could. Bending down and up, down and up, hurriedly hanging my things in the mahogany wardrobe then to and fro the window shelf, arranging my toiletries. All the time telling myself off for acting spoilt. I'm jolly lucky to have a roof over my head.

Done and dusted I flung myself down on the bed. The duvet bounced up at my feet and something fell to the floor.

A crusty, marble-eyed teddy bear is now in my hands and my heartbeat is rising. I can't shake off the horror of Chucky from *Child's Play* and those decal eyes. Mr Bear went flying up in the air, landed on top of the wardrobe and disappeared. He's gone. Phew.

I rested my weary head on the pillow and looked up at the bubbles of damp on the ceiling. It took me back to my childhood room where often I would make myself dizzy, circling my eyes around the wet yellow rings. Lying here now, doing the same, I suddenly remember I must text Mum. She'd been nervous about my journey today, despite the fact I've driven to Scotland several times before. All those trips with my ex, to visit his mother...Mum must have forgotten. No surprise. She's never given any weight to relationships past. Not her fault. My mother didn't have any boy-friends before Dad, so how can she possibly understand a broken heart?

I got out my mobile. There's no reception. Oh crumbs. I simply must find a solution for getting in touch, I know she'll have been waiting to hear from me all day – mobile on loud, in her pocket. Mum's anxiety is a new trait, born from our heart-to-heart at Christmas. As Dad had put it, 'this is a conversation for you and your mother'. Ever since, our relationship has been sticky. I can't afford to cause them any worry. I must let Mum know I've arrived safe.

I found the internet. No password – no neighbours, no need, I suppose. Mum refuses to use WhatsApp – 'Far too many lines of communication these days' – so I'll just have to Wi-Fi call her instead.

'Hello?'

'Hi, Mum.'

'Susie, everything okay? Have you arrived?' Her breath was short.

'Yes, yes. I'm here at last.'

'Oh good,' she sighed. 'I got your father to check the

weather. I think you're going to wake to snow. Oh love, I do hope you're going to be okay.'

Londoners eh. They think snow is a beast come to bring everything to a grinding stop. They see none of the magic, the pure white forming heavy quilts on pine trees, delicate crystals on window panes and billowing sheets across the landscape. To them it is a nuisance, grey slush, 'ankle dirt, unavoidable ankle dirt' is what my father calls it.

'I'll be fine. Please don't worry. I'm looking forward to the week ahead.'

'We'll be thinking of you and wait to hear when you're safely back in Sussex.'

I'd arrived, that's what mattered, now she could hang up. Neither of my parents use the telephone for proper conversation. The in-between details could wait until we were next face to face.

'Bye, Susie, have fun. We love you.'

'Bye. Love to Dad.'

I was glad I'd called. Hearing Mum's voice brought comfort to me in this strange house. As for them looking up *my* weather – fancy that. They really are living through me these days. I'm no longer a daughter out of sight, out of mind. What a happy thought, even if it is in a spoilt-only-child kind of way.

I took in a deep breath, hoping Mum's finally forgiven me for what I made her do. But I must not dwell on family issues; I've come to Scotland for a change of scene. To get away from life down south and take my mind off heartache. Thank goodness my mobile doesn't have reception, I won't be wasting time permanently checking if Dr Toby Cropper has been in touch.

Toby's a mortuary clerk I hooked up with in Dorset last year. He's so darn difficult to get off my mind. I honestly thought we were lifetime partners. But then, I found out he had a son. I wouldn't have minded if he'd been straight with me from the start. But he wasn't. We don't communicate any more, one non-committal scribbled postcard in answer to my loving letter put an end to that. He's frozen me out and I can't help thinking he's probably now breaking some other girl's heart.

I clenched my fist and punched the duvet...Why do I always fall for the wrong men?

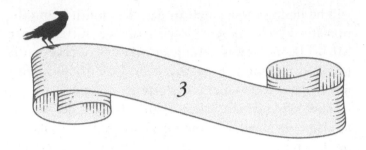

3

The dinner gong boomed through the house and I headed downstairs. Pinned up on the music room door was a new notice.

Daily Timetable
Breakfast 8.30am to 9.30am
Morning Tutorial 10am to 12.30pm
Lunch 1pm (buffet at the house or a picnic on location)
Afternoon tutorial 2.30pm to 5pm
Dinner* will be served at 8pm
Wednesday night ceilidh

* Paint-stained clothes are not permitted in the dining room, please wear appropriate dinner dress.

'No rest for the wicked,' came a self-amused voice behind me. Rupert was here. 'I heard the gong, a fine way to rally the troops.'

'Yes,' I smiled.

'Let's go through, shall we?' He led the way, pinning the doors open so I could walk through first.

The dining room smelt of gas, the culprit being the non-flued 1970s heater glowing orange in the corner. Mhàiri Bannoch was settling a final bowl of peas on the hotplate, nestling her way between Jane Atkinson, first in the queue, and Giles Chesterton – second.

Zoe doled out instructions. 'Susie, Rupert, do join the food line, shepherd's pie tonight. Fergus and I will take the heads of the table and the rest of you can sit where you like.'

No one other than me had changed out of their travelling clothes, something I like to do if I've driven a long way. The others are clean and tidy and, as for Zoe and Fergus, let's just say warmth comes before flair. I'm in a dress, no longer feeling the cold. I've had a lovely hot peaty-brown bath and with a bit of snooping I came across a blow heater in the broom cupboard; it's a bit naughty but I've smuggled it back to my room.

My tummy rumbled as I carried my full plate to the table and sat down next to Minty. I waited for the seat on my left to fill before starting, but no one came.

'Felicity's turned in for an early night,' said Jane across the table. 'She'll be better tomorrow, just needs some time to herself.'

This could have been a stab at having to share a bedroom but her sympathetic tone suggested Felicity was getting over the likes of a cold.

Fergus was last in line and with a plate full of food he took the long way around the table, whispering something in his wife's ear as he passed.

'Oh yes,' she said. 'So's we can save on washing up please remember the colour of your napkin ring; that way you can use the same one every day.' Anything to save a penny or two.

The turned-wooden rings were painted and the linen napkins dark enough to hide a week's worth of muck. I laid one across my lap and just as I was about to shove a forkful of food into my mouth a great scream came from the kitchen.

'*Aagh. Aagh. Aagh,*' hurtled through the wall.

Zoe and Fergus took off and as they burst open the swing door Mhàiri Bannoch's wail came to a grinding halt.

Shane and Lianne began to giggle and across the table a discussion began: 'Was it a burn?' 'Was it a dropped pot?' 'Was it an intruder?' 'Was it a ghost?'

'No,' said Zoe, re-entering the room. 'I'm sorry about that, Mhàiri just got a fright.'

'Yes,' confirmed Fergus, coming in behind her. 'Nothing to worry about.'

'What was it then?' said Lianne.

Fergus looked at Zoe and without a moment of doubt she told us, 'There was something in the kitchen but we've got it out now.'

'Like what?' said Shane but Zoe ignored him.

'Come on,' she said, 'eat up, the food will be getting cold.'

'You not hungry?' said Lianne, looking at Minty's spot of shepherd's pie and tiny portion of veg.

'I don't like to eat much before bed.'

Looking at her I don't think Minty likes to eat much most of the time. Although I do remember that age when things grew outwards, no longer upwards; puppy fat was hard to shed and Mum coined the phrase 'Rubensian beauty'.

Lianne, in contrast to her neighbour, had embraced the hormonal flux. Her curves, full cheeks and soft, fleshy figure had sex-pot written all over them – à la Titian's *Venus Anadyomene*. And as Rupert filled a glass with red wine I hoped Lianne could hold her drink.

Giles took it upon himself to take the bottle round the table.

'None for me,' said Minty.

'Fill it up,' said Shane, and so it went on, most people tucking into the free alcohol on offer. Getting their money's worth, this week costing an arm and a leg.

'Berry Bros. and Rudd,' lorded Rupert while tapping the label. 'They provide a good bottle of plonk.'

Louis' eyes rose to the ceiling.

'Yes,' said Fergus. 'We're drinking the remainders from the shooting season.'

'Marvellous to have some left over.'

'Well, with drink-driving laws so strict nowadays, far less is drunk.'

'I thought that didn't apply in Scotland,' said Giles.

'Scotland's worse than England,' said Rupert. 'They'd fine you on cough medicine here, wouldn't they?' He looked at Zoe, who charmed him with a chuckle. 'Do you let any days?' he asked, turning back to Fergus. 'Shooting's a frightfully expensive business in the twenty-first century.'

'It's all gone to a syndicate, grouse and pheasant. We provide lunch in the bothy and tea in the house.'

'Bothy?' snorted Giles.

'It's a small hut on the moor.'

'Letting your shoot is probably a nice little earner,' said Jane, hinting she was familiar with country pursuit sums.

'Yes,' said Zoe. 'But I'm full of ideas for making the most of living here.'

She proceeded to reel off endless suggestions: yurts, a plant nursery, craft courses, cookery demonstrations. When she mentioned 'spinning classes from local sheep's wool' Fergus's face fell. His wife was irrepressible in her ideas for making money, and as he subconsciously patted his tummy, one could sense him begging for a baby that would calm her down.

Loyally he said, 'Zoe's done wonders at thinking of all sorts of innovative ways to sustain living here. She's even taken the estate's accounts in hand. But, darling, we must remember limited internet in these parts will restrict the extent of what we can and can't do.'

'My husband,' Zoe teased, 'insists people expect to be permanently logged on.'

'He does have a point,' said Louis.

'You must have a book festival,' said Jane. 'They're terribly popular in the south.'

'Yes,' agreed Rupert. 'My wife simply loves our local affair. Makes her feel part of the intelligentsia.'

'Weddings?' suggested Minty, and Zoe answered before her husband could.

'No, no, that works in the south but here in the Highlands the weather's too unreliable.'

'Of course,' Minty giggled at her mistake.

'What about a film location?' said Giles.

'Our friends put us off that.' Fergus shook his head. 'Their Dorset estate featured in the adaptation of Jane Austen's *Love and Friendship* – they'd never do it again.'

'Why not?' said Lianne.

'They had to leave home for a month, no contact, and when they returned the place was a complete tip. That's enough to put anyone off.'

Shane's eyes lit up. 'I bet the money was good.'

'Still, it doesn't sound worth it to me.'

'Me neither,' said Jane and I wondered if she lived in a large house herself.

'Being a land agent, as I myself am,' said Rupert, 'one can imagine this place is very expensive to run.'

'Why don't you sell it then?' said Shane. 'You'd make millions.'

'No, no.' Zoe shook her head vigorously, and Fergus explained, 'This house has been in my family for over two hundred and fifty years, never been bought or sold, passed down through the generations by inheritance since 1761. I'd hate to lose hold of it. Zoe and I are one link in a larger chain and our primary aim is to pass it on to the next generation in good condition.'

'I have enormous respect for your ambition,' said Rupert.

'Do you have brothers and sisters?' asked Minty.

'One brother living down the back drive.'

Wow, I thought, if he's living bang next door, they must get on *very* well. I'd find it tough to see my sibling (if I had one) inherit all this.

'You have a brother?' exclaimed Rupert. 'Terribly unlike me but I never thought to ask. He must be the younger?'

'Yes,' Zoe gloated, clearly proud of having bagged the elder.

'I bet he's jealous of you,' Shane stared at Fergus and Louis smirked. I think we share a sense of humour.

Zoe diverted the conversation. 'We're adapting to the contemporary world.'

'Exactly, we no longer see Auchen Laggan Tosh as a private home,' Fergus declared.

'Really?' said Giles.

'Yes, this place is something we must share in order to afford living here.'

'That bloke,' Shane was pointing at a portrait of a general in full Blues and Royals rigmarole, 'has money plastered all over him.'

The colour drained from Fergus's cheeks. 'My grandfather,' he said.

I stared at the picture. I hadn't seen a portrait composition like it before. The head was in profile and the body was face on, and in my opinion they didn't meld together very well. The only quick explanation I could think of was that the sitter had a scar down one side of his face and decided halfway through the process to turn his head.

'Would anyone like second helpings?' said Zoe and when no one accepted she began clearing the plates. Minty and I jumped up too.

'Sit down,' she said with a kind but firm smile. 'There'll be plenty of opportunity for everyone to muck in. Fergus and I will do this course.'

'No, no,' I said, 'it's the least I can do.'

'*Angel*,' said Zoe firmly as she beckoned him with her free hand.

'What is it?' he asked without getting up.

'*Please*,' I said, 'let me help.'

Zoe had no choice but to accept, and with a handful of plates I grasped the opportunity to enter the kitchen.

Good Lord. There was a shattering of glass on the

linoleum floor and the stout woman standing amongst it looked utterly terrified on seeing me.

'Thank you, Mhàiri,' said Zoe, as she breezed in. 'That was delicious and how you knock it up in this restrictive space I'll never know. My mother-in-law's kitchen is the next step in our modifications, I promise. In the meantime, we *must* attach a blackout blind to that window.'

Mhàiri's hands trembled as she made space for the plates.

'Hello,' I said, with a sympathetic smile, realising a bird must have come in from outside, flying into its reflection and breaking the window as well as its neck.

'This is our tutor for the week,' said Zoe.

'Yes, I'm Susie, Susie Mahl.'

'Hello.'

'So Susie,' said Zoe, with a matronly tone, 'now you see why I didn't want you in here. I'd hate for you to cut yourself.' She turned to Mhàiri and asked, 'Have you called Stuart?'

'Aye and me husband, they're both going to come and patch it up. I'll see to it all.'

'Oh good. Thank you. Come along now, Susie, we must get out of here before the men turn up. Mhàiri...'

'Aye?'

'Pudding?'

'Oh aye, I made youse all a wee trifle.'

She thrust a Pyrex bowl of colourful layers into my hands and Zoe pushed me back through the swing door. Yuck. I really dislike trifle. This one had a discoloured crust on top and when Zoe sunk a spoon into it – deciding it'd be easier to serve people than have everyone get up – the mixture didn't wobble like it normally should. Unfortunately, I had to accept some. This food was made specially for us, and I hate to see things going to waste.

Rupert was holding up his spoon, calling down the table to Fergus, 'Is this your family's crest?'

Every piece of cutlery had a fish engraved on the handle.

'Not ours,' said Fergus. 'That's the Kelton family crest.'

Jane's eyes narrowed as she stared at him. Crumbs, do I have a short-sighted artist on the course?

'Then why do you have theirs?' said Shane.

'My father bought this silver when they sold it. He liked the association with salmon.'

'The river Trickle is a salmon river,' said Zoe, filling in the gaps.

'Kelton,' said Jane, joining the conversation, 'a kelt is what you call a freshwater fish after spawning and before returning to the sea. And,' there was no stopping her, 'if it were me hosting a house full of strangers, I'd have locked up the silver.' She glanced at Shane, which was embarrassing. It was far too early in the week for jokes like this.

After dinner, Jane and Minty went straight to bed and the rest of us piled into the sitting room, Fergus having suggested a dram. Haggis was curled up by the fire and as soon as I sat down in an armchair he jumped up onto my lap.

'Oh Haggis, you naughty boy,' said Zoe. 'Just push him off if you don't like it, Susie.'

'He's adorable.' I patted his soft coat, pleased to have him on my knee, sharing his affection at last.

Louis was slumped in an armchair, watching my hand

stroke the auburn fur. His arrogance rejected conversation so I didn't even try.

'Whisky, Susie?' said Fergus.

'No thank you.'

The wine with dinner had made me sleepy and I didn't plan on staying up much longer.

Shane and Lianne both said 'yes' and Fergus convinced them it was best drunk with a slug of water. Then, I presume exhausted by the formality of the evening, they rushed off to watch TV opposite. Giles wasn't exactly invited but followed too.

Zoe sat down next to me. She genuinely wanted to hear about my life. Here was a Countess with no airs and graces. She'd kicked off her shoes, snuggled her feet up under her kilt and asked me if I would draw Haggis this week.

'Yes, I'd love to if I find the time.'

'Great, that would be such a bonus. I saw the prices on your website. Such good value I thought.'

She went on to explain what *she* used to do. 'I can't tell you how pleased my mother was when I met the Muchtons again. My parents thought being an accountant was no way to find a husband. But, Susie, I liked working and that's why having quit my job I've thrown myself into making a go of things here. My training is perfect for turning a profit. I have no doubt I'll make this place work.'

Her enthusiasm was admirable but I cannot believe any of her suggestions at dinner will bring in enough money to sustain living here. Being an accountant, she must be fully aware of the sums involved. Now I'm thinking perhaps she has a much bigger plan up her sleeve? Even an idea she hasn't actually shared with her husband yet?

'You mentioned "met again"?' I said. 'Did you and Fergus know each other before?'

'Ha, well. I don't like to count it. But I did spend a night here when I was a child. My mother likes to constantly remind me, but Fergus wasn't even born then.'

Our conversation was abruptly interrupted by Fergus. 'Darling, listen to this, you'll never believe what Rupert's just told me.'

Zoe raised her eyebrows at me and turned to join in.

'He knew the Kelton family.'

'I didn't *know* them,' corrected Rupert. 'It was my first job, I'd just started working for Walker & Mackintosh. I was the land agent for the Kelton family estate and my colleague managed the contents sale. When you mentioned them at dinner their name rang a bell and I've just twigged why.'

'Father bought a lot of the contents,' said Fergus. 'It was thirty-odd years ago.'

'How amusing,' said Zoe.

'I'll never forget it,' said Rupert, crossing his ankles while making sure not to crinkle the creases down the front of his trousers. 'Hector Kelton was a tricky client.'

'Ooh do tell us more,' said Zoe, longing for a bit of aristocratic gossip.

'I'll fill you in later,' interjected Fergus. He clearly did not want his wife asking any more questions.

Zoe stretched out her arms and ran her hands through her wonderfully thick hair. 'I think I'm going to go to bed. Night, everyone.'

I pushed Haggis off my knee and got up to leave. But

when Fergus asked Louis how he'd heard about this week, Zoe blocked the doorframe, waiting for his answer.

'Ewen told me about it.'

'*Ewen?*'

Haggis gave a little yap.

'Yes.'

'Fergus's brother?' said Zoe, which was confusing… surely she knew who he meant?

Even I knew. Before arriving here, in the north of Scotland, at a big house, with titled owners, I'd done some shallow research on the current generation of Muchtons. Just enough to start a very basic conversation if needs be. Nothing invasive, of course not, it *would* be unfair to form an opinion prior to meeting. But I do know Fergus's brother Ewen is his twin – the younger twin. Imagine that. Missing out on inheriting all of this by a whisker.

'Yes,' said Louis.

Fergus stared at him. 'Why didn't you mention you knew my brother, at dinner?'

'He's barely been here a couple of hours, angel, give the man a chance,' Zoe giggled. 'Or maybe, Louis,' she tipped her head at him, 'you didn't want to say.'

Is there a problem between Fergus and his brother?

Zoe flicked her hair over her shoulder and walked out of the room. Haggis and I followed closely behind her.

'Night, Susie,' she said as she bent down to hold the dog back.

'Night, and thank you.'

'Haggis,' beckoned Fergus as I went upstairs. 'Come on, boy, let's go and look at the stars.'

'Think I'll join you,' I heard Rupert say as I turned under the arch into the children's corridor.

Stuart's words, 'Make sure youse lock your doors tonight', crept into my head and when a bedroom door creaked open I jumped on the spot.

'Susie,' said Minty, catching me fumble, 'are you okay?'

'Yes, sorry, I just got a fright.'

'Sure?'

'Of course,' I smiled. 'Sleep well.'

I'm actually quite a brave person at heart but this house has me on edge. From the moment I stepped through the front door I've been acutely aware of an unsettled feeling inside. And as friendly as our hosts are, there seems to be a string of surprises ready and waiting to pounce: Stuart in a fluster; Mhàiri's scream; Rupert's connection with the past; Louis knowing Fergus's brother – and that's all just from the first night. Is there some funny business going on?

Old Scottish houses often have a tale or two and I'm beginning to think I might enjoy working this one out. I have played amateur detective in the past. Me and Toby, should I say. He was a side-kick extraordinaire. But I'd love to solve a puzzle without him. Prove I can stand on my own two feet.

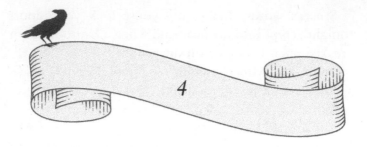

4

Monday morning is here and day one of teaching has begun. We're in the music room and I'm handing out orders as if I've done it before.

'Drawing boards behind the door. Easels over here, there's enough to go around. Just ask if you don't know how they work.' I counted everyone up. 'Anyone know what's happened to Louis?'

No answer.

'Anyone?' Still no answer. 'Well, Giles, as you're all set up please go and give him a shout.'

'Certainly.'

The class's work clothes told a tale. Jane and Felicity had matching smocks tied over calf-length skirts. Rupert had splashed out on a linen artist's apron, one with brush holders in the front. Clearly all three of them had been on a shopping spree up the Fulham Road. That's where the best art shop is, apparently – out of my budget so I've never been. Lianne and Shane were in paint-splattered boiler suits, Minty was in a man's shirt possibly belonging to a boyfriend, and Giles, who'd returned with no word of Louis, was in a tattersall shirt not in the least bit tatty.

'I'm afraid the model is going to be a bit late,' I explained. Zoe had filled me in after breakfast. 'Her car wouldn't start so Fergus has gone to pick her up. In the meantime, let's get everything organised. Shane and Giles, please can you move that chaise longue into the centre of the room? Then you can all make a circle with your easels around it, not too close, you'll need a wide angle.' My arms pointed left and right as the orders flowed. I was a natural. This confidence is alien, but I'm thrilled to have it within.

The room was warm. Someone must have been in early to turn on the gas heaters as they'd burnt off their initial smell.

'Lianne,' I said, 'grab those rugs in the corner and drape them over the back of the chaise longue, perhaps extend them onto the floor, you choose. *Minty.*' She was fiddling with her mobile. 'There are some cushions in a bag over there. Take your pick of colours and scatter them on the rugs, please.'

'Miss, I'm boiling,' said Shane.

'You're only drawing this morning so why not take your overalls off?'

Lianne followed his lead.

'Louis,' I said as he strolled into the room, 'is everything okay?'

'Just fine, sorry, I lost track of time.'

'Where were you?' asked Giles.

'In my room.'

'No, you weren't, I looked in there...nice room by the way.'

'I was also outside for a bit of fresh air.' Visiting his friend Ewen I bet. 'Anyway, sorry I'm late. What can I do?'

'Copy the others and set up an easel. Then tape a large piece of paper onto a drawing board.'

'There ain't no tape,' said Shane.

'We were meant to bring our own,' said Minty, having hidden hers.

'You can use some of mine,' offered Rupert as he dived into his picnic basket.

'Thanks, mate.'

Felicity's short arms were struggling to secure the tall board onto her easel.

'Here, let me get that.'

'Thanks, Susie.'

'I hope you slept well.'

'Yes, sorry I didn't stay up for dinner.' Her eyes dipped to the floor. 'I didn't feel strong enough.'

'Do you feel okay now?'

'Much better. Raring to go.'

Louis was by the windows looking out at one great big expanse of untouched snow with only a stone fountain in the centre peeking up as if gasping for air.

'Beautiful,' I said, sidling up to him.

He gave me a cheeky wink. 'It'll be gone by lunch. It's mild out there.'

The door to the room flew open and Haggis rushed in before Fergus's outstretched leg could stop him. 'Haggis, *Haggis*. Come here. Drawing isn't for doggies.' Minty helped usher the dog out.

'I'm *so* surry,' came an apology from the young woman strutting her fine figure into the room. 'Hiya youse, I'm Cailey Baird.'

Fergus hovered a second longer than necessary, then left, pulling the door closed behind him.

None of the students uttered a word.

'Hi, Cailey, I'm Susie, the tutor.'

'Hiya.'

I decided it was best not to introduce everyone by name. Getting on too personal a level with a life model can bring about all sorts of complications and the risks of this were rising by the second. Calling central casting, this blonde bombshell (think Nastassja Kinski in *Paris, Texas*) was now wrestling off her crimson mohair sweater. Baird by name bared by nature.

'I've put a screen up over there,' I pointed outside the circle of easels encouraging her to change behind it, 'bit of modesty for you.'

'Aye, Susie, I'll do whitever yous want. I'll teek me kit aff over there. Ne problem.'

Her smile was enthralling. Great big white teeth gleaming between shocking pink lipstick that had most definitely been applied up the bumpy front drive.

The room fell silent as Cailey's uninhibited figure appeared from behind the screen. Her skin was the colour of porcelain and even I had to remind myself life drawing is life drawing, *not* perving at a naked body. It's studying the beauty of the way light falls on the nude. The shadows in the crevasses and the darkness of the folds. Concentrating on the luminosity of skin and letting your eye travel across the figure.

'Right ya,' she said, 'where do yous want me?'

'Come, stand in the centre.'

As Cailey crept between the easels her tear-drop bosoms were the only things in the whole room looking towards the floor. Even the fire gave a crackle and a flicker.

'You must say if you want to do something different,' I had to get this class started ASAP, 'but I was thinking of six short poses to loosen everyone up?'

'Right ya. This kind of thing do?'

Cailey was lunging forwards, posed with her arms up in the air. A trained dancer I'm sure, no normal person has balance as good as this. Her figure was taut and the light streaming in the windows sculpted her every muscle. This room was perfect.

'Yes. That's ideal. Now, everyone, I'd like you to draw each short pose on the same sheet of paper. Try to get down the essentials of the figure, don't get tied up in the detail. Fluency is the thing here and lightning response.'

Jane exhaled loudly and Felicity asked if she could start.

'Yes, yes, get going. I want you to trace the outline of the body, get a feel for the extension of the limbs.'

I made sure not to mention Cailey's name, referring to her as an object not a person in the hopes it would help everyone concentrate.

It seemed to be working...

'Next pose please.'

'I haven't finished,' said Rupert.

'It's about practising not finishing. Don't worry. There will be a long pose after the break. These ones are just to get you going.'

Giles, Shane, Minty and Lianne drew fast. The scratching sound of their charcoal on paper intimidating the less experienced others who were, in my opinion, spending too much time looking and not enough drawing.

'Rapid sketches,' I said. 'One, two, three, it doesn't matter how many, just get your hand working. Another pose please.'

'This okay?' Cailey was crouching down with one leg extended.

'Perfect. Just great. Thank you.' She really was an excellent model.

'Susie?' said Rupert.

I went to his side.

'I don't know how to tackle this.'

Cailey's leg was shooting out straight at him, her crotch only just obscured by a conveniently placed thigh.

'Foreshortening is hard.' I stood behind him so as I could get a better view. 'Don't worry about the scale, just focus on the movement, get the muscles down. You can work on accuracy later.'

'Thanks.'

Jane's hand was down by her side, she'd given up. Time for a new pose. I got Cailey to perch on the chaise longue.

'If you can keep your back straight, Cailey, that'd be great. I want the class to focus on your centre of gravity.'

'Sure thing.'

When the exercise came to an end, everyone gave their drawing hands a good shake. I nodded at Cailey who disappeared behind the screen. Two seconds and she was back, pulling a satin dressing gown over her shoulders and not bothering to tie up the belt.

'Miss,' said Shane, 'I'm going to the toilet.'

Jane and Felicity left the room too.

'We'll start again at half past ten. Moving into a long pose. Come, Cailey, let's work it out.'

'Can she lie down?' said Minty.

'Everyone okay with that?'

Five heads nodded.

'Chuck us a cushion,' said Cailey. 'This settee's rock 'ard. Don't half smell too.'

'Moth balls,' said Giles.

'Hang on a minute, I'll go get a quilt from my car – it's comfy and it'll definitely smell better.'

'Cheers,' said Cailey, and I left the room.

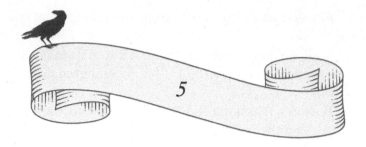

5

The sky was bright blue, the air crisp, and the cold hit me as I stepped outside. I rushed down the outdoor staircase full of glee that the class, so far, seemed to be going well. Louis had blithely ploughed his own furrow, drawing body parts on several bits of paper, but the rest of them had taken my instruction on board and drawn rapidly on one piece of paper.

A clapped-out Peugeot squeaked into the yard. Zoe was behind the wheel. Presumably back from visiting Stuart.

'Hi,' I waved as she parked next to my car.

'Hi, Susie.' She heaved a huge sigh as she got out. 'This buzz-box is hopeless in the snow. I'm so glad it's melting.'

Then, looking at my flat tyre, she joked, 'It's jolly lucky you made it here last night.'

'Yes, isn't it. I was going to tell you about that later.'

'Well, if you don't need to get away before, we'll make sure it's sorted by Friday.'

'How kind, thank you.'

'Class going okay?'

'Oh yes, great. I'm just getting something from my car.'

'Well, if you've time can I have a quick word?'

I stopped with surprise. Had I done something wrong already?

'It won't take long, it's just I wanted to mention Fergus's brother to you, in confidence.'

'Of course.'

'Ewen lives in a cottage down the back drive. He has done for years, although I'm sure he'll move on one day. He's very nice, *I* like him a lot,' – I'm detecting a bit of tension between Ewen and Fergus – 'but it's quite like him to decide he wants to join the course and I don't think that would be a good idea.'

'Okay,' I said, a little confused why I was being told.

'I just feel that for our paying residents it's unfair if family get to do it for free.'

'I quite understand.'

'Thanks, Susie, I knew you would. He's coming to dinner tonight,' Zoe looked happy at the thought, 'and if he mentions it, would you be kind and back me up and say there's no more room?'

'Yes, sure.'

'*Ow, ow, ow,*' she yelped. 'Good god, you little bugger.' There was a large black bird at Zoe's feet and as she kicked and shook her hands, a slinky gold bracelet slipped off her wrist. Before either of us could do anything the sly bird had snatched it in its beak. I instantly tried to grab it back but the scavenger flew, up, up and away. 'Oh no, it's taken your bracelet.'

'Thank heavens it isn't real gold.' She turned her ankle towards me. The bird had drawn blood.

'How absolutely awful.'

'Ravens are evil,' she huffed as if resigned to such things happening in the countryside. 'I'd shoot the damn thing myself if it wasn't illegal.'

Then, just as I was trying to think of something to say, a glazier's van arrived in the yard and diverted her attention. It was *Smash Bang Wallop* to repair the kitchen window.

I felt a little spooked by such an extraordinary event but as I grabbed my quilt from the car, I reminded myself: now I live in the country – if you can call over-populated Sussex that – I must pull myself together and get rid of these soft city roots.

'Isn't that gorjous,' said Cailey as I re-entered the music room. 'Real jazzy arrow deesin and wacky colours.'

'It's fun isn't it, and comfy.'

'What colour do yous call that?' She was pointing at a particular shade.

'Amethyst.'

Cailey could not get her tongue round the consonants and pulled all sorts of faces as she continued to try.

Louis reeled off a few more of the shades, 'Turquoise, citrine, jade, topaz.'

'Very fancy,' said Lianne. 'You a gem expert, are you?'

'*Gemmologist*,' said Jane.

'A photographer actually.'

'Then what you doing drawing for?' Lianne was quick to pick him up.

'Doesn't mean I can't draw.' Louis sounded hurt.

'Suppose not but a photography course would make more sense.'

Rupert volunteered an answer. 'He's a friend of Ewen's.'

'Who's Ewen when he's at home?' said Giles.

'Fergus's younger brother.'

'Fergus's twin,' said Jane, and as no one had actually mentioned he was a twin yet, I thought, like me, she must have done some research before she arrived. A bit of Googling perhaps or, if she owns a copy, a quick dip into *Who's Who*. Right now was not the moment to go over it again. 'Come on,' I said. 'Break's up. Time to start.'

'Marvellous,' exclaimed Rupert, and Louis flashed me a strangely affectionate smile.

I laid the quilt on the chaise longue and asked Cailey to lie down. 'Pop one arm behind your head, please. Yes. Look. That works well.'

'I'll dangle a wee leg on the floor too, don't yous think, open the pose up a tad?'

'Great, yes. This session will last until lunch, so just take breaks and have a move around whenever you need to.'

'Will do.'

I stepped outside the circle. 'Time to begin. This exercise is about looking at form in space and relating it to the surrounding drapery. If you get stuck, call me over. I'll be keeping out of the way on the sofa over there.'

I learnt as an undergraduate that the best tutors were the ones who kept themselves to themselves. They would set up the class with care for lighting, postures and framework and then encourage us to carry out our own interpretation of the subject. Sometimes one cried out to be shown how to do it but *they* knew best: teaching by example simply doesn't work, it stunts a student's chance to shine and turns them into a copycat.

Jane and Felicity were gossiping again. I went between them, '*Shh, shh.* Please save chatting for the break, it's unfair on the rest of the class.'

Jane gave Felicity a that's-us-told look. It was tiresome but I ignored it. I suspect these two have come here for a bit of a jolly and I don't want to spoil their fun. They are after all paying for the privilege.

Retreating to the sofa I suddenly thought now would be a good time to go and have a better look at that portrait in the dining room. The one with the head at a funny angle. It wouldn't take long.

'I'll be back in a sec,' I said and left the room. For all they knew I could be visiting the loo.

No one is in here. The table's laid, the water jugs are full. Mhàiri's job's done. I'm all alone. I crept towards the picture of Fergus's grandfather. It was hanging at one end of the room and the canvas caught the light in an unusual fashion. One side was bright, the other dull. My eyes traced the man's profile, lingering on his dignified hooter. The painter's palette was subdued and the beige background made it difficult to define the skin tones. So, I stood in front of the nearest window hoping to block out some light. My shadow cast across the canvas and an *eye* – an extra eye! – stared out from beneath the paint. It was right next to the man's profile, faded but unmistakable, I could see half a face next to his. I stepped to the side, it disappeared, I stepped back again, it reappeared. Disappeared, reappeared. This man's head must have been painted on top of a face-on portrait.

Ruff, ruff. Haggis's bark sent me rushing back into the music room. I don't want to be caught neglecting my tutoring duties.

I'd just got back when there was a *knock, knock* at the door and Fergus's head popped round it. In he marched, sidled up to Jane and whispered something in her ear.

'Bedford?' she said, with a frown. 'Does this mean there's no electrician coming this week?'

'I'm afraid not,' said Fergus. 'There's only one place in the UK where they make the particular part. There's no way we'll have it delivered in time. I do hope you and Felicity won't mind sharing?'

Felicity assured Fergus this would be okay. She then put her hand on her friend's arm and a sweet smile swept across her face.

'Cailey,' Fergus called out with glee in his eyes, 'I'll take you home whenever you're ready.'

'Are yous sure?'

'Yes, no problem at all.'

'Lunchtime,' I said and mayhem broke out, pencils went flying as easels were dismantled and people scrabbled around the floor trying to roll up their drawings.

Zoe popped her head round the door. 'I came to say I'll give the model a lift.'

'Don't worry, darling,' said Fergus, 'I've got it sorted.' He wasn't going to chuck away the chance of playing taxi driver again.

Cailey bounced across the room. 'Hiya, Zoe.'

'Hello.' She looked Cailey up and down with an air

of contempt. Zoe was jealous of this girl's youth, it seemed, but weren't we all.

Fergus pecked his wife on the cheek. 'Start lunch without me, I won't be long.'

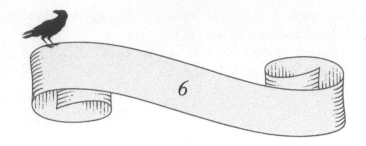

6

There had been a rush for lunch and I was last through the door after Zoe.

'Is your ankle okay?' I said to her under my breath.

'Absolutely.' She turned and gave me a firm smile. 'No need to mention it again.' Then with a far jollier expression she said, 'I do hope that went well. Come sit next to me. Tell me, was the model any good?'

'Yes, yes. Well done you for finding her. I think she must be a professional dancer.'

'Really?'

'Well, she could hold a pose for an unusually long time, so I reckon she's been trained to keep still.'

'Rather a lot of make-up I thought,' said Jane, joining the conversation.

'You could polish the floor with her she was wearing so much,' Shane snickered.

'It's actually a good thing,' I said. 'Just you wait till we get the watercolours out tomorrow. Colourful eye shadow and lipstick makes it great fun.'

A disagreeable sound came out of Jane's nose.

'Hard to understand her with that accent,' said Lianne.

'But I liked her all right.'

'Me too,' said Giles, inappropriately.

Lunch was what Zoe referred to as 'baps'. Floury white rolls, pre-buttered but unfilled. Covering the table were help-yourself-plates of breaded ham, sliced tomatoes, withered lettuce and half-eaten jars of chutney. Louis was cutting slices of cheddar and Rupert was passing everyone's napkins round.

I thought about mentioning the portrait. I really wanted to know the story behind it. But Fergus's reaction last night, when he told us it was 'My grandfather', and I'd seen the colour drain from his cheeks, stopped me. I must be sensitive at times like this.

Fergus walked into the room with a huge grin on his face. He went straight to his wife for a little tête-à-tête, and as I was sitting next to her, I heard their discussion word for word.

'You mean to say there's a show near here?' Zoe was saying.

'Yes, tomorrow night at eight. Cailey the model's taking part.'

'But angel, what about dinner?'

Fergus turned to me. 'Susie,' he said, thinking on his feet. 'Could we add in an evening drawing session at a local burlesque show?'

Louis was on my other side, all ready to throw in an answer. 'I'd be up for it.'

'But *Fergus*,' insisted Zoe, 'the menus have all been pre-arranged.'

'We can have high tea, darling. Don't worry about that. Susie, are you on for it?'

'Yes,' I mumbled. 'As long as it isn't going to cause a

problem?' I did actually think it was a great idea.

'No problem,' said Fergus, smiling at his wife. Then tapping a knife against her glass, he announced, 'Everyone, listen please. The model, Cailey, is part of a burlesque show reasonably near here tomorrow night, and if you all agree, we thought Susie could lead a drawing class there?'

'How marvellous,' said Jane. 'The costumes will be a hoot.'

'That'd be brilliant,' said Lianne. 'I'm in for sure.'

Minty, Shane and Giles were on board, Felicity said it'd be good for her to get out and Rupert guffawed.

Fergus leant over Zoe and picked up a bap. 'It'll be fun, darling – and good for *us* to do something local.'

'Yes, you're right,' she sighed.

I don't think Zoe wants to go.

'My brother,' said Fergus making his way down to the other end of the table, 'is joining us for dinner.'

'Excellent,' said Louis. 'I'd love to see him.'

'I thought you had already?' Zoe was confused. 'I saw you heading down the back drive this morning.'

'I didn't make it as far as his cottage.' Louis winked and Zoe fluttered her eyes in a way that made me think she's probably known all along Ewen's friend Louis was coming this week. It's just too much of a coincidence to believe Louis randomly got one of eight places.

I could ask Louis, but I kind of want him to pay me some attention before I go boosting his ego, letting on I've been trying to work him out. I've always found Frenchmen attractive and learnt the hard way you have to play it firm not to get taken advantage of. So, if Louis and I are going to be friends, he'll have to come my way first.

I took a big bite of my bun, and Rupert, halfway down
the other side of the table, did a napkin wiping motion
as if I might not know there was flour round my mouth.
The table was buzzing with chitter chatter and I thought,
how nice it is the Muchtons join in at meal times. It
suggests they don't have anything else to do but it also
adds a much-needed homely atmosphere and this all-
inclusive routine brings us all closer together. So, when
Felicity explained why she'd gone to bed before dinner
last night, saying, 'My husband died six months ago –
from lymphoma – it was all very quick – I still feel
completely drained from time to time but an early night
here and there sorts me out', it wasn't entirely surprising.
And whether intentional or unintentional, Fergus and
Zoe deserve a pat on the back. They've given a place to
someone in need and formed a trusting bond between
us all.

'Kind Jane,' Felicity turned to her friend, 'twisted my
arm to come here this week. I'm so pleased she did.'

'It's the least I could do,' said Jane, 'for my
book-buddie.'

Felicity and Jane are new friends, having met at a
local book club in Gloucestershire, and both admitted
(with an honest giggle) they don't have any friends in
common. No surprise. Jane's haughty manner and dis-
regard for personal appearance was a far cry from
Felicity's mellifluous tone and pastel colours. Maybe
that's why they've decided to trek all the way to Scotland
for a painting week, as surely Gloucestershire has a few
on offer?

The shrill of the front doorbell stopped my rumina-
tion. Zoe dashed out the room and soon returned,

telling her 'angel' he was wanted too. Rupert and I got up to do the clearing and found Mhàiri in the kitchen looking a lot calmer than last night.

'They fixed the window quick,' I said.

'Aye, they did that.' Mhàiri pushed Rupert away from the sink. 'Don't yous be getting yer hands dirty. There'll be nothing for me to do.' He chuckled and left the room.

'Zoe telt me aboot yous flat tyre, Susie. *That* drive I bet it's what did it.'

'Yes, I think you're right,' I smiled. Mhàiri and I were going to be friends.

'Well, hen, if yous have a spare tyre in the boot?'

'Yes.'

'Leave yous keys on the hall table this afternoon and I'll telt me husband to get it seen to.'

'Thank you very much.'

'Ne bother. I'll watch yer back if yous watch mine?'

She really was asking the question.

'Yes,' I replied, assuming it must be a friendly turn of phrase.

'Here yous go.' Mhàiri handed me a tray of coffee and flapjacks. 'Be a hen and take it through.'

'Sure.' I stuck my foot out and pushed open the swing door. Fergus was explaining he'd be taking us to the fishing hut this afternoon. 'I thought it'd be a lovely place to paint.'

Minty excused herself, and once Lianne and Shane had taken two flapjacks each, they also left the room.

'We'll meet in the hall at two-thirty,' I called out. 'Fully dressed in outdoor kit.'

'Right ya, Miss,' came hurtling back. I smiled; Shane's bumptiousness appealed to my humour.

'Surprisingly well behaved that Peckham pair,' said Jane as I bit my born-and-bred Kennington tongue, swallowing the words, 'Manners do stretch south of the river, you know.'

'I completely agree,' nodded Rupert, 'and on that note, I'm going to boot-up for the landscape painting. Golly gosh, I'm looking forward to it.'

'I bought fingerless gloves for the occasion,' Felicity literally bounced up out of her chair.

'Susie,' said Fergus, 'come with me and we'll work out how I'm going to get you all to the river.'

'You must take Haggis,' said Zoe, 'he *so* loves a trip to the fishing hut.'

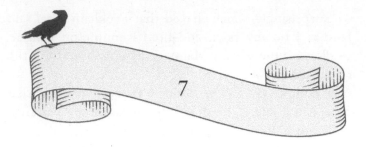

7

We all piled into the minibus, with Fergus behind the wheel, and halfway down the front drive he put his foot on the brake. Rupert then willingly opened a gate, Fergus pushed the gearstick into four-wheel-drive and we bumped on down a track towards the river. Most of the snow in the fields has melted with only a few humps remaining in the hollows. The trees have shaken it from their branches and the ground is soggy with excess water. Not that this is a problem, we all have our boots on. Minty's are by far the smartest. 'Dubarry's,' she told Lianne who looked upon them with envy – her hardware store alternatives are going to be cold.

The river Trickle is handsome and strong and as Fergus drove alongside it the water ran black, tumbling over and gushing round great big boulders of rock – I could see scum forming on the nearby grass. Fergus warned of a very dangerous undercurrent and when the wooden fishing hut came into sight, I thought thank goodness it's set back from the steep riverbank. The bus drew up behind it and together with easels and bags of equipment we all piled out. Giles, with a nudge from

Rupert, began to pull his weight, helping Felicity and Jane tread carefully across a particularly damp patch. Fergus turned over a stone and picked up a key.

'Here,' he said as he threw it to Shane, 'unlock the door will you. There's a table inside you can put your things on.'

Then, calling Haggis to heel, he told me, 'I'm just going to take this little chap on a potter.'

'Okay,' I smiled, 'see you later.'

'Have a look in here,' called Felicity. Her head was poking out of the hut's double door. 'It's terribly sweet and there's a mini woodburner we can light if it gets cold.'

Inside the place smelt of fresh pine, and Felicity was right: the curtains, made from Muchton tweed, a brown and green herringbone weave, gave the interior enormous charm.

'We must get going,' I encouraged; I didn't want people to start sitting down. 'Pick a view close by so you can hear me, and put up your easels.'

Shane wasn't happy. 'Miss,' he said. 'This is going to be impossible. I ain't ever painted countryside before.'

'I agree,' said Jane. '*How* do you expect us to work out here?'

'Can't we go for a walk instead?' said Minty, most likely longing to burn off lunch.

'I think you should give it a go. Just a small picture. I've got primed paper if anyone would like some?'

'Yes please', 'Yes please', 'Yes please', everyone replied.

Giles and Minty seemed confident they knew what they were doing, Rupert hadn't ever painted before, Jane came with pastels for her and Felicity, Shane told me video art's his medium, Louis was a photographer, as we know, and Lianne didn't care for painting – 'Performance art is more my kinda thing.'

'Well, today we'll all try oils and see how we get on. I have plenty of paint so hold out your palettes and I'll give you a splodge.'

'Are you sure?' said Rupert. 'I bought my own.'

'I'm sure. It's quicker this way. We've got to work fast, it's too cold to waste any time.'

'Quite right,' said Jane.

'Can I work separately?' asked Minty.

'Me too?' said Giles.

'Of course. No problem, but would you mind going over there a bit?'

They trundled off as I handed out the colours to everyone else. A hot and cold; red, blue and yellow. Some raw sienna, raw umber, burnt umber, a tiny bit of black and a small blob of titanium white.

'What about green?' asked Rupert.

'From red, blue and yellow you can make any colour.'

'Really?' said Felicity, genuinely surprised.

Louis coughed with disbelief and Felicity, worried he had a tickle, gave him a sensitive pat on the back.

'Yellow and blue make green; red and blue, purple; yellow and red, orange.'

'Yeah,' said Lianne, 'but what are the other colours for?'

'They'll lighten and darken the colours you mix. But don't worry about it right now, I'm going to talk you through step by step.'

'What a relief,' sighed Rupert.

'*Ahhh*,' squealed Lianne, '*ahhh, ahh, ahh*. There, *there,*

there.' She was pointing down the bank, turning her head away from whatever she'd seen.

Shane was finding the whole episode very funny.

'Good god,' shouted Jane. 'It's a *rat.*'

Everyone other than Minty rushed to take a look.

'Don't be ridiculous,' said Rupert, peering over the edge.

'Yeah,' said Giles. 'That's not a rat.'

The thing plopped into the water and out of sight.

'None of you can be sure,' said Jane, 'now it's disappeared.'

'I'm sure,' stated Giles.

'Lianne?' I called. She was heading round the side of the hut.

'I'm off to be sick.'

Shane laughed again.

'No, no,' said Giles. 'Honestly, come back, it wasn't a rat.'

'What was it then?' Lianne turned around.

'A water vole.'

'A *mole*?' said Rupert.

'A water *vole.*'

'Silly me,' he muttered, 'too much shooting's made me deaf.'

'We're very lucky to see one. They're a protected species these days.'

'Whatever,' said Shane.

'This one must be lost,' said Rupert.

'Why?' I asked.

'They live by slow-moving water. Very odd to find it here.'

'I see. Okay now, back to painting.'

'Great,' Louis was full of enthusiasm, sounding genuinely pleased we weren't going to talk about voles any more.

'I'd like you to do a rough drawing of the scene you've chosen.'

'With a pencil?' asked Felicity.

'Yes. Just a quick light sketch, it doesn't have to be accurate. You'll have plenty of time to change it when you start painting. Go on, do it now.'

I stood looking down at the gushing water. Scottish rivers really are beautiful. This one has carved a dramatic channel through the rock and as I took in deep breaths of cold, damp, fresh air I thought, I'm so happy to be away from home. I feel I deserve a break. I finished a commission of two cats last week – beautifully patterned marmalade pussies – and there's more work in the pipeline when I get home.

The initial melancholy I'd picked up on at Auchen Laggan Tosh seems to have sunk behind the homeliness of having people fill the rooms. The atmosphere has softened and I'm beginning to enjoy being part of the Muchtons' life.

I think Zoe's enjoying having me around too. She took me aside after lunch and let me in on a family secret. Apparently Ewen often mocks Fergus and she's worried about how he'll behave tonight. 'My husband's so wet,' she admitted, 'he never stands up for himself. He's full of guilt at having inherited all this.'

You don't say, I'd thought at the time. I've heard stories of jealous younger siblings causing havoc and if this one has chosen to live on the back drive, hang around and taunt his brother, he's obviously got a plan up his sleeve – some way of benefiting from his brother's bounty.

It's all beginning to make sense why Louis didn't let on that Ewen was his friend. But I'm excited about meeting him tonight, being in with a chance of working him out. I bet you he's charming. Younger siblings often are and if Zoe likes him that says a lot.

I'm pretty well practised in drawing people out. It comes from painting commissions. One has to get under the skin of the client, understand what makes them tick in order to produce a picture that'll strike a chord. So, I'll be all eyes and ears at dinner tonight and here's hoping I end up sitting next to Ewen.

Zoe had apologised for opening up. 'I shouldn't be so indiscreet about the brothers,' she'd said, 'but I don't often have women of my age around.' I'd empathised; it must be difficult being an English bride in rural Scotland and no doubt it will take time for Zoe to find friends.

'Susie,' said Jane, 'I'm done drawing so I suppose you want me to paint now?'

'No, no. It's best to do the mixing first. Colours change depending on what colours they're next to, so it's much easier to mix them all and line them up. That way you'll avoid having to remix and reapply.'

'What a top tip,' said Louis, mocking me from under the peak of his flat cap.

'You're going to *have* to tell me how it's done,' said Jane, as her arms dropped to her side.

'Start with the lightest colour, the froth. A bit of zinc white and a tiny bit of raw umber. Then the grass, lemon yellow, a tiny bit of cobalt blue and raw sienna. After that, look and see if you need to add anything to burnt umber for the water.'

'But Miss,' whined Shane, 'it's effing freezing.'

Jane tut-tutted, Louis laughed and Felicity said, 'It's not how I would have put it but I *do* agree.'

'Susie,' said Rupert, 'I think we should all stretch our legs, get the blood moving and then come back to this?'

'Okay then, let's all warm up.'

'Great,' said Minty, Giles too, and we all took off on a quick short stomp downstream. I fell into step with Rupert who unleashed a jeremiad on having recently 'got the boot from work'.

'How awful. I'm so sorry for you.'

'It's a right bugger, Susie. I've been a land agent for thirty-five years. To be made redundant in your early sixties is the pits. I have three children still financially dependent on Jules and me, two dogs, I'm part of a shooting syndicate, member of a golf club and would hate to have to give up one of our houses just because we can't afford it…Now I'm wittering, do tell me to shut up.'

'It's okay. It sounds tough for you.'

'I signed up for this course hoping it would take my mind off things, and now look, I'm the one bringing them up.'

'SUSIE. RUPERT,' shouted Lianne. 'Come, get in the picture.'

She had everyone in a huddle with a view of the house behind – like an eighteenth-century Dutch landscape.

'I've gotta post this. My friends will never believe where I am.'

'You should be in the picture then – here, I'll take it.'

I stretched my arm out and she handed me her mobile. Then, bouncing towards the group, she stood at the front with her hands on her hips and a smug smile across her face.

'Ready,' I said, and everyone apart from Louis smiled. It's not that he looked unhappy, he just didn't bother to join in.

'Another,' said Lianne, 'just to make sure.'

'I think I've taken about ten.' I handed her the mobile and turned to Louis. 'Don't like having your photo taken?'

'Why?' he said as we walked back to the hut.

'You didn't smile.'

'Ah, well, I don't look as good when I do.'

We both grinned.

'Look at you,' he said, 'your smile's so innocent.'

Miraculously I managed not to go pink. This tutor business has given my self-confidence a boost. I have a role, a part to play and, best of all, I'm in charge. Louis Bouchon is going to have to try a lot harder if he fancies his chances at finding out how innocent I am.

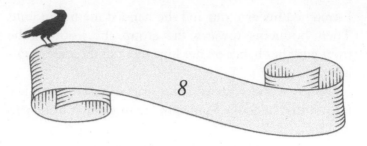

8

As soon as we were back at the hut I announced, 'It's time to apply the paint,' and once the beginners had all begun I went to have a look at what Giles and Minty had been up to. From the angle of their easels I presumed they were painting the same scene but the closer I got the fewer similarities I saw.

I had no idea what Giles was painting. 'That's an interesting take,' I said, hoping he'd explain.

'We have far more impressive trees in the arboretum at home but I thought I'd give that Japanese larch there a go.' He pointed with his brush towards the other side of the river.

'I see. Doesn't it look green to you?'

'Yes, but I'm painting this year's growth.'

Fortunately, I knew a year's growth of a conifer is the space between the outshoot of branches, so it was now clear Giles had chosen one particular length of trunk. He'd put a silvery-ochre almost straight line down the centre of his canvas and with a hog hair brush he was now scrubbing Payne's grey down both sides.

'They're beautiful trees, aren't they.'

'Yes, marvellous,' he said. 'Everyone loves a larch and that's why they're planted in places like this.'

'What do you mean?'

'Mixed through the wood for aesthetic reasons. They're deciduous, go a lovely colour in the autumn. Here they make the Scots pine less dense, and do you know a larch grows to maturity in forty years and then stands for a whopping hundred and fifty?'

'Wow, I didn't know that.'

'Well, it's pretty great isn't it, although lots have an awful disease so it's nice to be able to paint one before it dies.'

'Disease?'

Minty joined in. 'It's terrible. Daddy has such a problem at home.'

'Airborne,' said Giles. 'Blown in across the Channel from France. It's killed almost all Japanese larch in the West Country. We're jolly lucky it hasn't reached us in Suffolk yet.'

'It will,' said Minty, resigned to the fact.

Her lips were purply blue.

'Are you *okay*?' I asked. 'You do look awfully cold.'

'I'm fine. This isn't half as brutal as the Boxing Day hunt.'

'Fox-hunting?' I tried not to sound biased either way.

'Yes, I hunt with the Tynedale in Northumberland.'

'So, you're used to a rural setting.'

She gave me a sharp look. I put it down to her drawn features, but then she continued. 'Well, I don't live in a village,' she said.

It's not what I meant; she's the one who thought of villages as deeply infra dig, but I let it pass.

'We live in the middle of nowhere,' she softened, 'very like the Highlands in fact.'

'It must have been a long journey from Northumberland to here.'

'We're in Cumbria, but yes it was. Daddy drove me, which was *extremely* kind as he has so much on.'

'What does he do?'

'Sits on various boards but this week he's in the House of Lords. There's a bill he's trying to pass before Easter.'

Steering clear of politics, I asked how she felt her painting was going.

'I'm out of practice. Last term I spent all my spare time playing lax. It's why Mummy thought it'd be a good idea for me to do this course.'

'Well, you've got the perspective of the river spot on and your interpretation of the gorge is great.'

'I'm trying to stop myself using too many colours. I want the light to define the space.'

'It's really good. You could try using the other end of your brush to put in the cracks on the rocks.'

'Like this?' Minty scratched lines into her paint.

'Perfect.'

'Thanks, Susie.'

I could see Fergus with Haggis at heel, in the distance, heading back in this direction. So, leaving everyone be for a bit, forcing them to push on through any doubts they might have, I sped off to join him.

'How's it all going, Susie? I do hope it's all right?' He was as bad as Zoe with his pessimistic questions.

'All right now, but there was a bit of a ruckus at the beginning. Lianne thought she'd seen a rat.'

'A *rat*?'

'Yes, but Giles said it was a water vole.'

'How strange. They must be coming back. I've hardly ever come across one here but I saw a couple downstream as well.' Fergus thought for a moment and when he said, '*Hmm*, it is the breeding season,' I guessed he meant that's why there were more of them around.

Fergus planted his walking stick into the lush grass and, using it very much as a third leg, we began walking back through the field.

'Did you grow up at Auchen Laggan Tosh?' I asked.

'Yes, of course. I've lived here all my life. Well, in truth I had a base in London while I was in the army but as soon as I married Zoe I left the forces and we were up here in a shot.'

'How long ago?'

'Almost a year. Ma was thrilled to hand over the burden. My father died five years ago and she never enjoyed living here alone.'

'Where does she live now?'

'That's a whole other story.' Fergus pulled his cloth cap slightly up off his head. The thought of his mother had made him hot.

'I do hope the weather holds,' he said, looking up at the sky. 'I'd like to take you up to the bothy on the moor tomorrow. There's a wonderful view of heathery hills and a loch to boot.'

'That would be great. You live in such a beautiful place.'

'I'm so pleased you think so too.'

He stopped (again) to admire his fields and Haggis brushed his head against my welly boot, urging me on.

But I bent down to ruffle his ears and took the moment to ask Fergus what animals he farmed here.

'Funny you should bring that up, I was just wondering if we could see any.' He raised the pair of binoculars around his neck. 'Here,' he handed them to me, 'have a look through these and you'll see some Highland cows over there, on that distant horizon.'

'So there are. I've never seen one in real life.'

'In that case, we *must* incorporate a trip to them later in the week.'

Fergus put a hand out for the binoculars and walked on, while Haggis, excited to be on the move, rolled and darted through the stodgy grass.

'Do you have any sheep here?'

'Yes, on the back of the hill. Blackfaces and Bluefaced Leicester, if you're familiar with them?'

'No, I'm afraid not.'

'Hardy sheep. They're crossed and bred for meat but thank goodness that's nothing to do with me. There's very little money in stock these days.'

'Is the farm tenanted?'

'Yes, Willie owns the animals and pays me grazing rent for the land. Busiest time of year for him right now.'

'Lambing?'

'Yes, but not in the fields near the house. Haggis eats the afterbirth.' The dog looked back at the mention of his name. 'Nasty habit. Birds do it too.'

'All birds?'

'Mainly darn ravens; the savages sometimes pick out lambs' eyes as soon as they're born and right now we have a particularly mischievous one around.'

I knew better than to bring up Zoe's stolen bracelet so instead I asked about the fishing.

'We let all but this beat in front of us.' He lifted his stick and swept it across a section of the Trickle.

'Do you ever have trouble with poachers?'

'Why do you ask?' He sounded surprised so I decided to be honest.

'I was there last night when Stuart told Zoe about lights down by the river.'

'Wrong time of year for a poacher. I don't know what was going on. I had a good look on my walk downstream and other than water voles,' he chuckled, 'I didn't see anything unusual.'

Gosh, poor old Fergus, with so much to cope with here I don't think he has his finger on the pulse of what's happening. Stuart had sounded very agitated when I saw him crash into the house last night. Perhaps the lights down at the river have something to do with the water voles? Maybe someone's been doing a bit of guerrilla re-wilding? It is odd them being here. Though I loved seeing one – I grew up on *Wind and the Willows*, and Ratty was my favourite.

Fergus pointed his stick into the distance. 'There are brown trout in hill lochs over there.'

'Which you also let?'

'No, not them. Technically no one "owns" wild trout in Scotland and with the right to roam anyone can fish there.'

'Do they?'

'I've never come across a soul. Not many people round here.'

Ha, no wonder Stuart was in a stew that Donald

thought he saw someone last night. I'm beginning to think something fishy's going on.

We were back at the hut and Fergus suggested rather loudly that I could drive the minibus home when we were done as he wanted to walk back with Haggis.

'I'll drive the bus, no problem,' called out Rupert, and I didn't object…if he wants to carry the responsibility I'm quite happy to let him.

'Right you are then. See you later.'

I patted Haggis in the right direction and went to see how everyone was getting on.

Minty and Giles aside, all the pictures looked more like paint by numbers than anything else. But I was consoled by the fact everyone had *something* to show for the afternoon.

'I'm in desperate need of a cup of tea,' exclaimed Jane, waddling towards me in her calf-restricting boots. 'What do you say we call it a day?'

'Okay.' I raised my voice. 'If you're all happy to stop now, let's line the pictures up along the benches for a crit.'

Felicity looked terrified, and Jane refused, saying, 'No. No. No. *No* way.'

'Please,' I begged. 'You mustn't be inhibited. Discussing each other's work is a great way to improve. Honestly, it's such a useful exercise.'

'That sounds ominous,' said Rupert, as Shane slapped his board upright against the bench. 'Go for it, Miss. I'm going to take a video and turn it into a piece of art.'

Lianne split her legs and with one huge step she comically flung her arm over her head and placed her picture right next to Shane's. Then drawing her legs together, she put a hand to her mouth and blew a kiss straight into the recording mobile.

Felicity and Jane carefully rested their pictures side by side and Shane, unbeknown to them, took a wide shot of their behinds.

'You scoundrel,' said Rupert, wafting his hand in front of the camera.

'Keep going, mate, that's excellent footage.'

Louis handed me his picture and I began a new row.

'Minty, Giles,' I called out, 'we're having a crit.' They joined the group and both their paintings received compliments from the others.

'Well done. Look at all this work.'

'I like yours, Minty,' said Felicity.

'What is it you like about it?'

'The froth is *soooo* believable.'

'Minty, can you give us any tips on how you painted the froth?'

'Sure. I went for a mixture of zinc white, yellow ochre and cobalt blue to blend it into the water. Froth is much darker than one thinks it is. I know because home's on the Derwent.'

'Lovely river,' said Rupert. 'And you're right about the colour, but I never saw it like that.'

'Yellow ochre?' said Lianne. 'You didn't give us any of that, Susie.'

'I didn't want to introduce too many colours but maybe I should have. I'm sorry.'

'Whose do you think's best, Miss?'

'What's interesting is how you all see things. Jane has used a lot more green than the rest of you, Felicity's grey rocks are well observed, and then if we look at Louis', he's heightened the colours.'

'That's cos he's a photographer,' said Lianne. 'They're always enhancing things.'

'Artistic licence,' said Giles.

'But Miss,' nagged Shane. 'Whose do you think is the *best*?'

'All these paintings have successful elements and taste is personal.'

'Boring, you just don't want to say.'

'It's jolly chilly, Susie,' said Felicity.

'Let's pack up then.'

'I could murder a cup of tea,' said Rupert.

'What would you murder it with?' smirked Shane.

'Don't be so cheeky.' Jane prodded her finger into his back.

'*Ow.*'

'Don't worry, boy,' said Rupert. 'You're quite right, what on earth would one murder a cup of tea with?' He roared with laughter.

Louis and Minty had already packed up their bits and bobs and as they sat in the back of the minibus, out of the cold, they watched and waited for everyone else to do the same. Then as the group balanced wet paintings on shivering knees, Rupert navigated the bumpy track with confidence – I'm so glad he's taken control of the bus. Up the front drive we went and into the yard in front of the house.

'Rupert,' called out Louis from the back, 'I don't think you should park this close to the steps.'

'But it's where it was when we got in.'

'I know but it spoils the look of the house.'

'He's right,' I said.

'And he's talking at last.' Rupert released the brake and parked a little further away.

I stood in the yard looking up at the wonderfully self-confident house. This pile was not in the least bit subtle. The porticoed front door raised up above the ground gave it the grandest entrance I've ever seen – how nice it is the Muchtons regard their home as something to share. If Zoe's enthusiasm for public courses continues, many lucky people will beat a path here.

My eyes travelled along the windows of the top floor. 'Hey Louis,' I said as he was the closest. 'Why do you think the curtains of the locked wing are shut?'

'Don't know,' he shrugged.

'Do you think they're hiding something?'

I was joking but he snapped back, 'Don't be silly.'

'So, I'm right?' I wasn't going to let a Frenchman intimidate me. And anyway, he might have been here before so perhaps he knew.

'People with big houses don't like to heat it all…'

I finished his sentence, 'So the curtains are closed to keep it insulated.'

'Exactly.'

'Here,' I reached out an arm, 'I'll take your bag so you can carry the easel.'

'Thank you.' He gave me the sweetest smile and my tummy turned.

Oh crumbs, I must not crush on Monsieur Bouchon.

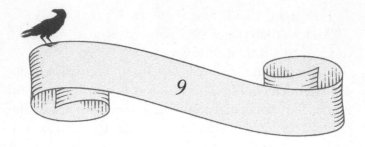

9

An absolutely essential part of a Scottish home, no matter how big or small, is the drying room, and if you've been into one you've seen them all. A seemingly windowless dark cavern, which has, dangling off-centre, a dim light bulb with a grubby shade. These uninhabited stuffy places have a universal cheesy-feet-cross-damp-wax-jacket smell. There's always a crusty insole in sight and a lonely glove to be found. And although spiders, mice and moths inhabit every other nook and cranny of the house, you'll never find any in here – it's far too hot with very little air. Slatted wooden shelves run up the walls, each haphazardly stacked with endless bits of outdoor kit, and, as is always the case, an enormous insulated water tank takes up most of the space. No hot cupboard (as they're also known) is complete without a 'pulley', a long wooden railed device attached to a cord. It's lowered, loaded with wet items and raised up into warmer air, muddy drips drip-dripping onto the floor. If you're lucky you'll find an out-of-shape coat hanger lingering in a dark corner. Despite the unpleasant components of this poorly lit dingy space it is excellent at drying out absolutely anything with rapid effect.

So, here I am in Auchen Laggan Tosh's drying room obeying Zoe's instruction for a tidy house, taking off my coat and welly boots. One thing's for sure, they'll be warm and toasty when I come to put them on again. Right now, though, I'm feeling cold, so I'm going to skip tea and scamper upstairs for a hot bath.

Zoe caught me on the landing. 'Susie,' she said, rather sharply, 'Fergus would like a word.'

'Okay,' wobbled out of my mouth.

I couldn't work out if she was exhausted or agitated, but either way her voice had definitely lost its lightness of touch.

'He's in our room at the minute but if you wait in the snug I'll give him a call.'

I turned back downstairs, my feelings retracing their steps. I'd felt nervous before this week, apprehensive when I arrived, gradually more settled, reached a state of ease this afternoon and now, curses, I was feeling on edge again. Why did Fergus want a word with me?

'Ah Susie,' he said, striding into the library and pushing the door closed. 'Do sit down, this won't take long.'

The corners of Fergus's mouth were twitching as if he was trying his best to hold back an almighty smile. This was a turn-up for the books. Maybe he had *good* news for me.

'Right,' he said and then took what seemed like forever to perch his bottom on the arm of the sofa opposite. 'I had a call this morning from an art dealer, renowned broker of fine arts in fact.' Fergus's smile was now huge. 'There's a Landseer exhibition coming up at the Scottish National Gallery.'

'How exciting. Do they want you to loan some pictures?'

'Did *she* tell you that?'

'Zoe?'

'Yes.'

'No, I just assumed it. I'm sorry.'

'Don't be.' Fergus could not stop smiling. 'Zoe thinks it's a bad idea but just this once I'm going against her.' He giggled.

'Fair enough. The oil sketches you have really are lovely, I'm not surprised the gallery wants them.'

'No, no,' Fergus wafted his hand and shook his head, 'we have four marvellous pictures. Just you wait. I can't tell you how exciting this is. My family have done their absolute best to keep hold of their collection. Never would a Muchton sell a painting.'

I smiled. Ewen wouldn't like hearing him say this. But, you know what, I feel just the same about my own limited collection.

'Fergus, I really would love it if there's any chance I might get to see the pictures?'

'Yes, definitely. Zoe's anxious about people knowing we own them. Silly really, as it is all out there on public record. But we've come to a compromise: they'll be loaned for the exhibition but none of the students this week will be told. I kind of get her point, one does not want too many people knowing exactly where they are.'

'It's so kind of you to tell me.'

'I had to push for that too.' He gave a light chuckle. 'But it seemed to me jolly unfair not to let a professional artist living under our roof see the pictures.'

'I'm thrilled, thank you so much.'

'They're sending over an art valuer very early tomorrow morning to assess the pictures for insurance purposes, and in order not to rouse suspicion I thought you could join him in the south-east wing before breakfast?'

Ah ha, the valuable paintings are in the locked wing.

'Yes please. That would be brilliant.'

Fergus rubbed his knees and stood up. 'Marvellous. Now don't say a word.'

He opened the library door and I skipped upstairs, grateful to find the bath free.

The peaty water consumed me as I rested my head back on the cast-iron lip. I'm so pleased to finally have time alone. A calm moment all by myself. It's just what I need to reflect on one of my obsessions – piecing together close observations of people so far. I've always been interested in human beings and I think I'm pretty good at working people out. I've practised the skill all my life. As a little girl in London I'd sit for hours gazing out the window of our front room absorbing the mannerisms of passers-by. The backwards-facing palms of simple folk, the spring in the step of young love, the untucked clothes of characterful children, the trembling onset of Parkinson's, and Trevor the tramp who always smiled. Trevor was a made-up name, I wasn't allowed to talk to Trevor. But from a very young age the seed was sown: what fun it is sussing out others.

Being cooped up in a large house this week as part of an intimate group might have its frustrations, not being able to escape for one. But with a hobby like mine, indulging in people's characters and how they behave, there could hardly be a better playing field. In fact, I've already worked out Jane's lifestyle.

I became curious at dinner last night when she hinted to Fergus she was familiar with country pursuit sums. I assumed she was a Lady of some grand manor herself and started to wonder where she lived.

Her surname threw me at first – Atkinson doesn't exactly smack of the gentry. But shooting estates these days aren't solely owned by old families and Jane's husband could have bought a country pile off his own back. Mr Atkinson might be a successful banker for all I knew, or actually, more likely, a barrister. They live in Gloucestershire don't you know. Jane's definitely not got a career under her belt, so unless inheritance bought them an estate, she's played no part in owning the home. But then, when Felicity told me over lunch that Jane's husband, Neville, is a farm management consultant, from that moment on I knew Jane had married outside of her class. She'd stepped down from the ranks of those who have assets (this is why she could identify with Fergus) to those who don't. If her husband Neville had land of his own he'd be running it, not consulting for others.

I enjoy getting under people's skin – it's instinctive, not nasty or malicious. An inbuilt reaction to being an artist. I'm simply unable to turn off my antennae.

'Knock, knock,' came Lianne's voice from the other side of the bathroom door. 'There's a queue building up out here.'

'Give me a sec and I'll be finished.'

'Cheers, Susie.'

Lianne was bang smack in my face as I opened the door and I very nearly stepped on her flip-flopped feet. She was in little tight PJ shorts and an even tighter t-shirt with a huge heart stretched across her breasts.

'What ya going to wear tonight?' she said.

Insensitive to the fact she might genuinely be looking for advice on what to wear to dinner in a house like this, I replied, 'I hadn't thought about it.'

'My mum said clean clothes for dinner might be a way of them telling us to be a bit dressy.'

The truth is, vanity influenced my packing and I came with a whole variety of evening gear. If the scene was trendy, I had stuff for that; smart, I could look sophisticated; party time and I could be sexy; plain clean clothes, I had them too.

'Well, I'm going to keep my best dress for Wednesday night's ceilidh, and tonight I'll wear a wrap-around one.' I looked down at my dressing gown. 'Much like this really.'

Lianne laughed. 'Thanks, that helps a lot.'

A great big deep gurgle came through my bedroom wall as the final glug of bathwater went down the plug. I lay down on the bed and sunk my head into the pillow. Lianne began to hum a tune. It sounded like something off a *Pure* relaxation CD. She clearly had a gift for melody. I'd better set an alarm in case I drift off.

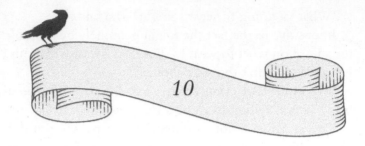

10

I could hear my name. 'Susie?' It was being called down the children's corridor. Thank goodness I'd kept an eye on the time. 'Susie?' My hair's dry, my make-up's applied and my dress is on. Whoever it is, I'm fit to be seen. 'Susie?' I opened the bedroom door.

'Louis,' I said, with a gulp.

'I've found you,' he said as he strode straight past me into the room.

'Oi. Don't feel the need to ask or anything.'

'Do you have something to hide?' He winked and sat down on the bed.

'Sabbia Rosa. Ooh la la,' came his best French accent as he read from a paper bag on the floor.

'Do you shop there?' I said, amused he knew the lingerie store.

'*Pfft*, if they should be so lucky. What a generous boy-friend you must have?'

'A girl can spend money on herself, you know.'

'So you go to Paris then?'

'I've been a few times, yes.'

'I live there.'

'Really?' I didn't believe him. Why would he be here if he did?

'My father's English but Maman's from Paris and we've always had a flat there.'

'So, you still live at home?'

'Don't be silly. I have a place of my own there now. Come on, it's time to go downstairs, everyone's missing you.'

I went to the window to shut my curtains. There was a blue van outside illuminated in the outdoor lights.

'Oh no, *Louis*,' I joked, 'someone's parked right by the front steps.'

'Oh no indeed.' He came to the window; our cheeks were now millimetres apart. 'That's Ewen's,' he said.

'Wouldn't he have walked?' I was confused how Louis could be so sure, but then again not everyone drives around in a van, and Ewen is his friend.

'Bit dark for that.'

'Hey...' I could see two men in the yard. It was Fergus, pointing his finger at Stuart. 'They look cross, don't you think?'

'Bit nosey, aren't you?'

I turned to pull a face and accidentally tripped over Louis' foot.

'Whoops.'

He caught me in his arms and gave me a quick squeeze.

'Probably just some landlord/keeper disagreement.'

'I *knew* he was the keeper.'

'Course you did, nothing to do with his tweeds or anything like that.'

'Ha ha. Anyway, how do you know Ewen?'

'We met on a photography course.'

'Recently?' I said as I closed the curtains.

'About seven years ago. But come *on*, it's time to go downstairs.' Louis linked my arm and marched me out of the room.

In the drawing room we found Zoe and Felicity huddled round the fire, Fergus now standing between them. Louis' 'everyone's missing you' was clearly an excuse to invade my room.

'Quick, quick, shut the door,' said Zoe.

Haggis ran from her feet to mine and Fergus wobbled the bottle of white wine in his hand. 'Drink, Susie?'

'Yes please, that'd be lovely.'

A husky, 'Hello,' entered the room. I turned to see Fergus's twin standing behind me.

'Hi,' I smiled, trying not to stare. They were identical. I find these genetics absolutely fascinating and almost haunting when two people still look alike when they've grown up.

'This is my brother,' said Fergus, handing me a glass.

'The better half,' said Ewen, closing the door.

'Equally good,' said Zoe. 'Now, would you like a drink?'

'Yes please.'

'Louis?'

'I have one, thanks.'

I sat down on the sofa and just as Ewen was offering me a bowl of nuts Louis pushed him out of the way and sat down beside me.

'Darling?' said Fergus, insinuating a drink.

Jane entered the room and caught the tail end of Zoe's answer: 'I think I'll save my one glass for dinner.'

'I know what that means,' Jane said, with a sing-song.

Fergus beamed and Zoe confirmed, 'Yes, there's a baby on the way.'

'Congratulations!' said Felicity and I at the same time.

'About time too is what my mother would say,' chuckled Fergus.

'She sure would,' said Ewen, his fingers tightening around his glass as he raised it in celebration. 'An heir,' he said, under his breath.

'People leave it much later these days,' said Felicity. 'Neither of my daughters are anywhere near mother-hood, unlike when I was in my early twenties.'

Jane lowered her bottom onto the largest chair in the room and launched in with, 'Young women who wear trousers only have themselves to blame.' Hmm, was she talking literally or metaphorically? Well, there was no stopping her now. 'My eldest daughter has always worn skirts or dresses and she was married at twenty-three. As for my youngest, I'm endlessly telling her to at least wear a frock for dinner but it falls on deaf ears, which is *such* a bore as I'm *longing* for grandchildren.'

Was Jane letting on her eldest daughter hasn't had a child and is struggling to conceive? Poor her if so. I have friends going through IVF and I know from them how unbelievably expensive it can become if it fails with the NHS and one has to go private.

Felicity grinned at Fergus. 'Your mother must be very happy,' she said, and then, taking hold of Zoe's hand, she added, 'I do hope you don't have the trouble I had.'

'Caesarean I bet?' said Jane, rather crudely.

'Did you too?' said Felicity, letting go of Zoe's hand and turning to her friend.

'Only with my second. Enough to put me off for life.'

'It's simply dreadful,' said Felicity, 'you can't walk for at least a week.'

'We don't want to frighten Zoe at this stage,' said Fergus. 'So, moving on then...' He went silent; he clearly couldn't think of anything to say, so helped himself to a handful of nuts instead.

Felicity let out a sympathetic moan. 'Dear me, if twins run in the family, caesarean might be your only option.'

Cough, splutter, cough, splutter. Fergus was choking. Zoe rushed to his side and whacked him on the back. In the commotion, I think I was the only one who noticed Ewen's fingers curl tighter round his glass. His knuckles went white, his face scrunched and he literally cracked it in front of my eyes.

'I'll get the water,' he said and scurried out of the room.

'Don't worry, I'm fine,' croaked Fergus, but Ewen had disappeared.

'Golly,' said Felicity as everyone flopped back into their seats. 'I thought you were going to keel over for a second.'

'That'll teach me not to be so greedy. Something my mother never got through to me.'

'Where does your mother live these days?' said Louis.

'Hampshire. Have you met her?'

Jane jumped in and put Fergus on the spot. 'Hampshire? Do you have family ties there?'

'No, she's, she's...'

Zoe finished his sentence. 'She's living with her boyfriend.'

Fergus's eyes dipped as Zoe, in a refreshingly

straightforward manner, told us, 'Fergus's father had a terrible drink problem, it's no secret. And angel, I think your mother deserves to have found happiness again.'

'I completely agree,' said Felicity.

Rupert's head appeared round the door. 'I'm sorry to interrupt but I can't get any blasted reception on my mobile and I must give Jules a call.'

'Here,' Zoe immediately stood up, 'let me show you where the landline is.'

Then, remembering I'd forgotten to thank Mhàiri for getting her husband to look at my flat tyre, I got up and explained where I was going.

'She'll be in the kitchen,' replied Fergus and I left the room.

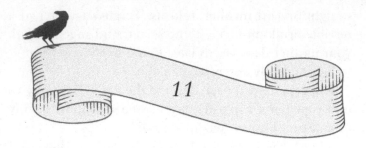

11

The kitchen smelt of lamb and there was a great big cast-iron pot bubbling away on a greasy Aga. The windows were steamed up and Mhàiri's grey fringe was stuck to her forehead.

'It smells delicious.'

'Lamb casserole. So many of youse I could nee fit the pot in the oven. Wee bit moisty in here.'

'Thank you very much for getting Donald to look at my tyre. I see he's fitted the spare one, so kind of him.'

'No trouble, Susie. I'm afraid he said the old un's slashed and you'll need ta get a new one fitted. Don't you go worrying tho, there's a local manny and he'll fix it for yous.'

'I should probably call him then and hope he can order it in.'

'There's no need for that, they've got them all there.'

I doubted they had every kind of tyre but as my modest car isn't some flashy indulgence, not that I could afford such a thing, I was hopeful they would have a fit.

'Enjoying yourself?' she said. 'You can be honest wee me.'

Mhàiri and I were staff, two peas in the same pod as far as she was concerned, and this made me smile. 'Yes. I've never taught on a residency before but it seems to be going okay and Zoe couldn't be more welcoming.'

'All right for some,' she said, and the sting in her tone worried me. We all know the cliché that Scots dislike the English; I've always had a good time up here, but did it stretch to Zoe? Have I slipped up and am I about to lose Mhàiri's trust?

'You having a hard time?' I asked, but she didn't reply, instead grabbing a dish cloth and furiously polishing an already clean surface. I now knew she wasn't going to tell me what was on the tip of her tongue.

I tried changing the topic. 'It's a pretty spectacular house this.'

'Needs a fair bit of work doing to it but I'm awfully fond of the place.' Mhàiri leant against the sink. I had her full attention again. 'How are yous students doing?'

'They're a good group and worked hard today.'

'That wee lad wee the spiky hair, he's a one. Likes me flapjacks so he does. Coming in here filling his pockets, you'd think he was feeding a horse upstairs. And whit's the upright gentleman called?'

'Rupert.'

'Well, he's fair got manners. He pokes his head round that swinging door at every opportunity to thank me.'

'How kind.'

'Aye. It's interesting the folk this week. We ain't had such a varied group afore.'

'What other groups have you had?'

'Ta be honest wee yous, we've only had day courses

afore. Garden open and what's not. Chatty posh ladies who dinee pay the likes a me or yous any attention.'

'I guess you see it all.'

'I fair do, Susie, nowt passes me by. That woman wee the cardigan wee gold buttons?'

'Jane?' I said. I was looking forward to a bit of gossip.

'Aye, that Jane. I swear she came here wee her folks when she were a bairn.'

'Really?'

'Unless it's her mammy reincarnated that's definitely the daughter of a woman who used to stay.'

Jane is one of many indistinguishable ladies in the English county set. A type. A woman with a lapsed figure, a short fuse, a bossy manner, a string of pearls and a tendency to visit a supermarket in her Schoffel. Take her off her home turf, deposit her at Auchen Laggan Tosh and Mhàiri instantly recognises her as the daughter of someone who'd stayed many years before.

'She hasn't said she's been here before?'

'She'll have forgotten, she were teeny weeny when they used to come. But I dinee forget, and that's her mammy's face for sure.'

'We could ask Fergus. He'd know.'

'Na, Fergus would nee remember, he was nee born.'

Now I was confused. If Mhàiri *is* right then I have my ages all wrong. Mhàiri must be in her seventies; she looks great for her age and I'd have to knock a few years off Jane and put her at about fifty.

'Hey,' I said swapping our subject, 'has Louis Bouchon been here before?'

'The foreign one?'

'He's half English,' I said, instantly sticking up for him.

'Aye, but wee a name like that he's gotta be a foreigner.'

I laughed. 'Has he stayed here before?'

'Nope.'

'Visited?'

'I canee remember. Over the years there have been a lot of people through this house.'

Ah ha, I'd got her. How could she remember Jane's mother from forty-plus years ago if she couldn't remember a foreigner in the last seven?

'Well, thanks again for the tyre and for all this delicious food.'

'Oh hen, yous dinee need to thank me.' Mhàiri touched my arm. 'But while you're here would yous mind giving me a wee hand and takin' these plates to the Belling?'

'Not at all, here.'

'You'll need a dish cloth, they're awfully warm.'

'It's okay, my hands can cope.'

'Surely not. Oh my. Look at that. Yous have a magic talent there.'

I stretched out a foot to push open the swing door and stepped carefully into the dining room.

'*Whoa*, Susie. You gave me a fright.' Ewen almost dropped the empty jug in his hand. A slight overreaction I'd say.

'Sorry.'

'Can I help you?'

'I'm just going to put these in there.'

Ewen slid back the door of the Belling and I placed them in. Then swinging the jug in his left hand, he told me he'd been on filling-up-the-water-glasses duty.

I giggled at the childishness of it and looked at my feet. There was a packet of pills on the floor. 'Piriton, how odd.' They were now in my hand. 'It's not really hayfever time of year.'

'They'll be Zoe's I bet.' He snatched them off me. 'I'll make sure they go back to the right place.'

'What if they belong to one of the students?'

'Nah, they would've said.'

Haggis came racing into the dining room, ragging around shaking his wet coat. Fergus was close behind him with a large torch in his hand. 'Here you two are,' he said. 'Ewen? Were you snooping at what's for dinner?'

'He was filling the water glasses,' I said, laughing under my breath.

'Really?' said Fergus, raising his eyebrows, and Ewen's matching ones rose in return. 'A house full of people to impress?'

'Quite right,' nodded Ewen.

'Susie,' said Fergus, 'I'm about to start a tour of the pictures. Everyone's gathered in the snug.'

'Marvellous,' said Ewen.

'It's not compulsory,' insinuated Fergus. 'Perhaps you'd like to re-park your van instead?'

'Ha, ha, very funny. Far too cold and wet to move it away from the steps and there's no chance I'm missing your tour.'

Ewen shadowed us both as we went to the library.

'For those of you who haven't met,' said Zoe, 'this is Fergus's brother, Ewen.'

'You don't say,' said Shane.

'Absolutely bloody *identical*,' shouted Lianne as both Ewen and Fergus shrugged their right shoulders.

'Fergus,' said Rupert, 'is that a Cotman to the left of the door?'

'That's not Cotman,' said Minty. 'It's too misty for one of his watercolours.'

'It's a nineteenth-century copy of an early Turner street scene.'

'In Margate,' added Zoe.

'Has anyone seen that film with Timothy Spall?' said Jane.

'Yes,' grinned Ewen. 'Got the measure of Turner spot on; very good painter, very dull man.'

Felicity giggled.

'Our picture collection is limited, but in good condition,' began Fergus. 'If there's something our father cared for it was paintings. He had a sort of eternal affection for the past and the Muchton collection tells a story. I'm going to take you round a selection and hopefully you'll make sense of this.'

Fergus crossed the room to the Victorian writing bureau, looked up at a trompe-l'oeil still life of a letter rack above it and turned on the torch.

'That makes a huge difference,' said Rupert. 'I can see every detail of the painting now. What a clever idea of yours.'

'Daddy always takes a torch when he goes to an auction,' said Minty.

'And mine,' said Giles.

Jane had a pair of spectacles on a string round her neck and as she forced them into an indent on the bridge of her nose, she held her face up to the painting and proclaimed, '1662.'

'Jesus it's old,' said Shane. 'And when did *you* take up wearing glasses?'

She prodded his shoulder. 'Some of us have to for reading.'

'Righto,' said Fergus, 'I don't want to spend too much time on this painting. It was bought by the 1st Earl and I only wanted to draw your attention to the overlapping playing cards in the bottom right. They allude to contemporary political issues at the time. Scotland with its lion and England with three lions…'

'That's because we're three times mightier,' Giles interrupted.

'Do you go to *Eton*?' said Ewen.

'No.'

'Ah.'

'Who's it by?' said Minty. 'I rather like it.'

'Thomas Warrender.'

'I've never heard of him before?'

'He was mainly a decorative painter. This is one of very few oil paintings by him.'

'Perfect place for it near your desk,' said Rupert.

'Isn't it,' exclaimed Felicity having only just twigged.

Fergus turned off the torch and as he led us out of the room behind the staircase, Ewen took it upon himself to set Giles straight. 'King James VI of Scotland unified the Scottish and English crowns in 1603. This is what the playing cards symbolise. Scotland was far mightier…and in charge.'

'Angel,' called Zoe from the back of the group, 'I'm going to leave you to it if that's okay.'

'Of course, you've heard it all before.'

Ewen caught my eye as he pulled the packet of Piriton out of his pocket and handed it to Zoe. Her brow ruffled, he whispered something in her ear and she slipped them into her pocket with a glance towards her husband. Ewen nodded at me. I smiled, he'd been right.

The torch was back on and Fergus drew our attention to a painting in the most elaborate gold-leaf frame. 'This scene painted by Allan Ramsay is of George III's coronation in 1761.'

'The original?' said Rupert.

Louis sneered at Ewen.

'It's one of many replicas. A very important marker for our family, as it was their loyalty to the King during the Jacobite Rebellion as well as their modest contribution to the cost of George III's coronation that bestowed an Earldom on them.'

'So, your family didn't support the Jacobites?' said Louis, with a huff.

'No offence,' said Ewen, tapping his friend on the shoulder. 'We were followers of John Knox, we're Presbyterians, so the Jacobites didn't hold any draw for us.'

'Did you buy your title then?' said Lianne.

Fergus launched into a lengthy reply. 'Our family were on the up, the Highland Clearances had gained momentum and, I'm not proud to say, the Muchtons moved away from loyalty and honour to profit, turning their back on the people who worked the land. Thanks to the union of the Kingdoms of Scotland and England in 1707 and the booming trade with the colonies they were well placed to capitalise on the sale of wool from their ever-expanding flock.' The effortless spiel was rolling off Fergus's tongue. 'The farm was making good money and a title raised their profile in society. Being aesthetes…'

'Eestheet?' said Shane, much to the amusement of Minty.

'Someone who appreciates beauty,' explained Jane.

Fergus continued: 'Contributing to the coronation, securing themselves a title, casting off old ties and embracing the new life as part of the aristocracy was an effective way for our ancestors to gain access to the best art and architecture.'

'Social climbing,' said Ewen, 'is what you'd call it nowadays.'

Giles grunted.

'I don't understand?' said Lianne.

'Having a title,' said Jane, 'brought the Muchtons friends in high places and all these friends would have spent money furnishing their houses with fine art.'

'But you don't have to have a title to have good art,' said Giles, I presume defending his own untitled although privileged family.

'We're talking about the eighteenth century,' said Fergus. 'In the midst of the Scottish Enlightenment, the best art collections belonged to those who could afford it, the rich aristocracy.'

'Did you get this house with your title then?' said Lianne.

'In a roundabout way.'

'For free?'

'No.' Fergus was amused. 'The 1st Earl built it.'

'It's an Adam house,' said Jane, 'it was explained in the starter pack for the course.'

Fergus clapped his hands. 'We're going to run out of time for more paintings. I'll tell you about the house another day.' He flung open the door to the larger drawing room and his tummy gave an audible rumble. 'Above the mantelpiece is a portrait of the 1st Earl's brown-eyed wife Ruth painted by Ramsay in 1764.'

'*Gaw*, she's beautiful,' said Giles.

'Ramsay was an eminent painter at the time, which is why I wanted to point it out, but we must continue. You can come back and study this another time.'

We were chivvied out and into the billiards room.

'Are you all familiar with the concept of the Grand Tour?'

'Rounding off the education for sons of the aristocracy,' said Giles, proudly.

'Exactly. Young men were sent to the Continent to...'

'Sow their wild oats,' Ewen interrupted.

Giles sniggered.

'More importantly,' said Fergus, 'to see first-hand the great paintings of famous artists such as Raphael and Titian, the cities of the Renaissance and the remains of classical civilisations.' He gave a great sweep with his right arm. 'All the watercolours hanging around this room were painted by the 2nd Earl under the tutorship of Gavin Hamilton.'

'That's the interior of the Pantheon, ain't it,' said Lianne pointing at one.

'Yes,' said Minty, 'and look, here's the temple of Athene – I love the Greeks.'

'How do *you* know all about the Greeks?' said Shane.

'We had an art history trip there last year.'

'Me too,' said Giles.

'What? Your school paid for that?'

'No, Mummy and Daddy did.'

'Fergus, did you say these were painted by your relation?' I asked and he nodded.

'So, are there still artists in your family?'

'I'm an artist,' blurted Ewen and I suddenly realised why Zoe had warned me he might want to join the course. Rupert, thank you Rupert, diverted our attention.

'I like that painting.' He was pointing towards a magnificent full-length portrait of a young man wearing the most beautiful blue silk and standing in front of a classical landscape.

'That's the 2nd Earl, painted by Pompeo Batoni.' Fergus shone the torch at the horizon highlighting the towers of the Vatican in the distance.

'Magical,' said Minty.

'Now, come, out of here and we'll do a quick circuit upstairs.'

'Were daughters ever sent on a Grand Tour?' asked Felicity.

'Occasionally, and you'll find a copperplate engraving by Francesco Bartolozzi hanging in the gents. It's of the 2nd Earl's daughters, Annabel and Mary, on theirs.' Fergus nattered away as we lined out on the landing. 'If you want to learn more about the Grand Tour, we have a very good copy of Boswell's *An Account of Corsica* in the library. Also, don't forget to look at the watercolours of Rome painted by Simone Pomardi on your way to the dining room later.'

'Which Earl collected those?' said Rupert.

'The 4th.'

'Now *his* wife's an interesting character,' said Ewen, winking at Louis, or me; it was hard to tell as we were standing one behind the other.

'These,' said Fergus, drawing our attention to the oil sketches crammed on the walls, 'are all views of the estate, painted by Landseer.'

I made sure not to catch his eye.

'Landseer?' said Shane. 'The guy who sculpted the lions at Trafalgar Square?'

'Yes.'

'And *The Monarch of the Glen*,' said Lianne. 'Our teacher gave us a quick run-down of Scottish art before we came.'

'Even an ignoramus like me knows that painting,' said Rupert. 'Comes from my love of stalking, you see.'

'Which Earl collected these?' said Felicity.

'The 4th again but it wasn't so much a collection as a gift.'

'Why?'

'Landseer was a popular visitor at Highland house parties and often in return for an invitation he would give his hosts a beautiful oil sketch he'd done over the course of his stay.'

I counted at least fourteen paintings. 'He must have been here a *lot*.'

'They're simply lovely,' said Jane. 'You're jolly lucky to have so many.'

'Isn't he,' said Ewen with a huge grin. 'They're all thanks to Countess Flora.'

'Perhaps you'd like to explain,' said Fergus, deferring to his brother.

'I've always admired Landseer,' began Ewen, 'his Highland oil paintings are my favourite. Theatre – that's how I think of them.' Fergus began to twitch. 'A performance within a frame. Stags, dogs, game and foliage beating their breasts on the stage...'

Louis got the giggles and Fergus interjected, 'What I thought Ewen was going to tell you is why we have so many more of them than most Highland houses.'

'Countess Flora, the 4th Earl's wife,' said Ewen, much

to Fergus's evident relief, 'had an affair with Landseer, and that's why he came to stay so many times.'

'And...' Fergus fed his brother the next line.

'Some of the dates on the backs of the pictures prove he came often even after her husband had died.'

'Why didn't she marry him then?' said Lianne.

'He was an artist,' said Minty, as if her parents had whispered something similar in her ear.

'Are you going to show them *all* the masterpieces?' said Ewen with a giggle.

'No,' said Fergus, irritated by his quip. 'I'm showing all we have time for.'

Does Ewen think his brother is boring on? As far as I'm concerned Fergus could continue as long as he wants, it's such a treat to be taken around a collection. These days one can probably look most pictures up online but digital versions always fall short of originals.

I'll never forget seeing Rogier van der Weyden's *The Deposition* in the Prado. The emotion in the faces of the ten figures made me tremble inside. No digital reproduction could ever move me like this. Modern photography just doesn't do a work of art justice, the vibrancy is lost, the size is misleading and the paint strokes are indistinguishable. Its only good use is in capturing intricate details.

What a joy it is to absorb the Muchtons' collection from life. I think everyone else thinks so too as not one of them has brought out a mobile to take a picture.

Fergus turned to Jane and Felicity. 'Would you mind if we looked at the portrait in your room?'

'Oh goodie,' said Felicity. 'I'd so like to hear the history behind her.'

Jane opened the bedroom door and rushed in first, planting herself in front of the dressing table.

'This is a portrait of Countess Antonia, the 3rd Earl's wife,' said Fergus. 'Gather round in a semi-circle and you'll get the full effect. It's a marvellously accomplished painting.'

The buxom woman was dressed to the nines and when Fergus turned on the torch, the sheer beauty of the diamond necklace, hanging like an armoured collar round her neck, glistened and shone as if it were real.

'I bet that's worth a bomb,' said Shane.

'It's painted by a follower of Raeburn so it's not worth a vast amount but isn't it beautiful.'

'I meant the necklace.'

'The necklace?' said Lianne as if he were stupid.

'The real thing,' said Shane.

'If only we still had it,' mourned Fergus.

'Family sold it I suppose,' said Rupert.

'It was stolen,' corrected Ewen and Jane grasped the dressing table with fright. Maybe she'd had jewellery nicked in the past.

'From the safe?' Felicity gasped.

'No,' said Fergus, 'our parents had returned home late from the Thane of Cawdor's daughter's wedding and got into bed without putting it in the safe.'

'Fools,' said Ewen. 'It was stolen in the night.'

'Burgled?' said Rupert.

'Yes, and the thief must have known exactly what he was after as nothing else in the house was touched.'

'Terrible, just terrible.'

'How frightful,' added Jane.

'Was it in their room?' Minty wasn't buying it. 'You're saying they didn't wake up?'

'Yes, that is odd,' said Rupert.

Fergus looked hurt and Ewen explained. 'Pa drank a lot and Ma often took sleeping pills.'

'Three cheers for insurance,' said Rupert, completely insensitive to the sentimental loss.

Fergus looked at his watch. 'There's time for one more picture. Come, out of here, we're heading for the far end of the children's corridor.'

'Who's sleeping all the way down here?' asked Jane.

We were outside my bedroom looking at a painting of the Annunciation.

'I am,' I said and blocked the door – I didn't want everyone peering in.

Fergus rushed into an explanation. 'This picture of the Angel Gabriel visiting the Virgin Mary is of little value but it has an interesting history in the context of the Muchtons. It was bought by our great-great-grandfather, the 6th Earl.' Fergus sighed. 'Our family have been as good at making money as they have been at losing it. The 5th Earl worked his socks off and thanks to him by 1873, when our great-great-grandfather inherited the title, the Muchton finances were in good order…'

'A role model for you,' interrupted Ewen.

Fergus continued unprovoked. 'You'd think my great-great-grandparents…'

'*Our* great-great-grandparents.' Ewen was at it again.

'Our great-great-grandparents had it all, but no amount of money in the world could buy them a son. They had three daughters, but were desperate for a male heir. So, despite the fact we're a staunchly Presbyterian family, they put their prejudices aside and bought this picture of the Annunciation.'

'Ooooo,' said Felicity.

'Jees, let me have a look,' said Shane, pulling Giles out of the way.

'The story goes,' began Fergus, 'that my, *our*, great-great-grandmother said a prayer in front of it every morning and every evening.'

'Did it work?' chuckled Rupert.

'Of course not,' said Ewen. 'She had twin girls and gave up.'

Louis found this particularly amusing.

'That's why *you're* twins,' giggled Felicity. 'Skips a generation, you know.'

'What happened to the title?' said Minty.

'On her father's death the eldest daughter became Countess Iona *suo jure*, in her own right.'

'But she's a woman,' said Giles.

'Muchton,' said Fergus, 'is one of a handful of Scottish hereditary titles that can pass through the female line in the absence of a son.'

'Did she have a son?'

'Yes, and so on her death it passed to him, on his death to our father and on Pa's death to me.'

Giles turned to Ewen and said, a little cheekily I thought, 'Bad luck you weren't born first.'

Ewen wasn't amused and neither was I. Giles's comment had made me feel profoundly sad, bringing the conversation I'd had with Mum at Christmas to the forefront of my mind. So, when Fergus announced, 'That's the tour over,' and began to march everyone back downstairs I nipped into my room to pull myself together.

I sat down on the bed and started to weep. I'm still finding it impossible not to, when I think about what I now know. It's not that I regret having faced up to my parents and asked them, 'Why am I an only child?' It's just their answer remains hard to digest.

It had been tough getting it out of them. First, Mum had avoided the question, jumping in with the usual, 'Susie, there's so much to do I think we should write a list, sort out the menus for the next few days, there isn't time for any chatting right now.' But I wouldn't let it drop, I wanted to know, and Dad, who was looking out of the window at the time mumbling about the lack of song birds these days, said, 'Marion, I'm going to pop out. Susie, this is a conversation for you and your mother.' Mum as good as collapsed into a chair, and I, too caught up in my own issues to offer sympathy, stared down at her drooping figure. It was then, with the smallest, saddest of voices, she told me about my other half, a little boy, who died at birth. After that she failed to ever conceive again.

Like Fergus, I came out first. He was granted primogeniture and I was granted life. I didn't dare ask Mum if a caesarean would have saved him. I'm sure in the past it had crossed her mind too.

Boom, boom, boom, the dinner gong sounded. I dried my eyes and said a prayer. *Oh Lord, give me strength not to get so upset.*

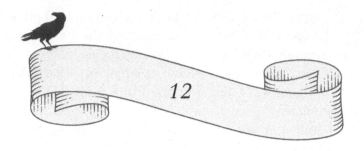

12

'You're very lucky to have married into this family,' said Felicity to Zoe at dinner. 'It's sooo interesting. Such a lot of history in those paintings.'

'Isn't there just.'

Felicity swung her head one hundred and eighty degrees and was now grinning at me. 'Don't you agree, Susie?'

'Yes,' I said, and although I was smiling back my eyes were watching Ewen and Louis who were sauntering into the room. If it wasn't a help-yourself-to-the-lamb-casserole-on-the-hotplate affair their tardy arrival would have been noticed. But everyone was shiffiling and shuffling, taking care not to slop their full plates as they chose a seat at the table. Felicity had sat next to me, and much to my relief Ewen, not Louis, sat down on my other side. I think Louis has been flirting with me (and me with him a bit) and although some fun this week would be exciting, it's only Monday, I don't want to rush into it.

'It *is* a treat being here,' said Felicity before I could so much as nod at Ewen.

'I agree. We are lucky to be in such a beautiful place.'

'I hope you won't have us painting the river again,' she tittered. 'Pretty as it is, it was a struggle.'

'Don't worry, we'll be visiting a new place each day.'

'Oh good-eeee. I'm so pleased Jane persuaded me to come here.'

I smiled; it was nice to see Felicity looking happy. 'You and Jane must live quite near each other?'

'Oh yes, neighbouring villages, although we always meet in Margaret's house, she's the one who started the club and has a sitting room big enough for us all. Are you a member of a book club, Susie?'

'No, but I like the sound of them.'

'Such fun, we all bring a bottle and some nibbles, it's more about the social than the book. I try to listen to whatever it is in the car, I never read them.'

'Do you drive a lot?'

'I used to take my husband to his train every morning and collect him in the evening so that made it easy, but now hardly at all.' Felicity blinked back a tear.

'I hope your daughters live near you?'

'Terribly close and they're ever so good to me.' She took a large gulp of wine and instantly perked up again. 'Tell me, Susie, is there a man in your life?'

'Not a steady one.'

'It won't be long, I'm sure.'

We both took the break in conversation as a good moment to tuck into dinner and when Felicity raised her head and looked at Zoe I grasped the opportunity to turn to Ewen.

'Susie,' he included me, 'Rupert on my left here was just telling me he knows where our cutlery comes from.'

'My wife,' said Rupert, 'couldn't believe it when I told her I was eating off the silver that caused such a hoo-ha on my very first job.'

'Red trousers here,' said Ewen, 'tells me my father bought the contents on the cheap.'

Rupert guffawed. 'I'm teasing you. It wasn't his mistake. The land sale I was in charge of fetched a penny or two but the wet-behind-the-ears chap selling the contents agreed a price without putting it past the owner. Legally he couldn't go back on his word.'

'Well done, Pa,' toasted Ewen with an empty glass. 'Can't say he has much else to show for the money he spent.'

Rupert chuckled. 'The likes of these,' he held up his knife and fork, 'won't keep Fergus and Zoe in their old age.' He then filled up our wine glasses and turned to his left to talk to Lianne.

Zoe stood up. 'I'm just going to get some more water,' I heard her say, 'I don't know who left an empty jug on the table.'

I gave Ewen a prod with my elbow.

'Whoops, that was your fault for distracting me.'

I smiled and he watched as I put a forkful of lamb casserole into my mouth.

'You'll never get any continental food here,' he said, 'but it's all delicious, that's for sure. I wish I had someone to cook for me.'

'You live down the back drive, don't you?'

'Glamorous, eh?'

'I didn't mean it like that,' I apologised, embarrased.

'I know.'

'It's nice you live where you grew up. It is your home.'

'*Was* my home.'

'Sorry, *was*,' I teased.

'Hey cheeky,' he said and then out of the blue, he asked, 'Are *you* a twin, Susie?'

My eyes glazed, my heart beat and my tongue clung to the roof of my mouth. I must not cry.

'So sorry, so sorry,' whispered Ewen, 'I didn't mean to bring it up.'

'Bring it up?' I said with total surprise; how could this man possibly know?

'I *am* familiar with problems between twins, you know.'

'Yes, of course.'

I was snappy because I was sad, and Ewen had touched a nerve. But he doesn't know this. I must be nice, and hey, dinner's when I'm meant to be working this man out. So, I went for it...

'Do you find it difficult living so close to the house you grew up in?'

'It's a bigger issue than that.'

'Go on...'

'You go first. There are too many questions coming my way.'

'My twin died at birth.' I said it. Straight out. No wobble of my vocal cords and no tears. Here's hoping my oversharing draws him out.

'*Susie*,' whispered Ewen, 'I really am so, *so* sorry. I've stepped out of line. That's awful. Terrible. Terrible. So sad.'

'It's okay, let's leave it.'

'Guess you're going to tell me it's my turn now?'

I was so pleased he was trying to lighten the mood.

'Yup, fair's fair.'

Now how was he going to soften the blow having brought up my dead twin?

'Rightfully I should be the 10ᵗʰ Earl.'

'Really?' I said, thinking, yes, Ewen is about to confide in me (or have a go at his brother).

He looked down at my plate. 'Since you've finished, I'll explain.'

Gads, what's he about to bring up?

'Here's a home truth,' he said matter-of-factly. 'Had Ma given birth naturally I would have come out first. But no, fifteen hours in she had a bloody caesarean, I was pushed into second place and Fergus suddenly became the heir.' He grasped his wine glass and I hoped for his sake he wasn't going to crack it again.

'That's extraordinary.'

'You're telling me.'

'I've never thought about such a scenario before.'

'Well, if you've no need,' he sounded much happier with another glass of wine in him, 'there's no point.'

'Hey, I could be the Duchess of anywhere for all you know.'

He laughed again. 'It *is* quite a sensitive subject, you know.'

'I'm sorry, I do understand.' I did. Because, even though people say male primogeniture is 'so last century' one can to this day drum up plenty of families who pass on estate, house and contents to the closest male heir. Here at Auchen Laggan Tosh it presents an acutely jealous case. When the previous Earl of Muchton died, the eighteenth-century Highland title and family estate all landed in his son Fergus's lap. Ewen, in the cruellest of twists, lost out on it all.

'Hey,' I tried to rally him. 'Why don't you prove everyone wrong?'

'What do you mean?'

'Go out into the world, find a vocation, reach the top of your game. Maybe even get your own title, end up in the House of Lords if that's what you want?'

'It's not.'

'Well, what do you want then?'

'My fair share.'

'That would mean selling the family home.'

'Nah, he could keep it. I mean the paintings. There's a fortune here, mouldering away on the walls. Why can't he sell a few and give me half? Fergus would have money to do up the house and I'd have some to get me started in life.'

'So you'd do the same if you were the heir?'

'Of course.' He gave an unconvincing grin. 'I certainly wouldn't have his hang-up about honouring our ancestors.'

Ewen looked down the table towards Zoe and I wondered if he'd been putting pressure on her? She gave him a glowing smile; there's certainly no hostility between these two. She seems to be thrilled he's part of the party. Maybe a wife warms to someone who resembles her husband? In looks at least. Fergus, responsible, and Ewen, footloose, don't seem to me to be cut from the same cloth.

'Don't you respect your brother for being a custodian, not thinking of this house and contents as being his to sell?' I wanted to get to the bottom of it.

Ewen gave me a go-on-then-argue-your-point look. So I did. 'Fergus doesn't want to be responsible for losing this estate. He's willing, they're willing, to do all they can to bring in enough money to keep it together and continue living here. That's huge pressure. Any money they earn will go into it, whereas any money you earn will be yours to keep.'

'Hmm, that's a new way of looking at it.'

'And an unspoilt one.'

'*Oi.* You're pretty blunt, aren't you.'

'Sorry, I couldn't resist.'

Louis, sitting much further down the other side of the table, caught my eye as if to say, I hope it's going okay with my mate Ewen. I lifted my glass with an it's-all-great reply.

'Louis checking up on you, is he?'

I blushed. 'You met him on a photography course, didn't you?'

'Is there anything you don't know?'

'Sorry, I can't help it, I'm interested in people.'

'I better be careful then,' Ewen smiled, and promptly stood up to clear the plates.

Pudding arrived on the hotplate and Shane could not get over the name Spotted Dick. He giggled and joked as Zoe and Ewen doled it out. Minty was offered some first and when she refused, Shane, without missing a beat, said, 'You can always have some of mine if you'd prefer.' Everyone laughed, except Jane.

I spent the rest of dinner listening to Felicity talk me through her uneventful plane journey here, and as soon as the first people rose to leave I took my cue and got up too. Fergus followed me out and whispered in my ear, 'The art valuer's arriving at seven-fifteen tomorrow morning. Best come to the hall five minutes before.'

I smiled and thanked him and said, 'Good night.'

A day of work and an afternoon out in the cold sent me straight upstairs after dinner. Jane was of the same opinion. 'If tomorrow night's burlesque and the following a ceilidh, I must get some sleep in advance.'

'Night, Susie,' she said.

'Night, Jane,' I called back. Then grabbing my toothbrush from my room, I glanced at the painting of the Annunciation on my way to the bathroom. Twin daughters granted to the Countess who longed for a son just shows our creator at times has a different plan. But I bet you her eldest daughter made a great Countess. A woman in a man's world. I must try and find a moment to ask Fergus about her.

I stared into the mirror above the sink, watching toothpaste foam in the corners of my mouth. Why had my parents decided I didn't need to know I'm a twin? I can't believe they kept this tragedy from me and it upsets me to think they've deceived me for thirty-something years.

I plodded back down the passage with heavy limbs and as I changed into my nightie and got into bed I felt drowned in unhappy thoughts. Lying under the covers in the foetal position I imagined myself curled up next to my brother in our mother's womb.

When I was little I had an imaginary friend, Luke. He kept me company as an only child. I never understood when Mum used to get short-tempered if I insisted on her laying another place at the table, buying two lollipops in the shop or making a bed on the floor next to mine. Now it's clear, I completely understand, but it makes me so cross they'd lied to me for so long.

I wish I'd been told as a little girl that the person I'd

been snuggled next to for nine months had left my side forever more. I think it would have helped me rationalise my emotions growing up, made sense of the total emptiness I've suffered. My brother and I were just bones, flesh and blood but I believe an emotional attachment was formed. That's why twins exist in-sync.

But my double act is never ever coming back. I lost the thing closest to me at birth. It's no wonder I'm afraid of commitment, unable to go out with someone for any longer than a year.

I blame my parents, I really do, but I don't want to hurt them. They obviously can't see how selfish they've been. My vulnerabilities are mine to get over; holding it against them simply won't help.

I stuck a leg out from the duvet, I was hot and fed up. In our family, supposedly, nothing is brushed under the carpet and left to be trampled on. When issues arise, we gather round the kitchen table and try to come to an understanding before causing too much emotional hurt. But, right now, an only child, out on a limb, I'm feeling lonelier than ever before. I bet my parents have other secrets under their roof.

My eyes stung with tears as I shut them tight and began to recite my night-time prayers. *Hail Mary, full of grace*, another in Latin, followed by a *Jesus, tender Shepherd, hear me* for old times' sake. I usually drift off to sleep midway through, but getting to the end of *Our Father, Amen*, I felt wide awake.

Drat. I sat up in bed, flicked on the light and stretched for *The 39 Steps*. I curled back the cover of an old friend and pleaded with John Buchan to take me on an adventure far away from here.

At last I was in someone else's imagination. Time passed, my eyes began to droop, then, as *always*, I felt the need to go to the loo.

Tiptoeing to the bathroom as silently as I could along floorboards that creaked with my every other step, I noticed a light shining out from under the door of the closed wing. Zoe's words came to mind: 'This wing is locked as it isn't used.' But I now know four valuable paintings are in there.

I looked at my watch: 1.04am. Presumably the light is a security measure, set to a timer as mine are when I'm away from home. Nevertheless, as I sat down on the cold china seat, I thought, wouldn't it be exciting if someone's up to something in there?

I stood in the unlit corridor listening for a sound, and when the locked wing door creaked against the wooden floor I stared at who was coming out.

Zoe couldn't see me – I was hidden in the dark. But I caught her leaving all right, wrapped up in a dressing gown, maybe just checking the place out, but even so, why now? She flicked off the light and then with a click something opened on the landing wall. I couldn't tell what but it was just to the right of the door. Suddenly a key pad lit up and I followed her fingers as they pressed a few buttons. The pattern they had taken lodged in my mind. She then closed it up and disappeared.

I lay in bed stock still, hoping to hear more. But nothing came: the house now slept in silence, and not even the wind blew. No chance of sleep though, too many thoughts buzzing.

Could Mhàiri have been right – has Jane really been here before? How odd she wouldn't say, but perhaps Zoe warned her not to, didn't want people thinking that's how she got on the course. Or for me to treat her any differently, for that matter.

I got out of bed and slipped on a pair of socks. I have a plan. If Jane has been here before, her name is bound to be in an old visitors' book. I need to find the one from forty-plus years ago. It can't be that hard, these big books take time to fill. Auchen Laggan Tosh must have a collection, a detailed account of every person who's ever been to stay. Even people who forgot to sign will have been pencilled in by the host. Everyone does it, no one is ever missed.

Now's a good time, John Buchan will be my cover: 'I can't sleep, I came to find another novel.'

I made it to the library door without a sound. No one was around and no lights were on. My hands trembled as I pushed it open. *Eeeek*, the blasted hinges let out a squeak.

Ruff, ruff, came Haggis's bark. He was somewhere nearby. Why wasn't he sleeping with Fergus and Zoe? I froze with my fingers crossed, pleading him not to do it again. Silence. My shoulders relaxed. Haggis had kept his trap shut.

I flicked the brass switch and the book cabinets lit up. Then scouring every row for the distinctive navy blue, claret red or racing green leather-bound books, a couple of hundred quid a pop, I realised no, no, no. There are none and what's more my hunt is in vain – I don't have a clue what Jane's maiden name is.

If Atkinson were aristocratic I could look it up in The Big Red Book. There's one of them there on the shelf, a sort of telephone directory for toffs. No addresses and numbers, just titles, names and lineage. I'd look up Jane's husband and find their marriage date and her maiden name. But no, a surname like Atkinson won't be in there, too ignoble to be part of the pack. My hunt has come to a grinding halt.

I put John Buchan back in place and took Edith Wharton's *Summer* down off the shelf. I haven't read this one of hers before, and it's slim enough to finish by the end of the week – a much better choice. My work here is done. I flicked off the lights and crept back to bed. Thankfully without another *ruff* from Haggis.

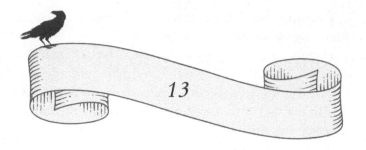

13

It's five past seven. I'm in the hall, ahead of time as always, but I'm far too excited to wait in my room. Spring light is flooding through the cupola showing up dust everywhere. I have a tissue in my pocket and as Fergus isn't here yet, and I like a job – I'm not very good at sitting still – I wipe the surface of the table.

'Susie,' said Zoe, swanning through the arch, her damp hair wound up into a bun, Haggis at her heel. 'What *are* you doing?'

'Nothing.' I stuffed the tissue in my pocket – it's actually rather rude to be cleaning someone else's house.

'It is so early,' she said. 'Fergus is sleeping. I didn't want to wake him so if you want to change your mind and go back to bed he'll never know.'

I tried to catch her eye. Has Zoe gone mad? Why would I ever turn down going around four great paintings with an expert?

She ruffled her damp hair and looked down at the dog. 'Landseer's pictures are out of fashion, aren't they, Haggis, I'm sure they're not Susie's kind of thing.'

'I definitely want to see them, please.'

Zoe shrugged her shoulders. 'Your choice,' she said as she flung open the front door.

Haggis wagged his way out beneath the Corinthian portico. Donald's pickup was leaving the yard. He raised his hand from the steering wheel to say hello. No sign of Mhàiri so I guessed she'd scampered in through a servants' entrance.

'Susie,' said Zoe, looking at her watch, 'I must take Haggis into the garden to do his business, but I'll be back before our visitor arrives.'

'Okay.'

It would have been nice if Zoe had asked me to accompany her, but I suppose I should wait here in case the man arrives. I stood on the top step breathing cold air up my nostrils until they stung. I wanted the shock to wake up my senses, help me get my head around why Zoe was up late last night, why Fergus had overslept and why Haggis was sleeping downstairs.

Fergus came storming out the front door wearing a scowl and rocking a bed-head do.

'Susie, thank goodness you're up. I don't know what happened, slept straight through my alarm, and as for Zoe, *where* is she?'

'Coo-ee, angel, morning.' Zoe was coming around the side of the house and no sooner had she greeted her husband, than a racing-green Volvo swept into the yard. The driver grinned and waved as if we were his audience in the gallery. I felt rather embarrassed on his behalf.

Fergus marched down the steps, making no attempt to stop Haggis racing across the yard. The young man (he couldn't be more than late twenties at the most) was too busy patting down his side-parting to stop the rascal jumping up. But totally unbothered by the paws on his off-the-peg suit, he seemed perfectly au fait with dogs and proceeded to greet Haggis as amicably as he'd greeted us.

'Come, Susie,' said Zoe, reaching the top step. 'It's freezing out here, let's go inside.'

We waited seconds in the hall and as soon as the door opened Fergus introduced us. 'This is my wife Zoe and this is an artist we have staying, Susie Mahl.'

'Hello, I'm Oliver Raylet.' He shook us both enthusiastically by the hand.

'Would you like some coffee, Oliver?' said Zoe.

'No thank you.' He turned to Fergus. 'If it's okay with you I'd like to get straight to it. I must make it back to Edinburgh this afternoon and the weather's not in my favour.'

'Is Edinburgh home?' said Zoe.

'Yes and no. I live and work there but I grew up in Bucks.'

'Buckinghamshire?'

'Yes. Although my great-great-grandfather was Scottish and so I'm trying to reignite the connection.'

'How lovely,' Zoe smiled, and Fergus chivvied us into the body of the house.

'Come, Oliver,' he said. 'As I explained on the telephone the house is full and I don't want our residents knowing you're here. We must keep our voices down.'

'Yes,' said Zoe. 'It's very important.'

'I understand,' whispered Oliver.

'Let's all go upstairs then and I'll show you the pictures.'

'Thank you, my Lord.'

'My *Lord*. For heaven's sake call me Fergus.'

'Fergus,' Oliver repeated, and I only just managed to suppress a laugh.

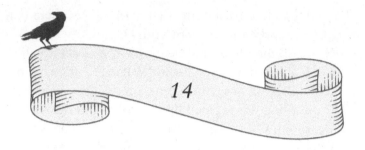

14

Oliver Raylet has the manners of someone who overthinks and underplays their sophistication. I blame it on his job. If you come, as I assume he does, from minor English public-school stock and are plunged into a sales role in a high net-worth department, it shapes you. Assuming the role of art valuer, you've become conscious of the price tag on things that were previously just stuffing in your parents', friends' or relations' houses. And like those before him − and car salesmen, estate agents and antique dealers too − Oliver has an inclination to dress up and flirt with his subject.

This performance began as the three of us, plus Haggis, which made four, trotted upstairs after Fergus, and Oliver said quietly under his breath, 'There's a rare harmony between the exterior and interior of your house, it's a delight.'

But Fergus wasted no time exchanging pleasantries, and it wasn't until he pulled a key out of his pocket and opened the door into a vast space, stretching the length and width of one entire wing, that he spoke. 'In we go,' he said, standing back. 'You first, darling, yes there you go, Oliver and Susie. *No*, not you, Haggis.'

'Haggis!' said Oliver and before Fergus could stop him the dog scurried into the room. 'What a fantastic name.'

'It amuses us, yes. But, come on, Haggis, here boy.' The poor dog was grasped by the collar and shoved out of the room. 'Off you go, no four-legged friends in here.'

Oliver giggled quietly as he took off, sliding in his penny loafers across the sprung wooden floor. He was headed for the first of four paintings, hanging one after another down the longest stretch of wall. Natural light flooded in through the handsome floor-to-ceiling windows opposite. Zoe must have come in earlier to draw the curtains.

Each painting was about five by three feet, maybe more if you included the frame, and all depicted stags, dogs or horses in various country settings. They were hanging from rails on brass chains, a lovely old-fashioned way to display a painting. Landseer, as is his wont, had encapsulated the grandeur and majesty of Scotland. Each one, I'd bet, would give *The Monarch of the Glen* a run for its money.

'What a spectacular room,' said Oliver.

Hey, I thought, why didn't he remark on the paintings first?

'It was in its day,' said Fergus, moving towards him and leaving Zoe hovering alone. She'd clearly seen these paintings many times before. 'Deemed the acme of taste. But now the parts that made it so, the panelled silk walls, the plaster ceiling, the gold leaf,' Fergus's hands dashed about above his head, 'the cornice, the paint, the velvet curtains, the ragged pelmets, all let it down.'

'But one *can* imagine the splendour,' said Zoe, turning to me, her friendlier self back with us.

'Yes,' I smiled; she was right, those three magnificent chandeliers spoke for themselves.

I wanted to comment on the perfect symmetry and how much I liked this particular element of Adam style. But now was not the time. Fergus was back on point. 'Rest assured,' he said to Oliver, who had his face right up close to a canvas, 'these paintings have been well cared for.'

'Much better seen from afar,' said Zoe. 'Come here, Oliver, stand back.'

'Oh yes,' he said, sliding backwards across the floor. 'So majestic, you're right, power really resonates from this perspective.'

Zoe beamed and Fergus put his arm around her shoulder.

I gave them a little bit of privacy and went to look at the painting furthest away. But without carpets in here sound travelled the length of the wall and I heard Fergus ask Oliver, 'When did you say the exhibition's going to be?'

'It starts at the end of July, and it'll run throughout the festival.'

'Marvellous, how many pictures in total?'

'I don't know, I'm afraid.'

'Aren't you involved in the show?' said Zoe.

'No, no. I just value Scottish paintings on loan for insurance purposes. That's the extent of my involvement.'

'Who else are you visiting?' Zoe wanted to know, and I felt a pang of jealousy for Oliver's free pass into other people's houses. Given my fascination with who people are and how they live, if I were Oliver I would have asked to visit the loo as soon as I arrived and certainly have accepted the offer of coffee – people's choice of china can tell you many a thing. But the opportunity to pry was wasted on Oliver. He'd come to do a job and stuck to it.

'We're trying to get the McMurray Jigs to lend some,' he said, moving back up close to a painting.

'Splendid name that,' said Fergus. 'In full it's actually Jig McMurray Jig.'

Oliver laughed, not too much – that would have been rude.

'Are they loaning their collection?' said Zoe.

'They have two great pictures but they're reluctant.'

Zoe looked at Fergus. 'Do we really want to loan ours, angel?'

Oliver spun on his heel. 'You must,' he said; he couldn't afford to lose his one and only deal.

'Yes, yes,' said Fergus. 'Don't worry about that. Now tell us, what else does your job involve? None of us have met someone in your role before.' Fergus smiled at me.

'Managing nineteenth-century picture sales, but I do like a job associated with an exhibition. It means I get to see the paintings without the crowds. I feel very lucky about that.'

Fergus swelled with pride. 'Well, you must just give us a call if you'd ever like to come and see our collection again. We're very open to that, aren't we, darling?' He turned to Zoe, who nodded with a half-smile. I'm not sure she likes the cut of Oliver's jib but then again it could just be she's tired *from a late night*.

'Which department do you work in, Oliver?' she asked.

'British Paintings, from early Tudor portraiture through to the early nineteenth century. I noticed you have one of Gainsborough's dogs downstairs.'

'Yes?' said Fergus and I perked up. This was a painting I liked a lot.

'There's currently strong demand for eighteenth-century artists, the golden age of British painting. Gainsborough is a favourite. You'd get a pretty penny or two for your picture.' Oliver's eyes cast over the peeling plasterwork as they traced his thoughts. 'And if you have any seventeenth-century portraits by, say, van Dyck, we've had record prices for these recently. Also, if I may...'

Fergus interrupted him. 'It's very interesting to hear about the current market but I want to stop you there as we Muchtons like to keep hold of our collection.' He put his arm around Zoe's shoulders. 'It's about the only thing in our family's history, other than the house of course, which has survived the ups and downs.'

'No problem, but our art dealership has an excellent relationship with both established collectors and new buyers.' Oliver looked hopeful.

'Not for us,' said Fergus and Zoe shook her head. 'Now if you're happy being left alone, we shall leave you to it?'

'Yes. I might need some time up here.'

'Susie,' said Fergus, 'I should think you'd like to linger a bit longer?'

'Yes please.' I turned to Oliver. 'As long as I'm not in the way?'

'No, not at all.'

Fergus explained he was going to lock the door from the other side, he didn't want people prying. He handed

Oliver another key. 'Use this if you need to get in and out. I'll come back in a while, see how you're getting on.'

'Thank you.'

'Yes,' I said, 'thank you so much for letting me spend a bit of time in here. I'll make sure I'm down for breakfast.'

'Please do, Susie,' said Fergus. 'I'd hate to have to lie about where you are.'

Gosh, he was an honest man.

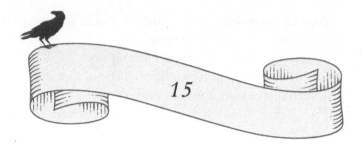

15

Oliver turned and asked me to point to my favourite picture.

'The first one up there, *Early Morning Stags on the Moor*.'

'Come then,' he said. 'Let's stand in front of it.'

Side by side we gazed at the dawn scene.

'What made you choose this?'

'You.'

'What?'

'*You* made me choose one.' I smiled but Oliver didn't get the joke.

'Why do you like it the most?'

'To be honest, I've never really liked Landseer but I'd never turn down an opportunity to see his work.'

'But you don't like it.' Oliver clearly wasn't a painter himself.

'One can learn a lot from well-known artists regardless of whether one likes their subject. I think Landseer's rather brilliant at the craft. The way the morning mist parts around the stag in this picture and the coat of the dog in that one over there are extraordinarily masterful pieces of painting.'

'Animal magnetism, that's what we call it. You're right, this is what makes his work popular.'

'I meant the brush work not the subject.'

'I see. That's something I know all about too. But first how would you sum up his pictures?'

'I'd say they were majestic Highland clichés skilfully portrayed.'

'Hmmm. He does divide people and you're correct in some sense, but the artwork's misty mountain background was almost always added later – like a nineteenth-century Photoshop. And occasionally the animals weren't even from Scotland.'

'Really?'

'Yes, after the National Gallery had paid several million pounds for *The Monarch of the Glen*, it was proved the stag was part of a herd in Cambridgeshire where it was painted,' Oliver sniggered.

'Surely the point of the scene is its association with Scotland, not where the work was done?'

'I disagree.' Oliver shook his head.

'So, if there was a picture of a Wiltshire man's bagpipes, painted at his house in Wiltshire, then they wouldn't be Scottish?'

'That's a different matter.'

I didn't respond; I don't want to bully this man.

'Don't you like any of Landseer's work?' he said.

'I suppose I only meant his breast-beating Highland scenes. I like the loose brush strokes of his oil sketches in the corridor. I don't know if you noticed them?'

'I certainly did. Very much of their time. A much freer style but Landseer no doubt. Tell me, surely there's a reason you chose this painting, *Early Morning Stags on the Moor*?'

'I like the way that sprig of heather sparkles in the light and,' I went up and touched the frame, 'this gilded wood is lovely.'

'Yes, his pictures are often presented well. You know the most famous frame, don't you?'

'I'm not sure,' I said as I wiped some dust off my fingers.

'That of *Neptune*, painted in 1824. It's made of beams taken from HMS *Temeraire*.'

'The warship that fought at the Battle of Trafalgar?' I was confused.

'Yes, in 1805.'

'Really?'

'Yes, it ties in nicely with the subject of a black and white Newfoundland dog on the seashore.'

Oliver did his penny loafer sliding motion as he moved to the second painting in the row, *Rutting Stags*, and asked me what I thought of it.

'It's okay.'

'Come on, you're an artist, you must have more to say than that?'

'I've always been a sucker for foreshortening so my favourite bit is the ridge of that barking stag's spine. It leads one's eye into the picture and I think it emphasises his dominance over the two less prominent ones.'

'The triangular composition. Yes, Landseer liked that.'

Oliver held his face right up close to the canvas and inhaled deeply. 'Hang on a minute.'

'Does it smell funny?'

He didn't laugh. Or speak for that matter.

'What are you doing?'

'I think there's,' he deliberated as he stepped back a bit, 'something not quite right with this.'

'The hanging of it?'

'It is a little low, but no.' He sounded irritated. 'I took an extra module in Landseer of this period.' His eyes were scanning the picture.

I have no idea what he's thinking.

'There's something uncharacteristic,' he began, moving his face back up close to the canvas, 'it doesn't look good enough to be by Landseer. It doesn't have the authentic Landseer touch. Another version would have different elements but this is the exact picture and I suppose therefore it may be a copy, I can't be certain.'

'A fake?' I said, instantly doubting the expert. Fergus is proud of his collection; there's no way this man can be right, we've barely been in here twenty minutes.

He cleared his throat. 'These revelations can come as a surprise but, well, I presumed you were here to see how my job works and as you're not the owner, or a close friend of the family, I thought I'd share my initial observations.'

'Yes, yes. But it's quite something to tell me they're fakes.'

'I wasn't suggesting it's a fake. I think something's up. It could be a second version Landseer painted or a copy. Though I wouldn't go as far as to say either yet.'

'A copy or a fake?'

'It might be a very accurate copy. Not a fake, no, not a fake. Only once a false signature has been added does it become a fake.'

'Are they all…' having already got in a muddle over fakes and copies I opted for, '…slightly dodgy?'

Oliver's right arm shot out. 'The final painting over there, *Dogs in the Moonlight*, has something odd about it too, but your favourite, *Early Morning Stags on the Moor*, and *Horses at Bay* are genuine Landseers, I'm pretty sure.'

'I don't understand.'

'Identifying legitimate paintings is all about whether or not they're good enough. The painter's hand is the first thing you look at when deciding what is an original and what is not.' Oliver moved along to the next painting on the wall, *Horses at Bay*. 'I'm familiar with the brush work of Landseer and this one here is definitely by him.'

'How can you tell?'

'One has to be on an eye level to analyse paint. Come here.' We went on to *Dogs in the Moonlight*. 'Look, I'm not trained in art fraud, I'm here to value the pictures for insurance purposes, but I know Landseer well enough to see there's something a bit wrong with these brush strokes.'

Once again, I wasn't sure what he meant and I began to wonder if Oliver's tentative suggestion it was a copy was because it's incredibly difficult to ever be certain.

The oil sketches on the landing have very different brush strokes. Even I can see that. So perhaps Landseer was bridging the styles when he painted *Dogs in the Moonlight*. Or having a bad day. Us artists do from time to time. Some pictures work and others don't. It's a constant struggle trying to achieve the best.

'Can you see,' he said, 'the brush strokes are all wrong in this picture, the texture of the paint with that plastic consistency is modern and I'll bet you it's on an acrylic ground – primer of that type has only existed since

1955. To me it doesn't look like old nineteenth-century paint.'

'Could they have had the pictures restored?'

'That's outside my remit but I don't think so.'

I could see a sheen on the surface and when I asked, 'Would you mind explaining the paint in more detail? It sounds interesting,' Oliver took the bull by the horns.

'When a painting has been around since 1840, and therefore it's almost two hundred years old, the paint begins to dry – craquelure. It starts to crack on the surface. This is very important when looking for an old painting. If it hasn't got the right craquelure it looks as if it's not a nineteenth-century picture.'

'Go on,' I encouraged.

I live in an old house, my studio is cold and sometimes I worry commissions will crack if clients hang them in a warm room. Oliver might be about to help me out.

'If you look at the first painting and the third, they both have a very obvious cracked surface, telling you the paint has been sitting on the canvas for a hundred years or more. Whereas, in this painting and the second one over there, there's no cracking effect.'

'Can one avoid paint cracking?'

'In a hundred years from now we'll know. Modern materials need to be tested over time, they haven't been around long enough yet.'

'I've heard of copiers baking the paint to make pictures look old. Much like dipping documents in tea. Is that true?'

'Copiers try all sorts of things to produce a craquelure effect, but it doesn't look right, you can always tell.'

'Do you really think two of these are copies?' My heartbeat rose as I said it.

'I'm not making it up if that's what you're implying. It drives me mad when people undermine an art history degree.'

'Oliver, I'm sorry, I honestly didn't mean that.'

'The Muchtons might well be thinking they can get away with submitting copies for public display.'

I tried to console him. 'Zoe and Fergus wouldn't do this to you.'

'Well, I've seen the provenance of the originals. Fergus Muchton owns them and I'm pretty sure two of them aren't here.'

'Could they have been sold by one of his ancestors? Maybe they had them copied and never said. Or maybe they sold the originals by mistake? These do look just like Landseer to me.'

'No fool would make that mistake. The owners will have sold the originals on the black market, it's the only way they'd get away with it under the radar. That's probably why Fergus has no idea.'

'Surely if you're going to be deceitful it's better to fool the black market than your relations?'

'Any underground specialists would have sniffed out a fake. By having them copied, they're gambling with the likes of me that they can pass off these as originals.' Oliver let out a long breath.

'What are you going to say to Fergus?'

'Nothing. I certainly wouldn't do it face to face and anyway it's not my job. When I'm back in the office I'll mention it to my boss. He'll give Fergus a call in a day or two to arrange a visit from Jamie Tumbleton-Smith, the current Landseer expert. It shouldn't be a problem, I happen to know Jamie lives in Scotland, not too far from here in fact. He'll come and give a definitive assessment and then we'll all know where we are.'

'Wow, I can't actually believe you might be right.'

'I've confided in you. I might be right, I might be wrong, these pictures are awfully good, but either way you mustn't say anything to the Muchtons.'

Is Oliver backtracking? I think he might be doubting himself.

'Yes, yes. I get that,' I smiled. 'Thank you very much for being so open with me. It is all rather fascinating.' I looked down the wall of paintings. 'Unfortunately I have to go to breakfast now. I'd so much rather stay and look a bit more. But at least you can get on without me asking more questions.'

'Well, it was nice meeting you,' Oliver smiled.

'I wish they'd let the students I'm teaching in here.'

'Nothing unusual about that. Quite a few owners closet their most valuable pieces of art away.'

'Lucky me then.' I hastily made my way to the door. I'm suddenly afraid Fergus might appear. I have been up here quite a long time.

'Bye,' said Oliver, retrieving the key.

He closed the door behind me and I paused on the landing. I wanted to know where Zoe had hidden the key last night. To the right of the door was a Landseer oil sketch and as no one was around, I thought, let's see if it comes off.

My fingers were pressed against the frame but the picture didn't budge until I released my hands and there was the sound of a click. I pulled at the bottom edge and to my amazement the whole thing hinged open to reveal a recess with a key pad. Easy as pie I'd found the hiding place. I clicked the picture shut again and took off downstairs.

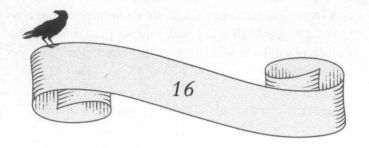

16

'Butteries for breakfast today,' said Zoe, sitting at the head of the table and pouring herself a cup of tea. 'Help yourself and pass the plate. *I* recommend Marmite on them.'

I sat down next to her. She reached across and stroked my arm.

'Thank you,' I said and she nodded with a smile. Phew, we've made peace over me seeing the paintings.

A plate of hot stodgy butter-drenched flat rolls came my way. Starting the day with a mouth full of calories is not my kind of thing but I had to try one and they did smell good.

'Now,' said Zoe, 'I should have said this to you all at the beginning of the week, we have a bandwidth allowance on the internet. I've had a warning to say we've almost used up our monthly allowance so *please* no more watching films online.'

'The Young,' tut-tutted Rupert, and Jane and Felicity nodded in agreement.

'I haven't been watching any,' said Minty.

'Nor me,' said Giles.

'Not me,' said Shane, to which Lianne replied, 'You have been Instagramming.'

'So have you.'

'Films will be the cause,' said Zoe. 'So please, no more.'

'Miss,' said Shane, 'I looked you up on Instagram.'

'And?' I knew he had more to say.

'Maybe you should be teaching us to draw hamsters.' He burst into a fit of giggles and Louis, who had been drizzling Marmite around his buttery, ignoring Zoe altogether, gave me a giddy look across the table.

'I draw people's pets from time to time. Yes?'

'Lots of pets @SusieMahl,' said Shane. 'Anyone got a hamster?'

'I bet there's good money in it,' said Rupert. 'And as we're talking about it, I'll commission you to draw our Labs right away.'

'Oh thank you, but you'd better look at my style first.'

'I'll show you,' said Shane, pulling his mobile out of his pocket.

'Not at the table,' said Rupert. 'Later.'

'You're excellent at it,' said Lianne. 'I looked up your stuff too.'

'If you want to draw animals,' said Zoe, 'we could organise a class amongst the Highland cows?'

'I'd be up for that.' Louis sounded keen.

'As long as we keep to the right side of the fence,' quivered Felicity.

The door to the dining room opened. 'What's all this?' said Fergus, grabbing Haggis by the collar and booting him out.

'Angel, there's some interest for drawing the Highland cows.'

'Well, I'll see if Willie the farmer can cordon off a section of the field for you tomorrow if you'd like?'

'I'm sure Willie will,' said Zoe.

'He's a willing chap then,' said Louis and I laughed.

'I'll go try him now.'

Fergus marched straight back out the room.

'Whose birthday is it anyway?' said Shane.

'Sorry?' Zoe was confused.

He pointed at a small pile next to her. 'All those gifts.'

There were chocolates, a scented candle, posh soap and a jar of honey.

'Oh these,' said Zoe, laying a hand on top of them all. 'They're presents from Felicity, Jane and Rupert.'

'But why?'

'Sometimes,' said Rupert, 'when one goes to stay with people one takes a present for the hostess.'

'House gifts to say thank you,' said Felicity.

'I never expected to receive any presents. These three have spoilt me.'

'Susie,' said Rupert, 'are we going for the usual start time, in the music room?'

'Yes, and we'll be using watercolour so please fill your pots, arrange your paper and have your rags ready by ten.'

Felicity looked flustered until Jane flapped her hand across the table and insisted she had enough to share.

'Louis,' Zoe smiled, 'you do look rather tired. Did Ewen force you to stay up awfully late? He's a terrible night owl.'

Louis winked at her. I was a little put out.

'We had a lot to catch up on,' he said. 'I'll perk up after another cup of coffee.'

Rupert stood up. 'I'm going to get a breath of fresh air before we begin. Anyone want to join me?'

'Yes please.' I jumped at the chance to see a bit more of our surroundings.

'Right then. I'll go get suited and booted and I'll meet you out the front.'

'Great.'

'Susie?' Zoe beckoned me to her side.

'Yes?'

'Have you found an opportunity to draw Haggis yet?'

Oh crumbs, I'd actually forgotten she'd asked me…'No, not yet.'

'If you don't mind me saying, maybe this morning's your chance. Take him on a walk with you now, then he'll sit still for you later. He should keep to heel so don't worry about a lead.'

It was a beautiful day, not a cloud in the sky, and as soon as we took off down the back drive Rupert told me my nose had gone pink.

Auchen Laggan Tosh sits in a copse of Douglas firs, planted, according to Fergus, in the eighteenth century to offer protection from the bleak winter weather. There was an abundance of lichen on the bark and Haggis was ferreting around, hopefully tiring himself out. I'd set the pace, I wanted to try and reach Ewen's house before turning back.

'Building up some heat in here,' said Rupert, unzipping his heavy tweed coat. Empty cartridges rattled around in his pocket prompting a rhapsody on shooting. 'I can never get enough of pulling birds out of the sky. Quite the best sport ever invented. I love it. Stalking too.'

We emerged from the Douglas firs and continued, guarded on either side by Scots pines. A rabbit ran across the drive and Rupert swung his arms as if aiming a gun.

'I'd have got that bunny for sure.'

I feigned an agreeable sound but it was drowned out by the piercing shrill of a bird. *Caw, caw, caw* stopped us in our tracks.

'What's that?' I looked up. 'I heard exactly the same noise the night I arrived.'

'Ghastly, isn't it. There. A raven.' Rupert pointed at a flash of sky between the trees. 'Oh look, there are two. Rather marvellous watching them frolic.'

A pair of birds, way up above us, were tipping and turning their wings as they croaked at each other.

'They're courting,' said Rupert. 'Monogamous like us.'

'How sweet.'

'Don't be mistaken. They're scavengers at heart. Can you see the twiggy ball at the top of that tree to the left?'

'Yes.'

'It's a nest, lined with rubbish I bet. They pick up anything twinkly. Would snatch a Kit Kat wrapper straight out your hand.'

'What about a piece of jewellery?'

He laughed. 'Only if you left it lying on the ground.'

Yes, I thought, this I've seen happen.

As we walked on Rupert didn't draw breath on the subject. 'They live off carrion. Would pick the tongue out of a dead man. Heaven knows why they're pro-tected. Highly intelligent but horrible birds. There seems to be an explosion of them around here.'

We turned a z bend and came upon a cottage.

'That must be where Ewen lives,' I said.

'Shall we rat-a-tat-tat at his door?'

'Why not.'

A few seconds later and Ewen was standing in the frame, wrapped up in a red tartan dressing gown.

'Wow,' he gasped, 'I did not expect to see you two.'

'Rather bumptious of us to appear on your doorstep like this,' said Rupert, grabbing hold of Haggis's collar, 'but Susie and I thought why not.'

'I'm sorry,' I said. 'We didn't mean to get you out of bed.'

'No, no. I'm up. Just not dressed.'

'Susie,' said Rupert, looking at his watch, 'we have precisely nine minutes to spare.'

'Oh,' said Ewen. 'Would you like to come in?'

'Yes please,' I said. 'That would be great.'

'Well,' Ewen yawned, 'leave Haggis in the porch and come this way into the sitting room.'

He flung open the curtains of the bay window and the early morning light lit up two lovely landscapes either side of the fireplace.

'These are very attractive,' I said, getting up close. 'Who's the artist?'

'Eerie,' muttered Rupert.

'Cameron,' said Ewen. 'D.Y. Cameron. They're twentieth century and if you look at this one,' I went to his side, 'the group of hills in the background are called Beinn Eighe. Not far from here. On a good day you can see them from Fergus's terrace.'

'Really?' said Rupert.

'Yes, the white quartzite sparkles.'

'I've never seen a mountain like that.'

'No mountains in Scotland,' said Ewen. 'They're either called hills, beinns or munroes.'

'I never knew.'

'Not many people do.'

'Hey Rupert,' I said, 'come closer and look at the subdued colours, they might help you this afternoon.'

'You'll have to give me more to go on than that,' he said, winking at Ewen.

'Okay then. See how few colours there are?' I asked.

'Blue. It's all varying shades of blue.'

'Atmospheric perspective,' said Ewen, taking over. 'As things recede their colour becomes less saturated. They assume the background colour. Bluer like the sky.'

'I see.'

'Unless you're painting a sunset. Then you make the object paler and redder.'

'I thought you were a photographer. Do you paint too?'

'I am an occasional painter. I did a photography course to help me understand paintings.'

'Why?' said Rupert.

'I knew if I learnt to take good pictures of paintings, I could then work from them back home. You know, dissect them, leave the emotion of the real thing aside and understand the technical details. It helps me get better quicker.'

'Yes,' I said, knowing exactly what he meant. Often when I visit art galleries I stand side on to a painting, getting as close as I can in order to see how the paint's applied, what ground it's on and whether it's varnished or not. Much like Oliver was doing this morning. I've always bought postcards in the shop to work from at home but I suppose a very good photograph would be better, that way I could zoom in, get really close to the detail.

'If you know how to work a camera,' Ewen directed his comment at Rupert, 'you can make an incredibly good reproduction and study it at home to your heart's content. Problem is,' he joked against himself, 'despite doing a course, I'm not very good at photography.'

'Well, if you paint,' said Rupert, 'you should join our afternoon class.'

'Susie doesn't look so sure about that.'

'The thing is,' I said nervously, 'everyone's paying to come on this week and I think if you were to join in it would change the dynamics and perhaps, if you don't mind me saying, it might appear as if you were taking advantage.'

'Good point,' said Rupert.

'That's exactly what it would be…me taking advantage of you being here. Don't worry, I'll keep out of it.'

'Thanks,' I smiled.

A loud whine came from the porch.

'Rupert, it's probably time we made our way back.'

He turned to Ewen. 'Would you mind if I had a quick glass of water first? I'm feeling rather parched.'

'Sure, come.' Ewen took us down a dull corridor into a mint green kitchen. 'Not a patch on my brother's pile, eh?'

'Easy to manage,' said Rupert.

There was a laptop on the table. I could just make out a progress bar on the screen – 'Downloading original. ZIP 500 GB 6hrs remaining'. What a *massive* file. I wonder if it has anything to do with Zoe's internet allowance?

'Susie?' Ewen snapped and I looked away. 'Water?'

'No thanks.'

'Jolly glad we knocked,' said Rupert. 'Any chance we can have a quick look at your studio?'

'Nope.'

'I'm sorry, I spoke out of turn.'

'Come on,' I said. 'We really must go.'

Ewen stood on the step waving us off as Haggis bolted back up the drive.

'Left right, left right,' boomed Rupert. 'We mustn't be late for class.'

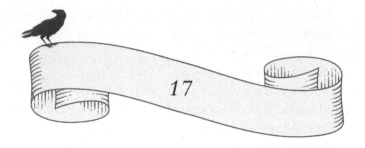

17

Cailey swaggered into the room, five minutes late, without an apology.

'Hiya everybody,' she grinned with a smile so huge one couldn't not be charmed.

'Cailey,' I said as she reached for her belt, 'there's no need to get undressed today. We're going to concentrate on your head.'

'Whatever yous wan't I'll do.'

'Thanks. Pop your bag over there and then come sit on this stool…'

Jane interrupted, 'So, we're painting a portrait, are we?'

'Yes, a head study in watercolour.'

Shane began to move his easel behind the stool. 'Don't be silly,' I said. 'You have to get a view of her face.'

He shuffled round next to the others and Cailey came to sit down.

'This do youse okay?'

'Absolutely great. You have such good posture, but can you really hold a pose like that?'

'I'll give it a wee go, Susie.'

'Okay, thanks. Right, everyone, you can either start by drawing a very light outline in pencil or go straight in with watercolour.'

'Which would you suggest?' said Felicity.

'I'd encourage you to do whatever you feel most comfortable with. Have you all used watercolour before?'

Only Minty said 'yes'.

Dammit, what a pain. I'm tired and lacking enthusiasm to run a step-by-step class. But I must, so when Lianne asked, 'Do you think you could show us, Susie? You can use my paper, I've got loads more,' I picked up a pencil and ran through the steps.

'That ain't look anything like her, Miss.'

'It will, I'm not worried about getting a likeness at this stage.'

Lianne handed me a brush. I dip-dabbed it in water and paint, and began building an impression of Cailey's colourful face.

'I reckon I can do that, Miss.'

'Well, there you go, but it's very important you only put down what you see. So, look hard and don't rush like me, we have all morning.'

'Can we play some music?' asked Lianne.

'As long as it's not ghastly modern junk,' said Rupert.

'What about jazz?' suggested Louis. 'I can get my iPod and speaker if you want?'

'If everyone's okay with that?' I looked around the room. 'Then Louis, do you mind if I go get it? I don't want you to fall behind.'

'Sure. It's on the dressing table in my room.'

Louis' bedroom, the Blue Room replete with light blue peely-wallpaper, curtains to match and a very ropey tasselled blue canopy over a mahogany four-poster bed, was like walking into a sensual cloud. The huge space was filled with the most delicious aftershave. I inhaled deeply. I *love* aftershave.

The iPod and speaker were next to a lovely old three-part mirror in a gilt frame. I bent down to try it out. The depth of reflection in this is so much better than modern equivalents. *Ow*, I blooming well stubbed my toe on something very hard. It was behind the curtain under the table.

I dragged it out, a big black case with a sophisticated camera and three lenses inside. It was nosey of me to have a look, but I wanted to know. I pushed it back in place, and with iPod and speaker in hand, I left the room.

The corridor felt cold so I put the things on the console table and rushed to my room to get a jumper.

I don't think it was the speed I was going that made me trip and I don't think it was my trip that loosened the floorboard in my room. It caught me unawares and I'm now a crumpled heap on the floor. The board stuck up like a wobbly front tooth, so I grappled my fingers round the front edge and, easy as pie, it came free. I can't actually believe it was that easy to do. If it had always been loose, I would have tripped up days ago. So, who's been in my room?

I pushed my hand into the shallow hole. There was nothing in it but dust, which I brushed off my fingertips as I popped the board back in place. After repeatedly stamping it down with my foot, failing to get it flush, I gave up and rushed back downstairs to the music room.

'Great,' said Louis, 'just press play, no need to change the soundtrack.'

Rupert was staring at my knees. 'Did you fall?'

'Just tripped on a loose board in my room.' I looked around the class. No one gave a flicker of guilt and as I bent down to brush the scuff marks off my tights Felicity made a concerned sound and Louis raised his eyebrows as if to say 'Are you okay?'

Break arrived and Cailey had a good shake, stretching out her jaw, relieved not to have to hold still a moment longer. I looked at everyone's pictures and as the talent varied considerably I decided not to open a discussion at this point – I didn't want to put anyone off.

'If you're all happy carrying this through till lunchtime then let's continue.'

Cailey nodded and the class resumed.

'We'll be stopping at half past twelve today as we're going up on the moor and we need to get back for an early dinner.'

'Youse all coming to see me show?' said Cailey.

'Yes,' I smiled. 'We're going to bring our sketchbooks too.'

'Youse'll have plenty of nudes to draw.'

'Lush,' said Giles and a few people giggled. Crumbs, I thought, maybe burlesque is different in Scotland.

The class was quiet, everyone was working hard, so I decided now would be a good moment to go and sketch Haggis. I don't need long, ten minutes or so to get an impression.

'I'll be out in the hall for the time being. Come find me if you're really struggling.'

The dog was slumped against the front door, basking in a spot of sunlight shining down from the cupola. This seemed to me a rather good pose, so I took the risk of not moving him in the hopes no one would enter for the time being. All I need is a sketch and some photographs. I much prefer to finish a pet portrait at home.

I crouched down and my rubber slipped from my hands, bouncing across the hall, disappearing behind an empty umbrella stand. Thankfully Haggis didn't flinch and when I went to retrieve it, I found lying next to it a spirit level – the perfect instrument for drawing an even-sided frame on my piece of paper. An outline helps such a lot with composition. So, sitting cross-legged, I began to draw. What a sweet dog he is. His left ear was raised, his head slightly cocked and his eyes glistened as I worked.

I scribbled down the composition and even managed to take several photographs before he moved.

'Good doggie,' I said as I placed the spirit level on the hall table and then bent down to stroke his soft coat. Haggis followed me to the music room door and I felt guilty going in and shutting him out.

When the watercolour session ended I had everyone lay their pictures on the floor for a quick crit.

'Do you mind if I scoot?' said Cailey.

'No, not all. Thank you very much for modelling today.'

'Byeee.' She grabbed her stuff and swaggered out the room on the tail end of everyone's thank yous.

'Right, come look at the pictures. You can ask me anything you want.'

'Are you single?' said Shane, and even I laughed.

'Well?' said Louis.

'Come on, I meant you can ask anything about painting. You've all put in such a lot of effort this morning.'

'What I want to know,' whined Felicity, 'is how Minty got such delicate colours.'

'Minty?'

'I think it's because I used a lot more water.'

'But I tried to use a lot of water and look at mine,' grumbled Lianne. 'It's all blotchy.'

'What sort of brush were you using?'

'Here.' She handed it to me.

'This is a synthetic brush. Minty, is yours sable?'

'Yes.'

'Sable holds water better than synthetic so it gives a much smoother, more even spread of colour.'

Lianne wrote down the name on the back of her hand. I didn't like to tell her quite how expensive these brushes are. Every artist, no matter how much money they have, has to weigh up performance and cost. The reality is, the more you spend the better the equipment and natural versus synthetic is no comparison.

'Louis,' said Rupert, 'why have you painted more of her jumper than her face?'

'I thought it'd be easier,' he shrugged.

'Cheat,' said Jane.

'Not true,' I said. 'Painting is interpreting what's in front of you any way you want. That's why pictures reveal so much about a person's character.'

'Yes,' said Jane. 'Louis is a cheat.'

'That's a bit harsh,' said Felicity. 'You and I would have done better concentrating on the jumper.'

Jane actually stamped her foot. 'I just wish you didn't all have to see my poor efforts.'

'Jane,' I said, trying to lift her mood, 'you mustn't say that. The hardest thing about creativity is the challenge.

There is no formula. No medicine to make things better when they're bad. It's not like learning something and knowing it forever. Each new painting or drawing puts you right back on first base and just because past drawings and paintings have worked doesn't mean future ones are going to.'

'Mine hasn't worked *at all* today.'

'Well, I think it looks like Cailey.'

'That's because no one else wears such wacky make-up,' said Shane.

'I'm hungry,' said Lianne. 'Can we go?'

'Yes, let's call it a morning. We're having lunch up on the moor and the minibus will be leaving here in ten minutes.'

I looked out of the window and my heart fell; grey clouds had swamped this morning's blue sky.

'Cheer up,' said Louis over my shoulder.

'I'm happy. I just don't want it to rain.'

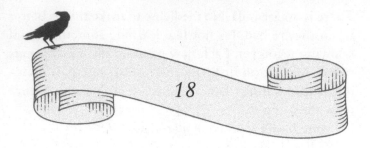

18

We've just finished a stand-up lunch of thick hot soup and cold lamb rolls in the bothy and are now out on the veranda, under an awning, contemplating the drizzle.

Stretched out in front of us is a loch, one long slick plane of deep brown sunk into the foreground of the heather moorland. The landscape behind tumbles for miles, eventually blending with the peaks on the horizon.

'*Look*,' exclaimed Rupert. 'There's a ptarmigan.'

'So it is,' said Fergus. 'Well spotted.'

'What did you say it was?' said Felicity, all giggly with confusion.

'A ptarmigan.'

'Spelt *P T A R M I G A N*,' said Jane.

'Blast, he's gone.' Giles was disappointed. 'I've never seen one before.'

'Over there,' said Minty.

'You's never seen a bird before?' said Shane.

'You'll only see *these* birds in the Highlands.' Fergus leant on the crook of his stick. 'They're a species of grouse. This one's a male. You can tell from the black feathers round his face.'

'I ain't see no black feathers.'

'It's a bit far away, but if you look closely you'll see them coming through his white winter plumage.'

'Only birds in Britain to grow completely white plumage,' said Rupert. 'Talking of which, there's a painting of them in my bathroom.'

'Yes,' said Fergus, 'it's by Thorburn.'

'And…which Earl bought that?' mocked Shane.

Fergus laughed. 'The Countess *suo jure*'s husband bought it. He was wounded in the First World War, no quality of life after and bought art to cheer himself up. He had been a particularly keen sportsman before the war. There are some of Henry Alken's wildfowl prints in one of the children's rooms, I think?'

'Mine,' said Giles.

Fergus clapped his hands and Haggis barked at the ptarmigan's rasp as it furiously flapped its short wings and grazed the heather in low flight.

'I'm going to leave you all to it,' Fergus said with a spring in his step as he bounced off the veranda into the heather. 'Haggis and I have some inspecting of the butts to do.'

'*What?*' shrieked Lianne.

'A butt's a camouflaged hide you shoot from,' said Rupert.

'What's a hide?'

'A place of concealment, disguised to appear as part of the natural environment,' said Jane.

'I bet you're good at Scrabble,' teased Rupert but she wasn't amused.

'It would be a grand place for a wind farm here,' said Giles. 'My parents are longing for their application to be accepted. They've got an eighty-foot application mast up, like that one over there.' He pointed into the distance.

'I can't see a thing,' said Felicity.

'I'm not lying, it's the tip of a mast breaking the horizon. I can tell.'

'Yeah right?' said Minty.

'Wind farms make you rich, don't they?' said Shane.

'Mega rich,' said Lianne.

'They're ghastly,' said Minty.

'Enough of this,' I cut in, 'it's time to begin and if you're all happy using my primed paper again, then help yourself to a sheet in the bothy. We'll be painting outside.'

'What about the rain?' mumbled Lianne.

'Yeah?' said Louis.

'You don't have to paint it if you don't like it.'

'Ha ha.'

I took a step down from the veranda onto the heather. It was only drizzling but everyone else stuck under cover. Rupert and Shane were squeezed in the doorway, Minty, Giles, Felicity, Jane and Lianne spread out over two benches, and as Louis bent to perch on the step he reached out his hand and caught a drip from the peak of my hood.

'Controversial subject these wind farms,' bored on Rupert.

'You should try talking to Fergus about it,' said Louis.

'Waste of time, there'd be no point applying for one here.'

'Why?' said Jane.

'The ornithologist would have a field day.'

'Who's he when he's at home?' said Shane.

'A bird expert,' said Jane.

'Of course, you'd know that.'

'Come on, enough of this.' I tried to stop the conversation but it continued.

'Why would an ornithologist have a field day?' said Giles, and Rupert opened a discussion.

'All of you must have seen the big black birds swooping around the house?'

'I told you, Jane,' said Felicity. 'There was one on our window sill the other night.'

'Do they make an *eeeee, eeeee, eeeee* noise?' screeched Lianne.

'Yes.'

'Well, *that's* been keeping me awake.'

'Me too,' said Minty. 'It's a horrible haunting sound.'

'They're ravens,' said Rupert, 'a protected species. There's a swell of them here.'

'And?' said Louis, clearly not well versed in wind farm regulations.

'Even without the necessary step in the application, they'd win the case for the antis.'

'How?' said Felicity.

'They're protected and any disruption to their flight path such as a collision with turbines,' Rupert could hardly sound smugger, 'would instantly put an end to an application.'

'Please,' I begged. 'We must get started.'

'What do you have in store for us this afternoon then?' lorded Rupert.

'Yesterday, we covered mixing colours and the basics of beginning a picture. Today we're going to focus on one colour.'

'Yellow,' said Shane.

'No. What's the dominant colour in the view behind me?'

'*Bleurgh.*' Shane's tongue followed the word out of his mouth.

'Blue,' said Rupert.

'Depends how much of the sky you're looking at,' said Jane.

'As a photographer I can tell you everything fading into the horizon is a varying shade of blue.'

'He's right,' said Minty.

'Yes, and this afternoon I want to try and teach you to create perspective using one colour.'

'Must we go out in the rain?' grumbled Felicity.

'If you're happy working on your knees you don't have to.'

'I'm going to sit here.' Shane plonked himself down next to Louis.

'And I'm going to brave the drizzle,' said Rupert. 'Nothing like a blast of bad weather to get one out of the post-lunch slumber.'

'There are easels in the bus.'

'Please grab one for me too,' said Minty.

'Won't their pictures smudge?' asked Felicity.

'No, water and oil don't mix.'

'So, you could paint in pouring rain?'

'I wouldn't recommend it.'

'It will only add to my picture,' said Rupert.

'What are we painting, Miss?'

'A view of the horizon.'

'None of this foreground?' said Giles.

'Not today. I'd like you to start your picture in the far distance, where things begin to turn blue.'

'I can't paint the lake?' said Lianne.

'Loch,' corrected Jane.

'If you really want to you can, but I was hoping you'd try this exercise first.'

'Anything for you, Miss.'

'Please can you talk us through it?' asked Rupert.

'Okay. Here goes…'

The endless questions were driving me mad but I kept my patience, just, and the class eventually began.

Jane and Felicity both tried really hard and Minty and Rupert stuck it out until the drizzle stopped, the temperature rose and hundreds of midges descended on us. Tiny little black dots bite, bite, biting any exposed bit of flesh. It was ghastly. The session fell apart, everyone rushed inside the bothy and, last in, I banged the door shut.

'I'm *never* coming to Scotland again,' said Lianne. 'That was the worst experience of my life.'

Felicity nudged Jane who was rubbing mosquito repellent all over her wrists. 'Give her some of your spray.'

'Hey, give us all some of that,' said Shane, stretching an arm out for the bottle.

'*Please*,' said Jane.

'*Please.*'

'Ladies first,' said Rupert and Jane handed the bottle to Lianne who took some and handed it to Minty who then handed it to me. I gave my neck and wrists a good spray and passed it on to Louis, he passed it to Rupert, on to Giles and eventually it got to Shane who thankfully saw the funny side.

BANG went the door and in stumbled Ewen with a bottle of sloe gin in his hand.

'Where did you come from?' said Rupert.

'Close the door, close the door,' squealed Lianne, reaching to push it shut.

'Thought I'd come see how you're getting on.'

Judging by the amount of mud on Ewen's boots he'd clearly walked here.

'I knew you'd appreciate some of this.' He held the sloe-gin bottle high in the air. I think he drank some on the way.

'Get in there,' said Shane, holding out his lunch mug.

'Yes please,' said Lianne, thrusting her mug at him too.

'Anyone else?' Ewen wobbled the bottle and, resigned to the fact the class had come to a crashing end, I thought why not round it off with a shot of sloe gin.

'Well, if the tutor's having some,' said Giles, 'I'll have some too.'

It wasn't ideal Ewen appearing like this but I had to hand it to him, he'd lifted the mood. Absolutely everyone accepted a shot and although it was not part of the curriculum, he couldn't have appeared at a better moment.

'What the hell are you doing here?' said Fergus, bursting through the doorway completely drenched.

'Uh-oh.' Ewen clenched his teeth for comic effect.

I was rather alarmed by Fergus's sudden strength of character. But nothing could have stopped the others charging for the bus, desperate to be off the moor and back at the house. Fergus, Ewen and I were soon alone.

'I'm sorry,' I said, taking the blame. 'The class ended early because of the midges.'

It sounded a bit pathetic out loud but it was the truth.

'Yeah, bro, I promise I didn't interrupt them, they were already in here when I turned up.'

'Okay,' Fergus said, then turned and left the bothy. Zoe was right, fundamentally he's wet.

'Susie?' said Ewen, his eyebrows raised like a cheeky little child. 'Do you think there's room for me on the bus?'

I couldn't hold back a smile, this man was a charmer. 'I'm sure there is, let's go see.'

He squeezed in the back, pretty much sitting on Louis' knee. I hopped in the front next to Haggis, and Fergus revved the engine. With wet paintings clasped tightly in cold hands, the bus was put through its paces, down the track and off the moor.

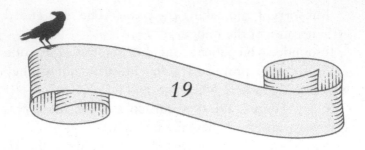

19

I've hidden myself away in my room. The smuggled electric heater is set to full blast, I've had a bath, got my nightie on and am lying under the bed covers wishing I had a gin and tonic in my hand. The failure of this afternoon's class, which was neither fun nor productive, is preying on my mind. I clench my teeth at the stupidity of not having thought about rain or midges. We're in Scotland for heaven's sake.

Refusing to let a tear creep out, I shut my eyes tight and think about what I'm going to do if there is worse weather to come. This week's residency advertised landscape painting and as the tutor I'm here to fulfil it. Oh help me, please, come up with a solution.

I roll onto my side and stare into the open wardrobe. What am I going to wear tonight? This decision always cheers me up. My new black mini skirt? Yes, I think so. Definitely my red satin underwear, it could hardly be more appropriate for a burlesque show and as it's cold I'll wear the matching camisole too. Would a see-through shirt on top be okay? Yes, loosen up, Susie, take the opportunity to have some fun. Now jewellery, I don't have much choice. Hoop earrings and some gold bangles should do. *Bangles*…Wasn't Zoe odd when I'd found her alone in the library before tea, musing over something on the Victorian writing bureau and I'd chosen my moment to suggest her bracelet could have been taken by a raven to line its nest. The tone in her reply took me by complete surprise: 'It *was* a raven,' she'd snapped and I'd jumped on the spot. Then, just as I was about to change the subject, Giles had come trundling in and Zoe, without another word, lifted up the front of the desk, inserted a mini key into a mini keyhole, locked the bureau and left the room.

Birds always make me think of Dad; he's a bit of a twitcher at heart and thanks to his spouting on the subject I've only ever associated ravens with the Tower of London. To this day there remains a small flock there, known as an 'unkindness', and the legend goes that if they leave, the Kingdom will fall. Highly unlikely considering their wings are clipped. When Dad first told me, the part I found most interesting was that breeding pairs must have their own territory, so cannot share the Tower's enclosure. The Wildlife and Countryside Act – stick with me here – states that we should not resupply from birds in the wild. Therefore there's an aviarist in the country, Alec Ronaldsay, with a dispensation for breeding captive ravens for the Tower of London. The sole purpose of this aviarist's job is to repopulate and ensure the Tower's precious flock thrives. How cool is that.

Lying here now, thinking about birds and that ridiculous discussion of wind farms this afternoon makes me want to prove Giles wrong. Surely Fergus, with his love for this place, can't possibly have a wind farm application in progress? Google I'm sure will back me up...I typed *muchton wind farm application* into my browser and...dammit...I'm wrong. The very first search result proves that.

> *Application for new onshore wind farm plans*
> *Planning application: 27/00126/EIA*

> <u>*The Proposal*</u>
> *Application for planning permission in conjunction with Anemoi Energy for a wind farm spread over 23 square miles of the Muchton Moor to include 140 turbines, associated infrastructure (site access roads) and ancillary development including turbine foundations, crane hard-standings, control building, grid connection and construction compound.*

Giles is right, Fergus does have an application in progress. The proposal went on and on and on – Size; Speed; Megawatts; Location; Construction; Connection; Site Access; Decommissioning; Environment; Risk Assessment; Hazardous Sites; Impact on the Countryside; Noise & Shadow; etc., etc. – and the substantial document highlighted just how many different angles opposers can come from.

A hundred and forty turbines does seem an awful lot. However, I know nothing of such things, so, let's see... Google: *largest onshore wind farm uk.*

> *215 turbines and a total capacity of 539 MW, with an average of 2.5 MW per turbine.*

Next I searched: *number of turbines in a wind farm uk.*

Wind farms can have as few as 5 wind turbines or as many as 250.

Here it is in black and white, Fergus is trying hard to make big money from this. The company website of Anemoi Energy, one of the more pretentious names I've heard, gave a bit of blurb about the project.

Application Pending
A section of Muchton Moor, part of the Auchen Laggan Tosh Estate, is Anemoi Energy's largest project to date, and is a joint venture between Anemoi Energy and Auchen Laggan Tosh Estate. The wind farm, located near the village of Muchton, Moray, will comprise 140 turbines – giving a total capacity of 322 MW of clean electricity, sufficient to power 200,000 homes.
   The proposed site is 53 miles west of Inverness with striking views over the Torridon Hills to the north and the Beinn Eighe to the west. There is a plan for a net-work of wind farm tracks to be built which, when the turbines are in situ, will be open for the public to visit and use.

I very much doubt that final perk will stand up against the opposition. I wonder if I can find any objection letters...
The first link I clicked on threw up a whole spread from five months ago reporting on campaigners laying out their opposition to the Scottish government's wind farm policy at an event organised by Communities

Against Turbines Scotland (Cats). The key speaker was an MEP, the Chairman an MSP and the opening statement read: 'The time has come for the government to think again about its wind farm policy.' It was far too political for me to read on so I went back to the search results and found over fifty individual objections from the public, against a single letter of support from Archie and Hilda Stewart. Fergus, believe it or not, had sent in a response and I'm afraid what with his address and title I don't think it will have helped him one iota. Here's what it said:

> **Fergus, Earl of Muchton, Auchen Laggan Tosh**
> *Looking at the problem from a broader angle, although we do not want these wind farms in the Highlands, we have come to the conclusion that, dire though the consequence of them coming is, for farms like ours to survive they are always going to be subsidy driven. Landowners with no private income do have to diversify and develop alternative practices to attract the subsidies on offer at the time. We cannot fight against opportunity for payment that would change landowners' lives principally because they would spoil the view. I object (as you would) to being told what I can and cannot do on my own land. So, I suppose what I am saying is that the real argument is with the government for getting it so terribly wrong and not with the people, who quite reasonably take advantage of what could be the biggest input of cash into their pockets for a generation. My wife and I would not want you to think we had no respect for the beauty of our surroundings and were motivated purely by greed.*

Beep, beep, beep. My alarm is going off, it's time to get ready for the night ahead. I pulled on my clothes, feeling a little bit guilty about looking up the Muchtons, especially while I'm still under their roof. But I know myself only too well: when I'm on to the scent of anything vaguely interesting, there's very little that will stop me prying. My biggest problem now is that I must not let anything slip. I wouldn't like anyone to know quite how nosey I am by nature.

Bang on six o'clock the gong sounded for high tea and, all done up, I headed downstairs.

'You go first, Susie,' said Fergus.

There were two huge dishes of Auchen Laggan Tosh lamb lasagne steaming on the hotplate. Mhàiri, standing proudly at its side, pulling off her oven gloves, said, 'Once yous have, Susie, would yous mind giving me a wee hand with the other things?'

'Not at all.'

I put down my full plate and skipped through the swing door into the kitchen.

'Only the one course the night. Baps to fill youse up and a wee salad for your greens. Will yous carry the butter and the wee salad, I'll take these baps and we'll come back for the others.'

We placed them on the table and as soon as we were back in the kitchen Mhàiri planted herself in front of me. 'I was right, Susie,' she said, her eyes wide with excitement, 'that lady Jane's been here afore.'

'How do you know?'

'When I went to clean youse bathrooms this morning, I found her in your corridor.'

'What did she say?'

'She said this big hoose with a children's corridor reminded her of growing up.'

'Not that she's been here before?'

'No but I bet you she has. How'd she ken the wains' rooms were down there and why was she looking at them?'

'You might be right,' I said to sweeten her. Mhàiri thinks she's right and I don't want to dampen her excitement even if I'm yet to agree Jane has been here before.

'I am correct, pet.' She winked at me and handed over the final bowls. 'Thanks fer your help.'

'That's okay.'

I re-entered the dining room and everyone was now seated around the table. The variety of clothing was very amusing. Jane, Felicity and Rupert looked as if they were out for Sunday lunch, pastel colours and high collars, a cardigan over the shoulders in case it gets cold. Giles had on a striped shirt with one too many buttons done up. Minty looked pretty in a thin person's floaty number, Lianne had an all hugging no hiding halterneck-top-mini-skirt combo going on, Louis was in his usual pale jeans and a white t-shirt under a dark blue shirt, Fergus hadn't changed and Shane was in a grey tracksuit, my goodness it looked comfortable. Zoe wasn't coming out. She felt queasy.

'You look great,' said Louis, rubbing shoulders with me as I sat down beside him.

'Thanks. Do you know if Ewen's coming?'

'Dressing up for him, are you?'

'No,' I grimaced.

'I don't think he is. Didn't go down too well this

afternoon. Just us lot. Funny crowd to be going out with but it is a *drawing* session I suppose. Would you like some wine?'

'Yes please.'

He filled my glass and held his up for a toast. 'Here's to the night ahead.'

I smiled and turned to Zoe on my other side.

'Rather nice for you all to get out tonight,' she said. 'I can't imagine anything spectacular but I'm sure you'll have an amusing time. Fergus *is* excited, he's even asked Donald to be the driver. I'd so love to be coming but the early stages of pregnancy aren't agreeing with me.'

Ever since I'd seen Zoe down the corridor, coming out of the locked wing late last night, I've been trying to work out what was going on. If she heard something in the night you'd think she would have woken Fergus, sent him out to see what's up. Not gone to check up on their most precious possessions alone. I'd certainly use a man as my protector if I had one in my bed.

It's not as if she's looking pale now and she's eating along with the rest of us, so maybe she has a plan for when we're out?

'Poor you,' I said. 'But we'll tell you all about it tomorrow.'

'Yes,' said Louis, leaning over me, 'you can get some rest while we're out.'

Zoe nodded and told him he could probably do without another late night.

'Another?' said Louis, looking confused.

'You and Ewen were up late, weren't you?'

'Oh yes, so we were,' he said as if he'd forgotten.

'Susie, I'm sorry he turned up on the moor this afternoon.'

'It actually lifted all our moods.'

'Oh good. Fergus was furious but I'm sure it will blow over, he's not one to drag these things out.'

'Honestly, it wasn't a problem.'

Zoe smiled. 'I'm sure Ewen didn't mean any harm. Up on the moor is where he gets his inspiration.'

'He knows a lot about painting, doesn't he?'

Zoe's face, that one which wears emotion so well, looked seriously doubtful.

'How do you know?' said Louis.

'Rupert and I stopped by his house this morning.'

'His house?' said Zoe, looking at Louis, and I wondered what was going on between these two.

'Yes.'

'He let you in?' Zoe was still looking at Louis.

'We had a bit of time to spare.'

'I see. Poor Ewen being woken so early.'

'He was, as he said, up, just not dressed. I did feel a bit bad but he honestly didn't seem to mind.'

'What makes you think he knows about painting?' Zoe wanted to debate the point.

'He *is* a painter,' said Louis, and Zoe laughed.

'Yes, and he gave Rupert a very good rundown on atmospheric perspective.'

Rupert was sitting on Zoe's other side. 'Ah,' she said, turning to include him. 'Did Ewen show you any of his work?'

'No, though I did ask to see his studio.'

'And he wouldn't let you in?'

I answered, 'He wouldn't let either of us in.'

'That's because he only lets his best of friends have a peek,' said Louis. 'Aye, Zoe?'

'I learnt my lesson the hard way,' she smirked. 'One day I was looking for him, and marched straight in. He wasn't very happy and has locked his door ever since.'

'Bit over the top,' said Rupert.

Zoe came crashing down in Ewen's defence. 'I don't see why he should have to show other people.'

'I didn't mean it like that,' Rupert apologised. 'I'd just like to know what kind of pictures he paints?'

'I'm not sure.'

'You must have an idea,' he cajoled. 'He told us he works from photographs.'

'Highland landscapes, I think.'

Where has Zoe's insouciance come from? Her conversation has really gone off the boil tonight. One minute she's engaged, the next she's offhand, almost as if there's something preying on her mind, coming to the forefront, receding and then surfacing again. Does this happen when one is pregnant? A downside if so.

'Hey Louis,' I said, 'maybe you've been taking photographs for Ewen?'

He stared at me unamused.

'I'm really sorry, I didn't mean to offend you.'

'When would I have had the time?' He was cross. Guilty I bet. If Louis *has* been taking pictures, the huge file downloading on Ewen's computer this morning could have been them. Which would figure…Louis exploited the broadband allowance. *Ha*. No wonder he didn't say.

'I love photography,' giggled Zoe. 'You must take your camera out when you're painting. I'm having a website designed for future courses and we could really do with some good pictures on it. I simply don't have the time.'

'Are you a photographer too?' Louis flattered her.

'I enjoy it when I do it.'

'So do I,' he said, winking at me.

'What's your opinion, Susie,' said Rupert, 'of people painting from photographs?'

'Well, I feel strongly that you have to sit in front of the real thing and at least do a sketch to get the atmosphere of the place. I wouldn't dismiss photographs,' I smirked at Louis, 'but only as an aid.'

'Do you ever use them?'

'Yes, for pet portrait commissions but only once I've been to meet the pet in question. I'd find it impossible to capture their character without.'

Louis looked at his watch. 'Nearly time to go,' he announced.

'I do hope you have fun,' said Zoe.

The ting of Fergus's glass silenced us all. 'Let's get a move on. Out of here and into the bus. The performance starts in an hour.'

'How long's the journey?' said Jane.

'Forty-five minutes at the most.'

'I'd better go and spend a penny then,' said Felicity and we all got up and left the room.

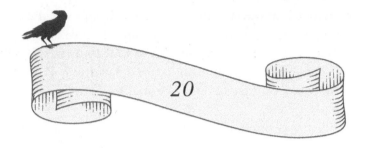

20

The town hall architecture was a Caledonian reading of the Gothic, a Scottish Baronial Revival building with a far-from-Baronial woman on the door. Ms let's-keep-the-show-on-the-road and don't stop and look at my cleavage even if you think it's asking for it ushered us out of the cold and into the building. She was wearing a two-sizes-too-small underaged outfit and as her head turned into the pitch-black interior save for a few flickering candles, her extended eyelashes pointed us on our way. 'Full house the night, come on, get a wee move on, in youse go, that's right, tickets to me, then youse can grab a table, roll up, roll up, on you go, keep movin'. Thank you, Sir. Ladies first.'

'*No*,' she exclaimed at the sight of Lianne's mobile. 'No taking pictures. This is a *private* show.'

'I was just using the torch to find the table.'

'Yous eyes'll soon adjust. No torches and no telephones, Missy.'

On we went, sticking close together, caterpillaring our way through occupied round tables. There were at least three lairy men to every done-up woman and as we crept our way to find a free seat it amused me to think, if only they knew we'd brought an Earl.

It was eight to a table so Fergus and Rupert spilled on to another and as soon as we'd sat down Rupert generously offered to buy the drinks. 'This one's on me.'

'That's really kind of you, mate,' said Shane, 'but there's no way I have enough cash for a round.'

'I'm sure no one will expect it, so don't worry about that. But I would like to. Wine for the ladies?'

We all bent across the crushed velvet tablecloth and tried in the glow of the tea-light to make out the list of drinks on the A4 sheet. Rupert meanwhile waved his hand at one of eight blonde bombshells buzzing around the room on roller-skates. It wasn't long before one rolled up and Rupert, unable to raise his eyes above her teeny-weeny kilt and fishnet suspenders, practically drooled on the table.

Jane and Felicity shared a bottle of white, Fergus and Rupert a bottle of red, a Diet Coke for Minty, a shandy for me and fizzy lager for the rest.

'Susie, what is it you're wanting us to do?' said Minty.

'Quick sketches of the performers is what I was thinking.'

'We're awfully close to the stage,' said Rupert.

'More like a catwalk,' said Lianne, quite rightly.

'So Miss, you're thinking they're going to appear from behind that curtain?'

'Duh, of course they are. That's what Susie wants us to draw.'

'Energetic scribbles of what's in front of you.'

'Doodles,' said Rupert.

'Yes. The rhythm of the music should help you get into it.'

And at the mention of the word a great big BANG came from all four corners of the room. A strobe light projected the rays of a rainbow on the ceiling and, with deafening volume, the R&B club song 'Hot in Herre' pounded out. A shriek came from the doorway, all heads turned and a lofty woman in a hooded cape wobbled her way towards the stage. The music quietened, lights went down and we were plunged into darkness. Wolf-whistling tore through the silence and then, boom went the speakers, up went the volume, on flashed the lights and here on stage, having abandoned her cloak to the words 'I want to get my clothes off', was the woman in a silver leotard and red stilettos. With a single split of her legs she was down on the ground and a buff man in silver buttock-hugging shorts appeared from behind her. He pranced a circle round her shadow, and with the spring of a leveret he leapt over her head, laying himself down *right* in front of us. His arm then stretched out towards our table and Felicity shrieked. The soundtrack took a clunky switch to Frank Sinatra's 'Come Dance with Me' and the woman, much to the relief of her crotch I would think, stood up and strutted her stuff down off the stage. She stopped, hovering over our table, beckoning Felicity's hand. Lianne bounced up out of her chair and with a 'Don't you worry, this one's on me' she willingly linked arms with the proposer and headed up onto the stage. She was presented to the man and with great cheers from the crowd they waltzed cheek to cheek up and down the stage.

The performance ended, the lights dipped and Fergus's, 'Isn't this great,' took me by surprise.

'It's not burlesque, that's for sure,' said Louis.

'I'm loving it,' said Giles, toasting Minty's glass. She gave him a half-hearted smile in response.

'Thank you, Lianne,' said Felicity. 'You really saved me there.'

'That's okay, I adore this stuff.'

There was a loud commotion as a group of late-comers entered the hall. A roller-skater led them to the only free table, one near us, and as they filed in I counted ten men. Eight sat down and two spilled over with Fergus and Rupert. One man had the most amazing curly mop of hair. I craned my neck to get a look at his face. Oh heck…what a nightmare…my heart raced out of control and, winded to the core, I shut my eyes. What on earth is Toby Cropper doing *here*?

A hand squeezed my knee and my body jumped.

'All right?' said Louis. 'I didn't mean to frighten you.'

I gave him a smile. There's nothing like revenge to turn up the attraction. Louis was going to be my target tonight.

The music began again, softly this time then gaining in volume as the pink strobe hyperactively dashed round the room. Onto the stage bounced two bodies dressed as Playboy bunnies, complete with big shiny-white front teeth. One masked figure had beautiful smooth legs, the other a hairy pair of tree trunks, and as they bopped around the stage, giving each other bum bumps, it all seemed quite innocent and fun. But then, DJ B's dance mix started and the performance turned into an orgy à deux. One bunny began humping the other from behind, the latter grinning as it aped eating a carrot. The whole performance was so amateur you couldn't help but laugh. Even Jane had a smirk on her face. Humpty hump hump they went until, completely exhausted, one cradled the other in its arms, stroking her ears until the soundtrack ran out. To uproars of applause and stamping feet the pair merrily hopped off stage.

When the lights came up I could see out of the corner of my eye that Toby was talking to Fergus. Suddenly he looked straight across at me. His eyebrows rose as high as a kite. Oh crumbs, he got up and was now coming around the table.

'Suthie,' he slurred as he bent down and kissed me. 'Never thought I'd see you here.'

'Me neither,' I replied as Louis stretched his arm across my waist.

'Louis Bouchon, nice to meet you.'

'Toby Cropper.'

Then, looking round the table, flashing his charming smile at everyone, he said, 'You're all on an art residency? Suthie's your tutor?'

'Yes,' grinned Minty, rising to his good looks.

'You must be a friend of Susie's?' said Jane.

Toby looked me up and down. 'Yes.'

'What are you doing here?' I asked.

'Stag do with that bunch over there.'

'Yours?' said Louis as my heart went into palpitations.

'Not yet,' said Toby with a laugh.

'If you want to catch up with Susie,' said Lianne, 'I

can swap places with you.'

No! No! Lianne you silly girl. My insides cramped up until Toby said, 'You wouldn't really want to, they're a rowdy bunch over there.' Then looking at his friends, who were having a right laugh, he said a quick, 'See ya, Suthie,' and was off.

Giles clicked his fingers and a waitress arrived.

'What can I get ya?' she asked.

'Lager for everyone?' said Giles. Jane and Felicity had hardly made a dent in their bottle.

We all nodded and pooled our cash.

'Bet you didn't expect to meet an old lover here,' Louis whispered in my ear.

I froze. 'Not much gets by you French.'

He winked at me and smiled as if he knew I needed a bit of cheering up.

'Has anyone done any drawing?' I asked.

'Jees Miss, you don't really expect us to draw *this*?'

'I can't take my eyes off it,' said Giles. 'That last girl was a real corker.'

'I've done a bit,' said Minty, laying her sketchbook flat on the table.

'And I've done this,' said Lianne, showing us hers.

Minty had drawn a looming figure in a hooded cloak and Lianne had done one big scribble. It was of the strobe lighting, I think.

'It isn't the drawing type music I imagined,' said Louis.

'It's nothing *like* what I imagined,' squawked Jane.

'I know,' I reassured them. 'It's out there, that's for sure, and don't worry about drawing if you don't want to. It's not the subject I thought it was going to be.'

Fergus got up and leant over our table. 'Everyone okay?' Some of us smiled.

'I take full responsibility for bringing you to this and I'm sorry. We could leave now if you want?'

'I'm not leaving,' said Shane.

'Me neither,' said Lianne.

The waitress arrived with a tray of drinks.

'Looks like we're here for the second half then,' said Fergus. 'Felicity, Jane, are you both all right?'

'We'll stick it out,' said Jane.

Then, suddenly, the room turned bright purple and Britney Spears's 'Hit Me Baby One More Time' came bursting down our ear drums.

The moment we had come for had arrived. Louis nudged my shoulder and I slipped my hand under the table and squeezed his knee.

'It's *Cailey*,' shouted Shane.

In a PVC catsuit with a provocative zip right down the front, Cailey Baird stood proud at the centre of the stage. Swinging her hips to the beat of the intro she curled the tail of a whip at her platformed feet.

'Oh baby, baby, I shouldn't have let you go,' she screamed at the top of her voice and then with a sudden crack of the whip, shocking us all, she shouted the words, 'And now you're out of sight, yeah.'

Cailey took the whip handle between her teeth and turned her back on the audience as the song got louder. Then with her behind on full display, black PVC straining, she flung her top half towards the floor. Bent double in front of us all, her arms, slowly, slowly, to the beat of the music, started to stretch through her straddled legs. Britney's voice singing 'Hit me baby one more time' came out of the speakers and Cailey's firm hands grasped hold of her buttocks.

The crowd roared, high voices and low, coaxing her on in her act. 'Go girl!' 'That's more like it!' 'Nice arse!' 'Show us your tits!'

I don't know if it was part of the plan or if it was the hype from the audience that encouraged Cailey. But here she was, on stage, looking as if she might strip her kit off. Her right hand tugged at the zip on the front of her suit. Down it went, her unclad bosoms popping out, following which, with the most provocative shoulders I've ever seen, she wriggled the whole thing off her waist. I didn't for the life of me think she wouldn't have any knickers on but as the PVC was peeled to the floor, a bare naked Cailey was revealed.

The eruption of cheers, whoops, wolf-whistles and screams rose above the music as the onlookers lost control.

Louis prodded me and nodded his head at the stag's table. There was a chap, with pink Y-fronts over his jeans, being pushed towards the stage by one of his friends. Cailey, catching what was happening, thrust her pelvis towards him as he began to stagger.

Jane shot up to standing, quickly followed by Felicity. 'We'll be waiting in the bus. I can't bear this any longer.'

For some reason I felt responsible and found myself getting up with them. But when the lights went down and the music stopped all three of us waited to see what everyone else had to say.

Rupert leant in between Lianne and Shane. 'If you're going, Jane, I think I'll come too.'

'I'm afraid,' said Fergus, 'I think we should all leave, it's too cold to keep people waiting in the bus.'

Not even Shane objected and to be honest I think all of us were embarrassed to be watching this together. It'd be different with friends, you could laugh no matter what, but here we were all sitting rigid in our chairs.

Toby stood up to say goodbye. It was a nice touch from a man who's ignored me for the most part of the last seven months. The woman on the door was no longer there and Donald, wrapped up in hat and gloves, looked so pleased to see us at last.

Fergus insisted I had the front seat, which meant I ended up next to him and not in the back with everyone else.

'Youse had a good time did youse?' said Donald to Fergus.

'Yes, such fun.'

'Looked an awfully lot of people.'

'It was full. Funny we hadn't heard about it till the model told us.'

'I heard something about it but dinee think to mention it. Youse not been out locally afore and I dinee really get the gist of the advert in the pub, said something I could nee read, the word began with b and had a q in it, wee a twist.'

'Do you and Mhàiri ever go to local shows?'

'We take the grandkids to the pantomime at Christmas but that's aboot it.'

Fergus turned to me and full of enthusiasm he said, 'I liked your friend. A lot.'

'Toby?'

'Yes. He loves Scotland, doesn't he?'

'I never knew. We know each other from the south.'

'Which makes it *all* the more amusing you bumping into each other tonight.'

'Yes,' I said, trying to sound cheerful.

'I hope you'll be pleased to hear, I invited him to join our ceilidh tomorrow.'

I gave a massive grin. I'm a pretty good liar when I have to be.

'I *knew* you'd be happy. He was delighted.'

I stared straight out the windscreen feeling absolutely wretched. The last person in the world I want to spend a night with is Toby. The headlights showed up one bend after another, never a long enough straight to get a clear view ahead. We were on a country lane in the middle of nowhere yet somehow, in some unfortunate way, Toby Cropper had wriggled his way back into my life.

'Well,' said Fergus, 'as we're a man short it couldn't have worked out better.'

'What about Ewen?'

'I had thought about that but Zoe tells me he's going away.'

'Away?'

'Yes, no idea where.'

I felt mildly smug at the thought it was me who'd encouraged Ewen to spread his wings.

Shane's voice came hurtling into the front. 'Are we nearly there yet?'

Fergus looked at Donald. 'Aboot another twenty-five minutes or so.'

'What's that?' called out Shane. 'We can't hear you,

Rupert's snoring.'

Fergus turned his head towards the back. 'We'll be home in twenty-five minutes.'

'Good,' said Lianne. 'I'm ready for bed.'

'Fergus,' I whispered, making sure Donald's aged eardrums couldn't hear, 'I'm a bit worried about tomorrow.'

'Tomorrow?'

'It's just, I don't know how to put it, I've been thinking, tonight and all.'

'What is it, Susie?'

'I don't think Cailey should continue to model for us.'

'Okay. You're the tutor,' he said merrily. 'Although I did book her for the week.'

'In all truth with the image of her from tonight in their mind, it would be very difficult, probably impossible, for anyone to concentrate on life drawing.'

'I hadn't realised there was a difference but I'll take your word for it.'

'Thank you. I hope I haven't caused a problem.'

'Zoe's bound to have a solution so don't worry about that.'

Donald's driving was cautious to a fault and when we eventually reached Auchen Laggan Tosh's front drive he travelled so slowly up it you'd have thought he was doing his very best to avoid coming to the end of the journey.

'Donald,' I said, 'I'm so sorry I never thanked you for putting on my spare tyre. *Thank you.*'

'Mhàiri passed on yer wishes.'

'Yes, but I really should have said something earlier.'

'Dinee ye worry, Susie. It was my pleasure.'

'Here we are,' said Fergus.

Donald finally parked the bus and we all tumbled out, ready for bed.

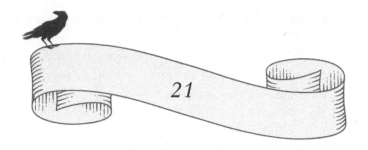

21

Louis grasped my hand on the way upstairs and told me I needed to come and '*get that thing from his room*'. Obviously, he was making it up, but I was on board.

'So, what do you want to drink?' he said as soon as we entered.

'Nothing.'

'Come on,' he pleaded. 'Just one.'

'Okay, one small glass of whisky and soda.'

'Great. I'll be back in a sec.' He kicked off his shoes, flashed me a smile and tiptoed out the door.

I sat down on the very large double bed and swung my legs, grinning to myself about the childish situation here. I feel like a teenager, not quite knowing what's on the cards but excited about being alone together.

'Pour toi.' He thrust a glass into my hand.

'Which language do you prefer? French? English?'

'I grew up in France. I went to university in England. When you have English and you have French, there is no comparison – French every time.'

He drifted across the room and picked up his camera.

'You look so beautiful, I'm going to take a picture of you.'

'Don't be so silly.' I put my hand over my face.

'Pleeeease,' he started to fiddle with the filters, 'you need a photo on your website.'

I felt flattered he'd looked me up, and found myself smiling at him rather than hiding my face. Blast, the black shutter began to blink and I lost count of the number of pictures he was taking.

'Stop it.'

'*Shh, shh*, no need to shout.'

He sat down beside me and the cushy mattress gave way. We both shuffled backwards giggling like children, doing our best not to fall off it.

'Can I see those photographs?'

'Sure.' He pushed the play button and held the screen towards me.

'Stop. You *have* to delete that one, I look awful.'

'No you don't, just shy. People always look a bit odd when they're caught unrelaxed.'

'Exactly, so delete it. *Please.*' I grappled with his fingers and won. 'I trust you'll delete it from the recycle bin?'

'You have to trust me; relationships are built on trust.'

'But you're French.'

'And?'

'French men always have at least two lovers.'

'Both of whom trust him,' he laughed.

'Can I see all the pictures you took of me?'

'Please?'

'*Please.*'

Louis handed me the camera and collapsed back on the bed.

Whoops, the dial spun and spun, many images whizzed by, and then suddenly they stopped on a rather lovely detail of heather.

'This is beautiful.'

Louis leant forwards. 'Oh that, it's nothing. Give it here.'

He obviously felt emasculated by such a pretty picture.

'I'm going to take charge of sifting through from now on.'

There were several terrible pictures of me and with a lot of persuasion I got him to delete them all.

'Why did you sign up to this course?' I asked as he went to put his camera down.

'I wanted to meet you.'

'Rubbish.'

'It's the truth.'

'I don't believe you.'

He picked up a sheet of paper from his dressing table and sped-read aloud: 'Susie Mahl is a figurative painter trained at the Ruskin School of Art. She is best known for her oil paintings but takes commissions for pet portraits. Her love of landscape and nature makes her well placed to teach this course. She's fun-loving, full of energy and is in no doubt that the richness and variety of Scotland's natural heritage will provide an infinite source of inspiration to all artists attending the residency.'

'*Where* did you get that?'

'It was part of the starter pack. Ewen sent it to me and I thought, why not.'

'You were lucky to get a place.'

'I sent in a photograph with my application.'

'*Seriously?*'

He laughed. 'Of course I didn't. Though I did say I'd like to give some more money towards it.'

'Really?'

'Yeah. I think it's a very good idea.'

'That's so generous.' I suddenly felt awkward knowing Louis must be rich. I didn't want him to think that's why I was keen.

He immediately made me feel at ease. 'I'm lucky enough to have some money to give away and when I heard about the sponsored places I thought it was a good cause. I would never have told you if you hadn't asked. But please, keep it to yourself.'

'Of course.' I smiled; it felt nice him opening up to me.

'Another drink?'

'No, no, I must go to bed.'

'Fair enough.'

Louis followed me to the door, and as I stretched for the handle he lightly wrapped his fingers round my right shoulder. Ever so delicately he motioned my chin towards his and as his hands felt for my cheeks he pressed his lips against mine with the most loving, soft, passionate kiss. I adored every moment of it and when he drew away he stretched his hand out and opened the door wishing me, 'Bonne nuit, mon amie,' on my way out.

I turned into the corridor with an incredibly happy feeling inside. There's nothing like a snog to perk one up, and I sauntered into my bedroom with my head in a hazy cloud of romance, until the blasted floorboard tripped me up again. Falling to my knees, full of confusion, I lay thinking, there must be a reason it's come loose. Then assuming it wasn't a trick on *me* – everyone's too grown up for April Fool behaviour – I began to wonder why.

I reckon it happened today, when Rupert and I were out walking – the timings make sense. Perhaps something was hidden and someone came to get it…Maybe it was Zoe? She could have stashed something in here when she stayed as a child or heard treasure was in the house and searched the locked wing last night and this corridor this morning. Unlikely – surely she'd do it when the house's empty?

Maybe Mhàiri accidentally sucked the board up with her Hoover and struggled to put it firmly back in place? Or, Fergus could have been looking into the electrics, it might be to do with that? I've never sleepwalked before, so it's highly unlikely but I suppose I *might* have done something in my sleep.

I stood up and got ready for bed and as I brushed my teeth then put on my nightie, progressively more absurd thoughts flew off the top of my head: Haggis had scratched the board until it came loose; Louis had tried to hide a present for me; a squirrel had sneaked into my room; the ravens somehow caused the problem; the teddy bear had come to life; the two-faced man in the painting had walked out the canvas.

I grasped my mobile and turned on the torch. Then, straddling the void in the floor, I bent right down and peered in the illuminated hole. A tiny speck in one corner sparkled back and I felt all zingy inside as I grabbed my tweezers to pluck it out.

A hard, pale, yellowish lozenge about five millimetres in length is now in the palm of my hand. Considering where I've found it, it's probably a jewel from a doll. But, no matter how insignificant, I'm excited to get to the bottom of who's been here and what they've taken out.

Right now, though, I must sleep. I can't be a hungover, tired tutor tomorrow. So, I popped the jewel in my jewellery case, replaced the floorboard and jumped into bed.

I'm lying in the dark, imagining Louis in his huge double bed. 'Mon amie,' I whispered with a smile. How much fun to have a Highland fling. Nothing long term, I don't want to be hurt again. I've lost my faith in finding true love. Lost it because of Toby. Oh Toby. Why are you tipping up here tomorrow night? How could you have accepted without asking me?

Grrrrrrr. I kicked a leg out from under the duvet. The more I think about it the more I cannot believe he's gatecrashing my fresh start.

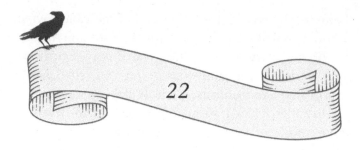

22

My morning alarm woke me with a fright. Where am I? Home? No. Scotland. It's morning. Really? Yes, morning. That was far too short a night. I reached for the snooze button and promptly fell fast asleep again.

Ten minutes later it began to beep. Unfortunately, I really had to get up now. I went to the bathroom and splashed my face with freezing water. Then, gently slapping my cheeks trying to get some colour, I whizzed through the hurdles I had to get over today – replacing life drawing with another activity; finding time to take my car to the garage; spending the evening with Toby; mastering the art of Scottish reeling. Oh God, give me strength for the day ahead.

I hurried back to my room and pulled on my clothes. I needed to give myself as much time as I could to put on my face. The late nights were taking their toll and my puffy eyes had terrible bags.

By the time I rushed downstairs I was behind schedule and last into breakfast. There's nothing like a hangover to heighten hunger. Even Minty was eating salty porridge this morning. I sat down with a bowl of my own and

Louis, all the way up the other end of the table, gave me a nod. I smiled back, not too much, just enough to get rid of any awkwardness. The great thing about hitting your thirties is you simply don't get that self-conscious nausea after a romantic escapade. It plagued my teens and my twenties when I often did things just to have done them and then felt desperately awkward the morning after a fumble. I'm not saying it wasn't good fun or that every boy who passed my lips was purely for practice. Just that the I-know-what-I'm-doing mature self now makes it so much less embarrassing at moments like this.

The breakfast conversation was buzzing with last night's show.

'Fergus told me *all* about it,' said Zoe.

'Did he tell you Cailey got her kit off?' shouted Shane.

'Yes, enough of that.'

'Not sure how I feel about drawing her today,' said Jane.

'You took the words straight out my mouth,' said Rupert.

'It won't be a problem,' said Fergus, staring at his wife.

'Not at all. As you all showed such enthusiasm for drawing Highland cows, we've cancelled the life class and this morning you'll be out in the field instead.'

'Brilliant,' said Shane.

'Yeah, I'd much rather be outside,' said Lianne. 'Means we don't have to listen to Louis' jazz.'

'What would you prefer? R&B?'

'*Anything* but jazz.'

'I hear you were on stage last night, Lianne,' said Zoe.

'She saved me,' cried Felicity. 'I'd have fainted if I'd had to dance.'

'Lianne loved it.' Shane tapped her on the back.

'I sure did.'

'So, you'll all be happy drawing cows this morning?' said Fergus.

'Not *in* the field,' exclaimed Jane.

'No. Don't worry, they'll be fenced off.'

'What a relief.'

'It looks jolly chilly outside,' shivered Felicity.

'Well, perhaps, darling, you could arrange some thermoses. Put something warm in them, you know.' Fergus revealed his undomesticated hand – surely he could pass this message onto Mhàiri himself?

'I'll get a basket of goodies made up.' Zoe fitted the bill of a classic wife (one with servants, that is).

'Susie,' said Rupert. 'That was a charming friend of yours we met last night.'

'Yes,' said Zoe, 'wasn't that a coincidence. I hear he's coming to join the ceilidh. Angel, I hope you offered him a bed?'

'He's staying in Buchtermuchty, you know, that clapped-out old building on the corner of the high street.'

'Poor him.'

'There was a crowd of them, I'm sure it's better than we think.'

Rupert's voice boomed across the table. 'He must be keen to see you, Susie, if he's deserting the stag party to come here.'

Shane wolf-whistled.

'He's just a friend,' I said through gritted teeth.

'I don't blame him coming here,' said Jane. 'It's terribly common this obsession with stag dos.'

'Part of the reason I invited him,' said Fergus, 'is he's all alone tonight.'

'How come?' asked Rupert.

'He didn't want to drive south on a hangover.'

'What a sensible chap.'

I could have told them, that's a trained heart surgeon for you. But no, I wasn't going to big Toby up, he could pave his own way tonight and I wouldn't be giving him an ounce of help.

Minty reached for my empty bowl. 'Shall I take that for you?'

'Yes please. Thank you.'

'Mine too,' said Shane.

Mhàiri came bustling through the swing door carrying a plate full of hot toast. The steam was rising in the cold air of the room.

'Do you want some, Susie?' said Lianne as she reached for a slice.

'No thanks.'

'Oh, go on,' said Louis, 'this marmalade's delicious.'

'I'm so pleased you like it,' said Fergus. 'My mother made a batch every year…well, Mhàiri made it but under my mother's instruction.'

The shrill of the telephone sent him scooting out the room and, full of inquisitiveness – the call could be the art dealer arranging Jamie Tumbleton-Smith's visit – I had a sudden urge to eavesdrop. So, I refused Louis' cajoling of a piece of toast and made my excuses and left.

I watched the library door close behind Fergus and searched for some plausible cover, an object nearby to look at.

My eyes settled on a long list of Muchton Earls carved into a wooden board just to the left of the door.

1715 Hew Angus 1st Earl Muchton 1760–1770
1737 Angus Hew 2nd Earl Muchton 1770–1791
1762 Malcolm Angus 3rd Earl Muchton 1791–1823
1787 Fergus Robert 4th Earl Muchton 1823–1847
1822 Malcolm Robert 5th Earl Muchton 1847–1873
1865 Robert Angus 6th Earl Muchton 1873–1911
1897 Iona Emma 7th Countess Muchton 1911–1943
1914 Malcolm Fergus 8th Earl Muchton 1943–1944
1938 Robert Hew 9th Earl Muchton 1944–2015

I couldn't hear a word from Fergus and ended up becoming genuinely interested in the Muchton peerage. I was working out at what age each head of the family inherited the title. Forty-five…thirty-three…twenty-nine…thirty-six…twenty-five…EIGHT, wow, that's young. I bet the girls threw themselves at him. Fourteen…the Countess…

'Susie,' said Fergus, giving me a fright. 'I'm *so* sorry, I didn't think you'd be standing right here.'

'My fault.' I looked straight at him but he turned away. So I stood, silent, hoping whatever he said next would give something away. But no, he looked up at the board and said full of amusement, 'There are certain names us Muchtons are keen on.'

'Countess Iona Emma breaks it up a bit.' Finally, I had an opportunity to bring her up.

'She certainly does,' he said and I jumped in with, 'I'd love to know more about her.'

'Ah well, there's an interesting story there. Iona got

married aged sixteen, imagine that nowadays, it was a ploy to get her pregnant before the First World War. Her parents recruited a suitable husband. However, unbeknown to them this pair were already in love. He was twenty-five years Iona's elder –' I knew she'd be a go-getta '– the bachelor uncle of her school friend. He gave her a son and then sadly got wounded. They weren't able to have any more children.'

'Did he die from his wounds?'

'Yes, poor woman, lost him in 1922 and then her only son died aged thirty.'

'Your grandfather?' I said, glad to be able to bring up the man in the portrait.

'Yes. Hence why my father inherited the title aged six.'

'That's so sad he grew up without his dad.'

'I agree, although he believed his father's spirit lived on in the house. Not that that was a good thing; apparently it used to haunt him in the night.'

'Seriously?'

Auchen Laggan Tosh is old and cold and in need of restoration, and although I sensed unhappiness in the atmosphere, I didn't feel spooked here at all. I'm susceptible to ghosts. I've never actually seen one, but I know when they're about.

'It's nonsense,' said Fergus, and I agreed.

Then, taking a huge risk, I said, 'The portrait of your grandfather in the dining room has been painted over, hasn't it?'

Fergus's face lit up.

'How on earth do you know that?' His brow furrowed as he stared at me intensely.

'I could see an extra eye.'

'Really?'

Fergus possibly hadn't noticed it before.

'Yes…just.'

'That's amazing. You're right, my father had the head re-painted in profile on top of the original face. He couldn't bear seeing his father looking at him down the dining room table. It worked as far as putting his mind at rest. He never mentioned the spirit again. But I had no *idea* one could tell. You must have unbelievably good eyesight.'

'It's a trick of the light. You have to know where to stand.'

Fergus's face froze. 'Don't go showing me. If this house was once haunted, I'd hate for it to become so again. You really cannot tell Zoe either, it took a bit of convincing to get her up here.' He raised his eyebrows. He must be serious.

'You didn't notice anything funny about the Landseers, did you?'

Fergus has cracked. Why would he ever jump to the Landseers unless he'd just had a call alerting him that they might be copies? Poor man; his face fell as he waited for an answer.

'No,' I smiled, 'nothing other than how wonderful they are.'

'Goodie.' His lips remained firm and he tapped my shoulder. 'Right, I must have a quick word with my wife. Zoe, darling, *Zoe*,' he called out, and from Haggis's bark it sounded as if she was upstairs.

I went to the music room to count up the easels.

'Susie,' said Minty, who was in there too, 'would it be okay if I paint this morning rather than draw?'

'Of course, it's entirely up to you.'

'Mummy wants me to make the most of painting this week. I'm out of practice, you see.'

'It's important you get what you want from the residency. I hope you're finding it useful so far?'

'Oh yes, very. I like the routine. It's good to have no distractions. If I was at home I'd be forever out riding, but here I'm quite happy being arty all day.'

'It's a good group, don't you think?'

'Yes, for a week. Turns out Giles and I have lots of friends in common. What a small world it is.'

There was a noise at the door. 'Ah Susie, there you are,' said Zoe. 'I just wanted to say…' She stopped as soon as she saw Minty.

'Don't worry,' said Minty, 'I'm leaving.'

Oh heck, is Zoe going to confront me about Oliver's visit?

'Susie, the Mahafi field…'

'Mahafi field?'

'Yes, all the fields have names.'

'Ah, okay.' My nerves settled.

'It's where the Highland cows are and it's reasonably near our keeper Stuart's house. Now, I don't want any of the class taking themselves off for a wander *anywhere* near his house.'

I swallowed, hard.

She elaborated. 'There was an incident on Tuesday morning, a roe deer was found in the woods.'

'Dead?'

'Yes, Stuart thinks a car hit it and the driver dragged it off the road. But I can't think who would've behaved like that. Anyway, my point being the gralloched deer is hanging in the game larder and it's not a pleasant sight if you've never seen one before. I'd hate to end up with a formal complaint.'

'Understood.'

'Thank you.'

Giles practically walked into me as I left the room. 'Whoops, sorry, Susie.'

'Don't worry.' I put my hand on his shoulder. 'Would you do me a favour and make sure everyone's taken an easel and a drawing board to the bus?'

'Certainly.'

'I'm going to put on my outdoor kit. I'll meet you outside in a bit.'

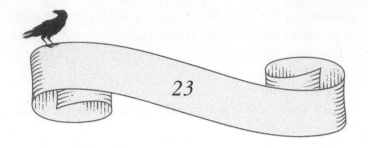

23

Rupert has taken charge of driving again and is following Fergus's directions to the field. We're
bumping down the front drive, dry weather in our
favour, and a lot of excited chitter chatter about the
beasts we're off to draw.

'Right here?' said Rupert, putting his foot on the
brake as we approached a track.

'Yes.'

'Look at that,' squawked Jane.

'Oh yes,' said Rupert, 'there's a buzzard on the fence
post.'

'It's gigantic,' said Lianne.

Shane banged on the glass and the enormous bird
drew up its heavy wings and launched into flight.

'Damn,' said Louis. 'I knew I should have brought my
camera.'

'You haven't brought your camera out at all,' said Jane.

'I'm too busy being a good student. Though I might
do this afternoon.'

'All you need is a mobile,' said Shane. 'Slip it in your
pocket and make videos wherever you go.'

'Nah,' said Lianne. 'The quality's turd.'

'C'est vrai,' said Louis.

I do like it when he breaks into a bit of French.

'Ah, here's the bridge Fergus mentioned,' said Rupert. 'Did he say we go over it?'

'*Yes*,' shouted Jane and we joined another off-road track.

'There they are,' squealed Felicity.

'Where?' said Shane.

'Over there.'

'Over where?' said Giles.

'Duh,' said Lianne. 'In the far distance, look, there's something orange.'

'That's far too small to be a cow.'

'It's a sheep feeder,' said Minty.

'It ain't got no horns,' said Shane.

We drove straight into a clump of trees and the discussion ended.

'Whose house is that, Miss?'

'The keeper's,' said Giles.

'Keeper like gate keeper?'

'No, game keeper.'

'How do *you* know?'

'All those antlers gave it away.'

We left the wood and Rupert announced, 'Here they are.'

He'd stopped the bus in front of a gate.

'Where?' said Lianne.

'*There*,' he pointed through the windscreen, 'in the next field. Susie, get the gate, will you?'

'Wow,' said Minty. 'They're *huge*.'

'Sick,' said Shane.

'We're not going *in* the field,' ordered Jane.

'No, no,' screeched Felicity.

'Calm down.' I was a little impatient. 'There's an electric fence around them. The farmer put it up specially so we can get close to them.'

'Susie,' said Rupert, 'the gate?'

I opened my door and put one foot on the ground. 'It's very wet here.'

'We mustn't get the bus stuck, what do you think?'

'I think we should walk from here,' said Giles, encouraging everyone to get out.

'Susie's in charge,' said Louis. 'Let her decide.'

'Yes, let's walk, it's not far. But leave your things here for now. I want to talk you through the class first.'

The closer we got to the cows the tighter they grouped together. Some were stamping their hooves and all had hot breath steaming out of flared nostrils. It's a bit intimidating but I must stay strong.

'Not very pleased to see us, are they?' said Giles.

'They'll settle down once they get used to it, just don't make any sudden movements for the time being.'

'I'm scared,' said Felicity, hanging back in the field.

'Don't worry.' I moved closer to her. 'They're not dangerous and I promise they won't cross this fence.' I coaxed her forwards to join the others.

'If we had a dog it would be a different matter,' said Minty. 'I'm jolly glad Haggis isn't here.'

'Are you sure we're safe?' said Felicity as she nestled herself next to Jane.

'Yes. They seem unfriendly at the minute, but look, they're already beginning to spread out.'

'Marvellous orange colour,' commented Giles. 'I think I'm going to use pastels.'

'You can use any medium you want. Minty's going to paint but I'd encourage the rest of you to draw. We don't have a very long morning.'

'Do you want us to draw the whole thing?' asked Lianne. 'Should we put in the background or not? You don't have any background in your pet portraits.'

'When I draw animals, I focus on their character. But here it's different.'

'Why, Miss?'

'Because you have an opportunity to draw a Highland cow in a Highland landscape. It makes for a nice picture.'

'You're going to have to give *me* more instruction than that,' said Rupert.

'Well, as with any subject, you must look very closely before you begin.'

'Frightfully long hair they have, no?'

'Yes, and if you look carefully, you'll see it's double-layered.'

'What?' said Jane.

'Their coat, the top part is oily and stops the rain seeping in.'

'The under bit is downy, isn't it?' said Giles.

'Yes, a warm lining.'

'I wish I had one,' said Felicity.

'Are you cold?' Rupert sounded concerned. 'You can have this if you want?' and without waiting for an answer, he handed her his scarlet cashmere scarf.

'Thank you.'

'Going back to their coat for a minute, I want you to notice it has a slight wave, it's not completely straight.'

'Like Jane's,' said Shane with a cheeky giggle and she furiously pulled her sou'wester more firmly onto her head.

'Why do they have such long horns?' said Minty.

''Cause they're horny.'

Lianne punched Shane's shoulder.

'They use them to dig for food during snowy winters.'

'And fighting?' asked Giles.

'I would if I were them,' said Shane.

'Can we go for a walk?' Felicity was feeling braver. 'I think it will warm me up.'

'Maybe we could all do a quick power walk to the gate and back instead.'

'Would you mind if I didn't?' said Minty. 'I want to get started.'

'Me too,' said Lianne.

'Okay then, but it would be really helpful if anyone who's not warming up could bring two easels each, please.'

'In that case I'll help.' Rupert took off towards the bus.

Jane and Felicity huffed and puffed to the gate and by the time they were back all easels were up and I was ready to start.

'I've been thinking,' said Louis. 'Why aren't *you* drawing?'

'I don't want to be shown up.'

'You can advise me then, I've never drawn an animal before.'

'Sure, I'll happily stand by your side.'

'Oi,' called out Shane. 'Minty, you're in my view.'

'Include me in your picture then.'

Shane, genuinely nice-natured, gave in and moved his easel.

'Can you tell us what you want us to do?' asked Jane.

'Of course. I would advise working out what size you want your picture to be and then draw a light frame in pencil on your paper. This will give you a boundary and help with your composition.'

'I think I'm going to draw after all,' said Minty. 'There's not enough time to paint. Can I share someone's pencils?'

'You can share my pastels,' offered Giles, 'but you'll have to come closer to me.'

Louis let out a faint wolf-whistle and I scowled at him.

'Do you have paper, Minty?'

'Yes.'

'Right, once you've all drawn a frame, pick one of these beasts.'

'They all look the same,' said Lianne.

'They're similar but just for now pick one.'

'What happens if it moves?' said Felicity.

'They will move and your drawing will change but try not to worry about that. It's a general impression we're going for. So, find your favourite part of the cow you've chosen…'

'What?' shouted Shane.

'Find the spark which draws your eye. It could be the nose, the horn, the belly, it doesn't matter, I just want you to choose your favourite bit as a starting point. When you have, work out the composition of your picture in relation to this bit and put a mark inside your frame.'

'Like this?' asked Rupert and I went to look at his picture.

He'd drawn a tuft of hair just off centre. Phew. He'd understood.

'Yes,' I said, 'exactly. Then, look really hard and see what and where things intercept it. You have to focus as much on the space around the cow as you do on the cow itself. Does that make sense?'

'Yes,' said Felicity who was clearly enjoying the process, 'but do I have to put the fence in?'

'No, you're the artist so put in and take out what you want.'

'Can you check I'm on the right track?' asked Jane.

Her drawing was so faint it was hard to make out but I could tell she had the right idea. 'Put your lines in with greater definition, it will enable you to see the whole picture more clearly.'

There wasn't nearly long enough for a proper break today so I went to get Mhàiri's basket from the bus and handed out a cup of coffee to those who wanted one.

'Isn't there a nibble?' said Jane.

'Yes, here – who wants an oatmeal biscuit?'

'These are getting better every day,' said Lianne. 'I normally ain't like ones without chocolate on them but I'm getting a taste for plain things up here.'

'Do you like my horns, Miss?'

'They're magnificent.'

Shane had drawn a huge close-up of a Highland cow's head.

'I'm going to have a go at drawing the tongue.'

'Good luck.'

'I'm finding the clouds terribly difficult,' said Felicity.

'I like the way you've drawn them, they're good. Don't do any more to them.'

'What next?'

'Focus on the foreground, it'll give your picture perspective.'

'Thanks, Susie.'

I really didn't want this morning to descend into endless questions so I asked if anyone would mind if I went for a short walk.

'You must,' said Rupert. 'You deserve a bit of time off.'

I headed in the direction Zoe had specifically told me not to. Back towards Stuart's house. But I'm not squeamish about a hanging carcass, so I'm pretty sure it'll be all right.

Up here, all around, stretch those barren landscapes Landseer must have loved when he came many, many years ago. I've really got to find some way of having another proper look at his paintings in the locked wing. The art valuer Oliver left so many more questions than answers. I'm no trained expert in the technicality of forgery, but I do know about paint, and I have a beady eye – maybe I can work out for myself if they are copies or not. Should I ask Fergus if I can take another peek? But then again, if he's already had a call from the art dealer, which I suspect he has, he'll probably jump to the conclusion that I know more than I've let on. I certainly don't want to land Oliver in it.

A dense wood encompassed Stuart's house. I was in it, off the track, wandering free amongst the trees.

'Whit the 'ell do yous think yer doing,' came a booming voice.

Stuart was stomping towards me, shotgun under one arm.

'I'm sorry, it's only me, Susie, the tutor.'

'Whit? Youse are drawing the cows so why the 'ell are yous 'ere?' He was so cross he could hardly get his words out.

'I'm going for a walk,' I said, trying to smile.

'Aye, aye, I bet someyun set yous up to this.'

'Honestly they didn't.'

A loud squawk came from above and a pair of ravens swooped right down to us and back up into the sky.

'Raven, eh,' I said, trying to find common ground.

'Yous have something to do wee this?'

'What?'

'Yous ken Alec Ronaldsay?'

'The ornithologist. The Tower of London aviary. Of course I do.' Thanks to Dad.

'Personally?'

'No, no. Although I'd like to meet him. Does he live near here?'

Stuart put a hand to his forehead. 'You dinne hay a clue, do yous?'

'I'm sorry, I should probably get back to my class.'

'All this started when youse arrived. Do yous swear me you dinne hay a clue?'

'I don't know anything at all, I swear.'

'Best get yourself out of here then.' Stuart pointed me back where I'd come.

'Of course, I'm sorry.'

I rushed through the trees, dizzied by our conversation and terribly confused about what was going on, but just as I was trying to get it straight in my head, stepping out of the trees back onto the track, I bumped into Louis who gave me an awful fright.

'Susie? What's wrong?'

'You surprised me.'

'I know, I'm sorry, but you look very worried.'

'An odd thing just happened. Stuart the keeper was here a moment ago. I think he thought I had something to do with the ravens.'

Louis started to laugh.

'What is it?'

'He thinks you released some, does he?'

'Maybe that *is* what he meant? There are an awful lot around, but it's nothing to do with me.'

'I wouldn't have thought it was,' Louis sniggered.

'Very odd. Anyway, why are *you* here?'

'I came to find *you*.' He smiled and tried to hold my hand but I wouldn't let him.

'We'd better head back.'

'Gone off me, have you?'

I elbowed him in the side. 'I'm not going to hold your hand.'

'No, I didn't think you were,' he said with a wink.

'So, how many times have you been here before?'

'Twice.'

'Long ago?'

'Over the last two years.'

'So, Zoe and Fergus were living here the second time you came?'

'Oh well, it must have been twice in one year then. The Dowager Countess was still in residence.'

'Did you stay with her?'

'No, Ewen's had his cottage for years.'

'Did you meet his mother?'

'So many questions. What is it you want to know?'

'I'm still trying to work out what's in the locked wing and I thought if you've been here before…'

He finished my sentence. 'I'd know what's in there.'

'Exactly.'

I was testing Louis. Seeing if he'd tell me the truth.

'Treasure,' he said.

'No, come on, seriously.'

'A ballroom,' he smiled.

'So we'll see it tonight?'

'I doubt it.' Louis looked cross but I think he was possibly just confused.

'Anything else?'

'Nothing I know of.' He gave my upper arm a gentle rub. 'Honestly.'

I believed him and he seemed trustworthy so I confided in him that I'd seen Zoe coming out the locked wing the other night.

'On Monday?'

'Yes.'

'That makes sense. Ewen and I were drinking late into the night. Zoe came downstairs in a dressing gown asking us if we'd been creeping around the house. She'd heard a noise apparently. I guess she was having a good look around.'

'Pretty brave of her to do it alone.'

'I think she thought Ewen and I were up to no good.' He gave a sheepish grin.

'Were you?'

'No. Only drinking. But I bet you Zoe didn't wake Fergus on purpose. I don't know if you've noticed but she manages the sensitivities between Ewen and Fergus very well.' Louis nudged my shoulder, we were almost back with the cows. 'I think you'd better attend to your class.'

I picked up my pace and went to see what everyone had done.

'I'm so pleased you're back,' said Minty. 'I was beginning to get cold.'

'Me too,' said Lianne who had packed up already.

I looked at my watch. 'Okay, let's stop.'

'Giles,' said Jane, 'would you mind helping me take my things to the bus, I don't want to do any more.'

'Sure.'

'Felicity,' said Rupert, 'I'll help you.'

'How kind you are.'

'When we get back, I'd like you to line up your pictures in the music room.'

'Oh Miss, not again.'

'We must,' said Rupert with a toot of the horn.

'I find your crits a frightfully useful exercise,' said Jane.

I was rather surprised.

'Me too,' said Minty. 'But that's because I'm used to it from school.'

'And you're the best,' said Lianne.

And, I said to myself, it helps to have expensive equipment.

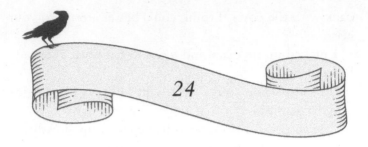

24

We were seated round the dining room table with bowls of hot barley soup and buttered baps. Rupert had made a great effort to bagsy a spot beside me – 'I haven't sat next to you yet' – and Zoe was on my other side.

'I'm so pleased your friend's coming tonight,' she said. 'I was worried about numbers being even.'

'Ewen could have always come.' I wanted to know where he'd gone. I really wish they'd asked him first.

'He's away.'

'Oh. Where's he gone?'

'We never ask.'

I didn't believe her, but she obviously didn't want to say. I would have liked to say goodbye; I liked Ewen but on the flip side I was still feeling smug he'd taken off.

'What did you and Rupert make of Ewen's house then?'

Thinking she meant the state of it rather than any comparison to hers, I joked, 'Pretty tidy.'

Zoe didn't laugh.

'Lovely building,' said Rupert, 'but it can't be easy having your brother-in-law living on your doorstep?'

'It's okay. Fergus finds it difficult, though I reassure him Ewen won't be here forever.'

Before any more was said, Zoe sent another question down the table. 'Louis,' she was saying, 'have you taken any photographs yet?'

'I'm going to this afternoon,' he called back. 'It's a good excuse to stop painting.'

'Stop painting?' I interrupted them.

'Yeah, I'm much better at taking pictures,' he smiled.

'One less member of the class,' said Zoe and I wondered if she was doubting my ability to teach. Not that I'm worried about that; I'm confident there will be plenty of work to show her at the end of the week.

Zoe got up to clear the table. 'Don't worry,' she said as I stacked Rupert's bowl on mine, 'I'm just going to take what I can to the kitchen and get the flapjacks.'

'Flapjacks,' said Shane, overhearing. 'I could do with a pocket full of them.'

'We're going to put on weight here,' said Rupert. 'You're feeding us so well.'

'I shall have to detox when I get home,' said Felicity.

'What are we doing this afternoon, Susie?' asked Lianne and the table fell silent for an answer.

'First,' said Fergus, 'I'm going to take you on a tour of the front of the house and then I think the plan is to paint out there.'

'Yes,' I nodded.

Zoe returned and Felicity, refusing a flapjack, said, 'I must go and put on an extra layer.'

'I reckon it will be cold…' I began.

'For a change,' interrupted Giles.

'…so layer up, put on your outdoor kit and we'll

carry our painting things round to the front of the house before the tour.'

'Better get going then,' said Rupert, leading the charge.

'Ten minutes and I'll be with you,' called out Fergus.

I went upstairs and, taking the long route round the landing, crashed into Felicity as she was leaving her room.

'Sorry,' I said as she giggled with fright.

'That's okay.'

The portrait behind her caught my eye and I asked if she'd mind me having another look.

'No, not at all, come in.' She turned to Jane who was sitting on one of two beds, slipping fur wrist warmers over her hands. 'Susie wants to have another peek at our Countess.'

'Fine.'

Felicity stood right next to me as I looked up at the picture.

'That's funny,' I said, 'I hadn't realised till now that the diamonds round her neck are yellow. They're so full of light, it's not easy to tell from far away.'

'So they are, oval too. Jane,' said Felicity, 'had you noticed this before?'

'Possibly.' Jane didn't even bother to look up.

'Aren't we lucky to be sleeping in here, Susie.'

'Yes, you are.'

We turned to Jane, who got up and, without a word, left the room.

'I'm not sure what's wrong with her,' said Felicity. 'She's been preoccupied and a little agitated.'

'Creativity can bring that out in people.'

'But her pictures are far better than mine. I get the feeling she's missing her personal space.'

'Are you okay?' I was now concerned Felicity wasn't enjoying herself.

'Yes, yes, I'm having a splendid time.'

'Oh great. Thanks for letting me have another peek in here. I'm just going to grab a jumper, and I'll see you downstairs.'

I rushed to my room with a wild thought: could that pale-yellow bead I'd found under the floorboard be in fact a diamond? Maybe even from *that* necklace. Perhaps Zoe really had found some treasure in my room.

I held it up to the light. It sparkled with the richness and fire you just don't see in costume jewellery and it was oval, an unusual shape for any ordinary bead. I know, I thought, I'll do a bog-standard test, see if it scratches the window glass. I had it firm between my thumb and fore-finger and slid my hand across a small lower portion of the pane. Crumbs...the jewel made a mark, almost too small to see but as I ran my fingers over it I could definitely trace an indent. This *is* a diamond...It can't be...It must be...I'd like it to be...If it is...was that necklace under my floorboard? I'll keep hold of it until I know the truth.

I put the *diamond* safely back in my jewellery case, grabbed a jumper and went down to the drying room. No one else's kit was in here so I hurriedly got dressed and rushed outside.

'Susie,' said Fergus coming down the front steps, Haggis hot on his heel and full of beans, 'do you want me to carry anything from the bus?'

'No, this is the last easel, they must have taken everything else round to the front of the house.'

'Can you manage it?'

'Yes thanks.'

'Come then, this way. I was thinking,' he said as we walked, 'maybe you could nip away this afternoon and get a new tyre fitted.'

'Are you sure?'

'If everyone else is, then yes. I very much doubt it will take long.'

'Okay, great.'

My keys, wallet and mobile were already in my pocket. I had been hoping to find the time today.

The others were lolling around on the terrace next to a pile of kit.

'Aren't we lucky with this lovely dry day,' said Fergus. 'Leave your things here and come stand back a bit and face the house. Line up, let me in the middle, I'm going to tell you a bit about the house and garden.'

Louis put his arm round my shoulder. 'Warm enough?' he said, squeezing me then letting go.

'Just,' I smiled as butterflies turned in my tummy.

'Right,' Fergus began, 'on this façade, you'll notice there's only one straight stone staircase leading into the garden, not two curved stone staircases as there are on the other side leading into the yard.'

'I never realised,' said Shane.

Lianne kicked his ankle.

'Stick with me,' said Fergus. 'There's a logic I like to follow.' He took in a pre-emptive breath. 'The similarities between the two sides of the house are their colonnaded porticos over the raised basement.'

'So, the ground floor's the basement?' said Shane.

'I suppose you could call it either but we've always

referred to it as the basement.' Fergus continued, 'A portico is this large central section you see here at the front of the house.'

'So the other side's the back?' said Lianne.

Jane huffed. 'Are we *ever* going to get through this afternoon?'

'We will,' said Fergus calmly. 'It won't take long.'

'It ain't make sense to me why you'd arrive at the back of the house.'

'It's a posh house, that's why,' said Shane.

'As a matter of fact,' corrected Fergus, 'it's a feature of the architectural style. Auchen Laggan Tosh was built by the 1st Earl of Muchton in 1761 to the designs of Robert Adam, a highly regarded architect then and now. This, a classical mansion of three storeys over a raised basement, is an excellent example of his style.'

'How fascinating,' said Felicity.

'Isn't it,' said Fergus excited by her compliment. 'Similar to the paintings in the house, influenced by the Grand Tour, Adam's architecture reflects elements from ancient Greece and Rome.'

'The harmonious proportions,' said Minty.

'Yes, as well as the detailing of the cornice and Corinthian capitals.'

'I've noticed lots of classical architectural details inside too,' said Rupert as if the rest of us might not have.

'Adam was adamant the elegant proportions of the exterior should be complemented with interior splendour.'

Louis whispered in my ear, 'Dilapidated interior matches dilapidated exterior.'

'Shabby chic,' I whispered back.

'Here,' said Fergus, 'we're looking at the uniformed windows of the first floor: dining room, music room and drawing room; and the top floors: best bedrooms and dressing rooms.'

'So we are,' smiled Minty. 'Home has a similar layout.'

'You live in a massive pile too?' said Shane.

'We live in a beautiful house,' said Minty, holding her own.

Fergus, with a spring in his step, set off towards a four-tiered fountain in the centre of a large sweep of mossy lawn and as he waited for us to catch up he ran his hand round the rim of the acanthus urn.

'This is B listed,' he said. 'The water drops down the tiers through the lions' mouths but I'm afraid we can't have it on in winter.'

'Because the water turns to ice and cracks the stone?' said Minty.

'Exactly.'

'Suppose you have one of these an all?' said Shane.

'Yes,' she snooted, although I think she was playing him for a fool.

Fergus marched on down the garden and Minty stuck right by his side.

Lianne turned to Shane. 'It's lucky my parents live in London, they'd probably have to turn their Jacuzzi off up here.'

'Nah,' he said, 'a Jacuzzi's hot.'

She giggled. 'I just wanted to let you know they have one.'

We stepped across a paved area and onto a great big long lawn. There were neglected flower beds either side

and as we made it to the end Fergus brought us to a halt.
'This,' he said as Haggis hovered over the edge of a vertical retaining brick wall, 'is a ha-ha.'

'Ha-ha?' said Shane, peering into the ditch.

'Yes,' snapped Jane.

'It was a common landscape feature in the eighteenth
century,' explained Fergus. 'The point of it is to give the
illusion from the house of an unbroken, continuous
rolling view into the parkland with its lovely old oaks.'

'But why do you need the ditch?' said Felicity in an
uncharacteristically perceptive state of mind.

'If there were sheep or cows in the park, it would stop
them from entering the garden.'

'What an awfully clever design. I must have a better
look from the terrace.'

'It's a shame you can't see the river,' said Rupert,
looking towards the trees in the distance, 'not that this
isn't a lovely view.'

'When the house was first built you would have seen
the river.'

'But that wood's ancient,' said Giles.

'Yes, Malcolm's Wood, planted in 1762 to commem-
orate the birth of the 1st Earl's first grandson, Malcolm
Angus.'

'But why there?'

'To give a bit of privacy, shield the house from the
drive.'

'Trees shield every view,' said Jane, looking to her
left and right. We were enclosed by sinuous-edged
woodlands. 'But,' she remembered herself, 'I suppose to
have the house encased in trees protects it from the
weather?'

'Exactly right. Although if you stand on the steps of the house you get a view of the Beinn Eighe hills in the distance.'

'You've got a topping variety of trees here,' said Giles.

'That's thanks to my ancestors' good taste.'

'What do you mean?' said Shane.

'The woods here have been carefully planned. They're a range of specimen trees, both broadleaf and coniferous. Such a pleasure to look at, particularly in the autumn. Unlike our neighbouring estates,' Fergus huffed. 'Their blanketing Sitka spruce ruin the landscape.'

'I quite agree,' said Giles.

Fergus led us back across the lawns, admitting the flower beds needed some 'TLC'.

'Are you going to have a kitchen garden?' said Minty.

'Well, that bit of broken wall over there,' he was pointing to his far left, 'is all that remains of the early nineteenth-century one here. But Zoe and I have every intention of reinstating it.'

'You've got a *lot* to do,' said Lianne.

Fergus was amused. 'We're aiming high. Not to mention the tennis court we'd like to build in that large space off to the right-hand side of the house.'

Louis raised his eyebrows at me and I nodded – these Muchtons are going to have to rake in the cash.

'I hope you all feel familiar with the setting now. I'll be very interested to see your pictures later.'

'You have such inspiring locations for us,' said Felicity, all giddy.

'I'm going to paint a picture of the house, for you,' said Shane, 'from the front garden, no, the back garden, no, the front…'

'We just call it the garden,' Fergus smiled. 'I'll see you all later. Haggis and I are going to stretch our legs, make sure the fishing huts are in order; the season's about to pick up.'

'Bye.'

'Hey Louis,' I called out. He was making his way round the side of the house. 'Where are you going?' I flapped my hand to get him back.

'I'm getting my camera. I don't want to paint.'

'Okay. Fine, but you could have said.'

'Sorry,' he teased and off he went.

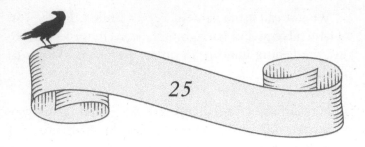

25

I started my rounds with Giles who was all the way down the far end of the garden looking out over the ha-ha.

'Are you going to paint more trees?'

'Yes, I thought I'd do a picture of this field with those ancient ones at the end.'

I helped him steady his canvas as he tightened the easel. 'I hear from Minty you have friends in common?'

'Yes,' he beamed. 'When I told Mummy who was here this week she knew all about the Froglan-Home-Mybridges.'

'Has she met them?'

'No but apparently they're some sort of cousins with my godmother. Once we established that, we tied up connections left right and centre.'

'How amusing.'

'It's funny, isn't it. Like you bumping into your friend last night. Small world.'

I fell silent. So far today I'd managed to block Toby out of my mind. But now, thanks to Giles, I began to dread his turning up tonight. The only incy wincy consolation is he hasn't been invited to dinner.

'Susie, how long do we have?'

'At least a couple of hours if the weather holds.'

I set off back towards the house.

'All right, Shane? Nice spot here on the paving.'

'Yes. All good, thanks, Miss.'

Minty was next, hovering by the fountain yet to put her easel up.

'Have you decided what you're going to paint?'

'The fountain. But I don't want to paint so I'm going to do a pen and ink wash drawing instead.'

'What a nice idea. In sepia?'

'Yes. I think the brown will work brilliantly with the stone.'

'Would you like me to help you set up?'

'No, I'll be all right, thanks.'

'You won't mind if I disappear for a bit, will you?'

'Where to?'

'I have to take my car to the garage.'

'What a bore for you. I hope it goes okay.'

'Thanks. See you later.'

Rupert, Jane and Felicity were gathered in a little trio on the top step of the house; goodness knows what their plan was.

'We're all going to paint the Beinn Eighe hills,' came a rush of enthusiasm from Felicity and Rupert.

'Can you see them clearly enough?'

'I think so, come up here and look for yourself.'

'Just.'

Jane was leaning against the wall with a frown on her face.

'Are you on board with this?'

'Well,' she said, '*I* was under the impression we'd be

painting landscapes and, without putting too fine a point on it, the garden is *not* a landscape.'

'You could join Giles down there and paint a picture of the field.'

'I'm fine here,' said Felicity. 'I'm going to paint the sky.'

'Jane?' I wanted to make her happy again.

'What?'

'Why not head down the end of the garden? There's a very nice view of some old oak trees.'

She looked at Felicity, who encouraged her to go. So, with Jane carrying her basket and me carrying her easel and canvas, we stomped across the lawns to join Giles.

'You're right,' she said. 'That *is* a pretty scene.'

'And I bet you'll do a good picture.'

'I hope so as it'll be my last.'

I felt winded. Was she giving up for good?

'What about tomorrow,' I said, 'and Friday?'

'I'm trying to change my flight. A week up here is such a long time and, just between us, I'm ready to go home.'

'Oh no, I'm sorry.'

'Not your fault, Susie. I've enjoyed it enough to be glad I came.'

'There are only two more days.'

'I've made up my mind, so don't try and persuade me otherwise.' Her firm expression said it all: this woman was not for turning.

'Haven't *you* heard there's more snow on the way?' she said, and I realised since being here it hadn't once crossed my mind to check the weather.

We're in Scotland. Time's only wasted looking up the forecast. Rain, sun, wind and (at this time of year) snow will all be on their way, interchangeable and wholly unpredictable. Not that natives take this attitude. *Every* Scottish household swears by a different weather app, and each time you visit they'll have discovered another. Always assuming it's better, rather than none of them being any good.

'I assure you there's more snow on the way,' she said. 'I should think you'll all be leaving early.'

Jane had one thing right: there's no way we'd ever be leaving late. For, as a visitor to a Scottish seat, lingering isn't an option. Just look at the efficiency with which the Muchtons addressed my flat tyre. If bad weather looms, I have no doubt they, like others of their sort, will have an array of strings to pull. You see, Scottish gentry are as good at filling their houses as they are at emptying them. Come Friday night, Auchen Laggan Tosh will have waved us goodbye. There's no such thing round here as outstaying your welcome. Invitations in advance give the dates, and most couples, however much they look forward to their friends arriving, always look forward to their departing more. You'll know this if you've experienced a north-of-the-border goodbye. The host family line up on the lawn in front of their house and frantically wave handkerchiefs as you sail down the drive. Then the moment before you lose them in your rear-view mirror, there's a mad performance as with outstretched arms they swoop around each other loop-the-looping, almost as if in celebration of your departure. There's nothing Scots enjoy more than having their 'hoose to themselves'.

I watched Jane wipe a rag across her palette, making doubly sure it was as it looked – clean.

'Are you happy painting here this afternoon?'

'Oh yes. I can manage one more stint, Susie. You can leave me now. Thank you.'

'Great.'

I turned and saw Louis, some distance away, pointing his camera straight at me. I rushed towards him. 'Oi,' I pushed my hand against his lens.

'We've got to have a picture of the tutor for Zoe.'

'Very funny, but there's no way to tell I'm a tutor.'

'You're Susie Mahl, everyone knows the great artist Susie Mahl.'

'I wish,' I said with a smile. 'Do you mind being in charge for a bit? I have to take my car to the garage. I won't be long.'

'Très bien.' Louis blew me a kiss and off I went, breaking into a slow jog round the side of the house.

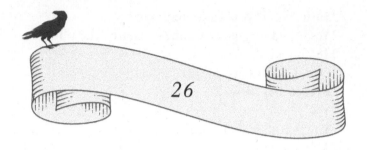

26

Bzzzz, my mobile vibrated. Four bars of reception just beyond the end of the Muchtons' drive. What a surprise. I was not expecting that.

Desperate to know who had been in touch – I'm more a letter-writer than a telephone-chatterer – I pulled over into a passing place.

1 new message Toby Cropper.

I slid my thumb across the screen and deleted it. Why would I want to read a message from Toby? He'd done enough meddling with my mood. I could not stand any more.

But, now I have reception, I think I'll give Dad a call. I know Mum will be out playing bridge and I want to ask him about ravens, so here goes.

Bring bring. Bring bring. Bring bring. Bring bring. Bring bring. Bring bring. It cut out.

I called back. *Bring bring.*

'Hello?'

'Dad.'

'Susie, was it you a moment ago?'

'Yes, I had to give you time to get to the phone.'

He chuckled.

'Dad, I don't have long…'

'Everything okay?'

'Yes.'

'Your mother will want to know.'

'All's good but let's keep this between us. I can fill her in at Easter. I want to know about Alec Ronaldsay.'

'*The* Alec Ronaldsay? Don't tell me you've met him? I wish I was with you right now.'

Dad loves anything to do with birds. Ronaldsay's a hero of his.

'I haven't met him but I need to know if he lives near here.'

'I'm not entirely sure where you are, dear.'

'Auchen Laggan Tosh.'

'Well, if Blah-di-Blah Tosh is anywhere near the river Trickle then yes, he certainly does.'

'Dad, I knew you'd know.'

'That all, love?'

'What can you tell me about ravens swarming?'

'How much time do you have?'

'Not much.'

'In that case let's save it for when we see you. I can't possibly cut my explanation short.'

'Okay, Dad.'

Learning about ravens isn't a key priority right now.

'See you Saturday, Susie. Bye.'

I rang off and got going. Mike's Motors was, as Mhàiri had told me, fifteen minutes from the end of the back drive. It was all alone, set back from the road. No houses and no sign of a village nearby. The makeshift reception was bolted onto the end of the garage and the bell on the entrance door tinged as I stepped inside.

'Afternoon,' said a sturdy little man. 'Nice of yous to come.' He wiped his brow with a very dirty sleeve and, leaving a great smudge of grease behind, he stuck out his hand. 'Mike.'

'Hello,' I said, not knowing what to do other than grasp hold of his grubby mitt.

'I've got the van round the back, all ready to go. New brake pads and all. It won't let yous down. Only twelve thousand miles on the clock. Yous must return it here, though.'

'I think there's a misunderstanding. I've come to see if you can fit a new tyre on my car.'

'Deerie deerie me. Thought yous were the woman hiring the Ford Transit. Said she'd be in to collect it this afternoon. Was certain I'd miss her so said I'd leave the keys round the back but then yous arrived. Not often I get a lady in here.' Mike slapped his own hand. 'Silly me ey.'

What a trustworthy place Scotland is; to leave keys and a hire van without feeling the need to meet the hirer is…staggering.

'Rightie ho then, what was it you're after?'

'A new tyre on my car if you can.'

We went out the front. Mike repeated our conversation to himself under his breath as he bent down to take a look at my tyre.

'Should nee be a problem. Got just the right yun round the back. Mind and drive round that wee corner there and I'll fit it the noo.'

Behind the garage was a large concreted yard and as I navigated bits of rubber, plastic-bottle tops and old pieces of gutter, Mike guided me between a silver van and three shabby cars parked nose to tail.

'Right yous are then,' he said, giving me an unnecessary though thoughtful hand out of the driver's seat.

'It should nee take me long. Yous in a hurry?'

'Not really.'

'Is that a yes or a no?' He winked at me. 'Where are yous headed?'

'I'm tutoring an art course at Auchen Laggan Tosh.'

'Wee the Muchtons?'

'Yes.'

'Aye, I heard they were doing all sorts up there. Some gud, some bad.'

'Really?'

'They're all at it. Raking in the money no matter whit.'

'Such as?'

'Not nice for the community. Divides people, yous ken.'

This was very much a one-way conversation...

'I'm not saying I condone whit he did.'

'Who did?'

'No, no, it was definitely bad whit he did.'

'Isn't it terrible when people fall out?'

'Oh aye. It's the worst. Yous have to keep the community on side.'

Finally, I had a rapport.

'It's selfish if not.'

'Shell fish? No, no, it's birds not fish.'

Mike plonked my spare tyre in the boot.

'So yous was saying it's art yous are doing?'

'Yes, it's a week of painting and drawing.'

'Oh aye, the lad Ewen's an artist I seem to remember.'

'Yes, he is.'

'To be sure with yous I can never work out which is Ewen and which is Fergus. They look affuy alike that pair.'

Mike dipped into the garage and reappeared rolling a shiny new tyre.

'This yun okay for yous?' he asked, nodding at me.

'It looks great.'

'I've only ever been to the big hoose once. Not in it, mind you. It's a stonking great thing, ain't it?'

'Yes, it's a lovely place.'

'Yous friends of theirs?'

'No, I'm just the tutor for the week.'

'Thank my lucky socks. I should nee have loosened my tongue. Yous a good girl, you won't tell them whit I said.'

I smiled but he wasn't watching, too busy tightening the wheel bolts to the tyre.

'That's a lovely job yous have, yous must be happy like me. Life's too short to do something you dinee want to.'

'I agree.'

'No, this ain't free.'

'No, no, I was saying I agree.'

'Acht youse English. There you go, lassie.' Mike lowered my car off the jack. 'All done fer yous.'

'Thank you very much.'

'On yous go and take it back round the front. I'll meet yous at reception.'

If I was going to get a puncture anywhere, here was the place to get it. A new tyre in Scotland was half the price of down south, and with a grateful 'Thank yous' from Mike for my payment I was back at Auchen Laggan Tosh in time to catch the last hour of class.

'Hi Minty, where's Louis?'

'I don't know, he was taking photographs earlier but he's actually been gone a while.'

Drat, I'd left *him* in charge. I bet he's gone to see Ewen. Say goodbye before he leaves.

'Oh well.' I walked up to her easel. 'Your picture's really lovely.'

'Do you like it?' She stood back.

'It's very accomplished. Have you ever tried glazing in oils?'

'The old-fashioned method?'

'Yes, the one where you build up a tonal scene and then wash very thin paint over it.'

'No, but I'd love to try. Maybe you could give us a lesson tomorrow?'

'What a good idea. I'll see what I can do.'

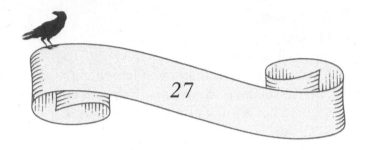

27

'Susie,' said Zoe as I emerged from the basement. I'd
been down dropping my outdoor kit in the drying
room.

'May I have a word?' Her finger curled as she called
me into the sitting room. 'Shut the door,' she said,
gaining the upper hand.

Oh crumbs, is she holding the art valuer's visit against
me?

The fire was crackling, the curtains had been drawn
and Zoe motioned for me to sit down. Yikes, she isn't
going to confront me about Louis, is she?

'Would you like a drink, Susie? I'm not going to have
one but I'm sure you could do with one to warm you
up.'

'You're right. Yes please, a little bit of whisky would
go down well.' I was grateful for something to settle my
nerves.

'Here you go then.' She handed me a glass. 'Now, I
really wanted to ask you...' She paused, took in a huge
breath and the words 'How do *you* think the week is
going?' rushed out of her.

'Really well.'

'Honestly?'

'Yes. Well, at least I think so.'

'That's exactly it.' Zoe lowered herself onto the sofa. 'It's unlike anything we've done here before. I, we've, never had a house full for this length of time, at least not one like this.'

'Like this?'

'Paying guests. Strangers. People one can't relate to.' Zoe took in another deep breath and I wondered where her parochial attitude had suddenly come from.

'Shooting parties and day courses work well, one knows the type. No one stays the night and the house becomes ours again at the end of the day. The problem I'm finding this week is keeping a balance between us and them.'

Zoe, much like Jane, seemed to be fed up of having people around her. But, if the Muchtons see Auchen Laggan Tosh as something to share, she's going to have to get used to life like this.

'Do you mean you're struggling to make everyone feel at home without becoming overfamiliar?'

Zoe had been so friendly to me on day one: as I'd said to Mhàiri, 'Zoe couldn't be more welcoming.' And she'd said, 'All right for some.' But as the week progressed Zoe's character had grown cold.

'Yes,' she said. 'I thought it was going so well, until today. But I've obviously been too much Madame and not enough Mum.'

'What's happened?'

'Jane's trying to leave.'

'I know.'

'*Why* didn't you tell me?' Zoe's face looked almost comical with a frown.

'I've only just heard. I would have told you. Honestly.'

She seemed to believe me, and we moved on. 'It upsets me desperately,' she said as her shoulders fell. 'I feel I'm wholly responsible for her having to share a room.'

'Don't worry about it. I promise you this week is going really well.' Then realising how unintentionally conceited this sounded I added, 'You've organised and put on a brilliant course.'

'Really?'

'Yes,' I smiled.

'Why is she leaving then?'

Hmmm, I had to answer carefully. I didn't want to suggest Jane was missing her personal space as I didn't want Zoe to blame herself.

'Some people like to do exactly what suits them. Jane I'm sure has enjoyed her time here, but having decided she's had enough, she now wants to leave.'

'Should we let her?'

'I think you have to.'

Zoe smiled at her mistake. 'Yes, of course you're right, it's not like I can keep her here.'

Her frown deepened. 'Will she expect to be reimbursed?'

'No, I shouldn't think so.'

Immense relief swept across Zoe's face and the mood in the room lifted just like that.

'How are you getting on with your picture of Haggis? Don't worry if you haven't found the time.'

'I should have mentioned it. I will definitely have a

drawing for you but I'd like to complete it at home, if that's okay. I've got a sketch and some photographs to work from.'

'Oh goodie. He is such an adorable little boy, my Haggis.'

'Yes, he is a sweet dog.'

Zoe stood up. 'There are drop scones in the dining room for tea if you'd like?'

'How delicious.'

'Come on then.' She flung the sitting room door open.

Louis was sitting at the bottom of the stairs.

'Hello there,' she said, 'do you have some photographs for me?'

'Yes, I do.'

'Wonderful. Let's all have a look then?'

'I'd rather sort through them first.'

'You artists are so closeted with your work.' Zoe looked at me and then back at Louis. 'Fair enough if you must, but do please come and have some tea.'

We were paraded into the dining room.

'Have a pancake, Susie,' shouted Lianne, shunting a plate my way.

'Thanks.' I took one and passed them on.

'They're called drop scones north of the border,' said Rupert.

'Squished scone would be better,' said Shane, and Felicity laughed.

'Rupert,' he said, 'if you're so good at Scottish, tell us some more.'

'Well, firstly you say *scotch* and if you look out of that window you'll see spiky green bushes with yellow buds.'

'Yes.'

'Tell me what you'd call them.'

'Never seen one in my life.'

'Gorse,' said Giles. 'That's a gorse bush.'

'Course?' said Shane.

'No, *g*-orse.'

'In Scotland,' said Rupert, 'they're known as whin. Like win with an h.'

'That's a fat lot of use,' said Lianne. 'Give us a word we'd use.'

'Zoe taught us baps,' said Felicity and Lianne's chest wobbled and wobbled as she tried to suppress a laugh.

'Sitooterie,' said Fergus.

'Conservatory,' translated Zoe.

'That's brilliant,' said Minty.

'Why don't you and Fergus have a Scottish accent?' said Shane.

'Scotch,' corrected Rupert.

'I'm English,' said Zoe.

'And Fergus?'

'He lost it when he went to boarding school.'

'On the way there or the way back?'

Even Jane laughed at this.

'There'll be no mistaking his roots tonight,' said Zoe.

'So he'll be in a kilt?' said Minty.

'Full rigmarole.'

'I wish I had an outfit to wear,' mumbled Felicity.

Lianne smiled at me, confident she had a dress for the evening.

'I could dig some things out if you'd like a swatch?'

'Swatch?' said Shane.

'A touch of tartan,' said Zoe.

'Can I have one too?'

'I might *even* be able to find you a kilt.'

Giles chortled. 'I'd love to see you in a skirt.'

'You might just,' said Shane, looking hopefully at Zoe.

'Let's go and have a look then.' Up she got. 'Anyone else want to come?'

'I will,' said Minty.

'And me,' said Rupert.

Felicity and Lianne joined in too.

Naturally the Muchtons have a bounty of Scots dress. Most heads of families do. A stash of gear ready and waiting to share when engagements are announced. The family-tartan kilts, jabots and shiny buckle shoes all handed down the lineage of eldest sons, with the unspoken prerequisite they are shared with other family members when occasions arise.

If you can picture a wedding snap of a landed Scottish family, you'll recall the distinctive dress of the page boys. This outfit isn't made especially for those ones, rather it comes out of a cupboard at the main house smelling of moth balls, having been donned at everyone's wedding. The same goes for tiaras – at times known to cause a scuffle if the bride's family own one too. Quite simply the largest is chosen, but this in itself can cause offence.

With fewer people in the dining room I chose my moment to ask Jane if she'd managed to change her flight.

'You're *leaving*,' exclaimed Giles as if he cared.

'I'm considering it,' said Jane with her nose in the air. She didn't wish to discuss the matter.

'Think I'm going to have a rest.' Louis got up and left the room.

'Me too,' said Jane.

Mhàiri burst through the swing door, prompting Giles's departure. Her rough hands were clasped round a tray and I immediately got up to help.

'You're a good lass, Susie.'

'We're being spoilt here. It's the least I can do.'

Mhàiri grinned a great big yellow-toothed grin. 'Are yous looking forward to the ceilidh the night?'

'Enormously.'

'You'll all enjoy it no doubt.'

'Have they done it here before?'

'This'll be Zoe and Fergus's first. But the elder generation they were always at it.'

Mhàiri' s tray was now full. 'Here,' I said, 'let me get the door.'

'Thanks.'

Together we stacked the dishwasher and once done Mhàiri rested her cushioned behind against the counter and asked me how the course was going. She wanted to have a bit of a chat.

'It's going well, I think.'

'Yous like teaching, do yous?'

'Yes, but I wouldn't like to do it all the time.'

'Ever done it afore?'

'No, but I am enjoying this week. Partly for the teaching but partly because I like meeting new people, getting to know them, learning about who they are, you know.'

'I certainly do.' Her eyes sparkled and she lowered her voice. 'There's an awful lot yous can learn about folk from what they bring in their suitcase.'

I could feel myself cowering with embarrassment at the misconnection. I certainly didn't mean spying on people – if that's what she was getting at. For me, going through people's belongings is an absolute no no, unless of course it's reading a letter left lying around. Or looking in a case on which I've stubbed my toe. This, one could justify, but not the other.

'The Frenchman ain't brought much with him,' she began, 'doesn't have a stable woman in his life, I can tell that. If he did, with her example he'd have hung his clothes in the wardrobe for sure. But nope. They've been in his bag fer the day he arrived.'

I was unable to stop her drawing conclusions from people's belongings; this cook-cum-daily was in full flow and on she went without a pause for breath. 'That, what's he called, Little Lord *Font-le-Roy* has his entire wardrobe ironed, briefs, socks, hankies and all. That rake of a lass, she's got a stash of pills in her spongebag, and as for the other yun, oh my, her underwear, yous ain't seen anything like it.'

Mhàiri used the tea towel over her shoulder to wipe a bead of sweat off her top lip. With a bucketful of trepidation I asked, 'What have you learnt about *me?*'

'Not you, pet. There's a trust between staff. I would nee go searching your room over my dead body.'

I was too alarmed by the thought to smile and when Mhàiri crossed the kitchen to check no one was listening through the door, I really did think, oh heck, what's coming next...

Her whole body was shaking with anticipation. 'Just yous wait and see what that lady Jane's bringing out the night. Quite something buried in her suitcase. Nearly fainted when I found it.'

'How thrilling,' I said, *only* to be nice. A line had been crossed and I absolutely did not want to hear any more. But Mhàiri was shuffling towards me and when she reached up on tiptoes and whispered, 'Diamonds,' in my ear, I actually thought her pupils might pop out onto the kitchen floor. Her eyes stretched to their absolute max and then snapped shut. 'I ain't telling yous any more.'

'Okey dokey,' I said with a smile as inside I let out a huge sigh of relief. 'See you later, Mhàiri, I'd better go and get brushed up for the evening.'

'I'm looking forward to seeing your outfit.' She grinned and turned to the sink.

I burst out the swing door. Although I love to work people out, there are lines you don't cross and gossiping is one of them. It makes me feel low, guilty and horrible all at once. I must not expose myself to that again. It's time to keep a little distance from the kitchen.

'Susie,' said Felicity as I reached the top of the staircase. 'Don't you want some tartan too?'

'Yeah,' said Shane, who was extracting plastic-wrapped bundles from a landing cupboard under Zoe's instruction.

'Behind these we'll get to the clothes, I'm sure,' she was saying through a musty cloud of unsettled dust.

'We'd better,' joked Rupert. 'It's the fourth place we've tried. Susie?'

'I'm going to leave you to it. I don't want to spoil the outfit surprise.'

Down the children's corridor I went, joining the queue for the bath. Next in line after Lianne, whom I could hear singing, 'It's all so beautiful', through my bedroom wall.

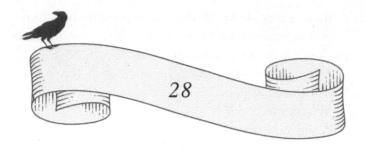

28

The drawing room was jolly chilly, even with a fire glowing at one end. I was late to the party. Everyone other than Fergus and Shane were here.

'I thought it a good idea to use this room,' said Zoe, holding court – an easy thing to do in a puffy ball gown. 'Gives us space to move around in our dresses.'

She looked lovely and the tartan sash, pinned over one shoulder with a Celtic brooch, was uncharacteristically elegant for Zoe.

'Susie would fit in anywhere,' said Louis, admiring my figure-hugging velvet number. I took a huge sip from my glass of wine; his attention was making me nervous.

'You do look lovely,' said Lianne and I returned the compliment.

'I envy your figure,' said Felicity and looking back at her I tried not to stare. The pleats of her skirt were inevitably falling unevenly over her waist.

'Where's Haggis?'

'He's safely tucked away in our room,' smiled Zoe. 'He'd only trip us up when the dancing begins.'

Shane entered and all the attention turned to him.

Lianne burst into a fit of giggles. 'Suits you that skirt,' she just about managed to splutter.

'Very comfortable too,' he said, showing off the Muchton tartan.

'What's under it?'

'A gigantic surprise.'

Lianne laughed again and Fergus entered.

'Oh my, oh my,' said Zoe at her husband.

'Three cheers for the host,' said Rupert, raising his glass.

'Talk us through your outfit, please, Fergus.' Felicity wanted to hear it top to bottom.

'First, though, darling, you'll *never* believe what I found.' Fergus went to whisper in his wife's ear.

'*Diamonds*,' she exclaimed, unable to keep the words in her mouth.

Jane bolted out of the door. I think she's suddenly remembered the ones Mhàiri mentioned.

Fergus gave Zoe a look as if to say, 'Don't mention any more.'

'Please talk us through your outfit,' begged Felicity again.

'As he pinched my trews,' Fergus said, looking across the room.

'They fit perfectly,' said Rupert, pulling at the waist.

Shane pointed at Fergus's left calf. 'What's that in your sock?'

'Let *him* talk us through the whole caboodle,' interrupted Minty.

Fergus beamed and as his hips swung the pleats of his kilt, he began to explain. 'This was my great-grandfather's. Worn ones always look nicer. My black jacket is called a Prince Charlie and is donned for formal occasions.' Fergus turned around, and pulled at the tails. 'These are short, which tells you it's for the evening.'

Zoe stepped forwards and stroked his sporran. 'Do tell them about this.'

'Ah,' said Fergus, flapping the fur bulge at his crotch, 'Donald made it for me. It's a squirrel.'

'Did *you* shoot it?' said Giles.

'Yes. Aged twelve.'

'Oh no, no, no, no, no,' said Lianne with her hands over her face.

'Don't worry,' said Fergus. 'It was grey not red.'

'Congratulations,' said Rupert. 'They're more like rats than squirrels.'

'May I touch it?' said Felicity.

'Of course.' Fergus held out his fur for all of us to feel.

Jane bustled her way back into the room. I looked her up and down – she wasn't wearing any diamonds.

'I like that dagger in your sock,' said Giles and Shane's face lit up.

'It's called a sgian-dubh.'

'Skee-en-DOO,' said Zoe.

'Can I have a look?' said Shane.

'No, no,' said Jane, 'it's terribly bad luck if he takes it out.'

I wondered how Fergus got it in his sock without taking it out but I suppose she meant the sheath not the blade.

'Sorry, Shane,' he said, probably thinking it would be

too risky to hand around. 'Just quickly, two other things worth mentioning are my kilt pin, basically a large nappy pin put here at the bottom corner of the kilt to stop it blowing up in the wind, and my shoes...'

'They must be Zoe's,' said Giles much to everyone's amusement.

'Their patent leather and silver buckles are pretty fancy for a man but they are wonderful for dancing in.'

'No doubt we'll judge that later,' said Jane, remarkably enthusiastic for someone who barely hours ago was all set to leave.

'*My* shoes are the best,' said Zoe, stretching a foot out from under her ball gown. 'They're officially called ghillies but really they're just soft black ballet shoes with tight laces tied up my ankle.'

Minty crouched down from the great height of her quivering stilettos. 'They're even nicer than the ones my friend has.'

The circle broke up and I turned to Louis. 'That's a nice waistcoat.'

'Soft green velvet, it goes with your dress.' He stroked my shoulder and I felt my face go hot.

'Angel,' said Zoe, 'I think we should eat.'

'Yes, come on then. The haggis, neeps and tatties will be waiting. Rupert, will you bring the wine, and Giles, put the guard in front of the fire, will you please?'

Zoe led the way to the dining room; no one hesitated about where to sit. We all plonked ourselves down in order and I ended up perfectly happily between Fergus and Giles. Lianne, Zoe and Rupert served the food and when a plate was put in front of him Shane exclaimed,

'Yuk.'

'Oi, don't be so rude,' said Giles.

'But it looks like a nutty turd.'

'Now you've spoilt it for all of us,' said Lianne.

'Why don't you just try it?' encouraged Zoe. 'You might be surprised.'

Shane put the tiniest amount on his fork and we all watched as he pushed it between his reluctant-to-open lips.

'Maybe it's not so bad.' He gave a massive smile.

'Well, if you like it that much,' said Minty, 'you can have a bit of mine.'

'No thanks.'

'You don't have to eat it all,' said Fergus. 'Just leave what you don't want, and we'll feed it to the namesake.'

'He won't get any from me,' said Rupert.

'Me neither,' said Felicity.

'Or Louis,' I teased. 'The French love offal.'

'Too true.' He beamed at me across the table and I wondered if we'd have another kiss tonight.

I quite like eating haggis once every five years and it's amusing that Zoe and Fergus are feeding it to us tonight. They're trying their best to give a Scottish experience and, as naff as it is, it adds to the occasion.

I looked across at Jane sitting on Fergus's right and when I overheard her say, 'You are fortunate to have help spanning two generations,' I leant in to hear more.

'Aren't we just,' he agreed. 'My parents taught Mhàiri and Donald the ropes and now Zoe and I are reaping the benefits.'

'It is marvellous they're not ambitious,' said Jane. 'My mother always maintained education's dangerous. It makes the likes of country folk want to move on, get up in the world. It's a real bonus for you if the schools are bad round here. It'll keep your staff loyal, you know.'

'I've never looked at it like that. But I do worry for our children before they're old enough to board.'

'You mustn't,' said Jane. 'The sophistication of life here combined with a little bit of,' she lowered her voice, '*nepotism*,' and raised it again, 'will see them sail through Common Entrance.'

'I do hope so.'

I'm rather surprised by Jane's sudden will to engage. It's not like she's made much of an effort to chat to the Muchtons before. But here, now, although I completely disagree with what she's saying, it's made me happy to see her in a good mood. It's almost as if a huge weight has lifted off her mind. Most likely she's managed to rearrange her flight and is in better spirits knowing this is her last night.

She complimented Fergus on his library and tucked into her food.

'Do you like reading, Susie?' Fergus asked.

'Yes, very much.'

'I try, but it tends to send me to sleep.'

'Very helpful in the right circumstances.'

'Indeed.' He looked at my empty plate. 'Would you like some more?'

'*Angel*,' called Zoe with an eye on his actions. 'I'm afraid we've started to clear. We mustn't let dinner drag on.'

'No, of course not. Here, let me help.'

The main course plates were stacked and steam pudding arrived to the delight of all. The whisky cream to drizzle on top looked particularly delicious, and if I were Mhàiri I would have made an extra portion to guzzle in the kitchen.

Felicity licked her lips. 'Mmm, mmm, such rich food you have here.'

'Like how much?' said Shane.

'Rich as in creamy. *Duh*,' said Lianne.

The swing door opened and in rushed Mhàiri. She whispered something in Fergus's ear.

'Susie,' he said. 'That'll probably be your friend.'

My heart jumped. Friend, yeah right. We both got up and left the room.

In the hall, filling more than his fair share of it, was a pot-bellied man with a bright red face.

'Davy?' said Fergus.

'Aye. Nice to meet you, Sir.' He shoved out his right hand. 'And you, Madam,' Davy nodded; he hadn't mistaken me for Zoe.

'Welcome,' said Fergus.

'I hoped to be here a bit earlier but we got caught up on your drive with a van. Had to reverse back, never an easy thing to do in the dark.'

'On *our* drive?' said Fergus, a little surprised.

'Aye.'

'How strange. Did you come up the front or the back?'

'It had a cottage a wee way up it.'

'Ah yes, the back. It must have been my brother. Now, Susie, would you mind showing Davy to the music room and I'll go and let Zoe know the band's arrived.'

'Of course.' I looked at Davy. 'Would you like me to carry anything?'

'No. I've got my accordion in here, and let me just give the others a wee shoot. They're a bit timid of a big hoose like this.'

Davy stuck his head outside and back with it came a girl tripping through the front door, violin case in one hand and a battery pack in the other.

'This is me daughter, Rosie.'

'Hi, I'm Susie, nice to meet you. Here, let me carry something.' She handed me the battery. 'We'll put this all in the music room, follow me.'

'It's humungous,' said Davy as we entered.

'It gets bigger,' I said. 'Would you mind helping me pull back the folding door?'

'That yun down there?'

'Yes.'

'A few of you here then?'

'Twelve in total.'

'You ken the reels?'

'I've done a bit before but not sure I remember them. We're all from the south so you'll have to talk us through it.'

'Aye, I thought so from your accent but you canee be too sure in a hoose like this.'

'Dad,' said Rosie, 'shall I go get the speakers? I think Jimmy needs a hand.'

'Aye, Rosie, go fetch him.'

Davy spun three hundred and sixty degrees on the heel of his buckled shoe. 'Quite a place they've got here.

Friends of the Muchtons, are you?'

'Not officially; there's a group of us on an art residency for the week. I'm the tutor.'

'Having fun, are you?'

'Yes, it's been great.'

Zoe came into the room and shook Davy's hand. 'Hello, nice to meet you. I'm Zoe. Is there anything you need?'

'No, you're fine. My wains will be here in a moment. They've got the rest of the kit. Give us ten minutes or so and we'll be ready for you.'

Zoe left and I hovered around to 'help'.

'So,' I said with a carefree breath, 'what was this van like you saw?'

'It was a silver Transit, you ken. Wasn't expecting that. Must have been lost.'

It sounded very like the one I'd seen in Mike's yard.

'Were there people in it?'

'Aye, just one and we were only late because I didn't want to have to make the lady reverse.'

'A woman was driving it?'

'Aye. That's why it would be in a muddle.'

I feigned a smile. I see no point in rising to comments like this, but, you would have to be a real fool to take a wrong turn off a tarmac road onto what could hardly be described as more than a track. And if Ewen's away, what was this woman doing? Very odd.

Davy's head turned to the door. 'Jimmy, this is Susie; Susie, Jimmy. Right, come on you pair, where shall we set up?'

Rosie and Jimmy looked a similar age, late teens I'd

say, their spotty faces and lack of a smile giving that away.

'Do you need any more help from me?'

'No thanks,' said Davy, 'just pass on to the host, five minutes and we'll be ready for you all.'

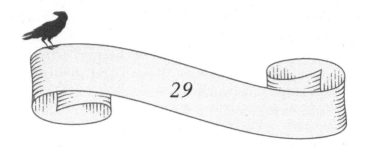

29

Dancing pairs were being drawn when the doorbell rang and Fergus rushed out of the drawing room. Toby had arrived. I was embarrassed – he was late.

'You're just in time, son,' said Davy as he and Fergus entered the room. 'Better get yourself a partner. I'm about to give a wee demonstration of the Gay Gordons.'

Jane looked astounded.

I've reeled a bit in the past and know enough to be privy to the snobbery of it all. There are a handful of easy-peasy fling-your-partner-around-the-room dances known to cause upper (class) lips to curl, Gay Gordons being one of them. But Fergus had asked Davy to choose the reels, saying he and Zoe would keep out of it.

With Toby's arrival numbers were now even, and Fergus, leaving no time for the rest of us to say hello, pushed him in Jane's general direction. She had to join in now.

Toby managed to grin momentarily as he moved past me and I gave a slight nod hello.

'Right you are then.' Davy put down his accordion, grasped hold of Zoe, and the demonstration began.

'That way, this way, no, this way, yes, that way…' This great big jolly man shouted out the steps and, good on Zoe, she threw herself into it. Davy's beer belly brushed against her midriff as they skipped and twirled and twisted around the room.

'That looks easy,' said Lianne smiling at Shane, as Louis, my partner, took my hand.

The music began and backwards and forwards we kicked out our legs in one giant circle.

'FORWARDS FOR THREE, SWIVEL, BACK-WARDS FOR THREE,' Davy shouted enthusiastically over the din. 'Hold your partner, that's it, step, hop, step, hop.'

The great thing about Highland music is the way the chords repeat themselves over and over, and as long as you can jump up and down while wiggling your body, you get away with looking like you know what you're doing.

But Louis was struggling, inhibition getting in the way. Every time I tried to speed up the twirling, get him to twist his arms over my head, he'd retaliate and stiffen up.

'Is something wrong?' I whispered and he looked at me as if I'd gone mad.

Jimmy and Rosie's bows were moving at a tremendous speed as they played along to their father's lead. I wonder if this is how they like to spend a Wednesday night?

The music reached a crescendo and cut out, the speaker crackled and Giles led us all in a round of applause.

'Louis?' I said before we parted.

'Yes?'

'What's up?'

'That was great. Thanks for being my partner.' He kissed me on the cheek and drew away.

'You weren't very relaxed.' I tugged on his arm.

'Ouch.'

'Sorry, are you okay?'

'Just pulled a muscle and it really hurts.'

'During the reel?'

'No,' he laughed. 'But I hadn't noticed it before.'

'That wasn't so hard,' said Felicity, bustling between us.

'It was embarrassing,' said Minty.

'It was a little,' said Rupert.

'Strip the Willow's next,' said Davy and brilliantly Shane asked me to dance. So far, I'd avoided having to even speak to Toby.

Jane took Fergus's hand at the top of the set and we were told that, as this reel involved only one couple dancing at a time, 'it's so easy, you can learn it on the trot'. The music started and Fergus and Jane elegantly swung their way down and back up the line, twisting and turning until we all felt dizzy. When their routine was over, Minty and Giles were next. Both of them had said they'd reeled before and took it upon themselves to demonstrate a sophisticated double-arm manoeuvre. When Shane, my partner, tried to copy, it resulted in the most complicated entanglement. We were literally locked together and to the sound of stamping feet and yodelling we abandoned proceedings and repositioned ourselves at the bottom of the set.

Once everyone had fulfilled their turn Davy suggested an encore, but no one's arms had it in them. 'Let's take a break,' said Zoe, and without waiting for an answer she plonked herself down on a sofa against the wall.

'I'll go and get some drinks,' said Fergus, already one step out the door. 'Back in a sec.'

Toby was coming towards me and when his mouth opened and he said, 'Sorry I was a bit late,' I wished he'd started his apologies many months ago.

'You're here now.'

'Yes.'

'I'm Giles Chesterton,' said Giles, thankfully coming between us.

'Toby Cropper.'

Fergus was back with the drinks and Toby, who has good manners, I'll give him that, offered to help.

'You take the water.' Fergus handed him a jug. 'Rupert's coming with glasses.'

I poured myself a large glass of wine. I need more alcohol to get through this evening.

When the music began again all us girls, other than Jane who was most definitely a woman, kicked off our shoes to the great relief of our heels.

Giles asked me to dance and I disliked myself for wanting to say no. He was dripping with sweat and I felt revolted by the thought I'd get its precipitation when he performed his complex twirling. But, so far, I'd avoided having to dance with Toby and that thought cheered me up.

'Eightsome reel,' said Davy, drawing shut his accordion. 'This one ain't as tricky as it looks. Trust me. My Lord, you must know it, don't you?'

'My Lord?' said Shane. 'Who's he when he's at home?'

'Do call me Fergus,' said Fergus modestly.

'Right ye are. I'm going to play very slowly and you and...' Davy paused.

'Zoe, call me Zoe.'

'...Zoe can walk through the moves showing the others.'

'This calls for a set of only eight people,' said Fergus. 'So, once we've demonstrated, Zoe and I will keep you straight from the side-lines.'

'We'll happily step out too,' said Jane, dragging Rupert with her.

'Okay, perfect. We can always have another go after.'

The demonstration began in slow mode.

'This *is* a difficult one,' said Felicity.

'But it's such a good reel,' said Minty.

'You've done it before?' I smiled.

'Many times. I go to the Highland Ball most seasons.'

'Now that's a marvellous dance,' said Jane, who was hovering *just* outside the set, ready to step in if anyone made a mistake. 'I went several times as a child.'

'Did you grow up in Scotland?' I asked.

'No, my parents had connections here.'

'Here exactly...or generally?'

'Don't be *silly*.' Jane avoided an answer.

Zoe and Fergus left the set and the music began. Round we all went in a circle for ten and back for ten. Jane couldn't help herself shouting out directions, 'SET, set, TURN your partner, SET, set, figure of eight. *Figure of eight.*'

Louis was on my right with his partner Lianne, and when she threw her arms up in the air for a twirl, I was pleased to see him flinch again. He really had pulled a muscle, it wasn't anything to do with me.

The Eightsome reel is a killer if, like me, you're shy at heart. The absolutely worst part comes when you have to stand in the centre of a turning circle, all alone, performing a little jig. Everyone's eyes are on you and the whole ghastly process seems to take an age.

'*In you go, Lianne*,' shouted Jane and the good-time girl burst into uncontrollable giggles. The momentum was lost, the set fell apart and I was unbelievably relieved to have missed my turn.

Davy wasn't going to let us rest. He coaxed his children to speed up the tempo and bellowed at us all to 'TWIRL' and 'CLAP' and 'SPIN' and 'BOUNCE', 'SWAP YOUR PARTNERS ONE TWO THREE.' It was mayhem but surprisingly good fun.

When the music stopped, Louis came and whispered in my ear, 'Save the last dance for me.' I smiled a smile full of joy – only because I thought Toby might be watching.

'Who wants another drink?' said Rupert, offering the bottle of white wine around the room. Rather too at home, I thought.

Louis, Lianne, Shane and Giles went outside to cool off and I glided alone up one end of the room.

'What a place this is,' I heard behind me and turned to meet Toby's sparkling blue eyes.

'Not bad.'

'I've just had a little snoop, pretended I was going to the loo. Kind of thing you'd do.'

I didn't react. It annoyed me he knew me so well.

'They've got some great paintings, haven't they?'

'They do.'

'Come on, Susie, can't we at least have a conversation?'

'Sure.'

'Okay then. Have you looked at the paintings?'

'Fergus gave us a tour.'

'Lucky you. Any particular gems?'

'I'd never seen any Landseer oil sketches before and there are a lot of them upstairs.'

'He used to give them as presents when he went to stay, didn't he?'

Why isn't there *anything* Toby doesn't know? I bet he was a right suck at school. Loser.

'Yes, he did.'

'Well, he must have come here a lot…Perhaps there was something going on?'

'Like what?'

'An affair or something.'

Grrr. This was going all wrong. I had no way out of the conversation.

'He was Fergus's great-aunt's lover.'

'Great-aunt? That would make him about a hundred and thirty-seven years old.'

'Very clever,' I finally smiled. Toby knew his stuff. 'Great-great-great-great-great-aunt then.'

His laugh made me laugh. It was difficult not to. I adore Toby, *had* adored Toby. His blue eyes, his curly hair, his ability to mingle in any company. He liked walking and swimming and cooking and being with me. My heart sank; would I ever find someone as companionable as that?

'Susie,' he said. 'I'm sorry if I've hurt you.'

Wow, an apology, he *has* grown up.

I gave him a sad smile.

'I kind of get the feeling I've hurt you.' He looked pathetic. 'But I don't know why.'

'You don't know *why*?' I was furious.

'No. I sent you a text the other night, and as you didn't reply I thought we were all cool.'

'Well, we're not.' I now regretted deleting his message. From here on in I'm going to have to improvise.

'How can I have done something wrong?' he pleaded. 'We haven't seen each other for ages.'

Tears began welling up inside me. There are so many things he's done wrong. He hasn't written to me; he hasn't been in touch; he hasn't apologised for leading me down the garden path; and to top it off he's come *here* tonight.

'*Yowch*,' came Lianne's cry and without answering Toby I rushed to the door. She was sprawled on the floor, her halter-neck dress struggling to keep her bosoms in check, and as I stretched out an arm, Shane found the whole thing highly amusing.

'Lianne,' said Zoe from the opposite side of the room, 'are you okay?'

'Yeah, thanks.' She got up and slapped Shane on the cheek.

'Time for more dancing,' said Fergus and I caught Louis' eye. But, at the very same time, Toby prodded my back and held out his right hand.

'*No*,' said Louis, striding towards us. 'I've booked Susie for this one.' He squeezed my shoulders and kissed me on the forehead. Crumbs, I kind of wanted to tell po-faced Toby there was nothing serious going on, but a large part of me loved that he was jealous.

Davy announced it would be Dashing White Sergeant, and I felt physically sick. 'You'll need to be in threes for this one,' he explained, 'two gentlemen and a lady, or two ladies and a gentleman.'

'Great,' said Toby with a huge grin. 'Shall we?'

'Sure,' said Louis, rising to the challenge.

Holding hands, me sandwiched between the two of them, the three of us walked into the centre of the room.

'What fun to have a threesome,' said Felicity, who was standing in-between Rupert and Giles.

Toby squeezed my hand and I pretended not to get the joke.

Dashing White Sergeant went on, and on, and on. I could not wait for our ménage à trois to break up. And when Davy finally decided to call it a day and his children's exhausted right arms dropped to their sides, I broke away without saying thanks.

I was headed straight for a seat against the wall but blooming Toby was on my tail and together we sat down side by side.

'I don't think you should trust that man,' he said.

'Louis?'

'Yes, he seems to like you.'

'Nah, he's just a flirt.'

'Exactly, he'll hurt you.'

How dare Toby dole out dating advice. I didn't even look at him let alone respond. What an arrogant so and so he is.

'You were talking about Landseer?' he said. 'His pictures go for a fortune in Canada.'

'Do they?'

'Yes, popular with Canucks who claim they have

Celtic roots. They'd buy anything to bolster their Scottish credentials.'

'But they'd have to have the money to buy Landseer, and anyway the Muchtons never sell their paintings,' I grunted, though my mind was whirling with the idea a Muchton ancestor could have sold two originals to a Canadian.

'I respect that. There must be a lot of family history wrapped up in the collection and you know how I like family history,' Toby smiled.

It annoyed me he'd referred to a conversation we'd had in the past. A conversation at a happy time. All memories with him were trashed in my mind. Toby had walked me down a happy path then dropped me into a lonely unhappy void. Anything we once shared together was now meaningless and made me feel sad.

I stood up. 'I'm tired. I'm going to bed.'

'Well,' he stood up too, 'sleep tight. We must try and meet up again soon.'

Oh my goodness, I wanted to scream my frustration at the top of my voice. Meet up? Soon? Is he joking?

Toby held my shoulders and looked into my watery eyes. 'I've missed you, Susie. Take care of yourself. I hope we can keep being friends.'

Keep being friends. Who says we're friends? Get out of my life.

We kissed goodbye on both cheeks and I dashed upstairs before anyone caught my tears falling.

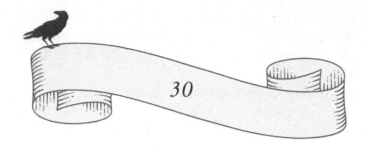

30

Oh God, I wish I could control my emotions. They just love to explode inside me when things aren't going my way and right now they're at an all-time high.

I haven't cried like this for at least a month and look at me now, bundled up in bed bawling my eyes out. Seeing Toby sparked it, but now it's the thought I might be flying solo forever. I don't need my friends around me all the time, I very rarely chat to them on the phone, but I've always wanted to share my life with someone and I had really believed that someone would be Toby.

I'm getting no further away from forty and I'm just as vulnerable as I always was. All my good intentions of abandoning the search for a long-term partner have gone out the window. I'm not suited to short-term flings. The truth is, I long to embark on a monogamous journey, say goodbye to the singles scene. I look forward to the security of a lifelong partner, the bond between two people and the opportunity it holds. Marriage for me is the only way out. I couldn't co-habit or 'go out' with someone for a long time, my religion would rub up against that. But I'd also never sacrifice true love to tick a few boxes. I couldn't get hitched to any old body, he'd have to be the *one*. But this idealistic view leaves me in a miserable place and I've only got myself to blame.

I'm now riddled with downcast thoughts and it's at times like this when I have to try extra hard not to lose my faith. One of the aggravating things about God is he doesn't strike deals. I can't bargain with him, say 'I'll never swear again' in return for something I want. He's tough like that. But if I desert him, omnipresent and all that, I really am alone. I *must* keep my faith however desperate life becomes.

Knock, knock, came through my bedroom door... *Don't* be Toby...

Louis entered uninvited.

'*Please* go away, I'm in bed.'

He flicked on the overhead light.

'Oi, get out.' I pulled the duvet over my head.

'Just wanted to say goodnight. Here, I'll turn off the light.' He bent down and turned on the sidelight instead. 'Susie, what's wrong?'

'I don't want to talk about it.'

'Okay, that's fine. Neither do I. It doesn't look like it'd be much fun.'

I popped my head out of the duvet.

'Come on, sit up, let's have a chat,' Louis smiled. 'In fact, I'm going to go get us a drink. Hang on a sec.'

He left the room and I let out a huff. *Grrr.* I don't want to see *anyone* right now. But I know he's coming back, I have no control over that, so I get up to put on a jumper. While I'm at it, why not apply a bit of concealer too? I might as well try and make myself look nice.

Louis breezed in the door and shut it behind him.

'Here you go.' He placed a whisky and soda on the side table, saying, 'I'll have it if you don't.'

He then kicked off his shoes and lay down on the other end of my bed. The mattress dipped and I actually quite liked the feeling of his legs pushed up against mine.

I took a sip of whisky. 'Thanks for this.'

'I'm good at reading minds, aren't I?'

'And getting into girls' beds.'

He smiled and leant forwards to toast my glass. 'Damn,' he winced as he leant down on his bad arm.

'How did you pull the muscle?'

'I don't know.'

'Yes you do. Don't worry, I won't think you're a fool.'

He raised his glass to his mouth and said nothing – the *vanity*.

I waited for him to talk. I wasn't in the mood to volunteer conversation.

'Where are you going after here?' He felt for my foot under the duvet.

'Home.' I wriggled away.

'Where's that?'

'East Sussex, just north of Brighton.'

'Long way to go.'

'Yeah, but I'd rather do it in a one-er – I need to get back and do some work.'

'Painting?'

'Yup.'

'What?'

'Two landscape commissions for neighbours. It's great, I don't have to travel far. They both want the view of the Downs from their house.'

'Nice job?'

'I'm looking forward to it. I love painting in spring. Then I've got to visit a cat in Dorset, two donkeys in Devon and a terrier in Oxfordshire.'

'No hamsters?'

'Oi.'

'What about Easter? Are you taking time off for that?'

'Rubbish. I'd completely forgot it's this Sunday,' I said, struggling to believe I'd failed to keep track of Easter.

'Well, it does tend to move around.' Louis winked.

'I told my parents I'd go to them.'

'In Sussex?'

'No, London.'

He nudged into my leg. 'Maybe we could meet up? I'm going there on Friday for a week.'

'Really? I thought you lived in Paris?'

'I live in London too. Where are your parents?'

'Kennington.'

'As in *Lambeth*?'

'As in Lambeth.'

'I'm in South Ken so we could meet there?'

I kicked him. 'That's my home you're talking about.'

'Your home is Sussex. Will you see me in London? Please?'

'Depends if my parents have plans.'

'You're right, I should check what my girlfriend's up to.'

'*Girlfriend?*'

'It's sort of on and off.'

'You're so naughty.'

Louis shuffled his bottom up the bed. '*Please* kiss me.'

I pushed him back as he leant towards me. 'You've just told me you have a girlfriend.'

'And?'

'I couldn't do that to her.'

He whined and shuffled back down the bed. 'You must live near Glyndebourne then. Do you ever go?'

'If someone else is generous enough to take me. I love opera.'

'Well, why don't I take you to Covent Garden?'

'On a date?'

'Just two friends.'

'Okay.'

Girlfriend or not, this was too big a treat to turn down.

Louis pulled his mobile out of his pocket. 'Give me your number then?'

I told him my number, adding, 'Text me, don't call me, please.'

'Why?'

'I don't like talking on the phone.'

'Comme tu veux. Although, I kinda like how blunt you are.'

'In that case, Louis,' I yawned, 'I really have to go to sleep.'

'No problem, I'll watch over you.'

I kicked his bottom and he got off the bed.

'Night.' He bent down and kissed my forehead. 'Sleep well.'

'Night, night, thanks for coming to see me.'

He closed the door and I turned out the light. A bit of flirting had cheered me up. I think I should be able to sleep now.

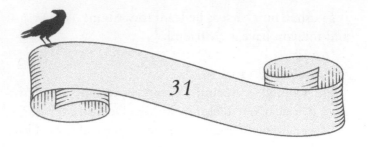

31

My tummy churned from the moment I woke. I'm in need of a hearty breakfast this morning.

Lianne and Shane were arguing in the corridor.

'What's going on? *Hey.* You two.'

'He's a smelly swine.' Lianne was grasping for his mobile.

'Morning, Miss. She doesn't get that it's *art*.'

'What's art?'

'He's got me on video in my PJs. Tell him to delete it. *Please*.'

'Can I see it?'

'Sure.' Shane handed me his mobile without a fight. 'It's a montage of the week. It's for my A Level course work. You can't make me delete it.'

'Yes she can,' said Lianne as I pressed play.

The video began with footage from the fishing hut and the wide shot of Felicity's bottom cut to a back view of Lianne trotting down the children's corridor into the bathroom.

'Jees, my bum is out,' Lianne wailed and before there was time to take in the full cheek of the scene it turned into Haggis jumping up, jaws wide open.

I pressed pause. 'Can we turn the sound up?'

'No, Miss, music's cheating. You get higher marks if you create atmosphere without it. Come on, you have to watch it as a sequence, no stopping.'

A series of split-second interior shots flashed across the screen, we were then outside a full circumference of the house, back inside, a speeded-up ascent of the staircase, and a flash of Louis' grumpy expression transposed with a clip of Mhàiri hoovering. This ended with a spiral effect of drawings and paintings from the week, then the grand finale, a Highland cow's behind.

'Very impressive,' I smiled at Shane.

'Tell him to delete it,' said Lianne. 'He has to.'

'You only show for a split second.'

'But everyone back home will know it's me.'

I looked at Shane. 'Is it easy to edit it out?'

'You're as bad as her, Miss.'

'*Pleeease*,' begged Lianne.

'I think it would be kind.'

'Fine then.'

'Thanks, mate.' She slapped his back and bounced off down the corridor. 'Breakfast time, toast and honey fill my tummy.'

'Shane, can I watch it through one more time?'

'To see Lianne's bum?'

'Don't be silly, I just want to check something out.' I pressed play.

'Oi, why've you stopped it again, Miss?'

I'd paused on the clip of Mhàiri hoovering.

'I think someone's been in my room and I want to see if you caught it on camera.' I thought nothing of being honest with him.

'Cool. Here,' he took his mobile back, 'you can zoom it in…Nah, Miss, you're wrong, no one's there.'

'Move it forward a split second.'

'*Jesus*,' said Shane, holding the screen right up to his face. 'You were right.'

'Let me have a look.'

'It's Jane,' he whispered as he handed me his mobile. 'I bet she was stealing from you.'

'I have nothing to steal,' I smiled.

'But you said someone was in your room?'

'I said I *thought* someone had been in my room.'

It was stupid of me to have told Shane the truth. There was no need for him to know and now he was hot on to Jane.

'I reckon she *was* stealing.'

'No, no, you've got it all wrong. She was just looking for me.'

'Yeah right, but whatever. Do you like my work?'

'It's great and will be even better when you take Lianne out.'

'Okay. I promise I will.'

'That's kind.' I smiled. 'Come on, I'm hungry.'

We went downstairs and Shane barged straight into the dining room before me. Then, in front of everyone, the little rat said, 'There's a thief here.' He pointed at Jane. 'We've got ya on record. There's no denying it.'

Despite the obvious sing-song in his voice, Jane took a hard line. 'Pardon me, young man. How dare you.'

It was embarrassing.

'Shane,' I said, trying to save the situation. 'Don't joke, it's nasty. Here,' I pulled out a chair, 'join me for some toast.'

Rupert, unusually sensitive to the atmosphere for once, made an effort to grab Jane's attention. 'You seemed to know all about reeling etiquette. Very helpful to the rest of us.'

'Oh yes,' she beamed and sailed into a lengthy reply.

'Shane,' I said under my breath, 'you shouldn't have done that.'

'But Miss, *she* started it. Saying I might steal the silver on the first night. I was just getting my own back.'

'She was teasing.'

'And so was I.'

'Okay. I'm sorry, I didn't mean to come down hard on you.'

'I'm going to ask her if she was looking for you. Just to make sure?'

'No,' I snapped, 'that's unfair, please leave it be.'

'Susie,' said Rupert loudly down the table, 'we were just talking about your charming friend.'

'I do hope he enjoyed himself?' said Fergus.

'Yes,' said Zoe with a yawn, 'it was lovely he came.'

'Thank you for having him. I bet he enjoyed it.'

Louis was staring at me, I think he was trying to read my thoughts. I smiled and, to my complete surprise, his lips puckered and pouted and he blew me a kiss. Crumbs, I blushed but I didn't actually care, it was so nice to have Louis here.

'Susie, would you like an egg?' asked Zoe. 'Mhàiri's got some on the boil.'

'Yes please, shall I tell her?'

'No need.' The kitchen door swung open. 'Here she is. Mhàiri, one more egg for Susie please. Shane?'

'Nah thanks.'

'So, Jane,' said Giles. 'Are you leaving today?'

Shane sat up.

'No, I've decided to stay.' She smiled and I wondered if last night's reeling had miraculously spun her into a better mood.

'Oh good,' I said, truly relieved. Jane's departure would have undoubtedly reflected badly on me.

'Well,' said Giles, 'it's so wild outside today, I wonder if *any* of us will make it home tomorrow.'

'I shall,' said Minty. 'Mummy's picking me up.'

'There's no need for the rest of you to worry,' reassured Fergus. 'I'll give Inverness Airport a call, and double-check the flights.'

'Don't worry, angel,' said Zoe, 'I'll do it before lunch.'

'What are we going to be doing today, Susie?' said Minty.

'Learning something new.'

'In the music room?'

'Yes, inside, don't worry.'

Louis sloped off and Rupert took the words out of my thoughts. 'He's a bit jaded this morning. Too much whisky I'll bet.'

'Susie,' said Fergus, 'do you need anything from me this morning?'

An energy bar would be good, I wanted to say, but instead I asked if there were a couple of objects I could borrow for a still life.

'Yes,' said Zoe getting up. 'Let's go and dig out some china.'

We found a sage green jug and a cerulean blue vase and I took them to the music room and arranged them on a high table ready for class.

Zoe popped her head around the door. 'Susie,' she said, 'as everyone's a little tired this morning I've suggested a quick blast of fresh air. Would you like to come?'

I gritted my teeth. Zoe was about to delay my class.

'You don't have to,' she said. 'Jane's staying here but the rest of us are going to brave the elements. Fergus wants to check on how high the river is.'

'I see,' I said, thinking, if Jane's the only one here, I can catch her alone.

I followed Zoe out of the room and into the hall.

'I don't think I'll come if that's okay?'

'Of course, Susie,' she smiled, and flung open the front door. Haggis yelped with excitement at being outside. Everyone else trundled after them, all dressed in wet-weather gear.

As soon as they'd left, I scampered upstairs and knocked on Jane's door.

'Yes?'

'Hi Jane, would you mind if I came in?'

'Why would I mind?'

I stepped into the room and got straight to the point. 'I know Shane spoke out of turn at breakfast, but *I'd* like to know why you were in my room.'

'Was I? I simply can't remember.' She plonked herself down on the bed.

'It was before class on Tuesday morning,' I said, leaving her in no doubt of the exact timing.

'Is *that* what Shane was on about?'

'Yes. What were you up to?' I sat down on the bed opposite, hoping if I settled in she would talk.

'Hmmm…I remember now, I did wander down the children's corridor. Briefly, yes, I spoke to Mhàiri.'

'Why were you down there?'

'That's right, I was looking for you.'

'But you knew I'd gone for a walk with Rupert.'

'Did I?' Her voice was steady but her pursed hands were now trembling.

'Yes, we discussed it at breakfast.'

Silence.

'Why were you in my room?'

She didn't answer.

'Please tell me.'

'There's nothing to tell.'

Her lips tightened. She was getting on my nerves.

'I *don't* believe you,' I said.

'It's none of your business.'

'It is, you were in my room.'

Her head dipped. I think a vulnerable side is surfacing.

'You can trust me, honestly you can,' I said, towing a sympathetic line.

I wanted to get to the truth.

Her expression gave briefly and I leapt in. 'I think you found something under my floorboard. Am I right?'

Bingo, Jane's shoulders slumped; I've almost broken her.

'Have you been here before?' I asked, thinking, why not get all my questions out at once?

'Why are you pushing me like this?' she moaned.

'I don't like to be lied to.'

We had eye contact again.

'I'm not lying.'

'Not answering is as good as lying.' I repeated the question, 'Have you been here before?'

'Yes,' she mumbled and stared at the floor.

Mhàiri was right.

'And you knew there was something hidden in my room?'

Silence.

'Jane?'

She sat up with a second wind. '*Stop* sticking your nose into my business.'

Help, she had a point. Blackmail is now my only option.

'I'm going to speak to Zoe about this.'

'Good god, girl, don't do that.'

I held Jane's stare until she gave in.

'I came to stay with my parents when I was very young,' she whispered, 'they were friends of Fergus's father, it was before he was born.'

On Jane went, sharing her secret. 'I was sleeping down the children's corridor and was woken suddenly in the middle of the night. My parents and Fergus's had been to a party. I never liked staying here. This house frightened me as a child and when Fergus's father came into my room, it terrified me.'

I felt a pang of guilt for drawing this out of her. But I now wanted to know more.

'*Poor* you,' I said. 'What was he doing?'

'It was an awful experience. I hid under the duvet as he made all sorts of noises, lifting a floorboard up.'

'Didn't he know you were in there?'

'Too blotted to have a clue. He was an alcoholic, you

know. The next day he treated me all normal. He never recalled a thing.'

Jane went on. 'He was stuffing *that*,' she pointed at the portrait, 'necklace in and stamping down the board again.'

Wow. I had found a diamond for sure and it dawned on me that if Jane now knew what he was putting under the floorboard, she must have the necklace.

'You've got the necklace?'

'I came here to get my own back.' Her voice was full of confidence again and I felt strangely flattered she'd told me the truth.

'How did you know it would still be there?'

'I was *certain*. I've never breathed a word about that night.'

'So, it wasn't stolen?'

'As good as.'

'But it *wasn't*.'

'Fergus doesn't know that and don't you go telling tales.'

'It's stealing.'

Crumbs, I'm an accessory-after-the-fact to a serious crime. What am I going to do?

'Hush, girl. You don't know the full story.' Jane put her fingers to her lips at which point the bedroom door flew open. 'Felicity! Susie was just leaving.'

'I hope you had a good walk?' I said.

Felicity's hair needed a good brush.

'Oh, we did, it was marvellous.'

I stepped out of the room, wondering why it had taken Jane so many years to return. And…I don't want to believe it, but…did Jane use Felicity's sob story as a way of securing her place on the course?

It's not in my nature to snitch and if I told Zoe and Fergus about the necklace now, I would be doing just that. Jane's right, I don't know the full story...yet.

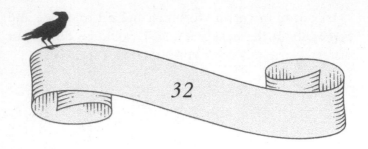

32

Louis was last through the music room door and I told him to tag his easel on the end of the semi-circle around the still life.

Where on earth am I going to drum up the energy to get through this?

'Susie,' said Rupert. 'Why don't I make some space and move my easel in front of the window there.'

'No.'

'That's me told.'

'Oh, sorry, but you'll get in the way of the light falling on the objects. I want it very bright on one side.'

'Miss, can we have music again?'

'Do we have to?' said Minty. 'My ears are still ringing from last night.'

'Me too,' agreed Felicity.

'Let's not. We've got to get going. Secure your primed paper on your easel...'

'I do hate primed paper,' interrupted Giles.

'Well, you have to use it today as the paint will dry quicker than on canvas.'

'Why does that matter?'

'So as tomorrow you can glaze on top of what you paint today.'

'What's that?' said Rupert.

'Tomorrow we'll do what we do tomorrow, but today I'm going to teach you about a trick of the light. Please get out four tubes of paint: zinc white, titanium white, ivory black and sepia.'

'Will this be a tonal painting?' said Minty.

'Yes, similar to the fountain you did yesterday. I'm going to show you a method I learnt at the Ruskin.'

'You went to the Ruskin?' Minty sounded full of surprise.

If you've been to the Slade or Ruskin, people always sound surprised. It's an indirect compliment in a funny sort of way.

'Didn't you read the brochure?' said Louis. 'Susie's talented, you know.'

I quickly moved on. 'This method's good but it's by no means the only way.' I smiled to show I meant it. 'Great masters of chiaroscuro like Rembrandt and Goya stuck to it.'

'Well, it must be the best then,' said Giles.

'Don't be stupid,' said Louis. 'There are many other skilful ways to paint. Which is what Susie has been saying.'

'Really?'

'Yes, Impressionism for example. Or Pointillism, since you ask.'

'Why are you teaching us kiro scuro then, Miss?'

'I'm just showing you an option. One that focuses on light.'

'What?' said Shane, staring blankly out of the window.

'It's the reflection of light that lets us see everything around us, and a trick of the light means what you are seeing is actually an effect caused by the way light falls. If you get to grips with this, you'll be well on the way to understanding and working out how and why things appear as they do.'

'Heavens above, Susie,' said Rupert, 'what *do* you mean?'

'I mean, forget about the images of jugs and vases you already have in your mind. I want you to record the facts in front of you. Only the facts, as they exist. You probably think the jug is green and the vase is blue, but if you look hard you'll realise you've jumped to a false conclusion. The evidence says differently.'

Just as Jane's lips parted I said, 'Look at the sides of the objects closest to the window – what colour are they?'

Shane squinted. 'White, Miss.'

'*Exactly*. The objects aren't white in our mind, but here, in front of us, there's no denying it. It's very easy to take sight for granted but you must be led by your eyes *not* your mind.'

'Beyond me,' said Felicity. 'But I'll give it a go.'

'To really stretch the point, we're going to forget about colour today and concentrate on tone. It's all about defining the light.'

Minty was nodding in my favour.

Here goes… 'I want you to use sepia to knock in the tonal values on your canvas, always working from dark to light, leaving only the area of white on your canvas where the light is hitting your subject. You then build form on this underpainting. Once this is bone dry, i.e.

tomorrow, you'll mix the colours and brush them over your tones. This then…'

'*Whooooa*, hang on a minute,' said Rupert. 'You're going a bit fast.'

'Very fast,' said Giles.

'Yes, Susie,' said Felicity. 'Any chance you could explain it a little more clearly? You are an awfully good tutor but that sounded terribly difficult.'

'I think it's safe to say,' grumbled Jane, 'we were *all* lost in your explanation.'

'Why don't you show us how it's done?' suggested Lianne.

Louis offered me his easel and paper and set another up for himself. I shifted forward so everyone could watch me and work behind – no time left this morning for a full demonstration.

'Do you all understand what I mean when I say white is warm when sunlight hits it?'

'Not much of that here,' said Jane.

'As a matter of fact, natural light *is* sunlight.'

'Well, *I* didn't understand what you meant.'

'No, I don't think I did either,' said Felicity.

Louis gave me a sympathetic smile and I moved towards the high table, hoping if I pointed at what I meant, it would make things clearer.

'The sides of the objects closest to the window have most light on them. Here. The sides of the objects furthest from the window have the least light. Here. Zinc white is warm and titanium white is cold. So, when you are painting the lightest side of the jug and the vase you will use zinc white because natural light is warm.'

'What about the shadow?' said Felicity.

'We'll get to the shadow, but for the time being these dark sides of the objects are not hit by sunlight and are therefore cold, so when mixing their tone you'll use titanium white.'

'I'm going to write this down,' said Lianne.

'That's a terribly good idea,' said Felicity, reaching for her sketchpad.

'It's *ridiculously* confusing,' said Jane.

Louis stepped forward and squeezed my shoulder.

Jane tut-tutted. I sighed. I wanted to scream: 'Listen carefully and *concentrate*.'

Oh dear, have I lost them? I'm a sucker for a thorough understanding. I really relish getting to the root of a problem. I like things to be proven before I buy into the result, and there are few things I enjoy more than studying life. Whether that be tricks of the light or tricky characters.

I tried to calm Jane. 'I'll talk you through the mixes and the easiest way to go about that is to work from dark to light. The further away from the sunlight the colder the tone. The blackest black, ivory black, is used for where light never goes.'

'There,' said Felicity, pointing to the correct place at last.

'Yes, and as the shadow extends it gets lighter. This cast shadow is a mixture of ivory black, zinc white and a hint of sepia.'

Lianne caught my eye. 'How do you spell that last one?'

'Any way you want,' said Shane

I laughed; fundamentally he's right. 'S E P I A.'

'And where's the name from, Susie?' asked Rupert.

'Originally, the ink came from the sac of a cuttlefish – sepia in Greek.'

'Yuck,' said Lianne.

'Oooh,' said Felicity.

'Hang on a minute,' snapped Jane. 'You are going to show us how it's done, aren't you?'

'I'm *just* about to.'

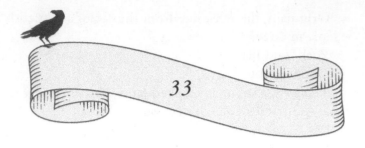

33

I'm exhausted. It's partly my fault for undertaking such an ambitious lesson but I so want to open everyone's eyes. Finally the questions have stopped and hard work has started so I'm going to leave them to it and grab five minutes alone in my room.

I face-planted my pillow. Blast Jane, she's testing my morals and it's wearing me out. I was in a similar circumstance only last week. One where I didn't know the full story. I'd gone on a blind date for dinner in Brighton, and across the restaurant I'd seen a friend, Ross. He was with a woman who was not his wife. I went straight up to say hello. They had menus in front of them, their food hadn't come yet, but I noticed the cutlery was ruffled on his left and her right. Drawing a swift but unfounded conclusion, I was pretty sure this pair had been holding hands. His reluctance to chat suggested it too.

It was upsetting to see a friend possibly cheating on his wife but it would have been presumptuous of me to tell her, Mary, without knowing the truth. She would have been terribly upset and where was the happiness in that? Instead, I rang Ross at work and put him under pressure to do the right thing. He insisted his relationship with the stranger was platonic and this I wanted to believe. However, I left him in no doubt how upset I was to come across him in a situation like this and hung up, leaving him to sort it out.

Right now, face down on my bed, I'm reminding myself: it's better to encourage the person in the wrong to do the right thing than go behind their back. My conundrum with Jane is: she's convinced she *deserves* the diamonds and I just don't know where that's coming from. Pure greed…or something else?

I went back to the music room and wrapped up the class.

'It's lunchtime.'

'Finally,' said Shane. 'I'm starving.'

'I'll race you to the dining room,' said Giles.

'First, you must clear up, clean your brushes, stack the easels, carry your paintings down to the basement and then you can go to lunch.'

'Oh, Miss. Really.'

'How did I do today?' said Rupert, showing me his picture.

'Very good,' I lied. 'There's certainly enough to go on tomorrow.'

'Where in the basement are we going?' said Felicity.

'The drying room so your pictures can dry.'

'Of course, how clever.'

Zoe and Fergus were already in the dining room when we arrived, piling shepherd's pie onto plates and putting them round the table. I made sure I sat a long way away from Jane. I couldn't bear to be near her right now.

'Can I have a small one, please?' said Minty.

Zoe spooned a final portion onto a plate and sat down.

'What are we doing this afternoon, Miss?'

'Drawing from paintings in the house.'

'Like copying?'

'It's called an equivalent not a copy.'

'Right you are then.'

Louis gave me a cheeky wink.

'Which paintings?' said Felicity.

'You can choose whatever you like.'

'Just one?'

'Yes, just one, in pencil on paper.'

'I think it's such a good idea of Susie's,' said Fergus. 'You can't possibly work outside in this weather.' He turned to look out of the window. 'That reminds me. Darling, you said you were going to look up tomorrow's weather?'

'Yes, I should have said, it's going to remain below freezing with a brief spell of sun in the morning.'

'*Brrr.*' Felicity's whole upper body shook.

'Good lord,' said Rupert, 'Jules will never forgive me if I don't get home to help with the dogs.' He looked genuinely worried.

'And I'm meant to be going skiing on Saturday.' Giles's shoulders slumped.

'Don't worry,' said Zoe. 'I've spoken to the airline and your flight's been rescheduled for the morning. Porridge and toast in here from seven and Donald will take you to the airport at eight.'

'How brilliant of you,' said Felicity.

'Well, I'd hate to think of you stuck up here.'

'Yeah,' said Shane. 'I like it and all but I want to get home.'

'You will. Inverness only has two flights south a day. The airport is quite used to bringing the evening one forward when the weather's bad.'

'This means we won't get to finish our pictures,' groused Minty.

'Blast,' said Rupert. 'So it does. I really felt I was going places today.'

'Susie,' said Zoe, 'is there anything you can do about this?'

I was glad to have an answer. 'It'll be easy to finish them when you get home, you just have to glaze over the tones.'

'*How?*' snapped Jane.

'Mix up two colours, green and blue, add a fair amount of medium to them and brush them lightly over the objects.'

'Will that work?' asked Giles.

'It should do.'

'Should do or will do?' said Jane.

'It will work as long as you keep your paint thin. You have to allow the tones we painted today to come through your greens and blues.'

'I'm definitely going to try it,' said Rupert.

'Does anyone want more shepherd's pie?' said Zoe.

'Depends what's for pudding,' piped up Giles.

Mhàiri stepped in to clear. Zoe looked at her. 'I think…it's blackberry crumble with custard?'

Mhàiri nodded.

'Help yourself from the hotplate,' said Zoe and everyone, apart from Minty, got up.

'Zoe,' said Jane, 'I do hope you won't mind having my pictures wrapped and sent south? I can't think how I'll manage them on the plane.'

The cheek.

'Hmmm,' mumbled Fergus. I think he was embarrassed they hadn't thought about this before.

'You could,' I said, 'fit them in your suitcase. They should be dry.'

'That's what I'm going to do,' said Rupert.

'I hadn't thought of that. I shall go right now and give it a try.' Jane got up and left the room.

'Would anyone like seconds?' said Zoe, and when Felicity joined a long line of takers I realised it was my moment to rush upstairs and have a bit more time alone with Jane.

Knock, knock…

'Come in.'

'Hi, Jane.'

'Susie, I don't want you bothering me again.'

I watched as she folded some clothes into her suitcase. The very one Mhàiri had found the necklace in. Jolly lucky for Jane Mhàiri hadn't recognised it from the portrait above. Although, even if she had put two and two together she'd never say she found a necklace in Jane's bag. Mhàiri's words 'I'll watch your back if you watch mine' gave me reassurance her relationship with Fergus and Zoe wasn't close. It's not like she'd confided in them about Jane having been here before. Hang on a minute…

'Jane,' I said. 'If your parents were friends of Fergus's parents, you must have come to stay once he was born?'

'*Were* is the key word there.'

'Did they fall out?'

'Don't you ever learn?' She stopped packing and turned her slitty little eyes towards me. 'Stop right now, poking your nose into my business.'

Eeeee, eeeee, eeeee, came the loud call of a raven. It was outside the window, sitting on the sill frantically flapping its wings. Jane got up and banged the glass.

'If you want a mystery to solve, young lady, off you go and work out what these blasted birds are doing here.'

'Fine.'

I walked straight out of her room adamant I'm going to get to the bottom of *everything* odd going on here.

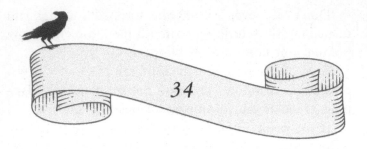

34

Although Zoe referred to the library early on as 'a snug' it will take a lot of renovation before Auchen Laggan Tosh gets anywhere close to cosy. However, for this afternoon's drawing from paintings the Muchtons have attempted to brighten the place up. Fires are crackling, chandeliers alight and Haggis is padding around, making people feel at home.

Rupert and Minty are drawing George III's coronation round the back of the main staircase. Lianne is in the library studying Thomas Warrender's trompe l'oeil and Giles has disregarded my instruction for the afternoon. I've just stumbled across him in the hall. He's got his watercolours out and is tackling the cupola, à la Gavin Hamilton.

'Didn't want to draw?' I said sarcastically.

'No, not on my last afternoon. We have rather a good painting collection of our own at home. I can draw from that any time.'

'I get your point. Would you like any help?'

'Do you think this is bad?'

'No, it looks a good start. I was just offering.'

'Thank you but no thank you,' he smiled.

I found Felicity in the drawing room sitting by the fire, under Ramsay's portrait of the 1st Earl's wife.

'Great choice. How are you getting on?'

'I,' her voice cracked. 'I,' she stopped again. I looked at her picture; most of it had been rubbed out.

'Felicity, you mustn't worry, anything good is hard work. You've come on such a lot this week.'

'But it's *so* difficult. I simply don't know where to begin.'

'Think of it like this.' I crouched down beside her. 'Fifty per cent is studying the painting, the tone, the brush strokes, the detail, and fifty per cent is drawing something that looks like what you have chosen.'

'If you say so.'

I changed tack. 'I bet you've never looked at the same painting for more than an hour?'

Her head shook.

'You'll be looking at this picture for at least an hour and a half.'

'So I will,' she giggled. I'd unwittingly cheered her up.

'When you look at the same painting for a long time it's very interesting how you begin to see it differently. All the intricacies start to etch themselves in your memory and the longer you look the firmer the image will stick in your mind. This helps enormously when it comes to drawing.'

'But where do I start?' She gazed at the portrait.

'First, draw a vertical rectangle inside the edges of your paper, roughly the same dimensions as the painting.'

'How?'

'Come.' I beckoned her up. 'Stand directly in front of

the picture, and hold your pencil out horizontally at arm's length. Now close one eye.'

'Which eye?'

'Keep your dominant eye open. Line up the end of your pencil with the bottom left-hand corner of the picture. Measure the width of the painting and mark it on your pencil with your thumb. This gives you the starting scale.'

Felicity's arm was wavering. I raised my hand to keep it steady.

'You can relax a bit.' I pushed at her elbow. 'It must be straight but it doesn't have to be rigid.'

'Susie, I'm terribly sorry but I don't understand.'

I let go of her arm and it dropped to her side.

'Oh Felicity.' I gave a sympathetic sigh. 'Would you like me to show you?'

'Yes, that would be best. I'm sorry I'm so thick.'

'Don't be silly,' I smiled. 'Now you hold the pad up and I'll draw.'

This was fun and worked rather well. Felicity at least looked as if she understood, her head nodding throughout my explanation. 'The width of the picture is two thirds the length of my pencil. So, keeping my thumb in place I'm now turning the pencil vertically, and counting how many times the width fits into the height. It will be a bit distorted because you're looking up at it but you can make allowances for that.'

'That *is* clever.'

'Yes, and now we know the height is two times the width we can draw a proportionally accurate rectangle on the paper.'

'Goodie. It's *much* clearer now. But why didn't you just draw a rectangle?'

'You mean without measuring?'

She nodded. *Harrumph*, nothing I'd said had gone in. I'm going to have to try to put it another way…

'If you mimic the proportions of the painting you can then, using your pencil, measure where objects are within the frame. Mark them off with your thumb and translate them onto your paper. This will give you a proportionally accurate drawing.'

'I get it,' Felicity smiled. 'May I use your rectangle?'

'Yes.' I agreed because although it would be good practice for her to draw her own, there's enough to contend with right now.

When I said I was going to leave, she begged me to stay.

'Just for a teeny-weeny bit? Help me with the next step?'

'Well this first step is very similar to the one we used when drawing the cows. Look at the portrait and choose your favourite thing.'

'Her pearl choker.'

'Good. Now stand still in front of the painting with your arm out again and re-find the width on your pencil with your thumb. Using this length, measure as accurately as possible the position of the choker in relation to the outside edges of the painting, and when you have, make a mark in the right position within your rectangle.'

Much to my surprise Felicity demonstrated she had understood exactly what I was saying. Wow.

'Next?' she smiled.

'Using the pearl choker as your anchor, look really hard at the painting and see what and where things intercept it. Then draw them on your paper. After this look what and where things intercept these things and so on until you reach the edges of the painting. Got it? I think you'll be all right on your own now, don't you?'

'I do hope so.'

'Well, if you're really desperate shout and I'll come back, but for the time being I must go and find Jane, Shane and Louis.'

Jane and Shane were upstairs arguing on the landing.

'You haven't started yet?' I said, full of disappointment.

'No Miss, she's refusing to let me in her room and I want to draw that portrait.'

'You can't invade our personal space,' said Jane.

Shane stood his ground wearing a grin on his face.

'Maybe you could work together in your room, Jane?'

I was trying to resolve things but she wouldn't budge.

'You're going to let him sit amongst Felicity's and my things?'

'Only if you're in there too.'

'*No*, and he doesn't *have* to draw in there.'

'I don't have to, you're right,' said Shane rather maturely for him, I thought. 'But I'd like to.'

'Please,' I added.

'Please,' said Shane and miraculously Jane stepped away from the door.

'You'll leave the door open, won't you?' I asked.

'No reason not to.'

I turned to Jane. 'Would you like me to find you a painting to draw?'

'I'm perfectly capable of doing that and as a matter

of fact I've already decided. I'm going to tuck myself away down the children's corridor.'

'Really?' I think she must have an ulterior motive. Why would she ever want to hang about down there?

'Yes, do you have a problem with that?'

'No, not at all. But let me get you a chair from my room.'

I went down the corridor one step ahead of her and as soon as I was in my room she stepped in after me and slammed the door.

'*Susie*, I have to talk to you. This can't wait any longer.' Her breath was short, her tone direct.

'Of course,' I gently rested my bottom on the window ledge, hoping to appear calmer than I felt inside.

'My husband Neville is seventeen years older than me; work that out and you'll realise he's a pensioner. He's set to be pushed out of his job sooner rather than later. Our eldest daughter is *desperate* for a baby and unable to afford private IVF and our youngest daughter wants to be a vet but can't afford tuition fees.'

Jane fell silent and as her shoulders slumped the pomp, pride and self-importance she'd carried about with her all week drained out. Standing with her back to the door, so wretched, she looked like she'd lost a stone on the spot.

'I'm very sorry to hear all you're going through.'

I stood up and took a step towards her.

'I'm not looking for your sympathy.' She flapped her hand and I sat back down. 'What I need is your understanding.'

'Okay.'

'That yellow diamond necklace is worth about three hundred thousand pounds.'

'Jane,' I said, shocked by the huge sum. 'I have a tiny diamond. Here.' I took it out of my jewellery case and without even looking closely she grunted and dropped it into her top pocket. 'I found it under the floorboard but I want rid of it. It's not my role to give it to the Muchtons. That's for you to…'

'*Let* me explain the calculation. Then hopefully, finally, you'll understand.' Jane held out her hand and ticked the separate elements off her fingers. Fore finger: 'Five years' tuition fees, that's forty-six thousand pounds, assuming annual fees don't increase, though they're bound to, so, accounting for that and living expenses, which we'll be covering too so that our daughter can study hard, I'll have to put aside one hundred thousand for her.' Middle finger: 'Twenty-five thousand for our eldest. IVF hasn't worked on the NHS so she must now go private. It's five thousand pounds a pop and with a twenty-nine per cent success rate it could take several goes.' Ring finger: 'Not to mention the likelihood of Neville being made redundant.' Jane wrapped her other fist round her little finger and her eyes shut.

'Jane, I'm worried about you.'

I felt a great need to put a hand on her shoulder but I didn't dare.

'I'm fine,' she said, brushing away my concern.

'Are you sure? Please sit on the bed if you'd like.'

'I'm fine.' She pulled a handkerchief out of her sleeve and blew her nose with great effect.

'I completely understand your situation.'

'Do you? Do you really, Miss Mahl? No. I don't think you do.'

This woman was something else.

She continued: 'I've waited years, literally years, for this opportunity. I swore to myself I wouldn't do anything until I needed the money. But that didn't stop me keeping a close eye on life up here.' Jane shoved the handkerchief back up her sleeve. '*Now* I desperately need the money. So when the painting residency was advertised I made damn sure I got on it. The half-wit Felicity's sob story was a great help with that.'

Blimey, my sympathy buckled just like that, and Jane's threat, 'There's much good to come from this and if you blow my cover, don't underestimate what I'll do', had no effect.

I accused her again of stealing the necklace. 'Don't you feel it's wrong to do this?'

'Before you got involved there was no right or wrong dilemma.'

'So you agree it's wrong to take it?'

She condescended to provide an explanation. 'The Muchtons got the insurance money from the necklace, Fergus said so himself. Other than sentimental value, which I think we can overlook in these circumstances, my taking the necklace won't leave anyone out of pocket. The fact it might be *wrong* is a minor consequence in a much larger philanthropic picture.'

'But Fergus would be thrilled to have it back in the family.'

'We can't always have what we want. You'd do well to remember ignorance is bliss. My family need the money much more than the Muchtons need their necklace.'

It was then I clicked: if the necklace is returned to Fergus, he'd have to declare it to his insurance company – pay them back what they'd paid out. The Muchtons simply don't have enough cash in their pocket to keep this necklace in the family.

I'm ready to give up, surrender, leave Jane to it. Follow her instruction: keep things simple, remain quiet, not say a thing. Maybe then I'd get rid of this horrible feeling inside me.

My fail-safe mantra in life when up against a moral problem is simple: answer *yes* or *no*. Everything, no matter what, no matter how complex, can be stripped back and there's your answer, *yes* or *no*. There is right and wrong, good and bad. Stealing is wrong.

But here, with Jane, I'm in a terrible muddle. Her daughters would benefit enormously from the sale of the necklace.

Is stealing for the greater good so bad?

I looked at her sympathetically. But there was no need, her fearful strength of character was in command. '*Please*. Leave me be. There's far more wrapped up in this than you will ever know. If I were you I'd get your little snout out of other people's business.'

I caught myself before any more words came out of my mouth. I'd forgotten there might be more to Jane's revenge. Her mission goes back a whole generation, to the day she was frightened as a little girl. My conscience has spoken: it's time for me to butt out.

I picked up the bedroom chair and carried it into the corridor. Jane settled herself down in front of the Annunciation, and when I asked if she'd like any guidance she said, 'Leave me alone now, Susie, off you go back downstairs.'

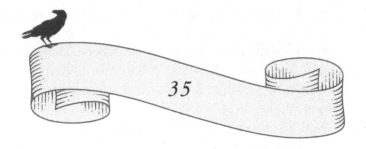

35

Louis. Oh Louis. Where is Louis?…Finally, I found him sitting at the dining room table with Zoe.

'Susie, I do hope you don't mind me pinching him,' she said all giddy. 'We're going through photographs and he's just so much quicker on the computer than I am.'

Louis grinned; he knew exactly what I was thinking: you're the same age, for goodness sake.

'Not at all,' I said.

'I thought it would be wise to get his advice on photographs while I still have him here. But I do want to get together, Susie, you, Fergus and I, to discuss how it's gone.'

'Very good idea.'

'How's the drawing from painting going anyway?'

'Everyone's begun so here's hoping they stick at it.'

'Can you spare some time and join us?'

'I'd love to.' Literally. I was longing to see some of Louis' work.

'Here. Pull up a pew.' Zoe moved her chair closer to Louis. 'You'll have a good idea of what sells the course.'

I sat down, pleased to be a part of it.

'We've downloaded all the photographs from his camera…'

'Transferred,' said Louis, 'not downloaded. That really would have taken you over your internet allowance.'

I felt bad; perhaps Zoe didn't know much about computers.

'Well, whatever he's done,' she said, 'we're looking at the pictures, narrowing down a selection.'

Louis started the slideshow and it became clear he'd spent yesterday afternoon retracing our steps from the entire week. Photographs of the river, the Highland cows, the loch on the hill, the garden, the back drive, the front drive…

'These are simply wonderful,' said Zoe, pulling a strand of hair from her ponytail and twiddling it between her fingers.

'Thanks.'

'You went miles yesterday,' I said, but he didn't react.

Interior pictures of the house were now crossing the screen. 'I like these a lot,' said Zoe. 'However, although we're happy to share what's personal to us with residents, I don't want the inside of the house splashed about online. Would you agree?'

'Yes, I think I do.'

Louis nodded.

'That reminds me, Susie, do you think we should include the Highland cows or will they put people off?'

'No, definitely include them. It's a real coup to have them here.'

'Oh look. It is pretty, isn't it?' said Zoe, admiring a photograph of Ewen's cottage. 'Whoever thought to put in ground-level windows certainly had an eye for aesthetics.' Louis zoomed in.

'But, once again,' said Zoe, 'I don't think we should include this.'

'No,' agreed Louis. 'Susie, what *are* you looking at?'

'There.' I pointed at the photograph; the front wheel of Ewen's van was reflected in one of the cottage windows. 'I think there's blood on his wheel arch.'

'Really?' said Zoe.

'In the reflection, see?'

'Zoom in more please, Louis.'

'I'm afraid that's not possible.'

She took it verbatim and I wasn't going to go against him, although I thought it a bit odd that he wouldn't.

'I bet my brother-in-law killed the roe deer,' said Zoe, jumping to the same conclusion as me.

'He did,' said Louis.

She looked shocked.

'I'm only joking. I have no idea who ran into it.'

I stared at Louis; how did he know a deer had been run over? He wasn't around when Zoe had told me.

'*Haggis,*' yelped Zoe; he'd appeared on the screen. 'We have to include that. Louis, I think you should start putting our choices into a designated folder.' She touched Louis' hand which was in control of the mouse.

'Susie?' Zoe sounded concerned. 'Are you okay?'

'Oh yes, I was just thinking about something. I'm fine, thanks.'

'Maybe you'd like a cup of tea?'

'I'm happy to wait until later unless you'd like me to get you one?'

'Louis?' said Zoe.

'Yes please.'

'Make that two and do get one for yourself, Susie.'

I entered the kitchen and Mhàiri pulled her hands out of the sink.

'Susie,' she said, wiping off the soap suds. 'I wondered how long it would take yous to come and tell me about last night.' Her eyes were very big and very round.

'It was good fun.'

'Aye. Ne doot. But how about the lady's jewels?'

Oh crumbs. *What* am I going to say now?

'She wasn't wearing anything special.'

Mhàiri's face fell. Thinking on my feet and trying to put her off the scent altogether, I said, 'Jane told me she's going to a black-tie do in London straight after here so maybe that's what they're for.'

Eeeek. I've just told a complete lie to protect a thief. I really am going to have to go to confession next week.

'So yous never saw them?'

'No. But I can imagine them.'

'Oh good,' Mhàiri smiled. 'Thanks to me?'

'Yes, thanks to you.'

'Whit is it yous want, Susie?'

'I came to make three cups of tea.'

'I'll do it for yous, I just had the kettle on the boil. Yous get a wee jug of milk and a tray ready.'

When tea was made I whisked up the tray and managed to spill milk everywhere.

'Dinne cry,' she joked, but little did she know she wasn't far from the truth.

I picked up a cloth and Mhàiri refilled the jug.

'Yous'll be needing your bed after this week.'

'I certainly will,' I said and left the kitchen.

As soon as they saw me Louis and Zoe immediately stopped talking.

'Tea,' I announced and handed them both a cup.

'Thanks, Susie,' said Zoe and then, catching me looking at a photograph of ravens on the screen, she forced Louis' hand and he flicked up the next photo.

'There are a lot of those birds round here,' I said.

Zoe looked at Louis who looked at me.

'What's going on?'

Louis waited for Zoe to answer, but she didn't.

'We,' he said, enjoying the intimacy of the remark, 'reckon someone's let a bunch loose.'

'Alec Ronaldsay,' shot off my tongue.

'*You know him?*' There was accusation in Zoe's voice.

Louis looked terribly guilty.

'No, I just know he lives nearby.'

'And that he breeds ravens?'

'Yes, exactly. I was putting two and two together.'

'Weren't we all.' She let out a sigh.

'Do you think it's a terrible mistake?'

'He could jolly well come and apologise if so.'

'I can't imagine why else they'd be swarming,' said Louis.

'Heaven knows,' said Zoe. 'I don't like to think about it.'

End of conversation.

'Susie, will you flick through the folder of photos we've chosen and tell us if you think anything's missing?'

'Of course.'

Zoe and I swapped seats and Louis, the rascal, slipped his hand under the table and onto my thigh.

'Your photographs are good,' I smiled.

'I know.'

'Any missing?' said Zoe.

'You could have a couple more to sum up Scotland.'

'Such as?' Louis sounded a little touchy.

'Oh, I don't know, the ceilidh?'

'But then everyone might expect it,' said Zoe, '…and it's inside the house.'

'I know what,' I looked at Louis, 'your photograph of heather.'

'Heather?' said Zoe.

'Yes.' I was excited. 'I saw it the other night.'

Louis reddened and Zoe shot him a look. For some reason he wasn't taking me up on my suggestion. I honestly think he was embarrassed.

'Come on,' I elbowed him in the side, 'you could use it as the background for the whole site.'

'I'm not sure about that.' Zoe's voice was firm.

'Me neither,' said Louis.

Their reaction was nonsense. A background of heather is a great idea. Zoe had asked for my advice and now she's agreeing with Louis, not me.

'Why not?' Regrettably I sounded cross. But I was hurt.

'Too much of a cliché,' said Louis.

'Yes,' nodded Zoe, 'we must think of something better than that.'

Felicity's head came around the door. 'Susie. There you are. I'm having a nightmare.'

I jumped up, relieved to have an excuse to leave these two. I didn't like them conspiring against me.

'I'm struggling *again*,' mumbled Felicity as we left the room.

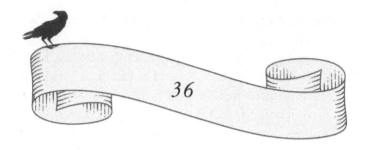

36

Hard work empties the stomach and the rush to tuck into tea proved how much everyone had put into their pictures this afternoon.

Hot buttered crumpets were devoured, tea was drunk and Zoe, who asked, 'Oh do please let us look at all your work,' got her way. 'Fergus and I will give you a moment or two to lay it out over the music room floor.'

'I'm not going next to you.' Rupert pointed at Minty. 'It would only make me look even less talented than I am.'

'Go next to Jane,' said Shane, thankfully under his breath.

'Don't worry,' I said, 'there's enough space for large gaps between everyone. Hey, Lianne,' she was struggling to carry everything to the far corner of the room, 'why don't you go here?'

'I was going to do a performance piece and I was thinking there'd be room up there for it.'

'Great,' I smiled full of joy. This was a welcome addition to the mix. 'Do you need any props?'

'Nah. Improvisation's more my thing.'

Zoe and Fergus came in and gazed at the work. 'What a marvellous result,' said Fergus, grinning at his wife.

'Yes, a huge achievement,' she replied with a hint of smugness between her lips, and I couldn't help thinking, there's still fourteen hours for it all to fall apart.

'What a success,' said Rupert, marching towards them.

'There's certainly a lot of work here,' said Zoe, evidently tiring of his manner.

Felicity then did what he should have done. 'Thank you very much. This has been a *wonderful* opportunity.'

Zoe grinned from ear to ear. 'I'm so pleased it's worked.'

'Didn't we do well,' said Rupert. 'What fun it's been to take up a new hobby. Susie,' he called out, 'you are lucky to be an artist.'

I feigned a smile. Art for me is not a choice. I have to do it. My soul thrives with creativity and my character fades without it. If I could go out there and get an office job, be well paid and have regular holidays – I would. How much easier a lack of vocation seems. But no. I'm made up of dreams, ideas, emotions and anxiety, all of which breathe through my art. If I didn't release them through my practice, my life would be meaningless. I'd quite possibly topple off the edge. Art gives me equilibrium (most of the time). By doing what I do each day, it helps me make sense of my being. I have a reason to be on this earth: to create. I doubt I'd exist any other way. Art is my life. Not some sort of permanent holiday dabbling in mediums, materials and colours. Rupert may have had 'fun' this week but being an artist full-time is far from this.

Everyone was tottering around the music room sniffing each other's personal pieces. Rather similar to dogs in a New York poop-park I thought. Some accepting each other – 'You have an interest in trees too?' said Fergus to Giles – and others rejecting one another – 'Video art is a waste of time.'

'Look at *her*,' said Minty.

Lianne was front-crawling her way into the room, arms going like the clappers as she headed towards the far corner.

'Oh no,' said Shane, 'it's the unidentifiable creature piece.'

She changed direction, now swimming towards him. Shane started darting from side to side. Lianne, unable to grab him, gave up and melted onto the ground instead. Then slowly, ever so slowly, she stretched out her hands and began dragging her voluptuous body across the floor.

'She'll be getting terribly dirty down there,' said Felicity, but nobody flinched. We were all witnessing something *quite* special.

Lianne reached the corner of the room and as she began to pull herself upright against the wall her body contorted as if she was physically stuck to it. Finally standing tall she flicked her long black hair over her face and let out the most unearthly wail.

Felicity's index fingers shot into her ears and Louis' hands erupted in applause. Giles, Shane and Fergus followed his lead. Zoe, Jane and Minty were rather slower on the uptake. I stood back and laughed inside. Lianne had successfully divided the room.

Zoe grasped Fergus's hand. 'Let's complete our circuit. We must look at everyone's work.'

'We must,' said Fergus and round they went. Nodding and smiling and dishing out compliments. Taking their time and saying all the right things.

'Well done, Susie,' came Zoe's congratulations as they headed for the door.

I smiled and waited for them both to leave.

'Come round, come round, everyone, don't pack up your work just yet.'

'But I'd like a bath,' said Jane.

'It won't take long. I was just thinking maybe it would be kind if you all gave Fergus and Zoe one of your pieces from the week?'

'What a nice idea,' said Lianne. 'I'll give them my doodle of the garden.'

'And I painted the house *for* Fergus,' claimed Shane.

'I can't think they'd want one of mine,' said Felicity.

'And I'm not giving any away,' said Jane.

'Everything I did is for my coursework,' said Minty. 'Isn't yours, Giles?'

'Good point, same goes for me.'

'I'm in Felicity's boat,' said Rupert.

'Me too,' agreed Louis.

The less you've got, the more you give, was ringing in my ears as everyone other than Shane and Lianne left my side.

'As you both won sponsored places here I think it is a particularly nice touch giving away one of your pictures, that's if you really mean it?'

'Jees yeah,' said Lianne. 'I'd like to do that.'

'Me too,' said Shane, 'but you can give it to them, Miss.'

They both looked terribly nervous.

'No, *you* must.'

'Now?'

'Before dinner would be a good time.'

'Okay.'

I smiled and said, 'Honestly, Fergus and Zoe will be thrilled.'

I gathered up my equipment, accepted Louis' offer to carry the quilt, and together we dumped it all in my car.

'You've got a long journey tomorrow,' he said as I reached to shut the boot.

'No longer than my one here.'

'Touché.' He jerked his head back sharply.

I was annoyed, and even more so when he grasped hold of my right arm and accused me of being off with him today.

'Sorry,' I relaxed. 'I didn't mean to be. I'm tired.'

'That it?' He let go.

'Yes.'

'So there's no problem.'

'Between us?'

'Yes, between us?'

'Not at all.'

He leant in to me and I accepted his hug. I had to, although I didn't really want to – news of his girlfriend had put me off any more frolicking together. Not to mention seeing Toby, whose charming manner and handsome face had set the bar high. And although Louis had rival looks, he was going to have to stop cheating before I let him cross the line.

'Bath time for me,' I said, pulling away.

'Together?'

'You should be so lucky,' I smirked and raced him up the front steps and into the house.

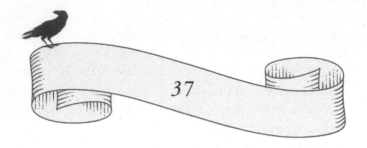

37

My suitcase is in the centre of the room, all packed and ready to go. One final night to get through, then I'll be off, heading south, back to Sussex. Home is on the horizon and I can hardly wait.

Tonight I must make it into the locked wing. It's my last chance to have a look for myself. I hate to think two Landseers are copies. It makes me so upset for Fergus and Zoe. But if they are, I'm mad keen to see if I can work it out. I set my alarm for 2.30am. I'll wake up in the middle of the night. Check no one's around and sneak into the south-east wing.

How ironic it is: if Zoe had got her way and the pictures weren't going on loan, the Muchtons would remain blissfully unaware. Fergus seems to be coping well, though. Taking the news in his stride. Not allowing himself to entertain the notion before Jamie Tumbleton-Smith has been. Zoe *is* lucky to have a calm husband. What a good dad he's going to make, only drawing conclusions about things precious to him when there's undeniable proof.

I bounced off my bed and headed downstairs. It was dinner time. Haggis was on his back outside the dining- room door. I rubbed his tummy with my foot and sent him roly-polying down the corridor baring his teeth in a grin. Moments like this make me think I'd like a pet of my own. But no, I travel too much, it'd be unfair.

'Now, Zoe, darling, have you explained about break-fast?' Fergus leant into the table as if it might help carry his voice to his wife at the other end.

'Yes,' she smiled. 'In here from seven, and Donald will be leaving at eight.'

'Good, good.'

Shane was on my right, teasing Lianne about what we were eating. 'It's lambs' bollocks.'

'Nah.'

'Pigs' brains.'

'Disgusting.'

'I bet you can't guess what it is,' I said.

'Yeah, Shane. Tell us what it is if you're so clever.'

He looked at me and Giles shouted, 'Venison,' across the table.

'He's right,' I said. It was probably the road kill.

'I can't believe you've all been tucking in not knowing what you're eating?'.

'I knew,' boasted Shane. 'I was just keeping quiet.'

'Yeah right,' said Lianne. 'It is good, though.'

Rupert leant across Felicity, who was on Fergus's left, and asked him where the name Muchton came from. I tuned in to hear the answer.

'It originates from the Norman French, early days of the Auld Alliance and all that.'

'It's very unusual. I haven't come across it before.'

'Our family's name is Hewson. Maybe you've heard of that?' said Fergus.

'Yes.' Rupert nodded vigorously. 'I think I might have.'

'On the subject of family names, I received the *most* extraordinary email today. Internet hackers are getting better and better.'

'Poor you,' I said, gripped. I like a hacking story, they can be so clever. Felicity was all beady eyed too.

'I'm wise enough to know better. It's other people I feel sorry for.'

'What was it?' said Rupert. 'I'd better make Jules aware. She's not always certain what's spam and what's not.'

'No need to worry,' reassured Fergus. 'I must have been a well-thought-out target. It came through our shooting syndicate website with the subject line "Muchtons of Auchen Laggan Tosh". Not something your wife will receive, I'm sure.'

'That's not hacking,' said Minty. 'It's spam.'

'Spam or hacking, all the same to me.'

'What did it say?' Felicity was giddy with anticipation.

'It began along the lines of how pleased they were to have re-established the Hewson family connection and how they hope to come poultry shooting here someday and whether we offer a discount for family. As if one would fall for that.'

Rupert gave a sneering snort and Louis asked whether the email said more.

'Yes, so devious, I think they wanted to strike up a correspondence about art.'

'Art?' said Louis.

'Yes, Landseer in particular. It went on about how pleased they are with theirs.'

Crumbs. Alarm bells are ringing in my head. Perhaps this pair own a Muchton original? But why isn't Fergus thinking that? He'd never be telling us this if he did. Maybe he hasn't had a call from the art dealer yet?

I wish I'd done 1471 on the landline. I could have so easily confirmed if he'd received the call.

'And,' said Fergus, 'they went on to say how much they're looking forward to the next one.'

'I think that's quite nice,' said Minty. 'It sounds as if they're trying to be friends.'

'Why would I want to be friends with Ethan and Chloe Hewson of Ice Lake Mansion, Canada, or so they say they are? I mean *poultry* shoot. Come on. Americans…' he corrected himself, 'Canadians can be so carelessly ignorant at times.'

Canadians struck a chord with me. Toby, oh Toby, has come up trumps, he'd suggested Canucks will buy up anything to bolster their Scottish roots. I don't think Fergus's email is spam.

Louis pushed his chair out from the table, stretched his legs straight and with a rush of thoughtfulness said, 'I'd delete it, Fergus. Much better it's out of your computer if there's the slightest hint of something suspicious going on.'

'Quite right, that's exactly what I did.'

'But,' said Rupert, 'people like to reach out in the modern world. The internet makes it possible. I rather agree with Minty, I'm not sure you've been "done" as they say.'

'Perhaps you're right.' Fergus's eyebrows rose. 'I never thought about it like that. I must put it past Zoe later, see what she says. I haven't actually told her yet.'

'What's that, angel?' said Zoe, attuned to her name.

'Oh nothing, I'll tell you later. Giles,' he called, 'keep the wine flowing, I don't want to be left with half-drunk bottles.'

'Will do.' Giles smiled a Burgundy-stained grin.

'Fergus,' said Felicity, 'what are you going to call your first child?' At the mention of babies I turned to Louis.

He was staring down the table at Zoe who was twitching her head towards the door. Louis got up and left the room. Zoe was now looking down the table at me; she shrugged her shoulders and left the room too.

'Shane,' I said, turning to my right, 'I'm so sorry, I'm just going to nip to the loo.' I really, really, really wanted to follow on.

'That's all right, Miss, you don't have to ask.'

Haggis stuck to my heel as I walked up the corridor, into the body of the house. Hovering behind the staircase, I could just see Louis and Zoe at the bottom of the banister. They were chitter-chattering under their breaths. Zoe had a hand to her forehead and Louis had his arm on her shoulder. Haggis yapped, they spun around and both bolted upright as soon as they saw me.

'Susie?' said Louis.

'Are you okay?' I played the I-was-worried-about-you card.

'He's fine,' said Zoe, giving the game away. She was trying her hardest to cover up their intimate moment. 'We were just having a chat.'

Are these two having an affair? It would be amusing *if I wasn't stuck in the middle of it.*

'Whatever,' I said. 'Didn't mean to interrupt.' Louis touched my shoulder as I went straight past them and on through to the downstairs loo.

There's a stuffed deer's head in here above the sink. Why do people put animals they've culled on display? Is it only the ones they've stalked or will the head of the road kill we've been eating tonight find its way onto a wall in this house?

I think there's a strong chance Ewen ran into that deer. He had blood on his wheel arch, I'd seen it in the photograph, and he was late home (according to Louis) on Monday night. He could have been drunk, embarrassed about what he'd done and not wanted anyone to know. So, dragging it into the wood at the time probably seemed the most logical thing to do. But can one man drag a deer or does its dead weight require two? Maybe Ewen got Louis to help and this is how he pulled a muscle in his arm? It's not as if we've been doing anything strenuous in class.

I went back to the dining room. Zoe was in her seat but Louis was nowhere to be seen. The plates had been cleared and I began to dream up my favourite thing for pudding.

Ting-ting went Zoe's glass and the kitchen door swung open to reveal Louis carrying an enormous chocolate cake.

'Bon anniversaire,' he began singing, and everyone, slightly confused, joined in with 'Happy Birthday to You, Happy Birthday…'

'Dear Fergus,' shouted Zoe.

'Happy Birthday to You.'

Louis settled the lit cake in front of the birthday boy, who took in a deep breath and blew out the single candle.

'How dare you, darling,' he said. 'I hate people knowing it's my birthday.'

'Had nothing to do with me,' Zoe grinned. 'Louis organised it behind your back.'

Fergus looked over his shoulder at Louis. 'That's the problem with being a twin.'

Mhàiri entered the dining room with a huge knife and Fergus grinned as he took it from her and began cutting up the delicious-looking cake.

Louis sat down beside me and slipped his hand under the table, onto my knee. I very nearly let out a yelp.

'What are you doing?' I whispered.

'Touching you. I like you.'

I looked down the table at Zoe and back to Louis.

'Non, non, non,' he shook his head. 'You don't really think so, do you?'

I shrugged my shoulders.

'You're so cute when you're jealous.'

'Well?'

'I'm not even going to answer that.'

The cake was delicious. Mhàiri had excelled. We all gobbled it up and as dinner drew to an end Shane ting-tinged his glass.

'Miss,' he said, when everyone was listening, 'I'm doing this 'cause I like you...'

For a conceited moment I thought he was going to make a speech to thank me. But when he got his mobile out of his pocket I feared the worst – he was going to take Jane down again...

'I want to know what you,' he was looking at Jane, 'took from Susie's room. She says you were looking for her but when I zoomed in on my video I can see you've clear as effing daylight got something up your sleeve.' Shane got up and thrust his mobile at Fergus.

'I won't have this bullying from someone less than half my age,' Jane said and burst out of her chair. 'Give me *that* telephone.' She waddled down the table and for some perceptive reason Fergus handed the mobile, which he hadn't looked at, back to Shane. (I bet if he hadn't, it'd be smashed by now.)

'Common little brat,' said Jane and stormed out of the dining room.

There was a shock of silence. What a dreadful end to the evening.

'Miss,' said Shane, 'I did it for you. She's got something of yours.'

'That's so thoughtful, but I've spoken to her about it.'

'She stole from you?' screeched Felicity.

'No, no, that's not what happened.'

'Damn well did,' said Shane. 'She wouldn't be making my life hell if she hadn't.'

'I'm sure there's a perfectly reasonable explanation for it all,' said Rupert. 'But I'm not prepared to sit it out so if you'd let me excuse myself I'm off to my scratcher. Better get some beauty sleep before seeing my wife.'

'Night, Rupert,' said Zoe. '*Angel?*' I think she wanted Fergus to rescue the situation.

He leapt in, 'Now dinner's over, please head to the sitting room, or the snug. I'd like to have a word with Susie and Zoe alone.'

People began to leave and I turned to Shane. 'It really is sweet of you to have played amateur detective for me.'

'Nothin' amateur about it, Miss. I have her on camera.'

'Yes, yes, I know but honestly I've cleared it all up.'

'What did she take?'

'It was personal so I'd rather not say.' This was a back-to-front truth. I really don't want to lie again.

'Susie,' said Fergus, 'come and sit by my side. Shane, please leave now.' Fergus patted the other seat next to him. 'Darling, are you okay here?'

'Yes.' Zoe came down the dining room with her head held high and I was pleased to see she didn't look in the least bit ruffled. Here's hoping it's something else Fergus wants to talk to us about.

'Look at me,' said Zoe, 'pregnant, hormones running through my body. It's put my character quite out of kilter. I reckon Jane Atkinson's at the other end of the spectrum, going through the menopause, battling with hormones too.'

Fergus stared at me as if for some ridiculous reason he thought I was going to open my mouth and confirm that his wife had hit the nail on the head.

'Susie?' he said.

'Yes?'

'Is there more to Jane's behaviour than you've told us?'

'Don't worry,' reassured Zoe. 'There was good reason why you didn't come to me before with things you knew, but...'

'What's this?' interrupted Fergus.

'It's nothing, angel, just a little blip. Jane had wanted to leave early.'

Zoe obviously does keep things from her husband.

'Right, I see. Susie, you must tell us if there's something else going on.'

Grrr, I felt so cross. Jane had well and truly dropped me in it. No matter how I go about this, I'll be blamed for holding something back. I wanted to burst into tears right here, right now.

'Susie?' said Fergus. 'What *is* it?' His patience was running out.

'I think it's best if you talk to Jane about it.'

'So, there *is* something going on?'

'Well, hmm, well…' I really did not want to tell another lie, so taking a deep breath I settled for, 'I'm in a very difficult position and I don't really want to say.'

'*Please*, continue.'

'I know too much about something someone else has done. What that person has done is, I feel, wrong, but I also think it would be wrong of me to tell you behind their back.'

'It *is* Jane we're talking about here, isn't it?'

'Yes,' said Zoe, longing for a conclusion. 'Has she hurt you, Susie?'

'No, not at all. I'm in a compromising position but it's entirely my fault.'

Fergus raised his voice. 'What have *you* done?'

'Nothing.'

'It doesn't sound that way.'

Zoe grasped Fergus's hand and rested it on the table under hers.

Bravely I looked them straight in the eye. 'I promise you can trust me, I've tried my very best to make this week a success and I'm so thrilled you asked me here to tutor. These little episodes with Jane are entirely down to something she's up to behind your back.'

'You *must* tell us,' said Fergus.

'Wait a second, angel,' said Zoe. 'Are you absolutely certain you're right, Susie?' She stared at me. 'I don't want you to say something you'll later regret.' Zoe's body stiffened.

'If you can confirm one thing, I can be certain,' I said, longing to rid myself of the whole Jane/necklace episode.

'Of course.' Zoe nodded.

I looked at Fergus. 'According to Jane her parents were friends of yours and they used to come and stay here with her when she was very young.'

'Nonsense. I'd remember.'

'You probably weren't born,' said Zoe nudging her husband in the ribs. If there's something a trained accountant's good at, it's numbers.

Their eyes were fixed on me. 'If you have a visitors' book from your parents' early days we can look back and see if Jane's family came to stay.'

'But we don't know her maiden name,' said Fergus, up to speed with tracing connections. His mother must have trained him well.

'But we do know she was young, so if we look up, say, forty to fifty years ago, and find the name "Jane" appearing with a mother and father, I'll bet that's her.'

Fergus rushed out of the room and was back in a matter of seconds with two leather-bound books. I wonder where he keeps them stashed?

'Well done, angel,' said Zoe as he laid them on the table and opened the first one. Page after page he whizzed through the signatures; he must recognise most of the writing.

'Nothing in that one.' Fergus opened up the book below.

'*There*,' I exclaimed. My finger hovered over a name.

'J A N E,' read out Zoe. 'Adorable squiggly writing.'

'I missed her by a decade,' said Fergus. His eyes were darting back and forth. 'Good god, her parents were Kelton.'

'Kelton?' I said.

'*Kelton*,' repeated Fergus as if he was trying to believe it. 'Kelton.'

'Who are they, angel? I vaguely remember a connection with Rupert?'

Fergus was speechless so I explained. 'Rupert managed the sale of the Keltons' land, his colleague the contents of the house. Your father-in-law bought some things.'

'What's the problem, angel?'

Fergus held his head in his hands. 'Jane's parents were great friends of my parents, in fact my father was her godfather.'

'What an unbelievable coincidence she's here,' said Zoe. 'Are you absolutely certain?'

'I'm sure,' said Fergus. 'His name was Hector, his wife Arabella.'

'How funny,' said Zoe looking back at the book.

'No, no, it's not good. They had a terrible falling out and never saw each other again. It was *ages* ago. I have absolutely no idea why she'd want to come here.'

'She must be up to something.' Zoe's voice held a wobbly combination of worry and fear.

Fergus reached to hold her hand. 'In the early days of my parents' marriage these Keltons – their great friends – fell on hard times. They had to sell their estate and my father bought some of the contents. Actually, rather a lot of the contents.'

'But how come they fell out?'

'I assume Jane's father didn't like the idea of his friend, my father, buying his things, carpet-bagging the estate they call it. I can understand. It would be difficult if you and me, darling, had to sell Auchen Laggan Tosh and Archie and Hilda bought a proportion of the contents. I don't think we'd be able to go and stay with them *ever* again.'

This Archie and Hilda, I remembered they'd written the *only* letter of support for Fergus's wind farm application. They are good (biased) friends.

'No, no, of course not,' said Zoe, stroking the back of her husband's hand. 'They're pretty much our best friends, they'd never do that to us.'

'One would hope not.' Fergus leant back in his chair. 'But my father did it to Jane's father, and even worse, he paid very little for what he got.'

'Did he realise that at the time?'

'Unfortunately, I'm sure he knew. But Pa couldn't resist a bargain. I doubt there was anything left for Jane in her father's will.'

'That's awful,' said Zoe, as if inheritance were all that mattered. 'It's hard to imagine being quite so cruel to a friend.'

'It's hard to imagine many things my father did in his lifetime.' Fergus squeezed Zoe's hand, as if reminding himself of a pact to lead a better life. 'Susie,' he said, 'aristocratic families with histories like this can be hard to understand, but I want you to know Zoe and I are trying our very best to create a home at Auchen Laggan Tosh where our children can retain their innocence for as long as possible and grow up good people.'

I smiled.

He went on, 'Do you know what…I'm not sure I really *want* to know what Jane was up to…'

'But angel,' said Zoe, 'that's awfully forgiving of you.'

He huffed, as if he'd heard this before. Zoe's subtle way of calling him *weak*. 'Jane's father was treated badly by mine. Digging up Pa's past is a can of worms. He was a selfish man and I never fully understood him. I don't want to cause any more problems. We have enough on our plate managing Ewen's jealousy. Please, darling, can we agree on this?'

'Agree what? Jane has been up to something behind your back. You deserve to know the truth.'

My heart was beating fast. If they want to know more, it's time they spoke to Jane. I've said enough. I don't want to go behind her back.

Fergus stroked his wife's hair. Her shoulders relaxed and she gave him a sympathetic smile. It was evident from her silence she understood her position in it all. Zoe's married into this family, she has no right to captain her husband on issues from his past.

Fergus turned back and forth between us. 'If Susie can reassure us no one has been hurt, she hasn't had something stolen and there will be no repercussions for you and me, I think it's best, Susie, if you keep the details to yourself. Jane deserves an apology from our family and if you think she has redeemed this then so much the better.'

I nodded. 'No one has been or will be hurt and I'm pretty sure once Jane's left you'll never hear from her again.'

Zoe was nodding too.

Fergus stood up. 'I'd like the three of us to leave this

room, and never mention this again.' He spoke fairly but firmly and Zoe didn't attempt to go against him.

I'm mightily relieved. My conscience can rest. I'll never *ever* mention it again.

Fergus thanked me and when Zoe stood up he held her hand. 'Quite something to end my birthday with this.'

She gave him a peck on the cheek and all three of us headed for the door.

'I'm going to go to bed,' I said, feeling completely drained.

'Night then, Susie,' said Fergus.

'I hope you sleep well,' said Zoe.

'Night, night.'

Oh my goodness, *what* a weight off my mind.

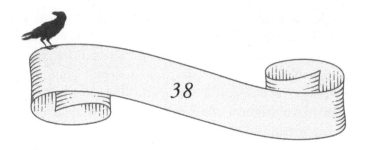

38

I grabbed my mobile and turned off the 2.30am alarm. I've been absolutely fast asleep. This week has worn me out. But I must get up, put some socks on. A jumper too and a spare one under my arm.

I turned on the torch and crept down the dark corridor – I cannot wake anyone up. I made it to the door of the Landseer wing without a sound and very carefully pushed the frame of the closest painting. The whole thing hinged open. I typed the number I'd seen Zoe put in and the box dropped open. Here was the key. I took it, closed everything back up and unlocked the door. Then I slipped into the room and locked it from inside.

I bent down and stuffed my spare jumper in the crack beneath the door. At a flick of a switch the picture lights came on and I turned my torch off. Alone and alert the stale smell hit me. A lack of air circulation – clearly the Muchtons never open the windows.

I went to touch the drawn curtains, to prove my point. Behind a fold of velvet, the blackout lining was speckled with mould. Already my eye is being drawn to things that don't fit.

I looked down at my feet as I walked across the room. If there's something on the floor I want to find it. I then craned my neck back and circled the ceiling. Rings of damp appeared where painted plaster had peeled. This neglected wing could do with a good blast of ventilation. Zoe really needs to read up on caring for an old house. Or let Mhàiri in here once in a while.

The pictures were stunning under the mounted lights. Far sharper than they were in natural light. I went to the first one, *Early Morning Stags on the Moor*. Oliver thinks this is genuine. Perhaps I should too. I need a prototype to start from.

My eye was drawn to the heather again and you know what, on second thoughts, to use it as a background for the Auchen Laggan Tosh Painting Residency website *is* a bit of a cliché. I laughed at myself agreeing with Zoe and Louis now. I guess I'd been jealous at the time of *my* Louis siding with Zoe.

The next painting, *Rutting Stags*, could be a copy. Though it looks a pretty brilliant piece of painting to me. The foreshortening of the deer, I wish I could do that. Oliver thinks it's been hung a little low, so I bent down to test his point.

The buff, virile beast burst out the canvas. Oliver's right. The picture came alive from this angle.

I looked up at the hanging chain. There's plenty of space between it and the light; this painting could so easily be higher. Hang on a sec, look at that, perfectly obvious in artificial light, there's a strip of faded silk above the frame. It's very similar to the green patches in the drawing room downstairs. Rupert drew attention to them on the orientation tour and Zoe said they'd recently moved the pictures to some of the spare rooms. How long does silk take to fade? I reckon a year or two. But with the curtains closed in here, it would be even more. Nevertheless, *Rutting Stags* at some point must have been re-hung, the s-hook joined fractionally too low down the chain. I quickly checked above the other paintings. There was no more faded silk.

Is *Rutting Stags* a copy? Oliver left a crack open for the real expert but I'm now thinking he's right. I mean, art fraud – it's as if the stars are aligning to get me on board. Giving me permission to play amateur detective again.

I touched the frame, dust came off on my fingers. It wouldn't take long for it to settle in this room but it does mean the painting's been on the wall a while.

I went back to the first picture. There was even more dust on its frame. The third, *Horses at Bay*, was dusty too. The last, *Dogs in the Moonlight*, had a little bit on the frame but as I moved my fingers along the bottom ledge there were obvious patches where no dust lay. Slightly bigger than the palm of my hand. It's as if someone's been clutching it recently.

I looked up at this painting of two spaniels, a grey-hound and a terrier of sorts. They're gathered on a clump of grass next to the stump of a felled tree. Oliver suspects this one's a copy too. He'd banged on about the brush strokes but if I want to prove it, I have to find some firm evidence tonight.

I leant my body up against the wall and pulled the picture out a little. It swung ever so gently on the chains.

I didn't want to pull it away too much. So I shone my torch behind it to see. There weren't any cobwebs but this doesn't exactly tell me much. If Oliver were here I wonder if he'd notice something unusual about the stretchers? Me, I have no clue. The wood is pine to avoid warping. It's what I use.

I released the picture carefully back against the wall and stood in front of it, scanning the brush strokes. I'm still struggling to work out exactly what it is I'm looking for. But if this picture is a copy I must have something in my armoury to winkle out the truth. Well, modesty aside I do have a keen eye and a bit of a knack for thinking laterally.

The dogs' fur is perfectly depicted. Each hair an individual stroke. So delicately painted. If only my drawings could be as subtle as this.

My eyes moved on to the stump of the tree. I counted the rings; this oak was some age. Landseer has picked out every wrinkle in the bark. His attention to detail is phenomenal. I can even see where he's painted a knot. The cracks are interwoven in a natural pattern. I've learnt a lot about trees this week. Giles is an authority and Fergus an enthusiast. Maybe I should think of planting some at home. I don't have an enormous garden but space for a maple at least or an outdoor Christmas tree, that would be nice. I've always found woods difficult to paint. I guess Landseer can teach me a thing or two. I stared at the colours. He'd used far more sienna yellow than I ever do. I must remember that. The knot on the stump is even lighter. I bet it's mixed with zinc white. But how did he get the balance with the cracks so right? What colour are those cracks?

Hang on a minute…this is very odd. Two letters are forming. I can see an E and an H within the pattern. Very subtle, but I can definitely see them. E… H… Are they initials? Landseer's? No, he'd be E L H, Edwin Landseer Harris, or E L at least.

E… H… E… H…E… H…

My lips wobbled as I mouthed the words Ewen, *Ewen,* Ewen Hewson.

I rushed along the wall to *Rutting Stags*. My whole body was trembly and overexcited. Are there initials hidden in this painting too?

My eyes darted all over the canvas. A subtle E H must be in here somewhere. I crouched down. I bet you they're hidden on the chief stag. Ewen, leaving his mark on the supreme being.

Its front hoof was poised on a rock and the misty bands of keratin covering were carefully depicted, stretching across the cloven foot. There it is. I can see it now. An E and an H in the strokes. The cross-bars of the letters in black, the stems in off white, each one slotted within the layers of the coffin bone hoof. Ewen Hewson, you've done it again. I've got you now. Caught in the act.

Suddenly my breathing quickened, I could feel my heart beating in my chest. The fear of being caught grasped me; how would I begin to explain what I'm up to? I must get out.

I scooted across the floor in my socks, turned off the lights and picked up my jumper. Then in the glow of my mobile I unlocked the door and with a shaking hand locked it from the other side. I popped the key back in the safe place and, desperately trying to get to grips with my breathing, I very quickly tiptoed to my room. *Creak* went the door as I shut it behind me. But it doesn't matter, I'm now safely back where I belong.

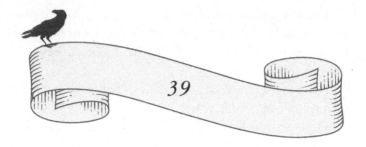

39

Rupert marched into breakfast brimming with news. 'Major breakthrough by the Tories,' he said. 'They've halted the spread of wind farms. Passed a bill last night putting a bar on onshore wind farm subsidies.'

Minty had told me her father was in the House of Lords this week trying to pass a bill before Easter. I wonder if it has anything to do with this?

'*Angel*,' said Zoe sharply down the table. 'Had you heard that?'

'No, I hadn't. Hmmm. On the news this morning I suppose?'

'Yes, just caught it on the box. I've been rather interested in the build-up and I had an inkling this would be the result.'

'You knew it was happening?' said Felicity. 'Why didn't you mention it the other day?'

'Wind energy's a controversial subject and, you never know, a debate on the matter could have divided us.'

'How sensitive of you.' Felicity missed the sarcasm in Rupert's voice, and when Giles asked, 'What's your opinion of them, Fergus?' she visibly cowered in her seat.

'I'm not against wind farms per se, they have a place both in the landscape and in our changing energy needs. However, where they are placed has to be chosen with the greatest possible care.'

'I was right, wasn't I,' said Giles. 'You have an application mast up, don't you?'

'How do you know that?' Fergus's eyes twitched.

'Told you so.' Giles searched the table. 'Hey? Minty. Where's Minty?'

'She's left,' said Zoe. 'Her mother turned up just after six to collect her. If it wasn't for Haggis's barking I would never have known.'

'*Six* o'clock this morning?' said Giles.

He's very surprised and so am I.

'Thereabouts. Didn't hang around. It was a last-minute decision due to the weather.'

'All the way from Cumbria?' I said.

'No, she spent last night with friends nearby.'

Quite nearby, I said to myself...these estates are enormous.

'Minty wanted me to pass on her goodbyes to you all,' smiled Zoe.

'Doubt I'll see Araminta Froglan-Home-Mybridge again,' said Shane with flawless timing, and all of us began to laugh.

'*Froglan-Home-Mybridge?*' Rupert was astounded. 'How could I have forgotten? It was *her* relation I saw on telly.'

'This morning?' snapped Zoe.

'Yes. It was an old clip of him banging on about wind farms blighting the landscape, damaging property prices and harming the local economy.'

'Really?'

'Yes, he's a Tory peer and it was footage from a previous moratorium on wind farm developments.'

'Minty's father?' said Fergus, not quite getting it.

'I should hope not. The man I saw is now under arrest.'

'Under arrest?' I said and Felicity tut-tutted.

'Quite unbelievable. Whoever it was, was up to all sorts of shenanigans.'

'Minty's relative?' asked Lianne.

'On second thoughts I doubt it was.'

I really hoped it wasn't, for Minty's sake. But it's hard to believe there'd be multiple people in the House of Lords with that name.

'What was he accused of?' said Zoe, staring fearfully at Fergus.

'Capturing water voles without a licence,' Rupert hooted and a crumb of toast shot straight out his mouth.

'I don't understand,' said Felicity.

'They're protected,' gloated Giles.

'Who cares?' grunted Shane.

'Wind farm surveys do. An application can fail based on an otter and water vole survey.'

'Was he releasing them then?' said Felicity, catching on.

Giles nodded at Fergus. 'Bad luck, for you.'

'Whoa, hang on a minute,' said Rupert. 'You're jumping the gun; the clip I saw said he was breeding them not releasing them.'

'Maybe it *is* Minty's dad,' said Lianne, terribly overexcited by the notion.

'Very clever to choose a water vole,' said Giles. 'All sorts of birds of prey feed off them. If released, the application would fail the ornithological survey too.'

'Angel,' said Zoe, 'I think you should give Stuart a call.'

Fergus took the order and marched out of the room.

'The ravens,' I whispered in Louis' ear.

'What about them?' He hadn't made the connection – these birds feed off voles.

'Nothing,' I shook my head. No point telling him my theory: water voles had been released here, they'd attracted the ravens and it's all happened at about the same time the art residency began. Mhàiri's husband Donald saw a light down by the river the night we arrived. The very evening Minty's father dropped her off.

Rupert changed the subject. 'That was a two-dog night if ever I've had one.'

'Such a marvellous saying,' giggled Felicity. 'What does it mean?'

'It means it was so cold you need a dog either side of you to keep warm.'

'I am sorry,' said Zoe.

'Not at all, I was exaggerating.'

Haggis rushed into the room; Fergus was back.

'Poor doggy,' said Felicity, stroking him at her feet, 'he's got icicles clinging to his fur.'

'Yes, it's a *very, very* cold morning. Donald's outside with the bus so chop chop, everyone, it's time to get moving. Fifteen minutes and you'll be off.'

There was a rush for the door. 'Jane, Felicity,' said Fergus, 'if you're all packed I'll get Donald to come in and carry your bags down.'

'Thank you, yes,' said Felicity nodding and Jane, without breaking her morning's silence, nodded too.

Rupert began to stack the plates. 'Don't bother to clear,' said Zoe. 'Mhàiri's here and you must get going.'

'Well, I'll just nip into the kitchen and say a big thank you.'

Rupert rustled his right hand in his right trouser pocket and pushed open the swing door. I knew: he was off to tip the cook. A sterling note stuck to his palm, all ready to transfer over to Mhàiri with a firm handshake. It made me smile to think how happy she'll be – and rather surprised, this isn't a standard move made by a paying guest. Rupert, dear Rupert's become overfamiliar to a fault.

I was last out of the dining room and raced upstairs, snatching some time to Google the news clip, before the goodbyes.

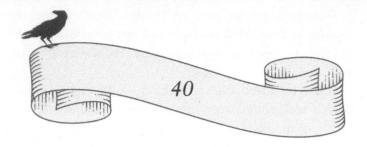

40

'For some time now the controversy of onshore wind farms has been a political issue with the Tories claiming many wind farms are blighting the land-scape,' said the short, clean-shaven man on my mobile's screen. 'A bill has passed to end subsidies to onshore wind farms from 1 October this year, a year earlier than set out in the previous coalition party agreement.' On he went, this spokesman from the Department of Energy and Climate Change, his hands clasped over his belt buckle. 'The change in timetable will not mean the Government can't meet its target for renewable energy. There are enough decisions in the pipeline to ensure targets are met.' Oozing confidence on this matter he added one final statement: 'There will be a grace period for projects that already have planning permission.'

The Energy Secretary then joined him to discuss the implications of the announcement, how it would affect investors as well as an agreement to press ahead with the intensification of offshore wind farms: 'The deal will look to seize on opportunities presented by the UK's seven thousand miles of coastline.'

Tagged on at the end was what I'd been waiting for, the short clip of Lord Froglan-Home-Mybridge, a tall lanky man with a big nose, grumbling away. He had a cleft chin, an inherited trait, the very same as Minty. He must be a relation.

The broadcast was preceded by a repeat of *News at Ten*'s coverage of his arrest. Not only had this man bred water voles (they were careful to mention there's no proof of releasing them) but he had paid Alec Ronaldsay, under the counter so to speak, a substantial amount of money to release several of his captive ravens into the wild.

Quote from a fellow peer: 'My associate and friend is not a malicious person. His actions were solely driven by his concern for the future of our beautiful island and the creatures that inhabit it. The excessive lengths he was willing to go to were driven by his commitment to the cause, not a means to target specific individuals. He was standing up for his principles; only in doing so was he breaking the law.'

A formal apology from the Conservative Party on behalf of their colleague was then read out, with the add-on, 'It is thought Lord Froglan-Home-Mybridge's good work as a member of the Lords will considerably reduce his sentence when the court makes its decision.'

Cor, what a story. So many things made sense now from beginning to end: the shrill in the dark sky when I first arrived; Stuart wanting to talk to Zoe urgently; the lights down by the river; I bet it was a captive bird flying into the kitchen window; Zoe's stolen bracelet; the explosion of ravens; Stuart's gruff manner when I met him in the wood. All from one man's conspiracy to stop the Auchen Laggan Tosh Moor wind farm. Or was Zoe behind it too? Had she teamed up with Ewen, the artist with a sensitivity for beautiful views, to terminate Fergus's application? The art residency would be the perfect opportunity to accept a Tory peer's daughter on the course and grant him access. Zoe even sent Stuart away that day – 'yous sent me to pick up a roll of tweed fer the mill'.

'*Susie?*' I heard Zoe shout along the corridor. 'Grab a coat and we'll go and wave goodbye.'

Whoops, I'd lost track of the time.

Almost everyone was in the hall and one after the other they were showering Zoe with appreciative thank yous and now I was here they moved on to me.

Lianne and Shane offered up a hug. 'Thank you so much, Susie.'

I smiled. I was sad to see them go.

Giles and Felicity both shook my hand. Then Rupert, having kissed Zoe on both cheeks, planted two on mine.

I reached to open the front door. Louis was on the other side.

'There you both are,' he said and welcomed Zoe's kiss. I took a few steps back at the sight but soon gloated when he gave me *four*. Credit to the French.

'Give me a text when you get to London,' he whispered as he stuffed a note in my hand. I smiled. All three of us stepped outside and no sooner was Louis down the steps than I thought, hang on a minute you arrogant so and so – surely *you* should be contacting *me*?

Zoe and I stood side by side.

'Have you all said goodbye to Fergus?' she called out.

Louis turned his head. 'Yes, he was here a moment ago.'

Then Zoe, suddenly remembering one other person, yelped, 'Where's Jane?'

Felicity stuck her head out the bus. 'She's already in here.'

'Wish her goodbye,' said Zoe.

'From me too,' I added.

The sooner Jane was gone the better and good luck to her trying to sell those diamonds on the open market.

Fergus and Haggis appeared from inside and joined Zoe and me, all ready to wave goodbye. He squeezed his wife's shoulder, the engine of the minibus started and all three of us threw our arms up in the air. No sooner had it left the yard than I dashed upstairs to get my stuff.

I returned the heater to the broom cupboard and picked up my suitcase as well as the Edith Wharton novel. I must remember to put that back.

I said a fond goodbye to Mhàiri and then found Zoe and Fergus in the library, slumped on the sofa with Haggis between them.

'We were just enjoying a bit of time to ourselves,' said Fergus, getting up. 'It is nice to think we'll be back to our usual routine soon.'

'I bet it is.'

Zoe got up too and Haggis stretched his legs out, making the most of the extra space.

'Thank you very much for inviting me here. I could not have enjoyed it more and you organised and ran it all perfectly.'

Fergus beamed and Zoe said, 'It was nice you and Louis got on so well.'

I blushed. 'Isn't he lovely?'

'We both thought so too,' Zoe smiled at Fergus.

'Now, now,' he said, 'let's not talk about people behind their backs. Susie, I'll take your bag.' He stretched out an arm. 'If you're going all the way to Sussex you must get on the road.'

'Haggis,' said Zoe. 'Time to say goodbye to Susie.'

She kissed me in the hall. 'Thank you so much, Susie. Safe journey.'

'Thank you for having me. I'll be in touch about the drawing.' I bent down to give Haggis a cuddle.

'Oh yes, I can't wait to see it.'

Fergus opened the front door and out we went.

'I do hope you'll make it home okay in this weather, Susie,' he said as he put my suitcase in the car.

'I'll go slow. It'll be fine.' I kissed him on both cheeks. 'Thank you.'

I waved goodbye as I left the yard and headed off down the long bumpy drive. Over a humpback bridge I went, saying a little prayer, *Oh Lord, give the Muchtons strength to bear the bad news…and help me please work it out.*

You never know, I might just crack it before Jamie Tumbleton-Smith visits. Easter weekend's in my favour – national holidays and all that.

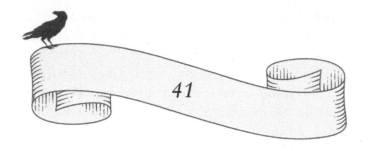

41

'ENGLAND,' I shouted out loud in my car. I'd crossed the border, it was time for a break. At last the outside temperature has risen above zero, the roads are motorways from here on in and, Yes, I'm definitely going to make it home tonight.

My most recently downloaded music has been on a loop, me singing and dancing in the driving seat, celebrating my first tutoring job. Will I do something like that again? Probably. The money's good and although I'm jolly glad it's over I did love spending time living with strangers.

A sign for a service station popped up and I took the next exit. The massive billboard in the car park boasted *First farm shop in the UK*. So, with my handbag over my shoulder I rushed in to find what goodies they had inside.

'What can I get for you, duck?'

'One of those sausage rolls, please. They look amazing.'

'Don't they just. Anything else for yourself? Slice of cake? Bit of flapjack? Double chocolate brownie? We have all sorts of beautiful things for yourself to choose from.'

'A bottle of fizzy water and that's all, thanks.'

'Right ye are then. Enjoy. Michelle will take your payment at the till over there.'

I smiled. Why is it northern service stations have such friendly customer service? Perhaps it's because there are fewer people in these parts and therefore those in services can keep up a fresh and friendly hello all day.

I paid Michelle and found a window seat. It looked out over a very muddy pond and on the vacant next-door table I spotted a coffee-stained business paper. I reached across and helped myself, hoping I'd find the Froglan-Home-Mybridge report.

I flicked the sheets – here we go. Lord Froglan-Home-Mybridge, husband of Patricia and father to Jonathan, Araminta and Harry – he *was* Minty's father. It was too much of a coincidence not to be true. I thought as much, but looking at it here, reading like a death notice, filled me with shock. My stomach plummeted. I'd read enough. *Poor* Minty.

I dug my mobile out of my bag. I'm not the most communicative of people when it comes to modern means, but two days without reception and I was excited to see who might have been in touch.

1. Vodafone with an offer.
2. Friend, Sam, saying my mum's invited him for Easter and will I please answer him.

He'd left a voicemail and two texts…You'd think he would have twigged I was out of reception. I'm sure I told him I was going to Scotland, but then again, we haven't spoken for a while. I'd better send him a text…

Hey Sam, I've been away, heading home now. You must come for Easter lunch. It's not like you haven't been for the last 4 years. Speak soon, Susie x

3. An excellent message from Jenny, a really great high-flying friend who's been working abroad for the last eight years.

Susie!!! I'm home. In London. For good. Let's meet up v v v v v v soon. SO much to tell. Hugs and kisses. J

Jenny and I go back years, all the way to junior school, and ever since then she's had her head down. I cannot *wait* to see her. Oooh, I wonder if her on/off boyfriend is coming over too. I'll be so happy if they've finally made it work.

4. A text from Toby...

My sausage roll was more tempting than reading this right now so I turned my phone over and took a big greedy bite.

Arghhh, the friggin' thing was absolutely piping hot. I spat into my napkin and looked around, luckily no one else was watching.

Bzzzz, bzzzz, my mobile vibrated.

1 new message Sam

Just thought you might not want me this year. I'll say yes then. Please call soon, it'd be good to have a chat before x

Urgh, Sam. *Why* do you have to make it complicated? I knew exactly what he was getting at…our drunken kiss before Christmas, standing on the pavement as I was waiting for a bus. It wasn't a long-drawn-out passionate number. Just a sort of whoopsie we-shouldn't-be-doing-this affair. It's never happened before, and why then, who knows? But surely we don't have to discuss it? N.B. call him tomorrow.

The sausage roll was delicious but I'd finished it. Time to get going. I weaved my way through the stationary cars and jumped back into the driving seat with a rush of energy for the next leg. I slipped my mobile into what used to be called the ashtray and, just before the engine started, I had a reconsidered thought: Toby's message was playing on my mind, it would be safer to read it now than resist it while driving. I picked up my phone. My fingers trembled as I unlocked the screen.

Susie, I know you'll be on the road south when you get this but I'd really like it if you called. We need to talk. Toby x

I chucked the mobile back and started the car. Oh heck, the engine let out an unpleasant roar as I missed the gear. *Grrr*, Toby, it's all your fault, your unbelievably manipulative text has got under my skin.

I looked at the dashboard. It's just after two. If in a moment of clear thinking *he* was going to call *me*, it would have happened in his lunch break, which is over now. Phew, I really don't want to talk to him and for at least the next three to four hours he'll be too busy working for anything else.

Radio 4 played for a change. Two theologians were discussing the meaning of Good Friday. *Blast*, I'd completely forgotten it's a public holiday...Toby won't be in the mortuary today. But a split second of thought and I concluded – he was never going to call me. His text was a fine way of turning the tables. The ball was in my court. He'd made darn sure if we never speak again then it's all my fault.

I give up. *Stuff him.* I don't need you in my life, Toby.

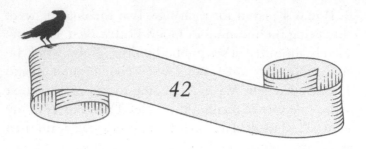

42

I turned the radio off – debating Good Friday isn't my kind of thing. And as I drove in silence, munching up the miles in the fast lane, I pin-pointed everyone's reason for being at Auchen Laggan Tosh. I have to make sure no one else was acting with Ewen. I can't just assume he was in it alone.

I remember a similar case of art fraud I'd heard of before. It happened in Ireland years ago, when a chauffeur faked a Canaletto under his employers' noses, selling the original and hanging the copy. Not that I think Mhàiri, Donald or Stuart are involved. Employee teaming up with a family member, no, I don't think so.

Very quickly names began to fall off the suspects' list. Jane's mission was to steal the necklace, Felicity her veil. They cancel each other out. Minty was a pawn in her father's plan and Giles, not the sharpest tool in the box, was sent by his mother to practise his art in the hopes he'd get at least one A at A Level. We can set them both to one side. Shane and Lianne were awarded scholarships so couldn't possibly have orchestrated their place and had Rupert been involved I have absolutely no doubt he would have accidentally let it slip. So, we can put him to bed too. Fergus has far too much pride in his art collection and surely wouldn't have risked exhibiting the copies. He's not a part of it. Louis, I fancied...but now I know he has a girlfriend Toby's words, 'I don't think you should trust that man...he'll hurt you', couldn't be more on message. We *are* a good team. But I bet you he'd never see it like that. Did Louis really pay over the asking price to get his place? Or had Ewen whispered he was a friend in Zoe's ear and she accepted him to keep the peace?

Bring, bring. Bring, bring. My mobile rang through the loudspeaker. A Sussex number flashed up, I better answer. I was just passing Birmingham on the M6 Toll, making good progress, well over halfway and predicting I'd be home just before seven.

'Hello?'

'Susie, is that you?'

'Yes.'

'It's Lavender Bell.'

'Lavender, hello. How nice to hear from you.'

Lavender is a friend, well, an absent friend really, of my mother's. Going back to when they were teenagers – that period in life when one has a large group of unidentifiable muckers. Mum's often talked of her but hasn't seen her for many years, the reason being my parents got married very late for their generation, and by then their contemporaries had drifted away. They were out of step. Almost all of their friends had entered into the complacent stage of marriage, done with popping out children and no longer keen on spending time with those in nappies. When I was born Mum had plenty of eccentric spinsters around to keep her vaguely sane, but I do feel a bit sorry for her, looking back.

Anyway, shortly after I'd made the move to Sussex, three years ago now, Mum told me Lavender lived there too. Something to do with her marrying a banker and bankers apparently – according to Mum – like to settle in Sussex. Property's expensive, this boosts their image and there's nothing like a national park to make them feel they own the land. Mum passed on my number to Lavender and ever since she's invited me for dinner twice annually. Full points to her for trying and nil points to me for genuinely never being able to go.

'Susie,' she squawked, 'I left a message about dinner on your landline. I'm sure you've put the date in your diary and just forgotten to let me know?'

One, I don't have an answering machine, but there was no point going into that right now, and two, I couldn't possibly refuse again…

'I'm sorry,' I said out loud in the car, 'I've been away. But I'm heading home now.'

'Oh, jolly good. That means you'll be able to come.'

'When is it?'

'Tonight.'

'Tonight?' I yelped but it fell on deaf ears. Literally. Many of Mum's age group are by now.

'Yes, come for seven forty-five, no need to wear any-thing dressy.'

'I might not…'

She cut me short. 'I know you might not know anyone but don't worry about that. They're very nice. There is someone I think you'll get on particularly well with, a much younger friend of mine, George, Georgina

Foss. I'm sure you've come across her? She is, or at least she's about to be, on TV. Now, you know where I am, don't you?'

'Yes.'

'Other side of Lewes from you, a Tudor cottage in Berwick.'

'Got it. Thank you. Bye.' I cancelled the call.

I don't have a clue who Georgina Foss is. I've never owned a TV and I often wonder when those who do have the time to sit down and watch it. Either George, as Lavender had so affectionately called her, is my age, or she has something to do with the art world.

Mum's friend has me hook, line and sinker. With only moments at home for a quick change I'll then be back in my car and off to dinner. Unpacking will have to wait until tomorrow and, as for a night off, that luxury has gone out of the window. *Harrumph*. Having promised Mum and Dad I'd be with them on Saturday and already predicting they'll guilt trip me into staying longer – 'Susie, I feel you just squeeze your father and me in when you can – It's not like you ever spend more than two nights with us – It would be good if you could stay till Wednesday – give us all time to rebuild our relationship as a family' – there wasn't going to be a moment to reflect. I must use the rest of this journey wisely. I have two and a half hours from here on in. I have to stick with art fraud while it's fresh in my mind.

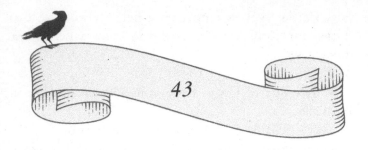

43

Collins English Dictionary, Puzzle: Solve or understand something by thinking hard.

Think hard I did, as Banbury, Bicester, High Wycombe and Crawley passed.

For Ewen, who knew that a medical procedure – the caesarean – could have such a profound effect on the inheritance of an ancient title? Copying and selling a few pictures would be a great way of taking revenge on his brother and getting his fair share, as he liked to put it, money being the main objective.

Ewen's a painter but realistically could he pull off the job without an accomplice? For one, swapping over the paintings alone seems pretty impossible. How do you hang a picture on two chains without someone to hold the other half? And as for the painting, did he copy it from life, set up his easel in the locked wing when Fergus and Zoe were away? No, far too much of a palaver getting all the equipment in...Much more likely via photographs.

He'd said himself, 'If I learnt to take good pictures of paintings, I could then work from them back home...

understand the technical details.' Then he'd admitted, 'despite doing a course, I'm not very good at photography.'

Ah ha...I've seen Louis' work, he has talent and if he was working together with Ewen, his friend, there would be no better combination for art fraud. A skilled photographer and an accomplished artist.

Let's say they hit it off on a photography course seven years ago. Ewen's father then dies and Fergus inherits. Ewen thinks, how can I make a lot of money for myself? He comes up with a plan and gets in touch with his mate Louis. They strike a deal to become partners in crime.

Louis told me he's been to Auchen Laggan Tosh twice before. I reckon the first time was to photograph *Rutting Stags* so Ewen could set to, painting a copy. The second visit was planned for when Ewen's equivalent Landseer was finished. Done and dry. Together they carried out a swap with the original, at the same time giving Louis an opportunity to photograph another, *Dogs in the Moonlight*. With only one elderly woman, the Dowager Countess of Muchton, in the house I assume it was a pretty easy thing to do.

The first original was sold, the transaction worked smoothly and Ewen got a taste for it all. But I think Zoe caught him out with his second copy. The day she referred to, stumbling into his studio. And although I hate to think Zoe's involved, going behind her husband's back, it is beginning to look likely to me. Everything from seeing her in the corridor on Monday night to not wanting the paintings to go on loan. I reckon she black-mailed Ewen to cut her in on the deal. We all know accountants are brilliant at hiding illegitimate cash on their tax return, and Fergus had proudly told us his wife had 'taken the estate's accounts in hand'. She wasn't ever planning to tell her husband.

Next step in the plan, Ewen's completed *Dogs in the Moonlight*: he needs a suitable moment for his photographer friend to return. The art residency was ideal. 'Now's our chance to swap the paintings and collar another.' I can hear Ewen saying it. 'You can stay in the main house with a bunch of strangers. No one will suspect a thing.' Zoe then sneaks Louis onto the course and their operation is under way. I've been suspicious of Zoe's friendship with Louis all along, and she boasted of getting on well with Ewen. All three of them, I'm now sure, are in this together.

I have to get my theory absolutely straight. So, going back to the start of the week I've decided the real reason Louis came late to the very first life drawing session on Monday is because he'd been down the back drive at Ewen's cottage, helping him carry a copy of Landseer's *Dogs in the Moonlight* from the studio to the van.

Now I think about it, when Louis asked Rupert to park the minibus away from the house on Monday afternoon on our way back from the river, he could have been making space for Ewen's van, later. It had to be right up close to the steps so as in the night, once the house party had gone to bed (when I saw a light on in the locked wing), this pair, supervised by Zoe, could swap an original for a copy. *Dogs in the Moonlight*, the painting with very little dust on its frame. Maybe Louis had pulled a muscle in his arm during the hanging. What's more they'd need a spirit level to get it straight.

The one I'd found under the hall table. One of them must have dropped it by mistake.

I can practically hear Ewen reassuring his accomplice, 'I'll send Fergus to sleep with Piriton, he'll never hear a thing.' Ewen must have crushed up a tablet when I'd caught him filling the water glasses before dinner. He'd even made a point later of confirming the drugs were Zoe's. She's involved, I know it. She'd even covered up the fact Fergus had overslept the next morning. With everything going on in the night, no wonder Haggis was shut away downstairs.

On Ewen would have gone, the leader of the two, 'When we're in the ballroom you must photograph our next project, *Early Morning Stags on the Moor*.' 'Yes, yes,' says Louis, beaming with excitement. Result: the photograph of heather on Louis' camera wasn't actually from real life. It was a detail by Landseer. No surprise I'd been shut down when I suggested putting it on Zoe's website.

If Ewen was in a bit of a fuss on the way home, heart beating rapidly with suppressed guilt, he could have easily accidentally hit a deer down the back drive. Then dragged it into the wood in a hopeless attempt to cover it up.

The huge file I saw downloading on Ewen's computer, when Rupert and I paid him a surprise visit, *were* Louis' photographs, details of *Early Morning Stags on the Moor* — they'd used up most of the bandwidth allowance.

Mention of an art valuer visiting had given Zoe the heebie-jeebies — she'd kicked up a fuss about the Landseers going on loan but she'd underestimated her husband's persistence. He was mad keen they should be shown.

Urgh. I feel so embarassed remembering how smug I felt when I heard Ewen had gone away. I really believed he'd taken my advice and gone to start his own life. But no, he must have fled, maybe before or maybe at the same time as the woman driving the silver van. The very one Davy bumped into. Odd at the time, but now, I think, she must have been transporting an original painting. Davy had said she was all alone...So where is Ewen?

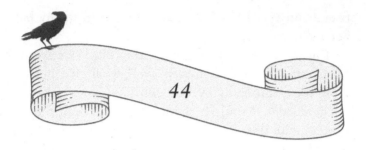

44

I rang the doorbell on the old-fashioned chain of
Downs View, Berwick. Thirty seconds later and no
answer, I let myself in. There was chattering in the room
to my left but as I've caught a view of the dining room
I'm going to put my box of chocolates in there. It gives
me an excuse to count up the places.

Ten people are coming to dinner and as I creak open
the small door to the sitting room it appears everyone
has arrived.

'You must be Susie, how marvellous to meet you.'
Lavender's eyeshadow matched her purple lipstick and
the baubles of her necklace and the studs in her ears. She
gasped towards me across the small room and the lightness of the pomegranate print chiffon dress over her
plump figure shimmered.

'You look just like your mother,' she said as she
embraced me in her bosom.

Up until now I've always been told I'm the spitting
image of my father's mother, not *my* mother. But this
kind of thing is what people say to make you feel like
you belong. Lavender was welcoming my looks as an old

friend and I told her how pleased I was to finally have been able to come.

'I nearly gave up asking you.' She rolled her eyes for comic effect. 'I said to myself, well, we'll give her one more try. Damned lucky I did, eh?'

I nodded and smiled, giving off all the right impressions despite the truth – I'd so much rather be at home in bed. Even Mum, when I'd rung to say I'd made it home, thought me going out for dinner would be an ordeal. 'They'll all be strangers double your age, poppet. No nice young men to keep you awake. You really should have said no.'

My parents will never tire of telling me what I should and shouldn't do. They just love to be the ones in charge, respecting my decisions if they're in accordance with theirs and kicking up a fuss if I go my own way. They've got it in their heads family mistakes are genetic. They're convinced I, their only child, will get a double dosage of theirs and their relations'. They're constantly trying to save me tripping up; the problem is, they leap in with opinions before I've even taken a step. But I'm soldiering on, living alone, being an artist and no doubt proving them wrong.

'Would you like some wine, Susie?' said Lavender. 'Or something stronger? Your mother was always fond of a tipple.'

'A glass of white wine would be lovely, thank you.' I grinned; Mum would not like me being told this.

'I'll do it, Lav,' came the dulcet tone of a dapper man next to the drinks cupboard.

'Do take your coat off, Suz, and when you're done just lay it on the sofa.'

As soon as I turned around, Lavender thrust a glass into my hand and introduced me to 'Georgina Foss'.

Rubbish, I'd meant to Google her.

'Hello, I'm Susie Mahl.'

Lavender left us.

'Do call me George, it's so much easier when one is amongst friends.'

'Okay.'

'I'm told you're an artist. Are you a painter, a writer, a sculptor, a dancer…?'

'I'm a painter. Or at least trying to be.' I gave a self-deprecating giggle.

'You must stick at it. I'd love to hear more about your work. That's if you don't mind?'

I went hot at the thought and moved a step away from the fire. 'I paint in oil, still lifes and landscapes mostly.'

'From life?'

'Yes, to begin with at least.'

'Good girl. I can't stand pictures from photographs. You can always tell. What's your style?'

'Well, hmmm, my paintings are, well, hmmm, always figurative but if you looked at a corner of one you might think it was abstract. I love colour.'

'They sound wacky.'

I'd failed, they're not. George had the wrong end of the stick.

'Not exactly. I'm too unrelaxed to be wacky.'

She laughed as if trying to put me at ease. 'Boy, I'd love to see some one day.'

'Thank you,' I said, returning her smile. 'It is kind of Lavender to have told you what I do.'

'It's only because she knows I can be *such* a bore about art. I guess she wanted to palm me off on you. Bad luck.'

'You won't bore me, I could talk about it forever.' Slight exaggeration but I was throwing myself in. If I want to leave early I must make an impression.

'What do you do?' I asked.

'I used to work for an antique dealer.'

'And now?'

'Now...' It was as if I should recognise her by name. 'Now I'm a presenter.'

'Sorry, I should have known.'

'Not at all. You will know. It isn't out yet.'

'When is it?' I said, implying I had a TV.

(A documentary on antiques – it's not as if I'd be missing much.)

'11th May, BBC Two, 9pm. Not the first time I've said that. It's been in a very long broadcast queue. Made it a year ago but apparently that's how these things go. I suppose the editing takes a bit of time and then there's the consents. Just so many rules these days.' She huffed.

'Is that for the owners?'

'What?'

'Is it consent from the people who own the antiques?'

George flung her head back and as her hand shook with amusement she miraculously managed not to spill any wine out of her glass.

'How hilarious you are. It's got absolutely nothing to do with antiques.'

I giggled as if it was the right thing to do.

'I'm the face of a documentary on art fraud.'

'*Wow*,' I was startled. I couldn't bring myself to say any more.

'Had me down as an *Antiques Roadshow* go-er, did you?'

'No, not at all.' My cheeks were burning.

'Don't worry,' she said. 'Why don't you tell me what you've been up to today?'

'Come on, you two,' came Lavender's order, 'break it up a bit.'

She nestled her ample behind between us and offered up a plate of cold cheese vol-au-vents.

'You mustn't keep talking to each other.' She shunted George's shoulder. 'Have you met James Crow?'

'Hello,' he said.

James Crow was very tidy, his accent hard to distinguish and the distance between his legs suggested he'd spent today playing golf. But before I could decide on any more, a sharp 'Hello, I'm Jessica Jones' came into my left ear.

This short thin woman in a stiff linen sack was clearly well practised in working a room. 'You're the only person I haven't met yet,' she beamed.

'Susie Mahl.' I smiled, thinking it unnecessary to shake hands.

Nevertheless hers sprung out and as our palms clasped she said, 'Mahl, that's unusual. Is it your married name or your maiden name?'

'Maiden name.'

'Ah, so you're a professional like me. How nice.'

I looked a little confused and she explained, 'When I met my husband I'd already established my career so I couldn't possibly have taken his name. Rather a bold move in my day.'

'What do you do?' I asked, assuming she must be a high-flier.

'I'm a part-time literary translator. French and Portuguese. And you?'

'I'm a painter.'

'You mean an artist?'

Amusingly, I think, Jessica is trying to confirm I'm not a painter-decorator without having to ask.

'Yes, an artist who paints.'

'And how do you know Lavender? She's so good at mixing the ages.'

'Tonight is the first time I've met her, but she knew my mother when they were young.'

'What a lovely connection.'

I gave a light smile and asked the same question back.

'Philip, my husband over there,' she pointed at a man whose podgy hand rose as his fingers gave a little flutter towards us, 'is her daughter's godfather.'

'So you're good friends?'

'Yes, I suppose I could have put it like that.'

'But you'd rather give him a role.' This popped out my mouth completely unintentionally. Oh crumbs, my thoughts are turning themselves into words, a sure sign I'm far too tired for this. I compensated with a huge smile confirming – for her – I completely agreed with how she'd put it.

'Dinner,' announced Lavender and I dived out the sitting room into the kitchen.

'Suz, be a star and put one of these on each plate, please.'

I looked down at ten sandy potatoes glued to a baking tray and when I stretched for the oven gloves I was told, 'Don't worry with those. Everything's been out of the oven a little while.'

For dinner we were having gammon steaks, baked potatoes and skin-on-the-top white sauce. The full plates were being fed through a hatch by which Philip stood helpfully laying them round the table. Names had been scrawled on pieces of notepaper and, once seen, people began to sit down.

'Oh no, Suz,' said Lavender, 'I forgot *this*. Do be a saint and take it round.'

She handed me a packet of pre-chopped parsley, curly – urgh – and motioned for me to take a saucer off the Welsh dresser. I followed her instruction and left the kitchen. Little pinches of two fingers and a thumb sprinkled it on top of the thick white sauce.

'Here you go,' said Philip, swapping the herb in my hand for a full plate in his. 'That's us all done.'

I sat down next to the dapper drinks server and the stump of the table. That's the end of the table with no one there. If it was my supper party I'd have had uneven sides, and a person at each end. Saving those like me from one-sided company and a high possibility of the conversation going dead. But come to think of it there's something wonderfully relaxed about Lavender's lack of pre-planning – or chaotic planning if you look at it like this. Doorbell – no answer; laid table – cold food; name places – uneven numbers. I'm all of a sudden rather amused by how this evening's going to pan out. A far cry from the Auchen Laggan Tosh timetable.

Opposite me was Paul, an unprepossessing man with no hair and enormous nostrils. I'd introduced myself briefly before dinner and was, to be quite honest, keen to avoid him. He had a whiff of I-haven't-washed-for-a-while about him but, now, sitting opposite, I thought I must be polite.

I tried to catch his attention as he looked up and down the table but our eyes failed to meet – he clearly didn't rate me much either. I watched as he punched his breast bone and drew a groggy lump up his throat. Poor Jessica beside him. Here's hoping the bearded man on her right has better manners.

'Hello,' said my neighbour who wanted to shake hands, 'I'm the son-in-law Stephen.'

'Hello, I'm Susie. Is Lavender's daughter here?' I was surprised. Why hadn't we been introduced?

Stephen laughed. A composed laugh but a laugh nonetheless and I realised what a ridiculous mistake I'd made. 'I'm sorry.' I laughed too. 'It's only Jessica mentioned a daughter. I haven't ever met Lavender before.'

Jessica looked up.

'It's okay,' Stephen nudged my knee. 'That's Chris there.'

Chris, the man with the beard, raised his mono-brow and nodded a 'Hello'.

'He's not feeling well,' whispered Stephen.

'Poor guy.'

'It's his mother's food. I think you'll agree.'

'I haven't tried it yet,' I smiled and he watched as I *attempted* to cut up my gammon steak.

All I can say is I'm extremely glad it was in a thick white sauce. So thick it didn't even wobble, let alone splatter, and as I literally sawed the piece of meat in half, I felt myself brewing uncontrollable giggles. Church giggles. Those ones I just cannot stop.

But Stephen's words set me straight. 'Be careful,' he

said as I wiped a tear from my eye, 'you can tease Lavender about a lot of things but never her food.'

I swallowed hard and pulled myself together.

It turns out both Stephen and I shared a love of cooking and we passed the time sharing tips. When everyone had, eventually, managed to finish their plates, we both got up and cleared the table.

Chris joined us in the kitchen.

'Hi, Susie, it's nice to meet you. Mum's been *longing* to get you over.'

'She's so kind. Thank goodness I've finally been able to come.'

'Have you lived down here long?'

'Nearly three years. What about you?'

'We're in London. But often visit. Don't we?' He turned to Stephen.

'Yes, Lavender adores company. When we're not around she's on her own.'

'On her own?' Chris joked. He looked pale. 'Mum's got more friends than the three of us put together.'

'How are you feeling?' Stephen asked him.

'Pretty dreadful.'

'You *must* go back to bed then. Come, I'll look after you.'

Chris turned to me. 'I am sorry to do this.'

I was just about to say don't worry, it's okay, when Lavender entered the kitchen. 'You youngsters chatting away in here,' she tut-tutted. 'Isn't it nice to meet Suz? Looks just like her mother when I first knew her. But, hang on, you're much older. What fresh looks you have.' She stroked my face. 'If I were you, I'd keep a hold of them.'

'Mum.'

'Yes, love.'

'I feel so ill. I'm going to have to go to bed.'

Stephen put his arm around his husband's shoulders.

'Poor pops. Thank you for trying to stay up. Off you go then. Night, night.'

They both left the room and Lavender sighed, 'Chris's father and I weren't a good example, nor was his step-father, but those two, you can't separate them. It's almost worse, don't you think?'

I shrugged.

'Single? Are you?'

'Yup.'

'Clever girl. Best way to be.' She opened the fridge. 'I've been on my own forty-six years. Here,' she handed me a tray of chocolate pots, 'help me take the lids off these.'

'Did you make them?'

'Me?' she frowned. I'd been trying to flatter her. 'No, no one makes dessert these days. Do they?'

I thought best go with the flow and replied, 'I doubt it.'

The lids were all off and as Lavender turned to the fridge for cream she said, 'Would you be kind and carry the tray? I get terribly unsteady with a drink in me.'

'Of course.'

'Potts & Co.,' announced Jessica seeing the tray; she'd obviously had this pudding before.

Lavender came through with a large jug of cream, then, noticing me out on a limb, she bellowed, 'George, move up a place so's you're next to Suz. Chris's ill. He and Stephen have gone to bed.'

'I'm *so* pleased,' said George as she shuffled towards

me, swapping over her glass and reaching for the bottle. 'Now you can tell me all about what you were up to today.' Her eyes were wide open, full of anticipation.

I don't believe in fate but I do believe in grasping opportunities when they present themselves, and here I was with a stranger who'd been the face of an art fraud documentary. I had so many questions up my sleeve. I did not want to waste time discussing my day.

'It's difficult to know where to begin today. There's not much to tell.'

'Just launch straight in. I don't need to know what you ate for breakfast.' George found herself slightly more amusing than I did. Not that I didn't laugh, just that I wasn't the one swinging back on my chair with my mouth wide open.

'I spent a lot of today in my car. It was dull. I'd so much rather talk about art fraud.'

'Great. Let's do that then. Do you know anything about it?'

'Not a lot but I've always wanted to know more.'

'Well, I'm afraid I was only the presenter but fire away with your questions and you never know, I might have the answers.'

This is great. George's indifference to where my interest came from allowed me the freedom to ask whatever I wanted. And so I began, 'I've often wondered how easy it would be to copy a nineteenth-century masterpiece and sell the original without anyone ever knowing.'

'It's not something generally kept secret. Many people have copies made of paintings before they sell them. You can go and see the process in pretty much any auction house. I can set up a visit for you if you want?'

'That's so kind of you but no, it's okay. I really meant, if a painting is copied by someone, not the owner, and that person replaces the original with the copy and sells the original, is it an easy thing to keep quiet?'

'Are you planning something?'

George was alarmed at my surprise. 'Don't worry,' she said, 'I'm only joking. In truth it's not an easy thing to keep quiet but it does happen and the less well-known the artist the more chance of getting away with it. Just you wait for my documentary, you're going to love it.'

'I bet I will.'

George took a glug of wine and I realised I'd forgotten to eat pudding. I put a teaspoonful in my mouth.

'It's good, isn't it,' she said.

'Sure is.'

I glanced up the table. Lavender gave me the happiest grin as if to say, 'I'm *so* pleased you and George are getting on'.

'Right,' said George as I finished my last mouthful, 'try me with another.'

'How easy is it to locate a painting sold on the black market?'

'As in find it?'

'Yes.'

'Practically impossible, I'd say.'

'Oh. What about tracing how and where it left the country?'

'If it's a painting you're thinking of, they're mostly transported by container ship. Less likely to get damaged than on an aeroplane. Various UK ports serve different countries. But you'd have to know where the buyer comes from, first.'

'What a muddle. Is your documentary about a painting?'

'No, no. The first episode, I hope there will be more, follows a vast sculpture of a horse. Harder to hide, easier to find. The producers had to give themselves the best chance at an ending. It does teach one an awful lot about the trade, though, which is the point.'

'Of course.'

'Now, Susie, I'm terribly sorry but I'm gasping for a cigarette. Would you like one?'

A large part of me wanted to say yes but it's been several months since I last smoked and I mustn't cave in *again* (just yet).

'No thank you. I think I might head home now. It was so great to meet you.'

'You too.' George kissed me on both cheeks. 'I hope one day we'll meet again.'

'Yes, I hope so too.'

I said goodbye to the table and Lavender saw me to the door. 'Toodle pip, Suz,' she said, steadying herself against the frame. 'Let's get together again. Give me a tinkle anytime.'

'Thank you so much, that was great fun.' I waved back at her as I crossed the gravel turning circle and got into my car.

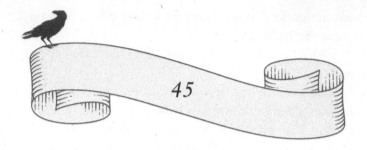

45

Yawn. It's Saturday morning, just gone nine o'clock. Last night I slept like a log. Straight through my alarm and I don't know what woke me, but something did. I've been downstairs and made a pot of tea and I'm now upright in bed basking in spring sunshine waiting for an answer to my call.

I've Googled two things this morning. 1. *where do containers from the uk to canada depart?* Answer: Portsmouth. 2. *who do I call to report an art fraud?* Answer: the local constabulary.

'Highlands and Islands Police Headquarters, how may I direct your call?' came the voice of a particularly cheery soul.

'Hello.'

'Yes, Missy? Whit's yous name?'

'Susie Mahl.'

'How may I help?'

Last night I'd worked out exactly what I was going to say and so without hesitation, I launched straight in. 'Officer, there's something I'd like to report...'

He interrupted, 'Yous fe England?'

'Yes, I am and I'd like to…'

'Right ye are,' he cut me off again, 'I can see from the code showing on the phone. It ain't a local number and with yous accent I put the two and two together.'

'That's so clever of you.' I *had* to get rid of this buffoon. 'Can I speak to your supervisor, please?'

'Yous'll have to tell me what it's aboot. I canee just pass yous on willy-nilly, yous ken.'

'I'd like to report a fraud.'

'Right ye are then, putting you through now.'

'Hello?'

'Hello, Officer.'

'It's Constable MacKinzie if you must.'

'Constable MacKinzie.'

'Name please?'

'Susie.'

'No other names?'

'Mahl.'

'What?'

'M A H L.'

'Right, why don't yous tell me why yous are calling and then I'll assess if we need yous details.'

Seriously? I think this station has scraped the barrel for fill-in holiday staff.

'Okay, sure…'

Before I could add any more he said, 'Pressing issue or emergency?'

'I'd like to report some art fraud.'

'Oh, looks like you're in luck, my boss has just arrived. I'll pass yous over.'

'Inspector Gordon, how may I help you?'

'My name's Susie Mahl, I'm calling to report an art fraud.'

'Right okay, give me a second, I've been caught up this morning and I've only just got to the station.'

I heard the sound of a chair scraping across a wooden floor, a desk drawer opening and a tin of pens rattling. A huge sigh came down the line. 'Right, you still there?'

'Yes.'

'Susie Mahl, Norland Lane, East Sussex. Correct?'

'Correct. How come you have my details?'

'Traced your phone number.'

'I see.'

'This is the Highlands and Islands Police HQ, do you think you've got the wrong number?'

'No, this is right. I was wondering if you've had a call about a local art fraud?'

'No comment.'

'So, you have?'

'Let's hypothetically speaking say we have.'

'Okay. It's to do with the Earl and Countess of Muchton at Auchen Laggan Tosh.'

'Yes, I know that.'

This man was easy to crack.

'I spent this last week tutoring on an art residency up there.'

'Aye, I heard about that.'

'I was there when the art valuer suggested two Landseers were copies.'

'Supposedly identified,' he corrected. 'According to Lord Muchton the art dealership rang on Wednesday morning to tell him the news. We don't have confirmation yet. There's a meeting in the diary for Tuesday with an art specialist but other than that there isn't a huge amount we can do.'

'Well, I'm observant by nature and over the last week I noticed quite a few things tied up with the copies.'

'If they *are* copies,' he reminded me again. 'You're going to have to explain yourself. The fraud was reported yesterday. If it turns out to be true, we have no idea which generation is to blame. This case is going to take months if not years.' A long breath came huffing down the line. 'As the station is affuy quiet today why don't you tell me a bit more about what you know? If you can aid our investigation, it's a red-letter day for me. The family aren't too happy.'

I've decided it would only complicate matters if I took Inspector Gordon through every step of my theory. I assume he's further ahead than he's let on. But I reached my conclusion behind the Muchtons' back, and I don't want to ruin my reputation, so I said, 'Inspector, I'd really appreciate it if I could remain anonymous going forward.'

He put me in my place. 'I'm not planning on mentioning your name to anyone. You tell me what you know, I'll keep it in the back of my mind and if it helps it helps and if not, so be it. You won't be getting a medal.'

'Great. Thanks.'

'Quick now, coffee time is approaching, give me what you've got.'

'Lord Muchton has a twin brother.'

'Aye, Ewen Hewson.'

'Yes. Ewen's an artist. He's the one who's been copying the paintings. I found his initials E H hidden in the pictures.'

'Did you now.'

This man doesn't believe me.

'I can guide the expert to the very spot. Anyone could miss them. But in the meantime if you search Ewen's house you'll find a projector, an array of specific painting equipment as well as a history of photograph downloads on his computer.' I'm putting myself on the line but, hey-ho, I have to nudge this man into action and to do so I must be bold. I wasn't even going to mention Louis. If he's involved, he'll be found out in the end, and as for Zoe, she may never be caught. I doubt there's enough evidence to prove her guilty. But a guilty conscience is hard to live with, her comeuppance will be served. So I said, 'I think an original Landseer is on its way to Canada.'

'*Now?*'

'Yes. In a silver Ford Transit on its way to, if it hasn't already arrived at, Portsmouth.' This was a guess but I didn't think Ewen would use his van, so it was all I had to go on. 'It left Auchen Laggan Tosh on Wednesday night. Mike's Motors, a local garage, will give you the registration.' I didn't mention the female driver. I hadn't seen her so I couldn't be sure.

'Never mind that coffee.' Inspector Gordon had clicked into action. 'I'm going to hang up, Miss Mahl, and get on to this right away.'

'One more thing, do you know about the email from Ethan and Chloe Hewson?'

'Aye, aye, Lord Muchton's told us everything. The email might be a hoax but it is, well, was, our main lead.'

Inspector Gordon ended the call.

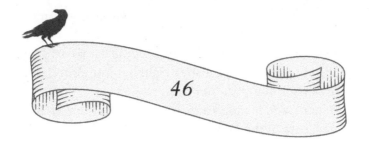

46

Mum, as predicted, persuaded me to stay on a few days after Easter. It's now Wednesday and I've only just left. Sam went down unsurprisingly well at lunch and thankfully forgave me for not calling him before. It wasn't intentional, I'd selfishly completely forgotten. He is forgiving like that and I do feel lucky to have him as a friend. Louis Bouchon was a different matter. I had not forgotten to text him and, however tempting a night at the opera sounded, I wanted him to contact me first. Of course, there was the whole art fraud issue but until he's locked up it wouldn't have put me off. Needless to say, he didn't get in touch. But guess who did... Yes. *Toby*. He called on Easter Monday morning and I was in such a good mood I answered before checking to see who it was. He'd been sweet. Refusing to hang up until we'd agreed on a date to meet. He wanted to see me in person, to talk things through. With a very full diary – the mortuary was busy – we settled on a place for lunch, halfway between us both.

That's how I've ended up here, on a Wednesday morning at Basingstoke railway station. Not really halfway from Sussex but I've come from London so it seems fair.

I'm sitting on a low-level wall of the car park basking in the spring sunshine. Toby's train has just pulled in and I must say I'm a little nervous.

There's a 9–5 shop outside the station. Almost all the newspapers in the rack have a picture of Auchen Laggan Tosh plastered across the front page. The headline, *Insincere Landseer Tears Twins Apart*, is jumping out at me in bold.

'*Susie*,' Toby shouted as soon as he saw me. He looked thin and tired.

I got up and his arms enveloped me in a huge hug. His shoulder felt bony under my chin. I thought I might cry. I didn't want to be here unless we have a future together and the thought there might not be made my bottom lip wobble.

'Thanks for coming all this way,' he said as he pulled himself upright and slung his satchel onto his back. 'Are you okay?'

I realised I'd forgotten to speak. 'Yes, yes,' I said, trying hard to smile. 'I'm so pleased we could make this work.'

'Have you ever been to Basingstoke before?'

'Nope.' I clenched my fists and filled myself with strength to get through the next hour or so.

'Neither have I but I've done a bit of Googling and there are plenty of green spaces.' Toby tapped his bag.

'You brought lunch?'

'Of course. If I was forcing you all the way here, I had to make your journey worth it.'

I smiled and waited for him to speak. Surely he'd seen the papers this morning – he must have joined the dots about Auchen Laggan Tosh. But I wasn't going to be the one to bring it up, just in case we never talked about anything else.

When he began, 'I didn't like how we left it in Scotland,' I practically tripped up on my own two feet. It was so out of character for him to address the issue that I suspected he'd been having relationship coaching.

He went on, 'I shouldn't have interrupted your teaching post and it was wrong of me to accept the invitation to that evening without asking you first.'

'It's not completely wrong of you,' I said, as usual dropping my guard. 'I didn't behave very well.'

Toby's brow creased slightly. He was surprised at my reaction but I knew I wasn't going to be able to hold up being sullen around him. Mainly because I think it's terribly bad practice to be cruel to someone you one day might love (again). Toby was that someone for me.

'When I accepted the job in Scotland,' I sighed, 'I felt it would be a breath of fresh air, a change of scene, and then you turned up and it upset me a lot.' This was brutally honest but it's how I am and I didn't want to pretend to be someone I'm not.

Toby took hold of my hand. 'Please will you give me a second chance?'

'Friends?' I said, getting in there first. I didn't want to hear the word come out of *his* mouth.

'Yes,' he replied, and I looked away. My heart has just broken for a second time.

He pressed the button on the traffic lights and let go of my hand.

'Susie,' he said without any feeling, 'you know me better than almost all my friends. Surely that's something we can build on?'

I forgot to speak, again.

'Can't we?'

'Yes of course.'

'Good,' he smiled. 'Hey, how do you think a blind person knows when to cross the road?'

I shrugged.

'Give me your hand.' He held it palm facing upwards under the black box. 'Can you feel a solid button?'

'Yes.'

'Keep touching it and when the red man turns green, it'll vibrate.'

He was right. 'That's so great.'

'Isn't it just.'

We crossed the road and I left my disappointment on the other side. I'm determined not to let my hopes spoil our time together. Who knows when we'll see each other again?

As soon as we reached the other side Toby pulled me down a gap between two buildings. Oh yes…I think he's going to kiss me. I've got it all wrong. Yes. Please do…

But when he said, 'I researched the parks on Google Earth. It's much quicker this way,' I realised it was a literal short cut and I plodded on, squeezing between barbed wire and into a wood.

'I wanted to see you today so I could apologise,' he volunteered. 'But I also just wanted to hang out and have fun like we used to do.'

He gave me a huge smile and I couldn't help smiling back. He looked so happy, a little boy in a grown-up's body.

We came out of the wood onto an expanse of grass with little bunches of yellow primroses and groups of people.

'If we head for that corner,' Toby pointed into the distance, 'there should be a bandstand and I thought we could eat in it.'

'Great.' I sounded reasonably enthusiastic.

We walked as a pair, neither of us talking. The calm atmosphere between us was enough to assure me things were going to get better from here on. I no longer felt the need to drag up the past. How he could have left me alone and upset, disregarded my sensitivities and cut off all communication. Today was Toby's day. He'd struck up the plan, taken it into his hands and although he hadn't spoken the word 'sorry' he had conveyed it in what he'd said.

I looked across at him and beamed. His blue eyes sparkled back as he ran his hand through his thick curly hair.

'It's so good to be out of the office,' he said, taking in a great big breath of fresh air. 'Working as a mortuary clerk is dead dull sometimes.'

'Yeah, I bet it's lifeless.'

He laughed, a lot. This made me happy. Toby was willing to let me in.

'Okay. Okay,' he said and stopped. The bandstand lay about ten feet away but there was obviously something pressing on his mind. 'I've been *dying* to say this but I wanted to clear things up between us first.'

'What?' I could hardly contain my excitement.

'Isn't it AMAZING what's going on with the Muchtons?'

This was a massive let-down. I honestly thought he was going to tell me he loved me. An unrealistic thought I know, but my emotions are all over the place and the most unlikely scenarios suddenly seem likely to happen at any moment. I have been looking forward to discussing the Muchton art fraud drama with him later, not now.

'It's a pretty great story, don't you think? I can't believe the brother got away with it.'

'He didn't get away with it, that's the point.' I began to walk away.

'Oi, oi, oi,' Toby pulled at my shoulder and turned me around. 'What's up? You can't just change the atmosphere like that.' His voice was now soft, kind, willing me to share whatever it was.

No matter what I said, I owed him a reply.

'You bringing up the Auchen Laggan Tosh mystery reminded me of us falling out in Norfolk over the death of that American girl, Hailey.'

Toby blew his lips apart with a puff of air. 'Susie, don't be so silly. Norfolk's in the past, and anyway, what's Norfolk got to do with this?'

His eyes strained as he fixed me with an anxious glare. I didn't flicker. I wanted him to get there by himself.

He stared and stared and eventually, forgetting he had a satchel over one shoulder, he threw his arms up in the air. Lunch rattled around but he didn't seem to care.

'You were involved, weren't you?'

'I didn't help Ewen paint them, no.'

He cuffed me round the head. 'You know what I mean.'

'But we're not a team any more.'

'*Please*,' he begged, 'don't be like that. I'm sure we can be a team again. Just this time we weren't but it doesn't mean I don't want to hear.'

I stopped myself from reminding him that last time we weren't exactly a team either. He'd given up believing in me halfway through the case and I definitely didn't want to bring up that argument again.

'How about I tell you over lunch?' I teased. 'I'm hungry.'

'Fine, have it your way,' he grinned and jumped up onto the bandstand.

I turned around to look at the view. I need to clear my thoughts. This morning I woke up in my childhood bed at Number 64 Cleaver Square: my week at Auchen Laggan Tosh had paled. Easter Day was good fun, Mass then lunch. Sam joined us for both. The next day my parents had taken it upon themselves to tell me a few family truths. 'Now you know you had a twin who died at birth, poppet, well, your father and I feel there are some other blips we should share with you.' None of these 'blips', as she so harmlessly put it, did I want to know, but they told me regardless. Consequently, yesterday equals deadly; I spent it sitting out the after-effects of what I now knew. But this morning...now that's a whole different matter. It's as if I've been granted a golden day.

At 9.30am I left Cleaver Square on foot to Waterloo Station. I had my overnight bag with me. After Basingstoke I plan to go home. I took a slight right turn onto Baylis Road and got caught in an almighty rush of people as I passed Lambeth tube station. Rather than fight my way through, with time on my side, I stood back for it to pass. I turned to a newspaper stand, the headline, *Insincere Landseer Tears Twins Apart*, caught my eye. I grabbed a copy and here's what it said inside.

The Daily News, *Wednesday 1 April*
ART FRAUD AT
AUCHEN LAGGAN TOSH
The Inside Story

The Honourable Ewen Hewson, 40, is by all accounts something of a gentleman rogue, although one with a true talent for painting.

The police are investigating an alleged fraud to do with copied Landseer paintings at Auchen Laggan Tosh, the Highland estate inherited by the Earl of Muchton, Mr Hewson's elder twin brother.

Mr Hewson, who lives on the estate, has been questioned under caution on art-forgery offences. His initials were masterfully identified within the paintings, thanks to the acute eye of an unnamed source, although formal charges are yet to be made.

We understand that a Landseer expert had raised doubts over the authenticity of two of the Landseers hanging in the main house. He refused to be drawn on the exact value of the original paintings, other than to say that each would be worth 'at least a substantial six-figure sum'.

A source close to the family told the Daily News *exclusively, 'To fake an artist's work, you need to love him. It looks like Ewen didn't love Landseer enough. His brother Fergus, the most honest man I have ever met, must be spitting feathers to have the family name besmirched in this way.'*

It is believed that the police are yet to uncover firm evidence of black-market involvement or money-laundering, and it seems that the original works of art were sold unframed and for an honest price, although it is also claimed that neither sale was sanctioned or known about by the Earl of Muchton.

The police say they have leads to the buyer(s) of the two original pictures, Rutting Stags and Dogs in the Moonlight, who are thought to be both resident in Canada.

Mr Hewson was apprehended at Portsmouth in possession of one of the original paintings, Dogs in the Moonlight.

When stopped, witnesses say that Mr Hewson was dressed as a young blonde woman, under the alias Rose Flowers, and he was placing the work of art on a container ship set for the Port of Halifax in Nova Scotia.

Mr Hewson and another man, thought to be his friend, photographer Louis Bouchon, are currently in police custody in Inverness.

The Daily News has approached the Earl of Muchton for a comment. Auchen Laggan Tosh is one of the largest privately owned estates in the Highlands.

Meanwhile, the Highlands and Islands Police Headquarters have expressed enormous thanks to their unnamed caller for 'vital information received' prior to the arrests of Mr Hewson and Mr Bouchon.

Acknowledgements

Gigantic thank you to: Andrew Festing, great friend, brilliant painter and Henry Wyndham my art-fraud adviser; all at Oneworld – everyone needs an editor and Jenny Parrott's the best; Jo Bending, the voice of Susie Mahl; Emily Carter for uncompromising honesty; and brilliant Sam, who never complains when I disappear to write – I love you from the bottom of my heart.

Ali Carter was born in Scotland and read art history at St Andrews. She first followed an eclectic career in investment management, retail and technology; then, in 2011, she had a catastrophic bicycling accident. After major brain surgery and a long recovery, Ali set herself a challenge to walk alone from Canterbury to Rome, a three-month pilgrimage she wrote about in her book, *An Accidental Jubilee* by Alice Warrender. From then she decided to follow her passion and become a fine artist, specialising in oil paintings from life with an emphasis on colour. Ali also draws pet portraits to commission and works from her studio in East Sussex. She is the author of *A Brush with Death* and *The Colours of Murder*.